About the Editor

Maxim Jakubowski was born in Barnet but brought up in Paris. He followed a career in publishing by opening the Murder One bookshop in London in 1988. He writes, edits and publishes in many areas of genre fiction, including SF and fantasy, mystery and erotica. He is an official advisor to several international film festivals, writes for a variety of publications including the *Observer*, the *Big Issue* and *Time Out*, and reviews crime in a monthly column in the *Guardian*. He is also contributing editor to *Mystery Scene*, a director of London's Crime Scene Festival and a winner of the Anthony Award.

D0756659

Also by Maxim Jakubowski and available from Headline

Past Poisons
Chronicles of Crime

Murder
Through the Ages

A bumper anthology of historical mysteries

Maxim Jakubowski

HEADLINE

First published in 2000
by HEADLINE BOOK PUBLISHING

First published in paperback in 2001
by HEADLINE BOOK PUBLISHING

10 9 8 7 6 5 4 3 2 1

ISBN 0 7472 6617 4

Typeset by Avon Dataset Ltd, Bidford-on-Avon, Warks

Printed and bound in Great Britain by
Clays Ltd, St Ives plc

HEADLINE BOOK PUBLISHING
A division of Hodder Headline
338 Euston Road
London NW1 3BH

www.headline.co.uk
www.hodderheadline.com

TABLE OF CONTENTS

Introduction

Many readers enjoy science fiction and fantasy tales for their sense of wonder and the many alien landscapes that stretch the imagination. However, without losing contact with reality, one can do no better than delve into the past – once defined by L. P. Hartley as 'another country' – for similar fascinating experiences where the locales can be varied and exotic and the state of affairs utterly different and unpredictable.

And when you add to the equation a clever dose of crime and mystery, the ensuing cocktail becomes an hypnotic mixture which holds the reader in a strong spell that few outside distractions can interrupt. No wonder then that historical mysteries are still so many people's favourite tipple and that, despite the passing of Ellis Peters who initially made the genre hers, it thrives on the bookshelves with new talents emerging almost monthly on publishers' lists, new periods being explored and an unending gallery of past sleuths beating the investigative trail.

In recognition of this enduring popularity, the first two volumes in this series of new historical mystery stories beginning with *Past Poisons* were dedicated to Ellis Peters, and the Crime Writers' Association instituted a new annual award, the Ellis Peters Historical Dagger, to be given to the best historical crime book of the year. I'm pleased to say that both the first two winners, respectively Lindsey Davis for her Marcus Didius Falco Roman series and Gillian Linscott for her Nell Bray, suffragette and sleuth extraordinaire adventures have appeared in this anthology series, albeit with new characters. Lindsey's story herein 'Investigating the Silvius Boys' offers a provocative new angle on the origins of ancient Rome, and Gillian Linscott was featured in our preceding volume, *Chronicles of Crime.*

Also in our roll call this time around are some of the most popular and enduring practitioners of the art of historical mysteries, including Paul Doherty, Peter Tremayne, Peter Lovesey (latest winner of the CWA Diamond Dagger life achievement award), H.R.F. Keating (another Diamond Dagger recipient and also President of the Detection Club), Edward Marston and Catherine Aird. In addition, some particularly distinguished contemporary crime authors gift us with what is, I think, their first ever adventure into past times, including Manda Scott (the only crime writer to have been shortlisted for the Orange Prize for Fiction) with a striking Viking mystery (coincidentally one of two in this collection; are marauding, murderous Vikings the next big thing?), California writer Michael Hemmingson and Lauren Henderson, creator of the Sam Jones series and leading light of the Tart Noir group, with a disturbing homage to 1940s film noir.

We have authors from England, Scotland, Wales, America and even Germany (and one expatriate who cannot tear herself away from the vineyards of Italy), a new Sherlock Holmes story by June Thomson and stories that span the globe and past centuries. A perfect menu of entertainment, thrills, dastardly deeds, treachery, bloody murder and fiendish puzzles I am confident you will enjoy to the full as they cleverly unravel.

So, follow this criminal romp through history and savour these nuggets of the past in the first year of a new millennium which will no doubt bring us more crime, sadly real but also fictional. I know I shall always prefer the latter.

Maxim Jakubowski

Who Killed Dido?

Amy Myers

Carthage, 10th Century BC

'**D**ido's dead.'

That little squirt Hermes, Olympus' messenger-in-chief, could barely hold back his smirk at ruining our lunch.

'What?' A scream as Heavyweight Queen Hera took in the bad news that all her scheming had been in vain.

'I didn't want her to kill herself,' I assured her, truthfully for once. I sat daintily on my dining cloud, sipping my nectar, knowing I was innocent of involvement (well, almost). As Aphrodite, goddess of love, I generally get the blame for any crimes of passion that result from my professional work, however unfairly.

'She didn't kill herself,' announced our Hermes gleefully. 'She was murdered.'

That put a fly in the nectar all right. Everyone choked on their ambrosia, especially Father (Mighty Zeus, king of Olympus) who doesn't like family meals interrupted by business – especially any not sanctioned by him.

'I've signed no death warrant,' he thundered, as we put our hands over our ears. 'Which one of you has been meddling?'

'This is your doing, Aphrodite?' Hera turned on me viciously – of course.

'No,' I shrieked. 'Oh, Father, it wasn't me.'

Dido had been queen of Carthage in Libya, and, I have to admit, both a beautiful and a good woman. Building her city and its temples to ensure her subjects' happiness was her sole mission in life after the death of her husband. And therein lay the trouble: temples. Dido, unfortunately, was the pet of Cow-Eyed Hera, queen of Olympus and my unesteemed stepmother, and was busily dedicating them to her – not to me. Okay, I can't win them all, but this one was particularly vexing.

Whoever thinks that being an immortal goddess is easy couldn't be more wrong. It's not all dancing around in gauzy dresses to Apollo's lyre; there are enough dirty politics on Mount Olympus to ensure none of us would get our work done at all if we put a finger in every honey-pot. Just because I'm the most beautiful and Father's pet, everyone has it in for me, except for those I'm sleeping with, or who are in need of my magic cestus to aid them in their sordid intrigues.

'Here we go again,' I thought, as every senior god present prepared to express his or her views on Dido's death – except for the king of the underworld, who is only allowed up here for a family lunch once in a while when Father can tolerate his gloomy face. He was licking his lips and negotiating with Hermes who is responsible for delivering bodies safely to Hades.

Unfortunately on this occasion I was in a sticky position, since it was my mortal son Aeneas (not to be confused with Eros, my immortal baby cherub) who was causing all this trouble. Not that it was entirely Aeneas' fault. It is the Fates who hold the real power round here, but we all pretend Father does, and he had decreed that Aeneas, after escaping from Troy when it fell to the Greeks, would found a new Troy, probably in a place to be called Italy, from which a great new race would arise. Aeneas himself would be safely in Hades by then, but his little son Ascanius, whom he had brought with him from Troy, would carry on the line. You bet he would!

Enter stage right Great Queen of Olympus Hera. She was a Greek supporter in the Big Match between the Greeks and

Trojans, and it did her ego no end of good when the Fates let the Greeks punch Troy out for the count. Consequently she was mortified when Father agreed to poor little me's petition that Aeneas should not only be spared but triumph in the end, and has spent the last eight years determined to stop him. Dressed in her best purple Dorian chiton to show off her oxlike legs, and smothered in pearls, she immediately hauled herself off to her chum Aeolus, god of the winds, and asked him to give Aeneas' ships a bashing.

I could do nothing since Aeolus skilfully avoids Olympus by living in a cave by himself, and he's so old that even if I hopped in naked he'd assume I'd come to pose for a statue. After seven years of getting nowhere they came up with a brainwave (this takes time for Hera). Yes, you've guessed it – an even bigger storm, and there was poor Aeneas, his fleet scattered and himself cast upon the barbarous shores of unknown Libya.

Old Fattie (sorry, Mighty Hera) then had another brainwave – she must have been taking Aesculapius' happy pills again. (He's our aged doctor.) Aeneas and Dido should fall in love, Dido could keep Aeneas chained to her side for ever, and he would never go to Italy and found New Troy. She had even boasted to me about it.

'What did Father have to say about this plan?' I had asked curiously. He is apt to throw the odd thunderbolt when his will is crossed.

'He doesn't know.'

'He will, darling, he will.'

'Then he'll also know it was you who foiled his plans to seduce that nymph by giving him a fake cestus.'

Point taken. I was on my own.

Mind you, Cow Lady's plan wasn't all bad, so I decided to go along with it. If Dido were to fall in love with Aeneas, it would certainly have the advantage that she wouldn't set her barbarian hordes on him to tear him to pieces. The snag is that I don't *like* Aeneas very much, and not even his doting father could make a case for his being a wow with the ladies. He'd even mislaid his wife Creusa in their escape from Troy (I'd always wondered how he managed it). Why on earth should Dido, a queen of decided mind and great beauty, who had turned down more suitors than I'd accepted in my bed, fall for my dull boring son? I had had to think quickly.

'Great Queen, your plan is so clever,' I had said to Stepmummy admiringly. 'And as love is my province, you can leave that to me.'

I realised I'd have to play an active part if this happy event was to take place. I decided first to convert myself into a passing virgin (a little hard, but I thought I remembered the script) in order to reassure Aeneas, still blundering around the sand dunes, that it was safe to seek out Dido. Secondly I'd summon his half-brother, dearest Eros, with whom unfortunately I also have an uneasy relationship. I call him my naughty little cherub but he's more of a mischievous adolescent now, I suppose. He's always obliging, but he leaves the dirty work to me, or, if he does deign to get his wings soiled, he leaves me to clear up the mess. There's sons for you.

Aeneas had been delighted to hear he might be in with a chance with a beautiful, *rich* queen of Carthage, with whose help he could resupply his ships, and, after a few days of her receiving the privilege of his sharing his body with her, depart with Ascanius to found the new race. Unluckily, as I departed, casually dropping my virgin's clothes on the ground, he recognised me (from my bare behind?) and a great wail went up about how I'd never been a proper mother to him and never had time for long chats. (I should think not. I'm a working mother. The way Aeneas chats, the rest of the world would be starved of love for years.) I gave him a beauteous smile, waved my long tresses at him and vanished.

My mission to Eros had been simpler. I'd pinch Ascanius for a while, I explained, put him to sleep so he didn't realise what was happening, and Eros would impersonate him. When 'Ascanius' went to introduce himself to Dido, she would dandle him in her lap to impress Aeneas with her motherly qualities. Ascanius was twelve years old, but she didn't know much about adolescent boys. While Eros was being dandled, he could shove a few of his love darts in her breasts as he chatted to her about his brave handsome father.

'I thought we were talking about Aeneas?' Eros asked cheekily.

'You underrate your brother, my little cherub.'

A chortle. 'Impossible,' he cried, and flew out of the boudoir window.

He did his job well, for Dido fell so much in love with Aeneas that the poor fellow not only had his life saved from barbarous tribes, but nearly lost it being devoured whole by its queen. No, that's unfair. Dido really was a nice woman, and though she did let passion take over from common sense, she could hardly be blamed since it was my fault. Moreover, I truly believe that Aeneas did fall in love with her, so far as he's able.

Unfortunately I'd made the most terrible mistake. I hadn't thought it through. There they were head over heels in love with one another, and so how was I going to prise Aeneas away to Italy?

'I've won,' crowed Hera, when she realised my dilemma.

'So you have,' I agreed, planning an appeal to Father, who had seen my point immediately when I casually waved my magic cestus at him. He had a date with a shepherd girl that afternoon who kept trying (with Hera's blundering help) to disguise herself as a sheep to escape him. In fact it meant Father could expect even more fun.

'Between you and me,' Father said unhappily, 'She of the Marital Bed is getting too big for her boots.' Not just her

7

boots. She's bursting out of every chiton she possesses; the Graces are kept busy running up new numbers. 'How dare she countermand me?' he continued mournfully. 'I'll send Hermes down for a word.'

'Oh, splendid.' I clapped my lily-white hands in genuine pleasure. Hermes could stir up trouble in the Elysian Fields. And he did. He went straight to Aeneas and pointed out it was time he was off on his travels again. He had a great destiny to fulfil and here he was wasting time with a mere woman. Did he want to be known as Dido's husband for the rest of his life?

That had done it. If there was one thing Aeneas loved more than Dido it was himself, so he switched on to the track of his glorious, foretold future. I've no doubt Ascanius supported him, not wishing to see any half-brothers appearing to queer his pitch. I almost prefer Aeneas to his son, who has all the makings of a pretty dictator. If that's going to be what the new dynasty's like, it won't get far.

Aeneas, busy organising his ships on the shore, with a course set straight for his own advancement, had suddenly remembered he'd better have a few courtly words with Dido, poor woman. I felt truly sorry for her, and even Aeneas seemed a little upset at her anguish. She pleaded for one last night in his arms, but my heroic son said he'd sleep on his ship to think things over, and come back in the morning.

Father, revitalised again by his shepherdess and several sheep, had the weird idea that Hera might be storming around seeking revenge for his afternoon's activities, so he sent Hermes down once again to interrupt Aeneas' snores. He pointed out that Dido was likely to turn nasty, and he should leave while the going was good, even though it was the middle of the night, before he found himself the centrepiece of a barbecue on the beach. Off he went and when poor Dido woke up, she saw the last white sails of the fleet heading for the horizon.

I may be a laughter-loving goddess, but every job has its downside, and broken hearts are part of mine. I couldn't bear to watch, however, and so it was Hermes who told us the full story, after he had shot his poisonous arrow about Dido's murder.

After Aeneas had broken the news of his departure to her, Dido had built a large pyre in the inner open court of her palace, put all her keepsakes of Aeneas on top of it, including his sword (how did he come to leave that behind?), gave the servants a night off, and booted everyone out save for her sister Anna. When she saw that he wasn't returning for the grand parting scene as he promised, but had made off at high speed, she climbed up on to the pyre, and killed herself with his sword. Anna came rushing in to find her dying, and Aeneas sailed merrily on his way noting with scant interest a tall plume of smoke licking the sky from Carthage.

Ox-Eyed Hera was sobbing her heart out at the tale, and I felt sickened myself though I had to defend my son somehow. Father hates to see Hera cry (and well she knows it) so I knew I was in for a rough chariot ride here.

'How do you *know* Dido was murdered, Hermes?' I opened my lustrous blue orbs wide upon him in admiration.

Oh, how he loved this chance to shine. He sat down with his feet on the table, quaffing his nectar, and not even Father objected, he was so eager to listen. 'After I left Aeneas, I was worried about Dido' (worried? *Hermes*?) 'and as Father' (yes, another step-sibling, though Hermes' mother was a *very* junior goddess) 'had loaned me the keys of the Earthvision Room for the night, I went to check up on her.'

There's a persistent rumour that on Olympus we are all-seeing, all-powerful. Not true, not even for Father Zeus. He keeps the keys, and the rest of us have to put in a chit for permission to look-see. It's a good system, I suppose, save that Father is absent a lot of the time on new fathering missions and we all slumber at night (or are otherwise engaged) so a lot escapes us.

'I logged on just as Anna lit the pyre,' Hermes drawled on, 'and seeing Dido dead, I whizzed off to have a word with Sister A. She told me she arrived too late to save Dido, ~~who~~ died in her arms.'

'So?' I queried hopefully. No proof of murder here.

'I showed Dr Aesculapius the Earthvision images, and he pointed out Anna had no blood on her clothing, nor could she have embraced Dido with the sword still in her. I myself observed there was no sword lying on top of the pyre, even though that was clearly how she died.'

He took a bow and everyone save me applauded. To Hades with that beastly image machine. It was Hermes invented it. He set mirrors up surrounding the hole in the clouds which permits Earthvision, got Apollo to magnify the strength of the light beams coming in by several thousand times, and smeared clear jellied ambrosia over the mirrors so that the images from earth were etched into it, and could then be peeled off for storage. Clever, I admit, but most inconvenient when one wants to make an incognito visit to earth. No wonder Zeus keeps the key.

'Who are the suspects,' I asked hollowly, 'apart from me?'

'None,' Hera chortled.

'Four, actually,' said Hermes, to my surprise. Preferring trouble-making to love, he's not usually on my side. 'First, there's Pygmalion.'

Father looked puzzled. 'Isn't that the fellow for whom you brought a statue to life, Aphrodite?'

'No.' Hermes blithely dismissed one of my greatest coups. 'He is Dido's brother, and rules Tyre like a tyrant, ho ho!' Hermes' puns are awful but we all dutifully laugh because it pleases Father. 'It was to escape Pygmalion that Dido fled to Libya after her husband's death – Pyggy killed him by the way

– and founded Carthage. He's never forgiven her, and he'll be after her throne now. Unless the king of Mauritania gets in first. He's a barbarian called Iarbas, with an obsession about Dido. He wanted to marry her not only so that he could grab Carthage, but because he had some personal grudge against her and saw marriage as the way to work it out.'

'The sister's still the most likely,' growled Father. 'Cherchez la femme.'

He picks up these outlandish phrases whenever Hermes comes back from foreign parts. This was some tribe called the Ligurians out in the land of nowhere.

'Sister Anna hasn't Dido's spunk. She'd shriek at the mere sight of a sword.'

'Father's right. She must be a suspect though,' I put in quickly in case Hera was thinking of a new heroine to look after her temples. 'The lack of blood could be explained some other way. My Aeneas is so attractive to women' (I heard a hoot from Eros, no doubt listening at the door) 'she could have fancied him for herself. She admits she was with Dido as she died. Maybe she held the sword, at least, took it away, and changed her clothes, which would explain the lack of blood on the mirror images.'

'I say, old bean, that's clever of you.' My husband Hephaestus roused himself from stupor. He may be the god of fire, but it doesn't extend to his loins.

'Why take it away?' asked Hera sweetly. 'There would be no point whether it was murder or suicide.'

'Anyone else in the running, Hermes?' Father intervened.

'Yes, Pa. Aeneas.'

The little rat. 'Aeneas was sailing over the horizon at the time,' I cried piteously.

'His ship was,' said Hermes smugly. 'Anyone see him on it?'

'You did,' I whipped back. 'Father sent you to give him a bad dream.'

11

'That was before he set sail, Aphro. He could have taken a boat back just before dawn to murder Dido.' (Mirror images have to be set up in advance, so there would be no immortal record.)

'Aeneas had no reason to kill her,' I cried, my wondrous orbs filling with tears. 'He was sailing off to find his *destiny*.' I couldn't help smiling at Hera as I emphasised that delightful word. Keep off my son's turf, big lady.

'Why didn't Dido ask for my help?' Hera wrung her hands, which look like Heracles' after he'd carried out all twelve Labours. 'She had only to sacrifice at my temple and I'd have been down like a shot to prevent that chump leaving her.'

'No one calls my son a chump but me,' I declared. 'Prove it.'

'That he's a chump?' enquired Hera. 'Easy.'

Father growled. 'Hera has a point, Aphrodite.'

Does she? She looks fairly rounded to me, but he knew the Hump best. I could see she was already working on a new scheme to blame Aeneas for murdering Dido, and proving it to Father, so that Aeneas' destiny would suddenly change. He and Ascanius would meet nasty deaths at the hands of sea-god Poseidon, who being Father's brother was always willing to do him a good ship overturn.

It was time to act if I was to save Aeneas, small thanks though I'd get for it.

I found grief-stricken Sister Anna trying on all Dido's clothes and preening herself in the mirror. She screeched when she saw me, partly because I appeared to have hobbled through a bolted door, and secondly because I was dressed as an old hag. What lengths we mothers go to.

'Who are you?' she asked faintly.

'I'm Aeneas' mother,' I told her truthfully, hoping she didn't know much about his family history. 'I've come to collect his belongings.' Her face went very white. 'His sword, dearie, and

12

any other knick-knacks Dido took with her on the pyre or left in her room.'

'They're all burnt.'

'Sword too? He *will* be upset,' I croaked. 'Is your old mother alive, dear, to see the sad death of your sister? I hope not. I know how a mother's heart suffers.' I was proud of my subtle introduction.

Anna promptly burst into tears and threw herself into my motherly arms. I did my best to live up to expectations. 'There, there,' I cooed, wondering whether to stroke her hair. One never knows what strange pomatums might be in use.

'Oh, Fortunate Mother of Mighty Aeneas, it was terrible. Dido loved your son so much. I could see her blood, and had to climb the steps of the pyre to see if she lived. Then a goddess swooped down and cut a lock of her golden hair, and Dido was dead instantly. I think it was Iris.'

I pricked up my ears. Iris was Hera's sidekick and it was normally the queen of the underworld who took care of the hairdressing rite to sever life.

'Tell me everything. Get it off your chest, my dearie,' I crooned.

She needed no urging. 'As soon as Aeneas left, the palace was surrounded by all sorts of horrid people. They're still there. There are barbarians under their king Iarbas, who first of all wanted to join Dido on the pyre and now says he's entitled to the throne instead. And there's a horrible peasant who keeps bribing my staff to let him in so he can seize the throne. And to cap it all, I've lost Aeneas.' She howled.

So she did have a yen for my son. Perhaps one of Eros' darts gone astray, though she seemed stupid enough to love Aeneas, dart or no dart. 'Tell me about Dido's end,' I said sharply, '*then* have a good cry. Why didn't you stop her?'

'I couldn't,' she blubbed. 'She built the pyre herself in the inner court and locked all the doors, so I couldn't get in.'

'Then how *did* you get in, sweet child?'

A pause. 'I climbed over the roof.'

A touching picture. 'Of course,' I said. 'Silly of me to ask.'

'I was almost too late.'

'Tell me,' I asked, 'did you see cuts on Dido's hands, as you cradled her in your arms?' Aeneas' sword would be a reasonable length, so unless Dido had very long arms, it would probably have needed steadying to find its full lethal way into her body – unless someone helped her do it.

'No. Her peerless hand fluttered to embrace me one last time, so I would have noticed.' Anna must have been sharper than I thought, for she gave me a distinctly old-fashioned look. I was forgetting I had inside knowledge. 'How could I know she was going to kill herself? She had told me building the pyre and lighting it was a trick to induce Aeneas back. She never said she'd be on it.'

'Really? And you believed her, even though Aeneas was heading out to sea?'

'She built the pyre the evening before,' Anna said sullenly.

'You'd have liked Aeneas to come back, wouldn't you? You're his sort.'

'Oh, he's *gorgeous*. Could I come with you to meet him again, please? I'm so scared of Iarbas and that peasant.'

'No, you could not.' I threw off my vestments.

'I knew it,' Anna shrieked. 'You're not his mother, you're a goddess.'

'Both,' I replied curtly, vanishing nude into a diaphanous cloud. I was sure Anna was hiding something, and we only had her word for how Dido died, but was she a murderess?

Tyre was not my sort of place at all. Far too industrial, with grim castles and bleak treeless wastes of land. No wonder the Phoenicians are always setting sail, trying to take over other people's lands. I saw a sizeable fleet drawn up on the beach

14

and popped down to inspect it. I took on the guise of a humble oarsman, scantily clad, and with hairy great tree trunks instead of my slender white limbs, and croaked to a passing officer, 'Take me to your king Pygmalion.'

'—off,' came a very rude reply which I was unable to obey owing to pain from his whiplash on my shoulders. In revenge, I revealed myself in my immortal glory, which instead of terrifying this odious mortal gave him far different ideas. Anything for Aeneas, I sighed as I submitted. Afterwards he was clay mortar in my hands, and I was led straight to King Pygmalion.

'I am a messenger from Libya,' I revealed to this slender, nervous-looking, and most unkinglike youth.

'What does my lord king report? Oh damn, I wasn't supposed to say that.'

'I take it you are not Pygmalion.' Just my luck.

'He's off on a business trip, goddess.'

'To Libya?'

'He did mention that name.'

'Could he possibly be disguising himself as a peasant?'

'He didn't take the clothes for it, but he could have killed one as soon as he got there. He's like that.'

I eventually tracked Pygmalion down in Carthage at a delicate moment in his wooing (if that was the word for the grunts and bangs on the palace kitchen floor) of a serving maid.

'I want a word with you.'

'I don't mind one with you.' He eyed my body through the Graces' spring fashion hit chiton, left a very grateful serving wench, and seized me.

When his arm went right through me, his jaw dropped as well as the upward inclination of other parts of this delightful man. 'You're a goddess,' he babbled.

'How clever of you, Pygmalion. You, I take it, are on a private visit to your sister.'

15

'You got it in one.' This brute of a man was far from cultured.

'Then why didn't you speak to her instead of trying to sneak through the servants' quarters? She didn't even recognise you.'

'She won't speak to me,' he said sullenly, 'just because I accidentally killed Dido's husband. It was years ago but they both still hold it against me. I'm as gentle as a lamb – aren't I?' He kicked the still recumbent body of the serving wench who moaned assent.

'So you didn't object to helping Dido to Hades?'

'Me? You must be joking. Brothers-in-law are one thing, but I stop short of murdering sisters.'

'Goddesses never joke. What would you give me for not revealing your plans to grab the throne?' I'd no idea what they were, but it was worth a go.

He abased himself. 'A temple, goddess.'

'I'm interested. Tell me more.'

'Two temples?'

'Better.'

We settled on three and a promise to tear down Hera's, and I left him. He could have done it. He was at the palace at the right time, and if Anna climbed over the roof so could he. He only had to bribe that moron Anna to let him in – that's if Anna was being truthful about her claim that Dido had been intending to remain very much alive – and bob's your uncle Poseidon.

Iarbas of Mauretania was only a trifle more refined than Pygmalion. I found him in his tent at the palace gates, biding his time to storm them, and passing it with a game of knucklebones. 'Loved that woman,' he growled. I had decided against disguise, and he had apparently decided against prevarication.

'Enough to kill her?'

16

'I had good reason. Dido cheated me, you know, when she first came here. Women! She told me she only wanted enough land as could be covered by one oxhide. We shook hands on it, as decent men do, and she promptly cut the oxhide into narrow strips, put them all round a perimeter of several kilometres, and built a whole bloody city on it. A man would never have done that – or thought of it.'

A new side to Dido. Or was it the Ox-Eyed Queen of Olympus' idea, so that she could get her temple built? That seemed more likely.

Talking of the Ox-Eyed Queen, it was time I nipped back for a quick word.

'O Mighty Queen Consort of Mighty Cronus' son,' I began. This took Hera a time to work out but won her over, and she was quite pleasant. 'You knew Dido was dead before Hermes told us, didn't you?' I continued brightly.

She lost some of her ox-cheek colour. 'So what? I thought she'd killed herself though.'

'And *you* sent Iris down?'

'Yes.'

'Summon her.'

There was a certain amount of resistance but she yielded after I threatened her with a High Court of Olympus Summons.

Iris is a dear, but a dimwit. You'd have to be to be close to Hera, and she looks after rainbows as well, so that shows you. 'Hallo, Aphwodite' – oh yes, and she lisps too. 'And hail Goddess Spouse of Whea's son.'

'Forget all that. Answer Aphrodite's questions, dear,' Hera snapped.

'You went to the inner court and found Dido dying on the pyre?'

'Yes.' A touch of nervousness here.

'What time was this?'

'Dawn. I twavelled shortly after Auwowa.' No wonder I

17

can't do anything for Iris on a professional basis. Even her husband Zephyr scarcely ever blows.

'That's odd, Mighty Queen,' I observed. 'You usually go to bed at dusk and get up at an hour or two past dawn. How come you were able to despatch Iris so early?'

Give her her due, Hera knew when she was beaten.

'All right,' she snarled. 'Dido actually killed herself the night before. What of it?'

'Dido climbed up to the pyre in the middle of the night, stabbed herself with a sword, and managed still to be alive when Anna found her at dawn and Iris came to collect the lock? Where was the blood if she was still alive? She'd still be bleeding. And incidentally, why despatch Iris at all, Mighty Queen? Did you know as early as that what Dido had done?'

'Perhaps,' Hera said airily. 'I did just happen to be in the Earthvision Room.'

Iris decided to put on her little girl act. 'Dido died in her tuwwet bedwoom,' she whimpered. 'Anna was there with her while I cut the lock off. It was about midnight.'

'Ah,' I said in deep satisfaction.

'It makes no difference,' said Hera, spoiling for a fight.

'Oh, it does. It means Anna has been lying through her pearly white teeth.'

'I'll slaughter her,' roared Mighty Ox Queen, hoping to divert blame.

'Stay thy hand!' Not often I have a common bond with Hera. 'We'll work together on this. Give it till next ambrosia time.'

My last port of call wasn't a port, unfortunately. It was Aeneas' ship and at his side was my grandson Ascanius.

This time I wasted no time disguising myself as an oarsman, but came down in a cloud of golden rain on the mess deck where they were busy having their lunch, despite the fact the ship was tossing and turning like Father with Hera in his bed (usually trying to escape her).

'Darling Grannie!' Young Ascanius' gleaming piggy eyes were laughing at me.

'Dear child,' I murmured. I'd sort him out later. 'Aeneas, did you know you were a suspect in a murder investigation?'

'No. Whose?' He seemed more interested in his lunch.

'The Olympus inquiry into Dido's death.'

He actually laughed. 'Not again, Goddess Mother. I'm free of Dido now. It was good while it lasted, but it's over. A higher mission calls me forth. I have Ascanius' future to think of.'

'Ah yes. By the way, Aeneas, what's happened to your father?' I suddenly realised that I hadn't seen Anchises wheezing and snuffling around for some time.

'I lost him just before the Great Storm.'

'How very careless, my son. First you lose your wife while fleeing Troy, now your father. You haven't been up to anything you shouldn't have, like—'

'No,' he quickly interrupted. 'Not in front of the child,' he hissed to me piously.

Child? Ascanius was a knowing twelve-year-old with both snaky eyes on his future.

'Dido actually died at midnight, not dawn when you saw the smoke of the funeral pyre, and not by her own hand. What were you doing after you'd broken the happy news to her that you were leaving her?'

'Getting the ships ready,' he bleated, suddenly very nervous.

'Witnesses?'

'Hundreds – I think. I can't remember exactly what time I went to bed—'

'Aeneas,' I explained kindly, 'I don't mean to split on you but I must know the truth.'

'She killed herself,' he shouted. 'She must have done. She was threatening suicide when I left her in her turret room.'

19

'Don't upset him, Goddess Grannie,' Ascanius piped anxiously. 'Please let us go. Daddy's got to find Italy this time. I can't wait another seven years.'

'*You* can't wait? Little slip, Asky?' I cooed. 'Nevertheless, I will be off. I have a murder to solve, remember?' I added in my best goddess tones. I just got away in time before I brought up all my ambrosia for the last two years. I'd never make a sailor (at least, not in that way).

Back at Olympus in my golden bower deliberating what to wear at ambrosia time, I felt better. Eros even made me a cup of hot nectar.

'How did it go?' he asked casually.

'I think Aeneas did it,' I said heavily. 'I believe Dido threatened not to kill herself, but to order her soldiers to kill him and the rest of the Trojans. The way he saw it he had no choice. He didn't come back to the ship till after midnight. He killed her and brought the sword away with him.'

'But why should Anna lie?'

'Maybe she was hoping he'd take her with him.'

It was puzzling though, for he went without her, and she still lied. She wouldn't keep the throne very long after Dido's death, and she was just about intelligent enough to know it, so Aeneas must have spun her some yarn.

'Will you tell Grandfather Zeus about Aeneas?'

'No. He's my son, after all.'

I caught a fleeting expression on Eros's face, which I interpreted as relief. *Relief?* Sons? The time of death? Of course. There was someone else whom Dido would have let into her bedroom besides Anna and Aeneas.

'It was Ascanius!' I yelled, and saw Eros trying to fly through the door. 'Come back here, you little monster. You had something to do with this, didn't you?'

'It was all your idea, Mother. It was you suggested I should impersonate Ascanius.'

'*You* murdered Dido?' This was terrible news. Almost as bad as though I'd been convicted myself. It meant High Court of Olympus Proceedings, if Father found out a god had killed someone without his royal warrant.

'No.' Eros looked terrified. 'I'm god of love, after all. I just impersonated him again on the ship so Aeneas wouldn't miss him, and while Aeneas was asleep after all the wine I gave him to drink, I impersonated Hermes and told Aeneas he should get moving right away. Hermes didn't care. He could stay in bed. Ascanius went up to see Dido and suggested she lit a funeral pyre to deceive Aeneas into thinking she was dead, and that he would ensure his father would come rushing back. Dido could step out from behind a pillar, and Aeneas would be so relieved to see her they'd be married. Then they could have lots of little babies and he, Ascanius, had always wanted brothers and sisters. It sounded all right to me. He didn't tell me anything about murdering her, though.' Eros began to look anxious, as well he might.

I saw it all. Our little Ascanius was so worried about his father's not getting to Italy, he decided to take steps himself. He ran her through with Aeneas' sword which he'd taken with him, then went hollering for Anna, to say poor Queen Dido had killed herself, and wouldn't it be a good idea if they put her on the pyre and set light to it? He told her Aeneas would come racing back, find Dido dead, and marry Anna instead whom he, Ascanius, would like for a mummy very much indeed.

'How did Ascanius get back to the ship?' I enquired sweetly. 'It was already under sail. Did you fly him through the air?'

'No, I thought you might not like that if you found out.'

'Too right I wouldn't.'

'Aeneas woke up with such a hangover I persuaded him we should leave last, not first, which gave Ascanius time to get back. Aeneas didn't suspect a thing. He's a bit dim, Mother.'

21

'You realise,' I thundered in my best imitation of Father, 'that I'll have to tell Mighty Zeus of this? Ascanius will have to be punished, and your brother's glorious future is going to be up for appeal before the Fates if Hera finds out.'

Eros looked stricken. 'Look, Ma, how about I promise Grandfather that I'll find Brother Aeneas a nice new wife and that *their* son could found this new Troy?'

I was all for it, as you can imagine. 'Darling boy, how clever.' That settled, I added grimly, 'And now tell me why you went to so much trouble to help that creep Ascanius.'

'Families,' observed my pious cherub, 'should stick together.'

'The truth, please.'

He fidgeted and then came clean. 'Ascanius said he knew this cute chick called Psyche . . .'

Chick? He may be growing up, but why the Hades did he have to take after his grandfather?

22

Investigating the Silvius Boys

Lindsey Davis

Rome, 735 BC

The location of the crime was critical. The scene was a marshy river valley, between low but significant hills. Alongside the river ran an ancient salt road. It came up from the coast, about twenty miles away, then continued into the interior towards a city which at that time ruled the neighbourhood. In a wide curve of the river lay an island which offered the first crossing point inland. This bridgehead made a natural halt, for it was about one day's journey for the beasts bringing salt from the sea. These factors had encouraged settlement. The hills were crying out to be defended – and someone had just begun surrounding them with a rampart wall. In the footings of the new wall the investigator had seen a recent corpse.

There had been no attempt to hide the body. As soon as he asked, bystanders told him freely that the victim was one of the two Silvius boys. They also admitted quite openly who had battered him to death. One of the oldest crimes in the world: a young man had quarrelled bitterly with his brother and killed him with a building tool.

That was when the investigator should have gone home. He was a visitor who had come merely to sightsee. But he knew something of the family involved and so he found himself intrigued. Being drawn in despite himself was a hazard of his profession. Once his interest had been caught there was no escape.

The purist inquirer likes a date for a murder. That posed a problem. Time had no set limits. The tribes north of the river maintained a rough calendar by banging a nail into a temple door every year. It worked well, unless the temple burned down, as happened fairly frequently. Here the people were more primitive. Even so they were practical, and quite capable of devising their own methods of reckoning. Very soon they would calculate everything from the most important date they had. So if you wanted to be pedantic, you could say that the man who was killed by his brother had died in the year time began.

Well, that was the kind of easy-to-remember fact which helps keep casework archives neat. This was, without any question, Case Number One.

Number One – with no arrest foreseeable. It did not bode well for the future of the profession.

On the driest and highest of the hills above the river's marshy flood-plain stood a group of shepherds' huts. They had a venerable, weathered air – and the shepherds who lived in them had a reputation for beating up strangers. As he climbed the hill, which was harder going than it looked, the investigator sighed. He hated shepherds. This collection were known to be formidable. They did not wait to be raided by bandits, like most countrymen who knew their lot was to lead a hard life and suffer. These themselves rode out in armed groups, attacked the bandits vigorously, and shared out their spoils. They were famous for flouting authority. They had found themselves young leaders who encouraged them to plunder the herds of neighbouring landowners, even including the royal estates. The investigator knew this because he worked for the king.

As he climbed towards the hilltop he noticed a flurry of movement. They had seen him coming. They knew exactly who he was. They also knew he was at a disadvantage. As he came up, gasping, he saw only a huddle of hostile people in rough sheepskin dress, who all looked surly and all looked the same. To a city man they had an obtrusive smell of woodsmoke and lanolin. It made him feel his own habits were over-fastidious.

'I need to speak to Faustulus.' He felt a taut knot in his belly. It was always the same at the start of something: dread of the unknown.

'What do you want?'

'Someone is dead.'

'What's it to you?' The man who spoke was being no more obstructive than usual. He just belonged to a group who took pride in being blunt. Like all such groups, outsiders judged them plain rude.

Faustulus himself had come out of a hut. The investigator knew him already because Faustulus was the previous king's herdsman. This had made for complications during the raids on the royal estates – for Faustulus was also foster father to the ringleaders who organised the raids. Now nearing the end of his working life, he was hardy, skilled and too intelligent for his own good. The stubborn, confident type, the type who breaks the rules. Twenty or thirty years ago he took home two abandoned infants when any sensible man would have left them to die. They grew up to be the Silvius twins.

It was clear from his eyes that Faustulus already knew that one of his rowdy foster sons was now lying alongside the new rampart with his head cracked open, and that the other was responsible. Those eyes said that, like any man who brought up children who came to grief, he was now wondering why he had bothered. But there was a hard defiance in their gaze as well. He would stand by the survivor.

The investigator gave him a courteous nod, then braced himself. 'Where's Romulus?'

A murmur ran through the crowd. 'Go back to your work,' ordered the investigator. 'Disperse. There's nothing to see.'

A woman rushed to the front, tear-stained and shrieking abuse. He ought to have known Larentia would not be far away. 'Get out of here! You're not wanted. Get back to Alba.'

She was younger than Faustulus, but well matched in spirit. She had a reputation for putting herself about too much. Maybe she did, though in a small, and small-minded, community any woman with character risks jealous talk. This one had never cared what others thought.

'Larentia, I'm sorry to find you in this trouble.' She checked herself, seeing that the investigator was a quiet and steady man who would not be swayed from his purpose. 'I have to see Romulus before I leave,' he told her levelly. He could take his time. Romulus belonged right here. He would not flee.

Larentia still looked ready to fly at him. If she appealed to the others the investigator would be lost. He knew this was the most dangerous moment. Walking up the hill alone had been stupid. His mouth dried, as if he had been chewing grapeskins to nothing. If these people decided to tear him apart he had no means of defending himself.

'Let Romulus be. He's grieving for his brother,' Larentia cried.

'I can understand that,' the investigator said.

'You don't understand anything!' Behind the spitting rage of a creature defending her young lay darker feelings. She was standing apart from Faustulus as if pain had erected a barrier between her husband and herself. She also knew that whatever happened she had lost not one but both her boys.

'I'm trying to understand,' said the man from Alba Longa. 'Maybe the best thing is if Romulus himself stops hiding in the hut behind you and comes out to explain.'

* * *

28

Romulus emerged of his own volition. If he wanted to remain a power in the community there was no alternative. Once he looked like a fugitive he would lose all powers of leadership.

Pushing past his knee as he ducked out of the hut came a large dog, growling fiercely at the stranger. The investigator stood his ground. Presumably a man who had been suckled by a she-wolf was good with animals.

The watchdog sat on its tail and fell silent. Romulus came further forward. He was strong and fit, past boyhood but still young. His expression was dark, but otherwise unfathomable. People said he made a happy companion exchanging stories around a campfire, but if you met him at market you would not attempt conversation. He was rural and close. That was how he set out to be, even normally, let alone on the day he had killed his twin brother.

Seeing him, the crowd relaxed. No one, including the foster parents, made any move to intervene when suspect and investigator walked to another part of the hilltop where they could talk in privacy. The two men were now looking south, across a deep cleft which divided the hill that would be known as the Palatine, the hill where the twins had been brought up, from the crag called the Aventine.

'I don't have to say anything to you!' declared Romulus. He sounded like anyone caught poaching on the royal estates.

'That's right.'

'You're wasting your time.'

'It goes with the job.'

The investigator surveyed him thoughtfully. Hardened and self-opinionated. A fighter, who could devise a plan and then organise the muscle to carry it out. A young thug. But then what else could he be, with that background?

The Silvius family, now the hereditary kings of Alba, claimed descent from Aeneas, that pragmatic old hero who escaped from Troy then pushed his way to power in Italy without a by-your-leave. His descendants were never renowned for peaceful living. The twins' grandfather had been shoved off the throne by his brother, who methodically killed all his nephews, then ordered his niece to become a vestal virgin. Instead of sticking to her intended life of chastity she let herself be raped – or, according to her, she was deflowered by Mars, the god of war (good story: a quick-thinking girl). The resultant sons had been ordered to be drowned in the Tiber, but the job had been bungled and Faustulus had found them in the flooded fields, being suckled by a she-wolf.

Well, the she-wolf tale was a ludicrous rumour. Romulus and Remus were just one more set of tearaways: a violent background, mother no better than she should be, unknown or absentee father, children pushed around between foster parents, unusual relations with animals. They had been brought up in dirt and poverty, always dreaming of the better life and striving to grab it the fastest way. Now one had come to a sticky end. The other was implicated. How long before he too met some sordid fate?

'What are you thinking about?' asked Romulus.

'I saw you, that night in Alba,' the investigator told him. 'The night the old king was killed.'

'Oh, that night!' exclaimed the old king's nephew in a soft, bitter voice. He seemed much older than he should.

'It looked like a happy ending for you and your brother.'

'Do you believe in happy endings?' Today, with Remus dead, Romulus clearly did not.

'I believe in order,' the investigator said. 'So when people get killed, I believe in calling the perpetrator to account.'

'You'll wear yourself out!' jeered the tearaway prince. 'I'll stick with believing in fate.'

Fate had certainly seemed to be on their side when he and his brother had come to Alba. At that time the twins had been at the height of their success as community heroes attacking bandits. One group, however, had set a trap for them. Remus had been captured by these robbers and handed over, first to the king of Alba, then to his deposed brother whose estates had been raided by the twins. So Remus had come face to face with his grandfather for the first time. The grandfather started to think.

Faustulus, who had long ago worked out the twins' royal origin, realised the truth was bound to come out. Back in the shepherd's hut there was urgent discussion. Romulus knew he had to act. With typical flair he infiltrated the city, rescued his brother, killed the usurping king, and saw their grandfather finally reinstated as monarch.

'So what went wrong?' mused the man from Alba. 'You had been greeted in triumph. You were princes restored to your heritage.'

'You can never go back,' said Romulus darkly. His expression cleared a little. 'We wanted space. We were uncomfortable in the old city that had once rejected us. We wanted our own territory.' He spoke as if fleeing the nest were some new idea. The investigator smiled. Alba was sorely overpopulated, all agreed. And the Silvius boys had always looked as if they were driven by unusual strength of will.

'So here you are. Back where you were found in the floods and brought up. About to found a new city that could rival all others – but now Remus is dead. Do you want to tell me about it?'

'No.'

The eyes of Romulus seemed to glitter as he stared out across the river. Was this simply the madness of a born killer? Or was it the set face of a man who had committed a horrific act by accident against the person he had always been closest to, a man who knew he now had to live with that for the rest of his life?

'It would be better if you told me,' repeated the investigator

31

quietly. The forces of right and wrong fought their old battle in silence.

Despite his previous refusal, the surviving twin began speaking. His voice was controlled but tense. 'The situation was impossible. No city can have two founders.' Why not? Well, any idea of partnership had always been lost on the Silvius family. Suggesting notions of brotherhood was just asking for a black eye. 'Because my brother and I were twins there was no seniority. We decided to ask the gods of the countryside to say which of us should govern the new city, and give his name to it.'

'So you chose to use augury?'

'One has to be civilised.'

'Of course.'

Augury was a rural art. In theory it was scrupulously impartial. To the sceptic from Alba it was open to misinterpretation, otherwise called fraud. The diviner foretold the future by looking at flight patterns of birds. That was random enough. The trickery entered when the diviner gave his opinion of what the patterns meant. At this point human error was inclined to creep in.

'I stood upon this hill here; Remus was on that one.' Romulus gestured to the Aventine. 'My brother spoke first. He had seen six vultures.'

He fell silent. The investigator had already heard what happened next. Immediately after Remus had made his pronouncement, Romulus doubled the tally and saw twelve birds. Well, that was what he said. Presumably Remus soon realised he had walked right into that one.

'Your brother's followers claimed priority for him, on the grounds that he had seen his sign first?'

'Yes. While mine did the same on grounds of number.'

'So nothing was solved!'

'Fighting broke out,' Romulus confirmed wryly.

'And is that when you killed him?'

'No.' Had the rediscovered prince not been so heavily sunburnt after his life as a shepherd, he might have looked as if he were blushing. An admission of the stupidity of it found its way into his voice: 'The majority seemed to agree that I should be the city's founder. I harnessed an ox and ploughed a furrow to set out a boundary. Then I set to, building a rampart. That was when Remus came over and jeered at my work. He jumped over the half-built wall, scoffing. I lost my temper and went for him.' Dangerous places, building sites. Not a sensible playground for such a pair of squabbling brothers.

To his credit, Romulus was not the type to inaugurate his city by sitting on a stool in a clean tunic giving orders from a chart. He would have been right in there with a hod or a mattock, stretching his muscles and getting his knuckles grazed. When his brother came and kicked at the newly mortared stonework with a maddening laugh, Romulus would have been hot, sweat-stained and covered with dust. After their tussle over the augury, his temper must have been stretched to breaking point. Remus never stood a chance. Still, he should have known that.

'So Remus is dead. What's your plan now?' asked the investigator cautiously. He thought he knew the plan. It could be unwise annoying a man who had just put a shovel through his own twin brother's skull for interfering.

'The plan,' stated Romulus, who also realised the fine points of the situation, 'is the same as before: I am founding a city. I mean it to rival all other cities. I shall fortify the hill on which we are standing, enclose ground, and attract manpower.'

'Mould the rabble into a body politic?' suggested the man from Alba.

'Your terms are a bit Etruscan,' said Romulus drily. He was referring to the tribesmen from north of the river, who traded with Greeks and had absorbed some exotic practices.

33

'Founding a city's more complex than herding sheep.'

'I realise that.' The prince was grim.

'For instance,' said his companion, 'you will have to address the issue of social order. Cities need rules. One rule which you may want to suggest to the community is "Don't murder each other."'

'I shall insist on it,' said Romulus calmly.

'Oh I see: "Don't do what I do, do what I say"?'

'That seems a nice definition of civic authority.'

'Now we're getting somewhere!' scoffed the investigator, who was after all a city man. He had a highly developed sense of irony, and was wary of people in charge.

Romulus had caught him gazing across the unwelcoming landscape. 'I'm going to make something of this place,' he declared. His tone was that of a visionary, as if he dreamed of ineffable empire. But since he came from rural stock, out loud he made only cautious claims: 'All you see now is wild country peopled by lawless tribes, but it will become far greater.'

'I wish you every success.'

'Why have you come to challenge me, then?'

'If whatever you're planning is meant to improve standards, maybe a murder is a bad way to start!'

'Prevent me founding my city, and there never will be anything here but the wilderness,' warned Romulus. 'You'll be interfering with history.'

'As special pleading, that's certainly different!' The investigator smiled. 'Normally when I tackle a suspect he says, "Put me away, and one dark night my pals will get you!" I have to admit, I wasn't expecting anything subtle from one of the Silvius boys . . . but it still leaves me as the high-minded idiot who has to allow you your second chance.'

There was a theory that if you gave hoodlums from a deprived background something to care about, they would come good. The man from Alba doubted it. On the other hand, not many roughnecks from difficult families were offered the chance to establish an empire as their sweetener to reform themselves.

'Think of it as an investment in the future,' said Romulus. Adding, 'As for me, I shall atone for Remus by devoting my life to the new city.'

'Ah – community service!' replied the investigator, inventing a dubious concept without intending to.

There was a short silence, which was not unfriendly.

Romulus stirred. As a man with a nation to found, he rarely stayed still for long. 'So is that all you wanted to ask me?'

'Yes.' The investigator's tone had a decisive note. 'Well, there's just one more thing—'

Romulus stared at him, unfamiliar with the concept of an investigator suddenly turning back with the unexpected question that overturns the alibi. Even so, he had a feeling he was about to be tricked. 'What's that?'

'Only—' For the first time a slight note of bashfulness entered the investigator's voice. 'If you're founding a city, you're going to need law enforcement—'

'So?'

'So I wondered if there might be a job for me.'

Decades later two grizzled investigators were comparing notes. The elder, retired now but still an expert in his own eyes, tried to cheer up his colleague by relating his own worst experience.

'Believe me, I know the nightmare: the witnesses clam up and the prime suspect is boasting that you can't touch him. There's unavoidable publicity; the whole population is watching and waiting for your big mistake. Mine had a royal connection – in fact, even the gods were taking an interest, according to some.'

'So what was this – a family case? Gang warfare? Or a

business partnership that went wrong?'

'Oh, all those! I'm talking about the Silvius brothers.' The name meant nothing. Time had moved on. There were new villains now. 'I knew who did the killing. There had been plenty of onlookers. He admitted the crime. The problem was, I couldn't touch him.'

'They all say that,' the young man disagreed. 'It's standard: "You've nothing on me! You'll never make it stick!" Normally once you've got as far as accusing them, you know you'll take them all the way to court.'

'Mine,' smiled the old expert, 'was never a normal case.'

'No case is normal,' snapped the rookie impatiently, as they turned down an alley (looking twice in case of muggers) then peeled off into a favourite bar. Immediately they both wondered why it had become such a favourite. The frosty girl who took their order growled with irritation at their greeting. She hated men in their line of business; well, she hated men in any line. She was suffering from an appalling cold. Her bar-room etiquette was to cough all over any drinks she was serving, then she coughed all over the customers. When they paid up, she fiddled the money.

Some things never change.

'No case is normal,' agreed the retired agent with a smile. 'Especially if you try to arrest Romulus!'

His young companion was choking on his drink. 'Romulus!' Now, sitting in Rome, which was already a leading city amongst its neighbours, with Romulus the great leader after a lifetime of wise public service, the idea of anyone taking him to task seemed unbelievable.

'He killed his brother. I thought he should account for it.'

'You set about him like a suspect – and then he gave you a job?'

The old expert looked diffident. When he had risked the

question, Romulus had suddenly smiled – the calm, confident smile of a man who knows he will fulfil his destiny. 'He said I had the right attitude.'

The young one spluttered again, but subsided in awe. 'Well, it all worked out.'

'Letting him off? Well, he wasn't going to offend again. We agreed what happened to Remus was all in the family – the fighting Silvius brothers doing what their ancestors did best. Unless their mother, the vestal virgin, had secretly borne triplets to the so-called god of war, Romulus had run out of brothers. I had two options: I could arrest him – if I wanted to be thrown off a crag by the mob. Or I could give him his chance.'

'So why do you call the case a problem?'

'I hate loose ends. Even when Romulus gave the city laws and made the populace respect them, when his own reputation had become impeccable, I could never forget that Remus was dead and nobody had answered for it.'

The younger man laughed. 'You're obsessed!'

'That's why it's a problem,' agreed the other quietly.

'Madness! He's built the greatest city in Italy. You're vindicated.'

The rookie's friend felt obliged to be fair: 'There was the business of the gang rape. I was never happy with our result on that.'

'The Sabine girls?' Surprised at first, the younger colleague forced himself to take the professional view. 'Well, yes; I can see there was a case – against Romulus as the ringleader, and every male in the city.'

'There had been a prior conspiracy; and the women were abducted and held against their will.'

'But when their fathers made a complaint, surely the victims all refused to testify?'

The retired officer shrugged. 'Marital rape is always tricky to prove in court.'

'They knew when they were well off,' said the young man, taking the robust Roman view. 'Husbands who were not bad, and life in a bright modern city.'

'Oh, I'm sure that's how they saw it,' agreed the old expert gravely. For a moment his young friend felt disconcerted. He sympathised with Romulus all those years before, standing on the edge of the Palatine and hearing this stubborn maverick suggest that the dead Remus should perhaps not be lightly passed off as a mere hitch on the road to destiny?

'Don't tell me you're still hoping to get him one day?'

Without comment, the retired investigator smiled and made ready to leave. In the doorway he paused for a moment. An old habit. Rome was a city, so it was full of thieves and fraudsters and people knocking each other on the head; sometimes there was a reason, but sometimes they did it just because they felt like it. Anyone who knew what he was doing stopped to sniff the air and look down the street before he stepped outside. That's what cities are like.

After he had gone, the younger man sat on, finishing the wine. When he rose, fumbling reluctantly for money, the miserable barmaid spoke: 'Your friend left a tip. He's not in the same line as you, is he?'

'He was once.' The rookie chortled, still amused by the story. 'That's the investigator who once tried to arrest Romulus!' The girl appeared impressed for a moment so the man added, 'Just think; if Romulus hadn't bashed his twin brother, we could be living in a city called Reme.'

'Get away!' said the girl.

'My pal would still arrest him, if he had a chance.'

'Too late.'

The rookie paid the waitress more attention. Rome's law-enforcement men had already learned the fine principle of picking up information from bored girls in tawdry bars. 'Why's that?'

'Romulus has gone.'

'What do you mean?'

'He vanished. Did you notice that nasty storm this morning? Romulus was out reviewing some troops on the Plain of Mars. A thick cloud of mist enveloped him, so nobody else could see him. When it cleared, he had disappeared. They reckon he was taken up to heaven in the whirlwind, and that that's the last we shall ever see of him.'

'Carried off by a whirlwind, eh?' The rookie sighed. 'You're right, it's too bad.'

He stood at the counter, staring into his own thoughts. The barmaid pretended to wipe down a table.

People don't just disappear. Being carried off by a whirlwind was about as likely as being suckled by a she-wolf.

Romulus had been a popular ruler, but only among the common people to whom he gave his own loyalty. The young man knew that Romulus had attracted jealousy from some of the city senators. Could it be that the senators had set upon Romulus and despatched him secretly? There would be a body somewhere; someone just had to hunt for it . . . The insistent voice of his profession suggested that the Plain of Mars incident should be looked into.

Another voice told him not to be a fool. Law and order men are not required to involve themselves in politics. This was one case for which he would never get civic funding. And if he was right, even if he discovered the truth, he would never be allowed to make it public or take any credit.

He knew what a sensible man ought to do. But when he walked from the bar, his feet were taking him towards the low plain alongside the river where Romulus was supposed to have vanished. His head was full of unanswered questions, and in his eyes was the haunted expression of a man obsessed.

Trunk Call

Marilyn Todd

Rome, 12 BC

When a man lies on his deathbed, it is, of course, customary to send for his wife. But with Rufus Vatia, purveyor of imperial elephants, wouldn't you just know that *three* women would turn up, each laying claim to the title? For two days now they'd been pacing his tiny apartment up on the Palatine, stiff with suspicion and hating each other's guts, yet these three women stuck like glue, fearful lest one gained an edge on her rivals.

The sun rose. The sun set. And now it had risen again, its fiery ball casting long autumn shadows across the seven hills of Rome, its heat swirling white mists over the Tiber, enshrouding the brown sludgy waters which churned beneath the arches of the bridges. Another month and there would be frosts twinkling across the city's red-tiled roofs. Would Rufus Vatia, the ultimate practical joker, live to see them? Or would Death have the final laugh?

On the table, in the corner, between a carved ivory jackal and a terracotta lamp, an old-fashioned cylindrical water clock relentlessly dripped away his allotted mortal span . . .

From time to time, the women took turns visiting the sickroom, returning, though, only moments later, thin-lipped and shaking their heads, but today the physician had taken the unprecedented step of banning all visitors. The only exception he'd made was for Milo, Rufus's almond-eyed steward, who continued to waft in and out with his trays on silent, padded feet.

For the first time, everything on those trays was coming back untouched.

So the three contenders sat.

And waited.

And watched.

The clock dripped on. Occasionally, one of the women would half rise, think better of it, then sink back into position, and Claudia, observing them from the corner of her eye as she leaned against the marble flank of a rearing Spanish stallion, was reminded of a pack of hyenas waiting for the stumbling beast to finally drop. The analogy was more than apt.

Africa had been the dashing trapper's life, and across his walls antelope and lion, wildebeest and zebra thundered across the open plain, while flamingos dabbled in the margins of a pair of double doors painted to resemble a lake.

Except that the young wine merchant with the flashing eyes and tumbling curls had not come to admire the artistry in the hunter's crowded apartment . . .

'I could be wrong,' whispered a baritone in her ear, 'but I have the distinct impression you've been avoiding me.'

'They do say that's the first stage of paranoia,' Claudia replied, although when he followed her behind the statue Marcus Cornelius Orbilio found himself completely alone.

'Claudia. Please.' He managed to catch up with her beside a painted hippopotamus. 'You've got to help me out here,' he hissed under his breath.

'My pleasure.' The young wine merchant smiled, keeping her gaze on a rampaging rhino. 'The exit's just past the flamingos.'

Orbilio contrived to have his head turned by the time his grin slipped out, and forced himself to ignore the gentle curve of her collarbone and the waves of her spicy Judaean perfume.

This was a professional visit, he reminded himself sternly. The Emperor, being as fond of the charismatic trapper as he was of the showpieces themselves, had despatched the representative from the Security Police with a single, clear-cut objective. To thwart any scandal, stamp it out. Orbilio rubbed his jaw with the back of his hand and tried not to reflect that failure would unquestionably result in some far-flung posting abroad.

'Rufus Vatia is dying,' he pressed, weighing up the prospect of scorching Nubian deserts versus cold, damp Pannonian plains. 'My job is to establish which of those three has a genuine claim on his estate.'

Claudia tilted her head at a painted giraffe. Was it her imagination, or did the poor beast have a squint? 'Knowing Rufus's sense of mischief,' she said, 'he would have married them all.'

'*Bigamy?*' Marcus felt his shoulders sag. That was all his career prospects needed. And suddenly, as he glanced across to Rufus's hard-eyed harem, his original notion of fraudulent claims seemed achingly appealing . . .

The hunter would be what – forty? forty-two? With half his year spent under hot African skies, trailing, trapping and transporting elephants for the Emperor's extravaganzas, it was obvious that that easy smile and lean tanned body was never going to settle for a good book on a long winter's evening and a ballad or two on the lyre.

Not when our friend Rufus could coax a sweeter tune from that sultry Arabian beauty buffing her nails in that high-backed satinwood chair.

. . . or test the voluptuous charms of the girl who now sprawled lengthways on his couch, one smoky sage-green eye keeping a permanent vigil on the water clock.

. . . and certainly not when he could melt into the soft, milky blondeness of the creature who stood twisting her rings by the window.

'You really think these could be bigamous wives?'

'Actually,' Claudia flashed him a wicked sideways grin, 'I know it for a fact.'

A fishhook clawed in Orbilio's gut, and he battled the urge to ask the question which was uppermost in his mind. Instead, he said levelly, 'Then I suppose I should turn my investigations towards which of the three Rufus married first?' He put strong emphasis on the *three*, but Claudia did not seem to notice.

'I wouldn't waste my time, if I were you,' she said. 'The whole thing's academic.' She began to edge away from her tall, dark, human shadow. (Dammit, the last thing she wanted was the Security Police sniffing around.) 'You'll find our man Rufus is as fit as a flea.'

'*Fit?*'

Orbilio followed so fast, she had to check that his belt buckle hadn't snagged in her gown.

'Claudia, his steward is laying cypress round the front door and weaving funeral garlands of oak!'

'Milo can run naked round the Forum for all I care,' she tossed back, 'but trust me on this, Rufus is *not* at death's door.'

Marcus smiled indulgently. 'I think you'll find you're mistaken,' he said. 'I've spoken to the physician and he's adamant—'

'I may have my faults, Orbilio, but being wrong isn't one of them.'

The young investigator might have been able to suck in his cheeks, but he could not disguise the twinkle in his eyes. 'Remind me again when and where you studied medicine, will you?' he said.

'One doesn't need to have taken the Hippocratic Oath to work this one out,' Claudia retorted. How many men do you know who, when they're supposed to be standing at the ferry landing about to cross the River Styx, suddenly lurch out of bed to pinch a girl's bottom? She resisted the urge to massage the bruises and said instead, 'Our handsome trapper is up to something.'

'I just don't know what it is yet.'

'Wait, wait.' Marcus pinched the bridge of his nose. 'Let me get this straight. You think this deathbed stuff is some kind of *prank*?'

'Oh, you can bet your fine patrician boots on that.'

Except you're not the only one who can play games, Rufus, my old mucker . . .

Outside, a horse whinnied as it stumbled in a pothole and a flock of goats not sold at market bleated their way back up the Palatine Hill, but Claudia was oblivious of both. Nor did she hear the squeals of children playing hopscotch in the street, or the foghorn voice of a pie-seller over the road. No, no. Whatever sport the wily trapper was engaged in, she could match him move for move, no doubt of that. What *really* bugged her was why he had—

The collective gasp of female breath made her spring round.

Three sets of kohl-rimmed eyes were fastened on the ruffled head of the physician, which had appeared round the bed-chamber door. His young face was the colour of porridge.

'I'm sorry.' He shrugged his thin shoulders to the assembly in general, though his gaze remained fixed on his sandals. '– I did everything I could . . .' His blue eyes were tortured. 'But – I'm really sorry – Rufus is dead.'

'Impossible!' Claudia barely noticed two of the women jump out of their seats, or the other slump to the floor. She was too busy pushing past the ashen-faced medic. 'No one drops dead from a simple cough and a sneeze!'

At first she'd thought it a joke. That Rufus would burst through the door, laughing. But there was no doubt the doctor was telling the truth. His face, his voice, said it all.

'It was the quinsy,' he murmured.

'Listen.' Claudia spun round to confront him. 'When I want a medical opinion, I'll go straight to the undertaker and cut out the cost of the middle man.' This clot typified the reason why she never called a doctor. Mistakes they bury, and judging from this one's nervy, twitching manner he had – incredibly – chalked up one more medical disaster. *What the hell had gone wrong?*

'A fever set in,' he began, but that was as far as he got, because the bedchamber door was firmly slammed in his face.

Damn! Somehow Orbilio had preceded her into the bedroom, no doubt slipping in while she'd been trouncing that idiot physician!

However, what caught Claudia's breath was not the sight of the aristocratic investigator lifting to peer under Rufus's eyelids. Rather, the overwhelming number of scents which were slugging it out in this simple room of woven drapes and wooden floor, bearskin rug and the writing desk strewn with scrolls and dice and shaving implements.

Slowly, Claudia identified the conflicting odours, one by one. Dark purple heliotrope in glazed pots out on the balcony. The heady aromas of the physician's ointments, his tinctures, rubs and infusions. There was evidence of some over-zealous beeswax polish. Burnt bread. Lavender oil in the lamps. And from the street far below, over-ripe peaches and pitch.

Alone, each scent could have laid out a horse, but the winner, on points, was surely the smell of death which clung to that motionless figure. The setting sun reflected off the only hint of luxury in the room, his great silver bedframe, and the light dazzled her eyes.

A perfect excuse, she thought, to turn away from the empty shell that had once been Rufus Vatia . . .

Around the walls, his adored elephants trumpeted and reared, their characters captured as clearly as the faces of their trainers. Some bore wooden castles on their backs, from which mock battles were fought in the arena. Others danced, or performed tricks, while the little ones endeared themselves merely by being babies. Moving round, she saw that the scene behind the desk recorded Rufus's skill in capturing the animals. The pits that he dug. The way he hobbled the beasts. The ships he carried them home in. Even the odd, tragic casualty, like when two elephants drowned after one boat capsized in the harbour, or when an Oriental assistant had been trampled beneath giant grey feet.

Claudia swallowed. So much death. So much unnecessary, excessive, *premature* death . . .

She stood for a moment, swaying, trying to make order from chaos. And then, while Orbilio was engrossed with his grisly inspections, slender fingers silently riffled the papers and scrolls on Rufus's desk.

Dammit, what she wanted wasn't there. Come on, come on, it's got to be here somewhere. Where have you hidden it, Rufus? Her stomach lurched. Oh, no! *Please* don't say it's under the mattress . . .

Claudia swivelled her eyes towards the lean, bronzed figure stretched out on what was now his funeral bier – only her gaze never reached as far as the trapper. The instant she saw the expression on Orbilio's face, ice exploded throughout every vein.

'You were right,' he rasped. 'Rufus didn't die from a simple cough and a sneeze. He's been poisoned.' He straightened up and spiked his fingers through his thick, dark curls. 'So I think now's as good a time as any for you to tell me exactly what brings a young wine merchant to this flat.'

Night had fallen. Claudia was in her own garden, where silvery trails of slug slime shone in the light of a full hunter's moon and there was not yet a chill in the air. The fountain gurgled like a contented baby, and somewhere a frog croaked to the bats.

The gate hinge had been oiled far too often to creak, but she knew it had opened behind her and she felt, rather than saw, him approach. There was a faint shadow of stubble on his chin and he poured himself a goblet of wine before settling himself beside her on the white marble bench, his back tight to the trunk of the sour apple tree. He smelled of sandalwood and ambition, leather and hope. An owl hooted from the garden next door.

'See that statue?' Orbilio's voice was thick as he pointed to the nymph and her amorous satyr. 'One kiss like that from you, Claudia Seferius, and I would be faithful to you for ever.'

'Well, thank you, Marcus. I appreciate the warning.'

In the darkness, she saw him grin and the tension drained from her limbs. Slowly – very slowly – the stars tramped their way across the heavens and Claudia pulled a wrap round her shoulders.

'You were right,' he said eventually. 'About who killed Rufus.'

Claudia watched a moth flutter round the vervain, a plant reputed to have sprung from the tears of Isis, before moving on to drink from the sweet blue blooms of borage.

'What happened when you broke the news to our winsome trio that Rufus was not the rich catch they believed they'd netted, but was actually up to his eyeballs in debt?'

The trapper was a man who worked hard and played harder, and his personal slogan of 'Live now, pay later' was fine . . . providing one remembered that there *was* a second part to that motto. Unfortunately, in Rufus's case, this wasn't as often as his creditors might have wished. Indeed, had it not been for his dire financial circumstances he and Claudia would not have been thrown together in the first place.

'Let's just say two of the women are already on their way

back to Ardea,' Marcus said drily. Ardea was the town south of Rome where Rufus stabled and trained his thumping great pachyderms, the place where he spent most of his time.

It would be a different town without him, she thought. No craggy smile, no easy laugh, no acted-out tales of his exotic adventures. Idly, she wondered whether the elephants would miss him, and had a mental picture of them shuffling in patient anticipation.

'And the third one?' she queried. 'The blonde?'

He shot her a sharp, sideways glance. 'I won't ask how you fathomed it out,' he said, refilling both glasses with wine. 'But you were right on all scores.'

Claudia twirled her goblet between her hands without drinking. It was obvious from the start that Rufus Vatia had been out to make mischief. This was autumn and, fresh home from the safari he loved and facing six months in a climate he hated, he'd very quickly grown restless. So much so that when he went down with that chill in his lonely apartment, he resolved to cheer himself up. Just a joke; nothing malicious; something to make the stablehands chuckle throughout the long winter.

Rufus would pretend he was dying.

And as if three bigamous wives pitched against one another wasn't enough, he'd summonsed the little blonde's lover, as well – that young buck of a physician – in addition to Claudia Seferius, his . . . his . . .

Well, never mind what. The point was, so absorbed had Rufus been in his own machinations that he'd failed to notice the shadow stealing over him. The shadow of someone who was aware of his charade – *and decided to cash in on the opportunity to settle a score* . . .

'I must admit, I was way off target,' Orbilio said, stretching. 'My money was on the blonde – especially when she fainted at the announcement that Rufus was dead. After all, her father *is* an actor at the Theatre of Marcellus. I simply assumed she was putting it on. It's a classic ruse to divert suspicion.'

'No, her distress was real, all right. Like me, she knew there was nothing wrong with Rufus apart from a few sniffs and snuffles, so when the poor sod was suddenly pronounced dead it came as quite a shock to think her lover had shortened the odds.'

'She thought he'd killed Rufus for the money?'

'Typical Rufus, feeding each of his wives the same line, that he was sitting on a fortune.' Greedy bitches. That was the only reason they married him. 'But you're in good company, Orbilio. Blondie was way off target in her suspicions, too.'

Claudia crossed one long leg over the other and leaned back.

'Blondie's boyfriend wasn't, as she imagined, looking sick and nervous out of guilt. The poor chap suspected *her* of bumping off her husband. He was genuinely mortified.'

She recalled the pitiful slump of his shoulders, the look of utter despair. *I did everything I could*, he'd said, and although his words had been addressed to everybody in the room, in reality it was a coded message to Blondie. Obviously, as a doctor, he'd realised at once that someone had slipped Rufus poison during his absence overnight and (this was the hard bit) he also knew that he was powerless to do anything other than make the unfortunate trapper's end as comfortable as possible.

That's why he'd banned visitors. That's why he'd disguised the fetid smell of baneberries with burnt bread and lavender, heliotrope and polish.

Believing the little blonde had killed her husband for him, the physician had gone to great pains to cover up murder.

As someone predicted he would . . .

'When did you realise the truth?' Orbilio asked, resisting the urge to massage her neck and rubbing his own instead.

'The minute I saw the exquisite detail on Rufus's bedroom walls.' Claudia sank half her wine in one go.

Every expression had been captured, every likeness reproduced with breathtaking authenticity. Especially the fresco recalling the accident where, boarding ship, an Oriental helper slips and is trampled by elephants. His injuries are truly horrific. His face twists. The scene is so vivid, you wince with him. Crowds gather round, men confer. The victim continues to thrash. Rufus steps forward. He slits the dying man's throat. When he's laid on his funeral bier, the dead man's mouth rests in a smile . . .

'The resemblance to Milo was unmistakable.'

And who, but the steward, would be privy to Rufus's hoax? *Who better placed to avenge his young brother's death?*

'Milo claimed there had been bad blood between the two men for several months,' Orbilio explained. 'In his view, what Rufus did was nothing short of cold-blooded murder and anything less accurate than the gentle euthanasia scene depicted on that fresco Milo could not imagine. His version is that his brother simply lost his footing on the gangplank and Rufus took the opportunity to kill his enemy, making up the story afterwards about him being trampled.'

'And as a slave, of course, bound to a master who, rightly or wrongly, he believed had killed his brother without conscience, Milo would be in a difficult position. The sense of injustice and grievance would grow, but to kill Rufus openly would only draw attention to himself. He had to either make it look like an accident or—'

'Or throw suspicion on to somebody else.' Orbilio chinked his goblet against Claudia's. 'Exactly!'

'I expect you'll find Milo's perception has been twisted by grief,' Claudia said. There were many accusations one might level against Rufus Vatia, but cold-blooded could never be one of them. 'I dare say once you start interviewing witnesses to his brother's death—'

'Ah.' Marcus wriggled uncomfortably. 'Unfortunately, the case file is now closed. We'll only ever be able to guess at what happened. You see, Milo fell on his dagger just as the soldiers arrived to arrest him, and the Emperor wants it left at that. Just – you know – in case there *is* any truth in the rumour.'

In the darkness, Claudia smiled. 'You mean, he doesn't want any taint of scandal attached to his imperial pachyderms?'

'Like Caesar's wife,' he grinned back, 'those elephants must be above suspicion.' A few moments passed, then Orbilio rubbed his jaw thoughtfully. 'Incidentally,' he said, 'you, er . . . never did tell me what you were doing at Rufus's flat.'

Claudia thought of the reason that had brought her and Rufus together. Two people, both in financial dilemmas. One with a product to sell. The other with a means of transporting it. She then thought of the formal, written contract which the wily trapper had insisted on securing before he would agree to ship any of her precious vintage wines to Africa unfettered, shall we say, by the burden of imperial taxation.

The self-same contract, in fact, that she'd whisked from underneath his mattress. And which now lay as a delectable pile of white ash in the kitchen . . .

'Oh, it was purely a social visit,' she purred, flicking a strand of hair from her face.

After all.

What's the point of having double standards, if you don't live up to both?

Who Stole the Fish?
A Sister Fidelma Mystery

Peter Tremayne

Co Laois, Ireland, AD 664

S ister Fidelma glanced up in mild surprise as the red-faced
religieux came bursting through the doors into the refectory where she and her fellow religieuses were about to sit
down at the long wooden tables for the evening meal. In fact,
Abbot Laisran had already called for silence so that he could
intone the *gratias*.

The man halted in confusion as he realised that his abrupt
entrance had caused several eyes to turn questioningly upon
him. His red cheeks, if anything, deepened their colour and he
appeared to wring his hands together for a moment in
indecision. He knew well that this was no ordinary evening
meal but a feast given in welcome to the Venerable Salvian,
an emissary from Rome who was visiting the Abbey of Durrow.
The patrician Roman was even now sitting by the side of the
Abbot, watching the new arrival with some astonishment.

The red-faced monk apparently summoned courage and
hurried to the main table where Abbot Laisran stood with an
expression of irritation on his rotund features. He bent forward.
A few words were whispered. Something was wrong. Fidelma
could tell that by the startled look which formed momentarily
on the Abbot's face. He leaned across to his steward, who was
seated at his left side, and muttered something. It was the
steward's turn to look surprised. Then the Abbot turned to his
guest, the Venerable Salvian, and seemed to force a smile

before speaking, waving his hand as if in emphasis. The old patrician's expression was polite yet puzzled.

The Abbot then rose and came hurrying down the refectory in the wake of the religieux who had delayed the meal. To her surprise, Fidelma realised the Abbot was making directly towards her.

Abbot Laisran was looking very unhappy as he bent down with lowered voice. 'I have need of your services, Fidelma,' he said tersely. 'Would you follow me to the kitchens?'

Fidelma realised that Laisran was not prone to dramatic gestures. Without wasting time with questions, she rose and followed the unhappy man. Before them hurried the red-faced brother.

Beyond the doors, just inside the kitchen, Abbot Laisran halted and looked around. There were several religieux in the long chamber where all the meals of the Abbey were prepared. Curiously, Fidelma noted, there was no activity in the kitchen. The group of religieux, marked as kitchen workers by the aprons they wore and rolled-up sleeves, stood about in silent awkwardness.

Laisran turned to the red-faced man who had conducted them hither. 'Now, Brother Dian, tell Sister Fidelma what you have just told me. Brother Dian is our second cook,' he added quickly for Fidelma's benefit.

Brother Dian, looking very frightened, bobbed his head several times. He spoke in rapid bursts and was clearly distressed.

'This afternoon, our cook, Brother Roilt, knowing that the Venerable Salvian was to be the guest of the Abbey at this feast, went down to the river with his fishing rod and line, intent on hooking a salmon to prepare as a special dish.'

Laisran, fretting a little at this preamble, cut in: 'Brother Roilt caught a great salmon. He showed it to me. It was just right for the dish to present to Salvian. It would show him how well we live in this part of the world . . .'

Brother Dian, nodding eagerly, intervened in turn. 'The fish was prepared and Brother Roilt had started to cook it a short while ago for we knew that the *gratias* was about to be said. I was in charge of preparing the vegetables, so I was working at the far end of the kitchen. Brother Roilt was cooking the fish over there . . .' He indicated the respective positions with a wave of his hand. 'A short while ago, the chief server entered and told me that everyone was ready at the tables. I looked up to see whether Brother Roilt was ready also so that the servers could take in the fish. I could not see Brother Roilt. I came down to where he had been cooking the fish and . . . and the fish was gone.'

Abbot Laisran gave a groan. 'The fish has been stolen! The delicacy that we were to present to the Venerable Salvian! What shall I do?'

Fidelma had not said a word since she had been summoned from the refectory. Now she spoke. 'The fish is missing. How do you deduce it was stolen?'

It was Brother Dian who answered. 'I made a thorough search of the kitchens and questioned the kitchen staff.' He gestured to the half-dozen or so brothers who stood gathered in their silent group. 'Everyone denies knowledge of the missing fish. It has simply vanished.'

'But what of the cook, Brother Roilt?' Fidelma demanded, irritated by the lack of explanation of the obvious. 'What does he say about this matter?'

There was a pause.

'Alas,' moaned Brother Dian. 'He, too, had disappeared.'

Fidelma arched an eyebrow. 'Are you saying that one moment he was cooking the salmon over a fire in this kitchen, with half a dozen others around him, and the next moment he had vanished?'

'Yes, Sister,' the man wailed. 'Maybe it's sorcery. *Deus avertat!*'

59

Fidelma sniffed disparagingly. 'Nonsense! There are a hundred reasons why the cook might have disappeared with his fish.'

Brother Dian was not convinced. 'He took such care with it because he knew it was going to be placed before the emissary from Rome. He caught the fish in the River Feoir itself, a great, wise salmon.'

'Show me exactly where he was last seen with this fish,' Fidelma instructed.

Brother Dian took her to a spot at the far end of the kitchen beside an open door leading into the Abbey gardens. There was a table below an open window to one side and next to this was a hearth over which hung both a *bir*, or cooking spit, and an *indeoin*, or gridiron.

'It was at this gridiron that Brother Roilt was cooking the fish,' the red-faced brother informed her. 'He was basting it with honey and salt. See there.' He pointed to a large wooden platter on the table before the open window. 'There is the platter he intended to put it on.'

Fidelma bent forward with a frown. Then she put a finger to the platter where she had seen grease stains and raised it to her lips.

'Which he did put it on,' she corrected gently.

Then her eyes fell to the floor. There were a several spots on the oak boards. She crouched down and looked at them for several seconds before reaching forward, touching one with her forefinger and bringing it up to eye level.

'Has anyone been slaughtering meat in this part of the kitchen?' she asked.

Brother Dian shook his head indignantly. 'This area of the kitchen is reserved for cooking fish only. We cook our meat over there, on the far side of the kitchen, so that the two tastes do not combine and ruin the palate.'

Fidelma held her red-tinged fingertip towards Abbot Laisran.

'Then if that is not animal blood, I presume our cook has

cut himself, which might account for his absence,' she observed drily.

Abbot Laisran frowned. 'I see. He might have cut himself and dropped blood over the fish and, seeing that it was thus tainted, might have been forced to discard it?'

Sister Fidelma smiled at the chubby-faced Abbot.

'A good deduction, Laisran. We might make you a *dálaigh* yet.'

'Then you think that this is the answer?'

'I do not.' She shook her head. 'Brother Roilt would not simply have vanished without telling his staff to prepare some substitute dish. Nor would he have deserted his kitchen for such a long period. There are more blood spots on the floor.'

Keeping her eyes on the trail of blood, Fidelma followed it to a small door on the other side of the open door to the garden.

'Where does that lead?'

'A storeroom for flour, barley and other grains. I've looked inside. He is not hiding there, Sister,' Brother Dian said.

'Yet the spots of blood lead in there.'

'I did not see them before you pointed them out,' confessed the second cook.

Fidelma opened the door and peered inside. There were several large cupboards at the far end, beyond the stacked sacks of grains. She walked swiftly towards them, having observed where the blood spots led, and opened the door of the central one.

The body of an elderly monk fell out on to the floor to the gasps of horror from those about her. A large butcher's knife protruded from under the corpse's ribcage.

'This, I presume, is Brother Roilt?' she enquired coldly.

'*Quod avertat Deus!*' breathed the Abbot. 'What animals are we that someone kills the cook to steal a fish?'

One of the younger brothers began to sob uncontrollably. The Abbot glanced across in distraction. 'Take Brother Enda and give him a glass of water,' he instructed another youth who was trying to comfort his companion. He turned back to Fidelma apologetically. 'The sight of violent death is often upsetting to the young.'

'I know who must have done this evil deed,' interposed one of the young men, who was wearing a clean white baker's apron over his habit. 'It must be one of those wandering beggars that were camping by the river this morning.'

The term he actually used was *daer-fudir*, a class of people who were more or less reduced to penury and whose labour was as close to slavery as anything. These were criminals or prisoners taken in warfare who could not redeem themselves and had lost all civil rights in society. They often wandered as itinerant labourers hiring themselves out to whoever would offer them food and lodging.

Abbot Laisran's face was grave. 'We will take our revenge on this band of miscreants if—'

'There is no need for that,' interrupted Fidelma quietly. 'I have a feeling that you will not find your fish thief among them.'

They all turned towards her expectantly.

'Abbot Laisran, you must return to your distinguished guest. Is there some other dish which can replace the fish that you were to serve him?'

The Abbot glanced at Brother Dian.

'We can serve the venison, Father Abbot,' the second cook volunteered.

'Good,' Fidelma answered for Laisran. 'Then get on with the meal and while you are doing that I shall make some inquiries here and find out how Brother Roilt came by his death and who stole the fish.'

The Abbot hesitated but Fidelma's expression was determined and confident. He nodded briefly to her and, as an afterthought, directed Brother Dian to obey all her instructions.

Fidelma turned to the table under the window and stared down at the empty wooden platter with the now drying grease marks on it. After a moment or two, she raised her eyes to gaze into the tiny plot beyond. It was a small, enclosed herb garden.

It was clear, from the blood spots, that Brother Roilt had been standing here when he was stabbed. He could not have walked to the store cupboard on his own. The killer would have had to drag him there, probably on his back, pulling him by his two arms. Had he been dragged on his stomach then the blood trail would have been more noticeable. The physical removal of the body would not have been difficult for Brother Roilt was elderly, small and frail in appearance. Indeed, he did not look remotely like the typical cook. But why had no one else in the kitchen seen anything?

She swung round.

The kitchen staff were busy handing platters to the servers who were waiting to take them to the tables in the refectory beyond.

There were six workers in the kitchen. It was a long, large chamber but, she realised, it actually was L-shaped. Part of it was hidden from the other part. Brother Roilt would not have been seen by anyone beyond the angle. Furthermore, the centre of the room, along its entire length, contained preparation tables and a central oven. The kitchen was fairly wide but, with a series of wooden supports running along its centre, it was obvious that certain lines of sight would be met with visual obstruction. Yet while these might obscure vision from various points, it was surely impossible that no one had been in a position to see the killer stab the cook and then drag him to the storeroom, even if the murder had been executed almost soundlessly.

That a murder could have been done in full view and no one had noticed it was also impossible.

She glanced back down to the platter. Who stole the fish?

Why kill someone to steal a salmon? It was not logical. Not even an itinerant worker would come forward and attempt such a thing in these circumstances.

She went to the open door and stood looking out into the herb garden. It was no more than ten metres square, surrounded by a high wall and with a wooden gate at the far end. She walked down the paved pathway towards it and saw that it carried a bolt. The bolt was firmly in place and this would have prevented any access into the garden from the outside. Furthermore, anyone leaving by this means could not have secured the bolt behind them.

She turned and walked back to the kitchen door. There was nothing unusual; nothing out of place. By the door stood a spade and some other gardening tools. Next to them, on the ground, was an empty tin dish. Presumably, the tools were used for tending the garden. Fidelma realised that there was only one conclusion. Brother Roilt must have been killed by someone who had been in the kitchen.

She was so engrossed in contemplating this fact as she re-entered the kitchen and took her stand by the empty fish platter that she did not see Brother Dian return to her side until he cleared his throat in order to regain her attention.

'The dishes have been taken into the refectory, Sister. What do you wish us to do now?'

Fidelma made a quick decision. 'I want everyone who was working in the kitchen to come forward,' she instructed.

Brother Dian waved the men forward. 'I was here; then there was Brother Gebhus, Brother Manchán, Brother Torolb, Brother Enda and Brother Cett.'

He indicated them each in turn. They stood before her looking awkward, like small boys caught in some naughty escapade and brought before their senior. It had been the youthful Brother Enda who had given way to his emotions at the sight of the dead body. Now he seemed in more control,

64

although his eyes were red and his facial muscles pinched in maintaining his calm.

'I want each one of you to go to the position where you were working at the time when it was noticed that Brother Roilt was missing.'

Brother Dian frowned. 'To be truthful, Sister, it was the fish which I noticed was missing first. I was, as I said, at the far end of the kitchen preparing the vegetables. Brother Gebhus was my assistant, working at my side.'

'Go there, then,' Fidelma instructed.

Brother Dian walked to the far end of the room with Brother Gebhus trotting after him. They were hidden from sight by the central obstructions but did not go into the area which was hidden by the angle of the L. She stood at the spot where the murdered man must have worked. She could not see the second cook or his assistant from that point.

'Now repeat your actions when you came to check on the readiness of the fish,' she called.

Brother Dian appeared around an obstruction at the top of the kitchen, hesitated, and then came towards her.

'What made you take the trouble to do this?' she enquired.

'The server who was to take the fish to the table had entered from the refectory. The door as you know is at the top end of the chamber near where I was working. He told me that the *gratias* was about to be said. That was why I turned and saw Brother Roilt was not at his position and when I came along I saw that the fish was missing.'

'How many entrances are there to the kitchen?'

'Three.'

'And these are . . . ?'

'The garden entrance, the door from the refectory and the one which leads into a small anteroom in which the servers prepare their trays and plates to go into the refectory.'

'So if anyone left the kitchen they would have to go directly

65

into the refectory or into the servers' room?'

'In which case,' Brother Dian pointed out, 'they would have been observed. The only way in and out without going through one of those rooms is through the kitchen garden. That is why I agree it was the itinerants who slunk in—'

Fidelma held up a hand. 'The garden is surrounded by a high wall. There is a wooden door which gives the only exit or entrance. That door is bolted from the inside.'

Brother Dian pursed his lips. 'The reason it is locked, Sister, is because I locked it. When I noticed the fish had gone, I went out to see if the culprit was still in the garden.'

Fidelma gestured in exasperation. 'And was the door shut or opened at that time?' she demanded.

'It was open. That was very unusual. Indeed, I clearly remember that when we arrived to start the meal this evening the gate was shut and locked. That's why I threw the bolt on it, to make sure no one else came through that way.'

'I am glad that you have told me.' She was reflective. 'It could have led to a wrong conclusion.' She did not explain further but turned to the others.

'Will everyone now go to the positions that they occupied?'

She saw that Brother Enda and Brother Cett immediately went into the area beyond the angle of the L at the far end of the kitchen. It was obvious that they could not see around the corner.

She called them out into her line of vision again. 'How long were you in that area, Brothers?'

The two young religieux exchanged glances. Brother Cett spoke for them both for the red-eyed Brother Enda was clearly still upset.

'This is where we prepare the fruit. We were washing and cutting pieces for the dessert course. That is our only task and so we were here most of the time. There was no reason for us to be anywhere else.'

'When did you last see Brother Roilt?'

'When we arrived in the kitchen to start to prepare our dishes. As head cook we had to report to him.'

'Stay there then.' She walked back to her original position. 'Now the rest of you . . .'

Brother Gebhus still remained out of sight at Brother Dian's original position. Brother Torolb stood on the far side of the kitchen in front of another big range supporting meat spits, while Brother Manchán took a position at the centre table next to some clay ovens where he had obviously been preparing bread.

Fidelma regarded their positions carefully. If Torolb and Manchán had been glancing in Roilt's direction, then they would have seen him, although with various obstructions depending on what they were doing. For example, if Brother Torolb had been bending to his cooking range he would have been facing the opposite wall, and even when he turned there would have been a central table with a low central beam from which a number of metal pots and pans hung which would have obstructed his view. He could only have seen the midsection of Brother Roilt.

She checked each of their views carefully before sighing in exasperation.

If everyone had been totally engrossed with their work, it might just have been possible for someone to enter from the herb garden, stab Roilt, drag his frail body to the storeroom and then steal the fish. Yet she was sure that the murderer had not come in from the garden. It made no sense. Why kill Roilt for a fish? The plate was by the window. If they were so desperate, they could have waited until Roilt's attention was distracted, leaned forward across the window sill and grabbed the fish. Why take such an extraordinary risk of discovery and resort to murder? And there was the matter of the gate.

Perhaps she was looking at this from the wrong viewpoint?

'I shall speak to each of you individually, starting with Brother Dian,' she announced. 'The rest of you will continue about your duties until you are called.'

With the exception of Brother Dian, the others, reluctantly it seemed, resumed their tasks in other parts of the kitchen.

'How long have you been second cook here?' Fidelma began.

Brother Dian reflected. 'Five years.'

'How long had Roilt been cook here?'

'Is this relevant? We should be searching for the itinerants,' he began, and then caught the glint in her eye. 'Roilt had been here for a year longer than I. That was why he was head cook.'

'Did you and the others get on with him?'

'Roilt? No one liked him. He was a weasel of a man.' He stopped, flushed and genuflected. '*De mortuis nil nisi bonum*,' he muttered. Of the dead say nothing but good.

'*Vincit omnia veritas*,' replied Fidelma sharply. Truth conquers all things. 'I prefer to hear the truth than false praise.'

Brother Dian glanced around. 'Very well. It is known that Roilt liked the company of the young novitiates, if you know what I mean. Male novitiates,' he added with emphasis.

'There was hatred towards him because of this?'

Dian nodded. 'Many brothers disliked his abuse of the young.'

'Abuse? Do you mean that he forced his attentions on them against their will?'

Dian gave an expressive shrug by way of reply.

'Did Roilt have affairs with any of the kitchen staff?' she demanded.

Dian blinked at the directness of the question. 'I must protest, Sister . . . you are here to find out who stole the fish . . .'

'I am here to find out who murdered Brother Roilt,' snapped Fidelma, causing Brother Dian to start.

'It is clear that he was killed for the fish,' Dian said doggedly after a moment to recover.

'Is it?' Fidelma glanced to the far end of the kitchen. 'Ask Brother Enda to come to me.'

Brother Dian looked surprised at being summarily dismissed. A moment later the youthful, red-eyed Brother Enda arrived at her side.

'Are you feeling better now?' Fidelma asked him.

The young man nodded slowly. 'It was a shock, you see . . .' he began hesitantly.

'Of course. You were close to Brother Roilt, weren't you?'

Brother Enda flushed and pressed his lips firmly together, saying nothing.

'Were you currently in a relationship with him?' demanded Fidelma.

'I was not.'

'He preferred someone younger?'

'He was the only person who was kind to me in this Abbey. I shall not speak ill of him.'

'I do not ask you to say anything that is not the truth and will not help us find out who killed him.'

The young man seemed bewildered for a moment. 'I thought he was killed for . . .'

'For the fish?' Fidelma's expression did not change. 'Did he have a current lover?'

'I think there was a young novitiate that he had just taken a liking to.'

'When did he end his relationship with you?'

'Six months ago.'

'Were you angry about that?'

'Sad. I was not—' The young man's eyes abruptly widened. 'You think that I . . . that I killed him?' His voice rose on a high note causing some of the other kitchen workers to turn in their direction.

'Did you?' Fidelma was unperturbed.

'I did not!'

'How about Brother Cett? He is your age. Did he have a relationship with Roilt or with yourself?'

Enda laughed harshly. 'Brother Cett is not like that. He loves women too much.'

'There is no feeling, beyond fraternity, between you and Cett?'

'We are friends, that is all.'

'I am told that Roilt was disliked. Perhaps he was disliked for his sexuality? Often people kill out of fear of things they cannot comprehend.'

'I can only tell you what I know,' insisted the young man stubbornly.

'That is all that is asked of the innocent.' Fidelma smiled thinly. 'Send Brother Torolb to me.'

Torolb was a man about twenty years of age. He was handsome and still in the vigour of youth, though not so young as Enda or Cett. He was dark-eyed and had determined features, an expression as though he would not suffer fools gladly. He wore a short leather apron around his habit.

'Your task is to cook the meat dishes?' she asked. Torolb nodded warily.

'How long have you worked in the kitchens here?'

'Since I came to the Abbey at the "age of choice".'

'Three or four years ago?'

'Four years ago.'

'So you learned your art in this kitchen?'

Torolb smiled thinly. 'Part of it. I was raised on a farm and taught to butcher and cook meat when I was young. That was why I specially asked to work in the kitchens.'

Fidelma glanced down at his clothing. 'You have blood on your apron,' she observed.

Torolb uttered a short laugh. 'You cannot butcher and cut meat without blood.'

'Naturally,' sighed Fidelma. 'How well did you know Brother Roilt?'

An expression of displeasure crossed Torolb's features. 'I knew Roilt,' he replied shortly.

'You did not like him?'

'Why should I?'

'He was head cook and you were under his direction. People have feelings about those they work with and an elderly man usually influences the young.'

'Roilt could only influence gullible youths like Enda. Others despised him.'

'Others, like yourself?'

'I do not deny it. I obey the law.'

'The law?' Fidelma frowned.

'The law of God, the Father of Christ Jesus,' replied the young man fiercely. 'You will find the law in Leviticus where it says "If a man has intercourse with a man as with a woman, they both commit an abomination. They shall be put to death; their blood shall be on their own heads." That is what is written.'

Fidelma examined the saturnine young man thoughtfully. 'Is that what you believe?'

'That is what is written.'

'But do you believe it?'

'Surely we must believe the word of the Holy Scripture?'

'And would you go so far as to carry out the word of that Scripture?'

The young man glanced at her, his eyes narrowing suspiciously for a moment. 'We are forbidden to take the law into our own hands and to kill. So if you are trying to accuse me of killing Brother Roilt, you are wrong. Yet if those who are given authority under the law had said he should be executed, then I would not have lifted a hand to prevent it.'

Fidelma paused for a moment and then asked: 'When you came here as a young novice, did Roilt make any advances towards you?'

Brother Torolb was angry. 'How dare you imply—'

'You forget yourself, Brother Torolb!' snapped Fidelma. 'You are talking to a *dálaigh*, an advocate of the Laws of the Fénechus. I ask questions to discover the truth. Your duty is to answer.'

'I tell you again, I obey the laws of the Faith as given in Scripture. Anyway, you forget one thing in desperately seeking to find the guilty.'

'What is that?'

'The missing fish. If I were called to be God's instrument to punish Roilt, what reason would I have to steal a fish that I did not want? Or would you like to come and search my cupboards for it?'

Fidelma gazed coldly at him. 'That will not be necessary. Tell Brother Manchán to come to me.'

Torolb turned away, his attitude one of barely controlled anger.

Brother Manchán came forward smiling. He was a fleshy, bright-faced young man, scarcely older than Torolb. He gave the impression that he had just stepped from a bath and was freshly scrubbed. His smile seemed a permanent part of his features.

'And you, Brother, I observe, are the baker of this Abbey?' Fidelma said in greeting.

Manchán wore a pristine white apron over his habit, yet this had not prevented the fine dust of flour settling over his clothing like powder.

'I have been baker here for two years and was three years assistant baker until the death of poor Brother Tomaltach.'

'So you came here as a young novitiate five years ago?'

Manchán bobbed his head and his smile seemed to broaden. 'Even so, Sister.'

'How well did you know Roilt?'

'I knew him well enough, for he was head cook here. Poor Brother Roilt.'

'Why do you say "poor"?'

'The manner of his death, what else? Death comes to us all but it should not visit us in such a terrible fashion.' The young baker shuddered and genuflected.

'Any untimely death is terrible,' Fidelma agreed. 'Yet I believe that many in this kitchen do not feel grief at this man's passing.'

Manchán glanced quickly in the direction of Brother Dian, still at the far end of the kitchen.

'I can imagine that some would even feel pleased at it,' he said quickly.

'Pleased?'

'A matter of ambition, Sister,' the young man replied.

'Do you imply that Brother Dian was ambitious to be head cook here?'

'Isn't that natural? If one is second then it behoves him to strive to be first.'

'I was not particularly thinking about ambition.'

Brother Manchán regarded her for a moment or two and then grimaced. 'I suppose you refer to Roilt's sexual inclinations?'

'What were your views?'

'Each to his own, I say. *Quod cibus est aliis est venenum.*' What is food to some is poison to others.

'That is laudable, but not a view shared by some of your colleagues.'

'You mean Torolb? Well, pay no attention to his fundamentalism. It is so much baying at the moon. Who knows? It may even be an attempt to hide his own inclinations, even from himself?'

'Yet a man who can wield a knife and slaughter an animal might have no compunction in slaughtering a human being.'

Brother Manchán reflected for a moment.

'Are you really sure that Roilt was killed by one of us? That he was not killed by itinerants determined to feed well on the salmon that disappeared? After all, wasn't the garden gate open and unbolted? One of the itinerants must have come in.'

'And you can think of no other explanation?' countered Fidelma.

The young man raised a hand to rub his chin thoughtfully.

'Anything is possible. I agree some did not like Roilt. But I think you are wrong about Torolb. Brother Dian coveted Roilt's position as head cook and disliked him because he thought himself a better cook.'

Fidelma smiled. 'But Brother Dian was at the far end of the kitchen. He would have had to leave his position and walk down the length of the kitchen to where Roilt was cooking his fish. He would have been seen by either yourself or Torolb or, indeed, by Brother Gebhus who was working beside him and would have noticed him leave.'

'But he did come by me. He did leave his position,' pointed out Brother Manchán.

'That was when he went to check whether the fish was ready; when he noticed that the fish and Roilt were missing.' Fidelma frowned as an idea occurred to her. 'Did you see Dian pass by?'

Brother Manchán nodded. 'I had my head down rolling dough but I was aware that he passed my table.'

'How long was it before he announced that Roilt was missing?'

Brother Manchán thought for a moment.

'I think that some time passed between my being aware of him passing my table and the moment I thought I heard a door bang. That made me look up and go to the corner where I could see without obstruction. I saw Brother Dian standing by the kitchen door. He was looking rather flushed, as from exertion. I asked him what was wrong and that was when he said that the fish was missing and that he could not find Brother Roilt.'

74

Fidelma was thoughtful. 'Thank you, Brother Manchán.'

She went forward to where Brother Gebhus was standing nervously awaiting her.

'Now, Brother Gebhus.' She drew him to one side of the kitchen, away from where Brother Dian was now intent on ensuring the fruit dishes were being handed to the servers.

'I don't know anything, Sister,' the young man began nervously.

Fidelma suppressed an impatient sigh. She pointed to a hearth where a fire crackled under a hanging cauldron.

'Would you like to put your hand in that fire, Brother Gebhus?' she asked.

Brother Gebhus looked startled. 'Not I!'

'Why?'

'I don't want my hand burnt.'

'Then you do know something, Gebhus, don't you?' she replied acidly. 'You know that the fire will burn your hand.'

Brother Gebhus stared blankly at her.

'Think about the meaning of what you are saying before you answer my questions,' explained Fidelma. 'I need them to be answered with accuracy. How long have you worked here?'

'Two years in this kitchen.'

'You assist Brother Dian?'

He nodded briefly, eyes warily on her.

'How well did you know Brother Roilt?'

'Not well. I . . . I tried to avoid him. I did not like him because . . .' He hesitated.

'He made advances to you?'

The young man sighed deeply. 'When I first came to the Abbey. I told him that I was not like that.'

'You were standing here when Dian went to look for Roilt?'

'He went to look for the fish,' corrected Gebhus. 'The chief server had come in and said that the *gratias* was about to be said and Brother Dian turned and looked down the aisle there to where Brother Roilt was cooking the fish for the guest of honour. He could not see him and so he went to find him.'

'And you remained here?'

'I was here from the moment I came into the kitchen this evening.'

'Was Brother Dian with you the whole time?'

'Not the whole time. He had to discuss the meal with Brother Roilt before we began and once or twice he went to consult with him and the other cooks.'

The refectory door opened at that point and Abbot Laisran came in, looking worried. He approached Fidelma.

'I just had to come to see if you had any news. Have you decided who stole the fish?'

Fidelma smiled her curious urchin-like grin.

'I knew who stole the fish some time ago. But you are just in time, Father Abbot.'

She turned and called for everyone to gather around her. They did so, expectantly, almost fearfully.

'Do you know who murdered Brother Roilt?' demanded Brother Dian, asking the question that was in everyone's minds.

Fidelma glanced swiftly at them, observing their growing anticipation.

'Brother Manchán, would you mind removing your apron?' she asked.

The young brother suddenly turned white and began to back away.

Brother Torolb grabbed him and tore the apron off. Beneath the pristine white apron, Brother Manchán's habit was splattered with bloodstains.

Abbot Laisran was bewildered. 'Why would Brother Manchán kill Roilt?'

'Reasons as old as the human condition: jealousy, love

turned to hatred; an immature and uncontrollable rage at being rejected by a lover. Manchán had been Roilt's lover until Roilt turned his attentions to a new young novitiate. Roilt rejected Manchán for a younger man. Presumably Roilt was neither sensitive nor tactful in bringing an end to his relationship and so Manchán killed him.'

The young man did not deny her accusation.

'How did you know?' asked the Abbot.

'Brother Manchán was very eager to point an accusing finger at others in the kitchen and out of it, especially at Brother Dian. I realised that he was just too eager.'

'But you must have had something else to go by?' Brother Dian asked. 'Something made you suspect him.'

'Brother Manchán was, of course, best placed to kill Roilt. When everyone had their attentions fixed on their tasks he seized the opportunity. He went forward, struck so quickly that Roilt did not have time to cry out, and then he dragged Roilt to the storeroom. He even went into the garden and opened the wooden gate, which was usually kept shut and bolted, in an attempt to lay a false trail. He pointed out to me that the gate had been open. Yet Dian, finding it so, had shut it and bolted it again almost immediately. How had he known that it had been open?'

'And he also took the fish to lay a false trail?' suggested Brother Dian.

Fidelma shook her head with a smile. 'He did not have time to do that. No; the fish was actually stolen by someone else. The opportunity to take the fish was seized when Roilt was no longer there to prevent it.'

'Just a minute,' interrupted Abbot Laisran. 'I still do not understand how you initially came to suspect Manchán. Suspicion because he tried to lay the blame on others is not sufficient, surely?'

'You are right, as always, Father Abbot,' conceded Fidelma.

'What alerted me was the problem of his apron.'

'His apron?' frowned the Abbot.

'Manchán would have us believe that he was working away making bread. Indeed, there was a fine dust of flour over his clothing with the exception of his apron which was clean; pristine white. It was clearly not the apron that he had been wearing while he was working. Why had he changed it? When Roilt was killed blood had splattered on the floor. It would have splashed on his clothes, especially on a white apron. He changed the apron in the storeroom, covering the bloodstains that had seeped through on to his habit. Seeing that clean white apron made me suspicious and his eagerness to point the finger at others simply confirmed my instinct. The reference to the gate merely confirmed matters. Now you have the proof,' she added with a gesture at Manchán's bloodstained robes.

Abbot Laisran stood nodding his head thoughtfully as he considered the matter. Then he suddenly looked at her in bewilderment. 'But the fish? Who stole the fish?'

Sister Fidelma moved across to the kitchen door and pointed down to the empty tin dish by the door.

'I noticed this earlier. It looks as though it is used to contain milk. Therefore, would I be correct in presuming that there is a cat who frequents the kitchen area?'

Brother Dian gave a gasp which was enough acknowledgement of this surmise.

Fidelma grinned. 'I suggest that a search of the garden will probably disclose the remains of the fish and your cat curled up nearby having had one of the best meals of its life. It was the cat who stole the fish.'

The Fury of the Northmen

Kate Ellis

South Coast of Devon, Britain, AD 997

'From the fury of the northmen, O Lord defend us.'

I lay on my mattress in the corner of my father's hall with Father Ordulf's words echoing in my head. Before sunset the people of the village had crowded into our new stone church and I had smelled the sweat of fear upon their bodies as I shouted the amen with the rest.

I had heard much of the northmen who came raiding and ravaging; the men whose sleek, dragon-prowed boats flashed like eels along the coasts and up the rivers, burning, robbing and forcing tribute from the terrified and defenceless.

As I listened to my mother's gentle snores and the sounds of the night, I lay still on my straw mattress and held my breath. If the Danes were coming to our village, I wanted to hear them.

I was drifting towards sleep when I heard the gentle sound of horses' hooves, slow and soft as raindrops dripping from a roof. Did the Danes ride horses? If they did, I told myself, it was unlikely they would be so quiet about it.

I had to be certain, so I rose from my bed and walked softly to the window. As I pushed at the shutter, a dog whimpered at my feet. I put my finger to my lips and it looked at me with pleading eyes, then laid its head back on its paws as I stood on tiptoe and looked out into the night. There was a good, bright moon and I could see the man clearly. He wore the habit of a monk and he was knocking on the door of Father Ordulf's cottage which stood next to the great bulk of our church. I took a deep breath of the night air that seeped in through the window, and relaxed: Father Ordulf's visitor could hardly be a threat to our village.

I was weary so I returned to my bed and fell into sleep almost at once. Sometimes now I wish that I had stayed awake and watched into the night. But even if I had, I fear I could not have prevented the bloody death of Brother Frithstan.

As my father was away fighting for King Ethelred (whom men call Unready, or of evil council), it was my brother, Oslac, who took charge the next day when the foul murder was discovered. The people look to the son of their thegn for leadership – and Oslac is seventeen years of age, a man in the eyes of most, though I would that my brother were of stronger character. I, his sister Ymma, am wiser in the ways of men.

'The Danes came among us in the night,' Father Ordulf announced. His voice was unsteady and I thought him close to tears. 'They killed a brother of the Abbey who arrived in our village after darkness. They killed him in the crypt while he was praying before the relic of our saint.'

'The Danes arrived, killed the unfortunate brother and then departed leaving the rest of us unharmed?' I heard myself saying in disbelief. 'Did they steal from the church?'

The priest turned towards me and regarded me with sad brown eyes. I knew Father Ordulf well. He had taught me to read and write and this I did now as well as any holy brother. 'I speak the truth, Lady Ymma. They departed without harming the village for which I thank God. But they stole from our church.'

'What did they take?' I asked. I glanced at my brother Oslac who was staring at me resentfully. But someone had to ask the questions and I knew that he was not man enough to do the task himself.

Father Ordulf shook his head, close to tears. 'They took fourteen shillings in alms and tithes and a silver chalice.' He looked at me nervously. I knew there was something else. 'And our holy relic . . . St Wulfgar's finger.'

The villagers had been edging closer, listening to every word. Now they gasped. The blacksmith's mother began to weep. Several lips moved in prayer.

'They took the casket?'

The priest nodded. I chided myself. It had been a foolish question. What self-respecting heathen raider would take a few small bones and leave behind the valuable jewelled casket which housed them?

'I was watching from my window last night,' I said. 'I saw the brother arrive at your house.'

'He was returning to the Abbey from Winchester and he sought shelter.'

'Our village is out of his way.'

'He and I knew each other many years ago when I too was at the Abbey. He thought to visit me.'

'Were you with him in the church when the northmen came?'

'So many questions, Ymma. Let the poor father rest after his ordeal,' my brother said in his piping voice. I turned and gave him a withering look.

'I will answer the lady's question.' Father Ordulf attempted a smile. 'I stayed in my house while Brother Frithstan went to the church to give thanks for his safe journey. It shames me to say that I fell asleep and I did not know that anything was wrong until the morning. When I realised Frithstan had not returned, I feared that something was amiss so I went to the church.' He looked away, distressed. 'Frithstan was lying in the crypt before the altar. He had been killed, most likely with

83

a dagger. I ran from the church to raise the alarm. I can only give thanks that the heathen did not set fire to our church as they have done to others.'

'And much thanks be to God for that,' said the blacksmith's wife, her arm about her mother-in-law.

'And nobody saw these Danish raiders?' I looked around at the people of the village. All manner of men and women, slaves and freemen, young and old, shook their heads, stupefied. 'So the furious northmen left us all safe in our beds?'

'Enough, Ymma.' It was my mother who barked the order. 'They robbed the church and they killed. The good brother's blood and the holy treasures were enough for them last night. Let us give thanks for our deliverance and pray that they do not return.'

I saw the determination in my mother's face. The subject was closed and I knew better than to argue. My brother nodded vigorously and whispered something to Wilfrid the bailiff who grinned slyly. I do not like Wilfrid . . . and I do not trust him. But my brother, Oslac, hangs upon his every word.

We departed after Father Ordulf had given his blessing and I noticed Wilfrid the bailiff had slunk off to join his brother, Aelfrid, at the church door. How I mistrusted that pair with their sly looks and their secret talk.

My brother also was most secretive that night. I suspected he was hiding something and I prayed it was nothing that might bring shame on our family or grief to our dear father. But I feared the worst.

The next day I made bread with the women: I kneaded the sticky dough and punched it about, imagining it to be my foolish brother's face. It is a task that never ends for we all need bread to eat . . . and it is a task that falls to us women. But it is also a time of talk when the news of the village is relayed and chewed over. And that day the talk was of Brother Frithstan's death and the heathens from the north.

Gunhilde, the blacksmith's daughter, swore she had heard them come to the village. She heard their bloodthirsty cries and saw the light of their flaming torches through the cracks in her shutters as they passed. She said she heard them saying that they would see what treasures were in the church. When I asked her how she understood their heathen tongue her cheeks reddened and she fell silent. Gunhilde is always one to invent stories: she has listened too often to the tale of Beowulf and imagines monsters in every shadow.

I asked if anybody else had witnessed anything that night. It is well to ask the women of the village for they know all that goes on. But nobody saw anything amiss, which I thought strange. It is the desire of the Danes to drive terror into our hearts; to make us afraid for our homes, our possessions and our lives so that they can exact tribute from us. Villages are burned, people taken as slaves, women ravished and men killed most brutally. We live in fear and dread, yet I have never heard of the Danes robbing and killing by stealth.

That morning my father returned, riding his fine horse through the village, the bridle jangling and glinting in the sunlight. How I rejoiced that he had not met his death serving in the king's war band, the fyrd, defending our land against the raiders from the north. I lose much sleep worrying and offering prayers for his safety. I ran to him, my hands still covered with the rough-ground bread flour, and he jumped down from his horse and took me in his arms.

My thoughts had been for my father but then I saw there was another horseman with him. Edmund, the son of a neighbouring thegn, was a young man I had known since childhood. He smiled shyly at me from his horse. I had not realised he had become so handsome.

Father Ordulf rushed from his house. As the priest had

grave news to impart, my greeting to Edmund would have to wait.

'You have told your father of the raid?' he asked.

I shook my head. My joy at seeing my father had put Brother Frithstan's death from my mind for the moment. I allowed Father Ordulf to tell his story. My father listened, a frown clouding his face.

But it was Edmund who spoke first. 'I had not thought them so close,' he said, puzzled.

'What do you mean?' I asked.

'We encountered a band of these Vikings some way around the coast. We fought them off and they fled eastwards. I fear that they will reach here in time, but I do not think it possible that they could have outrun our forces and headed this way.'

'There may be more than one force of these heathens.'

Edmund shook his head. 'Surely we would have had word of it.'

My father led the way to our hall where ale and mead would be served to the weary warriors. I knew there would be work to do: there would be a great feast to prepare for that night so I followed, walking by Edmund who talked of this and that and spoke of bravery in battle with a becoming modesty. As we walked, I saw my brother Oslac skulking in the shadows of Wilfrid the bailiff's doorway making no effort to greet our father, home from battle. I would have words with him later.

My father confirmed what Edmund had said. No Danish raiders had been seen anywhere near our village . . . as yet. Perhaps there was a rogue band, separated from their fellows . . . but somehow I doubted it. The northmen would have wreaked more destruction on our homes and people; the thatch of our roofs would be set on fire and our folk slaughtered. I began to fear that Brother Frithstan's killers might be found closer to home. But I said nothing. Let the Danes take the blame until the truth could be discovered.

I sat by Edmund at the feast and he talked of love and warfare. I like him well but of late I have been drawn to a life of prayer and scholarship and I have contemplated joining a house of holy nuns. Yet I am young: I have time to make my choice. And that night I enjoyed Edmund's company greatly as we drank the ale and listened to the poets telling of brave and noble deeds.

My brother, Oslac, sat at my father's right hand. But when the feast was near its end he excused himself and went down the hall where he was soon deep in talk with Wilfrid, the bailiff. Oslac was most likely up to some misdeed. I watched my mother gazing at him: her only son had always been her favourite and in her eyes he could do no wrong. If my father hadn't been away so long fighting the Danes, Oslac might have been guided by a firmer hand and not been spoiled by our mother's devotion.

I left Edmund's side and walked around the smoking hearth to where my brother stood. Wilfrid saw me and slipped away, quick as a ferret, to join his brother Aelfrid.

'What are you doing, brother?' I asked.

Oslac scowled. 'It is not your concern, Ymma. Go back to Edmund. It is time you had a husband to tame your shrewish ways.'

'It is time you had a wife to teach you manners and manhood. Why is your business with our bailiff and his weasel brother so important that you desert our father on the night of his return?'

'Keep your nose out of what doesn't concern you, sister.'

I could have struck him across the mouth for his bitter words but I had no wish to distress my father on the night of his homecoming. I resolved to watch Oslac closely. He could hide nothing from me, his sister who knew him so well.

* * *

Later that night I lay awake, pinching myself each time my eyelids closed in sleep. My brother was planning something and I knew that wrongdoers prefer darkness to shield their evil deeds. My cloak was by my side and if Oslac chose to leave the hall by stealth, I would hear him and follow.

My patience was rewarded. At the very dark of night when only hunting owls and those with ill intent are abroad, I heard somebody moving, stepping over the sleeping servants in the hall. I pulled my cloak about me and followed, walking on tiptoe out into the night.

It was my brother. I recognised his figure and his gait as I recognised the men who waited for him outside our hall. I kept back in the shadows, certain that I could not be seen.

They talked for a while; Oslac, Wilfrid and the weasel Aelfrid. Wilfrid the bailiff is a wealthy man, trusted by my father . . . but I fear his wealth has not been gained honestly. As the three began to walk to the edge of the village, I saw that Aelfrid carried a sack and Wilfrid carried what looked like two spades. I followed, keeping to the walls of the cottages, drawing my dark cloak about me. I was too far away to hear what my brother and his companions were saying but I knew their words were not those of honest men. Honest men do not behave like thieves in the night: honest men have nothing to hide in the darkness.

They reached the trees near where our pigs are kept. The pigs set up a noise, grunting and squealing, and the three men – if I can call my brother a man – froze until the beasts quietened before they crept on among the trees. I followed, flattening myself against a thick trunk, and watched as they took the spades and began to dig. The hole must have been shallow for they did not dig for long. When they were done they placed the sack carefully inside and covered it with earth.

As they walked softly back to the village, I stayed silent

against the tree. I waited until I was sure they were out of earshot before I moved. I had no spade but hands that can make bread are strong enough to dig a shallow hole in soft earth. I found the sack and pulled it out, staring at it a while before I emptied the contents out on to the ground.

There was still a full moon and the precious metal gleamed, reflecting its light. Coins spilled out around the silver chalice from the church. And beside it lay the fine casket, adorned with jewels of every colour, that contained the blessed finger bones of the saint.

My hands trembled as I searched to find its clasp. I had looked upon the finger of St Wulfgar only once. My father had given money to build the crypt that would house the relic and people came from far around in the hope of a cure. Many miracles were wrought and Wulfgar's finger had brought wealth to our church as people made offerings to the saint. Now I was to gaze upon it with a prayer that Brother Frithstan's killer would not go unpunished.

I found the clasp and opened the precious box with care. I expected to see the tiny bones lying on their bed of soft blue cloth. The cloth was there but the bones were gone. I sat for a while on the cold earth, staring into the empty box. Had some ignorant heathen discarded the holy relic?

But if my suspicions were correct, the unbelieving Vikings had nothing to do with the theft of the treasure at my feet. My foolish, grasping brother and his dishonest companions had decided to seize the church's treasure to enrich themselves. I shuddered. My brother's evil deeds would break my father's heart. If it were merely the theft, I would have ordered Oslac to return the treasure to the church and said no more. But there was Brother Frithstan: a human life had been lost and it pained me to think that my own kin was a murderer.

I searched for the missing bones without success, then filled the empty hole with earth. As I walked back to the hall with the sack of treasure, I pondered the best course of action. Whatever he had done, Oslac was my brother, my kin. Yet if justice were to be done he would have to pay the price for Frithstan's murder.

I entered the hall quietly and crept to where my brother lay. He appeared to be asleep but I knew better. I shook his shoulder and he sat up with a start. There was fear in his eyes as I held the sack up for him to see. It was best that we talked outside or else we would wake the whole hall. I led the way, Oslac following in terrified silence, and when we were outside I waited for my brother to speak.

'We found it,' he began.

'And the wild boar in the woods fly like birds,' I replied. 'Try again, brother. And give me no lies.'

'It is the truth. I was hunting with Wilfrid and Aelfrid and we found the sack in the hollow of a tree. I will show you that tree, Ymma. Please believe me.'

I looked into his desperate eyes and something told me that he might be telling the truth. But then a frightened boy with murder to hide would do his best to feign innocence. 'I will take these treasures to our father,' I said. 'If you are guilty of that holy man's murder you will pay the price like any other. Father would have it no other way.'

'I am innocent. I know nothing of the brother's death. I swear it.'

'Would you swear it on the finger of St Wulfgar?'

'Gladly.' He reached his hand out to the sack.

'Did you open the casket to view the holy relic?' I asked. There was something in Oslac's manner that gave me some hope.

'No. Why do you ask?'

'Swear on the relic, then.'

I fished the casket from the sack and held it out to him. He placed his right hand on it and swore that he told only the truth.

90

'What of Wilfrid and Aelfrid? Could they have taken the treasure?' I thought it unlikely that he would tell tales on his friends but I had to ask.

'They were as amazed as I was when we found it in the hollow tree.'

'Who found it first?' I asked, thinking that the accidental find might have been deliberate. Had my brother been taken for a fool to provide those two men with a plausible tale?

'I did. They were some way behind me when I spotted it.'

My fine theory was disproved . . . if Oslac was speaking the truth.

I put the casket back into the sack. 'The matter cannot rest here, brother. A man has lost his life because of these things.'

'It was the Danes,' said my brother hopefully. 'They left their loot in the tree and they will return for it later.'

I looked at my brother's youthful, hopeful face. 'We must tell others of this, Oslac. It is not something we can keep between ourselves. Our father must know.'

I returned to bed that night with a sense of dread, knowing what would become of my silly young brother if he were proved to be a murderer.

The next morning I handed the treasure to my father and told him all I knew. I would not have wished to distress him so on his return from the fyrd but I had no choice. He called for Oslac and I thought it best to leave the hall.

While I strolled through the village, lost in my own thoughts, I saw Aelfrid with his sly weasel's face, cutting the throat of a pig. How he relished the deed and smiled as the blood spattered out and spilled on the ground. I imagined him thrusting a dagger through the heart of Brother Frithstan. If Aelfrid was the killer, then my father would ensure that justice was done.

A few hours later I had word that Wilfrid, Aelfrid and my

brother had been taken and were denying their guilt. They would soon go before the court and the penalty for deliberate murder was death. Whatever Oslac had done, he was still my flesh and blood. And the thought of my father's distress moved me to tears. What man wants to see his only son hanged as a murderer?

That afternoon in the churchyard I knelt by Brother Frithstan's new grave, which lay next to the chancel on the south side – the most favoured place – and brooded on my brother's fate. It pained me that I had brought his part in the crime to light. Perhaps I should have left the matter well alone for our parents' sake. Justice is all very fine until it hurts your own kin.

My knees were sore from kneeling. I stood up but I had no wish to return to the village and the company of the chattering women. I wanted to see Father Ordulf, to make my confession and ask his good advice. I looked into the church but it was empty and I guessed that he would be praying in the crypt that had been built to house St Wulfgar's relic. Although my father now had the relic's jewelled casket in his safe keeping, there was still no sign of the finger itself. My father was organising the men of the village to search the woods for it that very afternoon and I prayed that it would be found safe and returned to its rightful place.

I entered the cool, silent church and made for the small arched doorway near the chancel. A small flight of steps led down to a narrow, candlelit stone passageway. A stranger to the church would not have known of the crypt's existence without a careful examination of the building and I was now certain that it was not the Danes who had come to our village that night. Brother Frithstan's killer was one of our own. Our bailiff and his brother perhaps, aided by my foolish Oslac . . . or another?

If I could talk of my fears with Father Ordulf, it might help me to think, to remember anything odd that had happened in the village recently. I thought of the inhabitants, but forty souls. Had anybody been behaving strangely? The blacksmith? The churls who farm the land? Any of the slaves who might have hidden the treasure against the time when they made a desperate bid for freedom?

I walked slowly down the narrow passageway, my skirts brushing the rough stone walls, and I found Father Ordulf kneeling before the crypt's small stone altar in the flickering candlelight. The niche above the altar, formed especially to house the precious relic, was empty. The sick from villages for miles around had come here to this tiny airless chamber to pray to St Wulfgar for a cure. Now hope had departed with the bones of the saint.

The priest turned as he heard my footsteps. He smiled. 'Ymma. It is good to see you, my child.' His expression became suddenly serious. 'I heard the news of your brother. I cannot believe such a thing of him and I shall tell the court so. Wilfrid and Aelfrid were always ungodly men, but—'

'It may be that my brother has fallen under their influence.'

The priest nodded sadly. 'I fear it may be so.'

'But the church will get back its treasures: my father has them safe. The saint's niche looks so empty.' I walked slowly over to the niche, my eyes on the void where the richly jewelled casket had lain. Then I stopped dead and my heart leaped at what I saw.

I turned to face Father Ordulf who was watching me with fear in his eyes. 'You always were my brightest pupil, Ymma. I cannot hide the truth from you, can I?' He smiled gently but I felt a shudder of fear.

'The bones are back . . .'

'Such tiny bones . . . the little finger of the saint. Yet they hold so much power.'

'You stole the treasure?'

'I intended the folk of the village to think that the heathen had robbed our church and killed Brother Frithstan in the course of their evil work. I put the church treasures in a sack and hid them in a hollow tree. But the bones themselves had to rest in their rightful place ... had to be treated with reverence.'

'You killed the brother?'

He paused and looked at me. I could see the first signs of tears in his eyes. 'It was for our village ... for our people. For all the sick who come with no hope but our saint.'

I began to see the truth. 'Brother Frithstan was from the Abbey ... he wanted to take our relic back with him?'

The priest nodded.

'But he had no right to take it from our village,' I said indignantly, forgetting for a moment the situation I was in.

'He had every right, my child. When I left the Abbey resolved to become a priest, I took the finger of St Wulfgar with me. Oh, I left its beautiful casket and just took the bones – your father was good enough to endow the saint with another, equally rich resting place. Nobody at the Abbey discovered that the bones were missing until recently when word of the cures and miracles St Wulfgar was performing in our church reached the Abbot's ears. The brothers looked inside their casket and, behold ... no bones. Brother Frithstan guessed the truth and came to take the relic back.' He walked forward and took me by the shoulders. 'I could not let him take it, Ymma. You understand, don't you?'

'But you killed a man.'

'I did it for the saint ... I did it for our people.'

'And you would let my brother hang?'

His grip tightened on my shoulders. He was pushing me down to the ground. Soon I would be kneeling helpless before him. 'I had no choice, Ymma. The saint chose to come to our village. I could not allow a mere man stop the saint's work.'

'And what of God's work?' I shouted. 'What of His commandments about stealing and killing?'

He didn't seem to have heard me . . . or he had heard and rejected my reasoning. His fingers crawled around my throat and slowly, almost gently, he began to squeeze.

I had a choice – to resist or to die there in that cold, stone crypt. I was never one for giving up without a fight so I feigned a swoon then sprang up, shrieking like a devil from hell. I bit and struggled then I thrust my arms between his and he lost his grip long enough for me to slip from his grasp. Pushing him away, I ran down the narrow passageway but I could hear his laboured breathing behind me. He was getting closer.

I reached the steps and saw the daylight flooding through the church windows. I had lost the first rush of fury and power and now my legs felt like lead as I willed them to carry me faster towards the safety of the village.

I felt a tug on my skirts. He had caught me and I fell to the ground, closing my eyes and trying to summon my last reserve of strength.

Then nothing. I lay there a full minute, waiting for the death blow or for those great hands to choke the life from my body. When I allowed my eyes to open I saw a face close to mine. Edmund. He asked me what had happened but I cannot recall my answer. Then I asked what had become of Ordulf, and he told me that the priest had pushed past him and rushed from the church. Edmund helped me back to the hall but I was in a daze and can remember no more.

A few days later Father Ordulf's body was found upon the shore. Most said he died by some accident. Some said he met with a band of Danes who murdered him. There were a few who said that he died by his own hand. I said nothing to the folk of the village but I had to tell my father so that no innocent men paid for Ordulf's crimes. It was put about that a pair of Danes, split from their fellows, came looking for booty to take by stealth and killed the innocent brother as he defended the church's treasures; that they dropped those treasures in the woodland and that Oslac found them while hunting. It was better that the gossips did not know the truth and I begged Edmund to keep his silence. The man was dead and it served no purpose to blacken his name when he would be suffering God's judgement.

Oslac returned the treasures to the church and put the bones in their fine casket as the village rejoiced.

It is half a year now since Father Ordulf's death. We have a new priest and Oslac is gone to join the fyrd with my father and Edmund. It may be that the boy will return a man. I, Ymma, am drawn more strongly now to the scholarly life of a holy nun. Perhaps I must be grateful that Father Ordulf gave me a love of learning before he turned towards evil. Yet Edmund is always in my prayers and I look to his return. I am still young and must choose my path with care.

There was word today that the Danes are coming around our coast once more. From the fury of the northmen, O Lord defend us.

Raven Feeder

Manda Scott

Orkney/Norway, AD 999

I burned my father at dusk on the day after the summer solstice in the year nine hundred and ninety-nine.

It was not a good day to be building a fire. We were in the aftermath of the worst summer storm the Orkneys had seen in my lifetime. The rain was less than it had been overnight and the wind had eased from an ear-battering, mind-numbing gale to something where at least we could shout one to the other with a chance of being heard but it was, nevertheless, not easy to find wood to hold the flame. Because it was my father, the men crossed the island to Kirkwall to bring stored timber from the earth houses there and I used what kindling there was left from the Great Hall at Orphir. Very little of that was dry. Very little of anything anywhere was dry in the wake of a wind that had lifted the thatch from the rooftops and destroyed three ships on the rocks offshore before we could make fast the fleet. Still, we gathered in the wet with the less wet and we poured on oil from the lamps and goose fat and tallow and ropes from his ship and, lastly, we laid on his shield.

I lit the first brand as the sun hit the waves. Fire met fire with the churning water between and it was as he would have wanted it. We did not fire his own ship. She was the biggest of all our ships, twenty benches, six men to a bench, three men to each sweep, one great-hundred of oarsmen to row her forward and more to man the sails. He had her built in the year of my tenth birthday and called her *Tranen* which means the Crane and she was the joy of his life next to my mother and, I believe, me. In other days we might have fired her for him but not now when we were so close to war with Norway; he would not have wanted that. Instead, we used one of the three smaller ships that had part foundered on the rocks. She was a good ship and the wind was strong and she sailed west towards the sun with nothing to block her path. I stood at the prow of the *Tranen* and saw, then smelled, the body of Thore, son of Skule, son of Svein, father to Arne and husband to Ranveig, leader of men and feeder of ravens, burn in a tangle of damp wood to the stench of sheep fat and goose grease and a great black sweep of smoke that caught the strength of the wind and surged forward ahead of his boat so that his last voyage into the sun was down a tunnel of tarred soot that led all the way to the edge of the world.

I could not have asked for a better omen. In that time, men were talking a great deal about the omens and their meanings. As the Christians counted it, there were a scant six months until their Day of Judgement fell on the land and they would have had every man, woman and child following the new religion or dead by that day. That was the measure of Olaf Trygvason's visit to Orkney; he sailed by chance into the harbour as Sigurd Hlodvirson, earl of all Orkney, rode out a storm and when he sailed out again, Sigurd and – nominally – all of Orkney were sworn to the White Christ. Just to make sure, Trygvason took with him Sigurd's youngest and most favoured son, Hlodvir. The Norwegians named him *Hundi*, which means dog, or *Hvelp*, which means whelp and is worse, and they held him hostage in perpetuity for the continuing faith of the Orkneys.

That was three years ago and we were the first. When he left Orkney, Olaf Trygvason sailed straight to Norway and killed the earl Hakon Eirikson and had himself made king in his place, and since then he has spent his summers hunting throughout his fiefdom for all who keep the old way and the old laws, and those who will not convert he takes his pleasure in killing slowly. It is his belief that men can drop the true gods and pick up new ones at his word as a skald might pick up a new harp at a nod from his master. Some of them do. Some of them don't care and will do whatever seems politic. The rest of us know that the gods are not changed on the whim of a single man and we wait for their words in the cry of the gull or the flight of the raven – or the sign of a flag of black smoke running to the edge of the world before a ship manned by the dead.

So I spoke, then, with the stench of burning flesh all around us and the sky black with the storm clouds and with the ending of my father. I spoke to Einar Sigurdson who was my closest friend and whose brother languished in Norway, and beyond him I spoke to all the men of the islands who had gathered to honour my father's passing. As I raised my voice, so the wind fell and the furthest of those gathered on the boats of the fleet or on the shore could hear me. This, too, I counted a gift from the gods.

'Men of Orkney; men of Odin, men of Thor and of Freya, listen to me. The Christian priest who builds his church on our islands will tell you that black smoke is a bad omen, a sign that my father will burn for ever in the fires of the Christian hell. This is one of the many things that sets us apart. For him, white is good which is, I believe, because the White Christ comes from the hottest part of the earth where white is needed to shield them from the midday sun. Here and in Norway where the true gods lie, white is for ice and for snow and the grey-mawed wolf of winter who takes entire families without pity or mercy. For us, black is the warmth of the earth mother, of Frig and the Norns, and is the blessing that guides our nights and our days. The raven is black, he who is the messenger of the gods. The dark earth is black, that feeds us and holds us. The wolf of battle is black, who takes us all in the end. For us, black is the best of signs as my father was the best of men. Know now that, however he died and whatever was done to him after his death, he has gone to join the true gods in the afterlife as he deserved.'

I was nineteen years old and it was the longest speech I had ever made in public in my life. I stopped to see how it was taken. All of those present had sailed or fought with my father and there was a shout of greeting and agreement that made worse the sting of salt in my eyes. It was not a time for grieving and I think only Einar will have seen that I did so. I let the sound die with the falling breeze and went on.

'Men of Orkney; you who know my father will know that he never left the true gods. How could he, married to my mother? All of you, who fought with him, know that he was the greatest of fighters. How could he not be, with a ship like the Crane?'

Again, for both of these, the cheer went up. This time I raised my voice above it.

'And so I ask you, any of you, who saw my father with me, to say how he died?'

It was Einar who spoke, as it had to be because he was the only one with me when we found the body. Einar, my soul-friend, who is first son to Sigurd and will one day be earl of all Orkney. He came to join me at the prow, beside the head of the Crane. He was not as tall as I am, but broader in the shoulders, and where my hair is black of an Icelandish mother his was the red-brown of a fox in winter and it shone like copper in the evening sun. He had a voice like a bullhorn and he used it.

'Men of Orkney, I will speak now, who was with Arne Thoreson when he found his father. It was this morning, an hour after sunrise when we were all but done with securing the fleet. Had the night been other than it was, we would have found Thore earlier and we will each carry the pain of that for the remainder of this life because his body was still warm in the places where the rain had not cooled it and the blood still flowed freely from the axe wound that killed him, which means that he had died while we were fighting to save the long ships. We had each cursed him for not being there to help us. We will carry that, too.'

He hung his head and men stood silent, knowing what it does to curse a friend already dead. He lifted his head again.

'I have to tell you what we found. You all knew Thore Skuleson as a man who had never turned his back in battle. This morning, that man lay with his axe still in his belt and his arms by his side and a great wound here' – he brought the heel of his hand to the side of his head, on the left, above the ear – 'in the place where an axe struck on the backhand would hit from behind. He was struck only once and he fell forwards on to his face. This we could tell by the pattern of mud on his skin and his tunic. Then . . .' he paused and gathered himself and the men leaned forward to hear him better, 'then he had been turned over and dragged to a new place and when he was laid down again a cross of the White Christ had been placed on his chest.'

He stopped then because the noise was too great to go on; the noise of men aghast, in soul-pain, in anger of the kind that drives a battle. Out of it all came a voice that was pitched to carry: 'Where was he found, Einar Sigurdson? Where did you find him?' and the men grew quiet to hear the answer.

'Not where he fell. There was mud on his heels and his calves from being dragged through the mud. We have searched and we cannot tell where he fell first; the rain has washed the signs to nothing. All I can say is that he lay finally by the foundations of the Christian church that the Saxon priest is building at Kirkwall.'

The shout that went up then was the shout of a war host, nothing less. Einar and I stood together in the eye of it, as in the eye of a storm, and felt it hammer our ears and our hearts. I wept without shame and Einar with me. He put his hand on my shoulder. 'There are fewer of them Christian now than there were this morning,' he said. 'We may have enough, now, to sail with us to Norway.' Even then, it was his heart's dream to sail east and take back his brother.

I shook my head. 'If all Orkney is with us, there are still not enough for that. And before all else, we must find who killed my father.'

He looked grim, as I must have looked grim, peering through wind-lashed tears and the after-haze of smoke. 'Is there any doubt?' he asked.

I said: 'There is always doubt until the gods have spoken.' And that was when, in the presence of all the true men of Orkney, a raven flew from the land and, calling, circled three times round the mast-head of the *Tranen*, my father's ship, and then flew east, to Norway. If there was doubt in my mind, it was answered. The smoke I had prayed for and then planned for and prayed for again. For the raven, I would not have dared ask.

We rowed the ships to shore and beached them with care in the face of a possible return of the storm. The men were not to be held and neither Einar nor I tried to stop them as they ran through the surf and up past the first row of cottages. Sigurd is earl and he is the one who allowed the Saxon priest to begin building his church when he knew that he had already killed three men in Iceland for failing to turn themselves to Christ. It was up to Sigurd, therefore, to decide whose laws to follow – those of the old ways that say a man is a man and may not be killed unlawfully, or that of Olaf Trygvason which says that any man who is a Christian may kill any man who is not with impunity. I walked with Einar up the shoreline and we watched four shiploads of men turn on the Great House and demand word with Jarl Sigurd.

Einar was pensive. 'They will kill him,' he said.

'Only if your father permits it.'

'He won't dare turn them down.'

'Then we had best get to your brother before word reaches Christ's Wolf in Norway that his favourite heathen-slaying priest has gone to meet his god with his head in his hands and a hammer of Thor burning his chest.'

At the door to my mother's house we parted. The last thing I heard as I entered was the odd, high-pitched voice of Thangbrand, the Saxon, denying that he had ever killed anyone. And that, at least, was a lie.

I was afraid of my mother. In a different way, I am still afraid of her now, knowing the full measure of what she can do. My mother is a Singer which gives her more power than any man to know the will of the gods. In the years since that day, I have travelled to the far north and sat with the reindeer herds and flown to the beat of their drums and seen the things that they call out of the smoke of their fires. I have ridden to the east and spent a winter with the keepers of horses and slept in the hide of a new-foaled mare and dreamed the dreams of the all-mother that showed me the ways of the afterlife. But I am not a Singer and never will be and I have never met anyone who lived closer to the true gods than my mother. Even Sigurd, with Olaf and his martyred saints on his back, would not presume to convert Ranveig Gunnarsdottir. He has more sense than that.

I knew nothing of that on the day of my father's burning. I stooped in through the door skin with the sight of a circling raven filling my mind's eye and fear turned my legs to water and my water to running wine. I stood with my back to the door post and searched the dark of her home with my eyes. She was there, sitting in the farthest corner with her back to me watching the colours of her fire. On a night when every other home in Orkney was fighting to find a roof, never mind dry wood to burn, my mother's fire burned strongly blue, the colour of the morning sky. Then, as I watched, she cast her hand at it, with possibly some powder, and the blue turned to red, the colour of blood in water.

'Is it done as he would have wished it?' Her voice resonated like a struck harp. I stood straighter.

'Yes.' I stepped forward into the room. 'May I sit?'

'Of course.' She smiled in the dark so that I could hear the new chord in her voice. Her hands withdrew and the fire glowed the colour of any fire. 'Was it hard on you?' she asked.

I thought about that and answered honestly. 'Less than I thought it would be.'

'Good.' She turned so that I could see her face in the firelight and she was, indeed, smiling. 'Einar looks well with the sun behind him.' This was one reason we feared my mother. She was not within sight of the *Tranen* when Einar spoke. 'He with the sun behind him, you with the moon. Remember that.'

'I will.' I remembered everything my mother said. One day, it may kill me. In the meantime, it has saved my life more times than I can recount. 'Did you send the raven?' I asked.

She shook her head. Her black hair turned red in the light of the fire. Her voice came as if from somewhere else in the room. 'I don't send,' she said. 'I ask.' A cat moved in the far corner and if you watched closely you would think the voice came from it. I am used to this. I sat still. She watched things move in the fire. In time, she raised her head. 'You will sail three days from now with Einar and the fewest possible men you can take to sail in safety. His father will stay here so that, if all fails, he can claim no knowledge and Orkney may be spared the wrath of the Christ-wolf.' I said nothing. If we took

106

the *Tranen*, lightly manned, we could sail her safely with a half-hundred men. Sailing was not the problem – it was what we might meet at the other side that worried me. Still, I am not one to argue with my mother when she is speaking. I sat in the quiet of her room and let her finish. The fire glowed low to the coals. Her eyes reflected the colour of it. Her voice flowed in dissonant chords from many places. 'You will berth north of Nidaros,' she said. 'The Wolf will not be there but you will meet a man called Eyvind Kelda who will know of your coming. Treat him as you would treat me.'

She turned. Her voice came out of her own mouth. 'They are asking for you now in the Great Hall. Go and tell them what you may. We can pray even yet that your father did not die in vain.'

Only at Yule have I seen so many men, women and children in Orkney's Great Hall as I saw that evening. At a time when every one of them should have been using the last of the light to make fast their homes, they gathered to hear of the death of my father and to judge the man who had killed him.

Thangbrand the Saxon is Olaf Trygvason's man. He always has been and it is true that he was sent to Iceland to bring them to Christ and returned to Norway thrice a killer and with Iceland still for the true gods. That the king sent him next to Orkney says much about the stability of our relations with Norway and everything about the nature of his priest. He is a big man, a hand taller than me and as broad as Einar or his father. He has the wheat-gold hair of the Saxons but he crops it close across the forehead in the way of the Christian priests. In the manner of his fathers, he wields a Dane axe in battle that has a handle as long as his height and he can kill a man with the haft on one side and the blade on the other. They had brought his axe with him from his place near the new church and Sigurd stood with it now, holding it beside him like a standard, a single man standing quiet above the chaos that raged amongst the people below the dais. It took me a good push and a lot of shouting to fight my way to the front. He saw me as the men thinned out and gestured with his free hand.

'Arne! Come up and talk of what you know.' Einar was there ahead of me and his father would know as much as he did but it was necessary that I tell it again to the crowd.

I vaulted on to the dais and found, behind the earl and the priest, in the darker place where the torches didn't reach, twelve men assembled which meant they were holding a court in the old way and that it would be the men, not the earl, who would pass judgement on the Saxon's innocence or guilt. It took a moment to look over them; men who were deemed not to have been tainted by evidence one way or the other which means, in this case, that they should have been neither for the old gods nor for the new and that they had not seen the wound on the body of my father. In the former there was more difficulty than the latter; we had called for four men to help us carry his body back to my mother but most of those who had helped build the pyre had seen him lying in state on his shield after she had done dressing him in his war gear. The presence of his helmet on his head meant that the killing wound was not readily seen. Thus the men had not been tainted by the evidence in the way that they would be by their vows. Running my eye along the line, I saw that Sigurd had chosen six who had turned to the White Christ and six who still spoke for the gods. It was the only thing he could do.

When I turned back, he was waiting for me. He had given the war axe to Einar and held the bible in one hand and the Hammer in the other. Now, he offered both to me without a word. I took the Hammer. The priest turned his head and spat.

Sigurd held up his hand for silence, his eyes on me. 'Tell us,' he said. 'Speak the truth as you know it.'

And so I did. Before they had heard it from Einar, now they

heard it, not much different, from me; a brief recital of the moment when we found my father. I was heard through in silence. It didn't take long. At the end, Sigurd turned to the twelve. 'Does any one amongst you wish to question this man?'

None did. It was not as if they were hearing anything new.

Sigurd turned to the priest. 'Thangbrand the Christian. Give account of yourself. Where were you last night?'

The man was more angry than I had ever seen him. More so than when my father and I refused to take on the White Christ. His face blotched red and white in uneven patches. His veins stood out as if carved on the rock of his temples and neck. He said nothing. Sigurd asked it again. In the old laws, a question asked three times and not answered is a sign of guilt. The man knew this. Sigurd waited. Where before there had been a hum of voices, now there was silence. The wind soughed through the cracks in the walls. The torches crackled. A dog, left outside, scratched at the door to come in. All else was quiet.

In the length of the quiet, Sigurd asked it the third time. His voice rang off the walls.

The Saxon took a breath. He was more white now than red. He lifted the bible from Sigurd's hand and held it up. 'I was asleep,' he said.

The silence became a wall. Sigurd stared at him and said: 'The roof came off half the homes in Orkney last night. Doors were wrenched from their hinges. We lost three boats of the fleet. No living being could sleep through a storm such as that.'

The bible shook in the Saxon's hand. 'I would not lie on Christ's bible. I tell you again. I slept from my evening meal until long after daybreak. I was not awake when the heathen died.'

'So then can you kill in your sleep?' That was Einar and he

spoke out of turn but no man there would have stopped him.

Sigurd looked around the hall. 'Did any man or woman here see the Saxon during the night?'

The wall pressed in. Harald Half-hand raised his stumped arm. 'I knocked on his door to ask for help as the storm was at its height and got no answer. I thought him already out. I did not think to go in and see if he slept.'

Sigurd turned back to the man at his side. His brows met together in the centre of his forehead. 'How could you sleep through that?' I think he was genuinely puzzled.

The Saxon lowered his book. 'Ask the witch's son. The roof came off my cottage as it did all the others except for his mother's. I woke this morning as wet as if I had been down to the floor of the Pentland Firth. And yet I did sleep. Ask Arne, son of Ranveig, how this could be so. I know nothing of witchcraft. I am a mere man of God.'

He might have drawn them to his side, had he not said that last thing. Not the accusation of witchery – my mother is a witch and proud of it. I would not put it past her to make a man sleep through his own burning if needs be, nor to call up a storm to cover it, and there were others who might have believed as much even if they would not believe she could set a man to kill her own husband. But the Saxon was no *mere* anything and he was known to have killed in the name of his god. In that he made his mistake. The wall that had been holding the voices broke as a dam breaks before the melting snow and the noise was the same as that on the ships when my father burned, only contained by the Great Hall as in a vessel of sound.

Sigurd rode it as he would ride a ship in a big sea. When the calm came, he spoke again to the Saxon.

'Thangbrand, favoured of Olaf Trygvason. Do you deny that you threatened Thore Skuleson and his family with the wrath of the White Christ for failing to take your baptism?'

110

'For failing to take *Christ's* baptism. I am the intermediary, not the son of the god. No, I do not deny it.'

'And do you deny having called down the wrath of your Christ, with the aid of your Dane axe, on Thorvald Veile and Veterlide the skald and of one other man while in Iceland?'

'I do not deny it. They, too, refused the baptism of the White Christ.'

They had done more than that. Veterlide had composed ten long-verses relating what he thought of Thangbrand and his new god. It was for that he had died, but men sing the verses still in all the lands of the north.

Sigurd took the Hammer from my hand and gave it to his son. He turned me round to face the front of the hall. 'Einar,' he turned to face the back. 'Einar Sigurdson will bring the charge,' he said. It was not for me, as the blood relative, to seek to charge the facts with my anger.

The twelve men sat still at the back of the dais. In all of this, they had remained calm. Einar used his voice as he had used it on the ship so that it carried back to the far end of the hall behind him.

'Men of the Orkneys. We all knew Thore Skuleson and we could sing songs in his honour. Now is not the time for that. In this, there are only two things that matter. First that Thore, though a great man, no longer had eyes and ears as sharp as they had been. All of you will have known how often he had to ask twice when you bade him good morning.' They nodded at that and some smiled. My father's encroaching deafness was a source of constant comment from his peers, as is every failing sense in those growing old. Very few knew of his eyes, but that was true too.

Einar went on. 'The other thing beyond question is that he was a warrior born and no man would best him had he the mind to defend himself.' They nodded for that, too, and it was true. 'Therefore I bring this charge before you: that

111

Thangbrand the Saxon, in the darkest and hardest part of the storm, did come upon Thore Skuleson in stealth and did take his life from him, using the coward's blow from behind against a man who could not hear his enemy coming and therefore did nothing to defend himself. I ask therefore, in accordance with the old laws and those of the bible, that we take an eye for an eye and a life for a life – that the Saxon has forfeit his right to live.'

It is not given for the men on the floor to influence the assembly. Still, the groundswell was with him.

Sigurd turned and lifted the bible in the Saxon's hand. 'You may make your plea,' he said.

It has never been suggested that the Saxon was not a brave man. He held the bible high and his voice carried every bit as far as Einar's. 'I swear before Almighty God that I slept through the night and that I did not take a hand in the killing of Thore Skuleson. I have killed before. God willing, I will kill in His name again. But not this time.' He lowered his book. 'Nevertheless, I have no proof of this if you will not take my oath on the bible. Therefore I offer a decision in the old ways. I will fight Arne son of Thore in single combat and let my god and his show who is speaking the truth here.'

Men drew breath at that. It was a clever move. Without it, he was a dead man. With it, either one of us could have been. But I had the black smoke and the raven and a full moon rising in the black sky above Orphir. The words of my mother rang in my ears. I stepped forward and took the Hammer again from Einar.

'I accept your offer,' I said, and heard the echo of my words come back from both walls. 'There are men here who need to be tending their homes and their families. Let it be done now, under the light of the moon, before the storm returns to harry the fleet further.'

He was thirty-four years old and a man in his prime who

had killed men beyond counting. I was three days after my nineteenth birthday and it was well known that I had not yet taken my first man in battle. For the rest of my life I will remember the size of his smile.

There are rules for these things but not all of them are rigid. Einar was the one to suggest that, because we were both skilled with the axe but the Saxon had clearly the longer reach, it would be more even if we fought with the sword, with which we were both less familiar. I would have thought the priest would have turned that down but he accepted it, as he accepted other things one would not have thought of him. It was later that my mother told me he had been raised in the horse herds to the east and had lived with their customs, which are not unlike ours, before he ever came north to be the long arm of Christ's Wolf in Norway.

It was a cold, clear night with almost no wind. A poor night for sailing but the best of all possible nights for fighting. The moon was part risen above the Great Hall's roof ridge and it lit to daylight the flat ground they chose for us to the west of the hall. Beyond the land, the water lay quiet after the chaos of the storm and the first sliver of moonlight slid across it as milk across a floor. The ground itself was flat and smooth from years of threshing corn and most of the stones had been taken long ago. Those that had not stuck proud from the ground and their shadows lay crisp to the side of them so that there was no danger one might stub a toe and lose footing. I stood at the northern end of it, as was my birthright, and had Einar bind the lengths of boiled leather around my forearms and calves and another around my brow to make tight the fit of my helmet. I raised my arms above my head and he lowered the chain mail over them so that it settled on my shoulders and hung partway to my knees. He tied my belt to my waist and slid into it the haft of the small throwing axe that had been

113

allowed as the second weapon. If we had been going to battle, he would have brought me my shield and then I would have dressed him likewise. As it was, the gods and their truth were our shield and there was no need for Einar to dress in any way other than he already was.

Sigurd stood in the centre of the field. When I was ready, I walked to him. The Saxon joined us from the south side. As we met in the centre, the moon rose clear of the roof ridge so that the light of it painted a single stream out across the oil-flat water and the voice of my mother rang in my head. *You do well with the moon behind you. Remember that.* How could I forget? And then, as with all memories, the cry of the raven filled my ears and I looked up, which was nonsense, because ravens do not fly at night, and yet on this night one did, flying up the silver line of the moon, heading east for Norway. It called three times as it passed overhead and when the noise died away, Sigurd stepped back into safety.

You will know of battle. In the moments before, it is good to hear the war cry of the host and to feel the bodies of one's companions on either side. In single combat it is different. Then there is only the beat of the heart, not the beat of the drums, the cry of the sinews as they move into action, not the cry of other men. There is the taste of metal in the mouth and the churning of guts and the moments of coming to terms with the single man who will kill you if you do not kill him first. A full battle is about seeing before you are seen. Single combat is about believing. At the moment when I believe I am going to die, then I will do so. On this night, I stepped forward under the light of the full moon with the cry of the raven in my ears and for one long moment, Thangbrand the Saxon shrank before me to the size of a child.

Still, a child may kill if it chooses and when he launched the first blow it was with the strength of a full-grown man against a nineteen-year-old youth and I knew that whatever my mother had said, I could die as easily as had my father. I blocked the blow and cut down towards his knees so that he jumped back to give me space. Still striking, I stepped sideways three steps, to put my back to the west and hold the light of the full moon behind me. The Saxon paced with me, eastwards, so that his back was to the sea. The light shone on his sword, marking out the Christ-cross engraved on the blade. Mine stayed black in the shadow. I sought his eyes. In the light of day, they were grey. In the moonlight, they were clear, as if looking down a tunnel, and quite empty of feeling. In battle, one cannot afford to feel. His sword came at my head, at the height of my ears. I ducked and struck forward and then pulled my blade urgently sideways, just in time to block the full impact of his back swing. The shock of it made my teeth clash on my tongue and I tasted blood. I jerked the short-axe from my belt and regripped my sword one-handed to give me use of both weapons. His blade swung in a double loop, twisting in the centre so that any one of the four cuts could have killed. I took two of them on my blade and one on the back of the axe, and the last I let swing clear to pull him off balance before I threw my own attack at his knees, his chest, his skull, his elbows. Not one of them made contact with anything but steel and the force of it spun us both to the edges of the clearing to take breath and come in again.

I have no idea how long we fought. Time drew down to the end of a blade and the small edge of a hand-axe. We both drew blood, neither of us badly. We both tasted salt and iron and the acid of exhaustion. We both tired, but equally so that one was not slower than the other. Around us, the men, women and children of Orkney stood in silence, giving us due respect – all bar my mother who watched it all in her fire.

It was she who made the difference, in the end. The Saxon made a half-feint to my knees and brought his blade up at a sharper angle than he had done before, aiming for a cut to the thigh on the back stroke. I brought my sword hand down to block it and, as the blades screamed on the strength of his stroke, the light of the moon caught on both and was blinding. I jumped back out of reach and looked upwards. The moon was very close to being straight overhead. My mother spoke in my ears as she had done before. *You do well with the moon behind you.* Behind. Not above, or in front. I thought she was warning me to keep clear of the sun or to watch Einar if he took to battle in darkness. It had not occurred to me that, instead, she had been warning me to kill before the moon reached its height.

The Saxon had taken pause to breathe and to think. I looked again at the moon and let the whole understanding of it show on my face. He saw it and did not understand, but he was weary and his wits were not as sharp as they had been at the start and he looked to the moon anyway, to see what I had seen. In that was his death. It is said that Olaf Trygvason can kill two men at once with a spear thrown from each hand. I use my sword in my left hand and have done so since birth – I am, after all, a witch's son. But I am also the son of my father and I can throw my small-axe with either hand. I used both, then. The hand-axe spun forward, aimed for his head. The sword sliced in a killing arc a hand's breadth down from his neck. He saw the first and ducked. He could not have seen the second. With a shock down my arm that was quite different to the clash of iron meeting iron, the blade bit in the gap between his helmet and his mail and hewed into his neck. I did not take off his head – the only man on the island with the strength to sever that head was the man on whose shoulders it rested – but the full length of my blade cut across the full width of his throat and his life flowed in its wake. He was dead before I finished the stroke. Dead, and, by extension, guilty.

* * *

I remember nothing of the hours that followed. I woke in my mother's home, lying in a shard of broken sunlight with a cat asleep on my chest. A bandage replaced the boiled leather on my left forearm and the smell of groundwort and pig's fat came from beneath it. Something else burned on the fire and turned the air sweet. A raven with a single white feather in each wing sat on the roof beam and watched me, or the cat, or both. I tried to remember if the raven of my omens had white feathers but it had flown too high and too fast to know. My mother moved from her place at the foot of the bed to a place where I could see her smile. 'Welcome back,' she said.

I tried to sit up and she stopped me. 'Not yet, hound of my hearth. You are not all the way back yet.'

'Where have I been?'

She smiled. Her eyes were violet beneath hair the colour of the raven, with a white streak at the crown that I had not seen before. Her skin was perfect. I have no idea how old she was. 'I don't know,' she said. 'I was hoping you could tell me.'

I lay back and looked at the cat. The cat looked at me. It stuck up one hind leg and washed the curve of its flank. I closed my eyes and brought back the dream. 'I was running,' I said. 'In Nidaros. There was a man with black hair and a white streak like yours. He flew ahead of me.'

'How did he fly?'

'He used his drum to carry his spirit. He flew to the lair of the Christ-wolf and then to where he keeps Einar's brother. He brought me back a token of his hair.'

My mother was kneeling by my side. Her smile was the smile of a mother at a child who, in learning to walk, has taken the full width of the room and is ready for more. 'Let me see it,' she said.

I opened my left hand, my sword hand. A single red-gold hair lay across it that could have been the Saxon's. I chose to believe that it was. My mother lifted it with great care and

117

carried it back to her place by the fire. I saw the flames burn black and an oiled green, the colour of a magpie's back. I saw a man's face in the flames and then blood.

'The man with the pied hair was Eyvind Kelda,' she said, and it was as if the name had been part of me since my youngest days. 'He is waiting for you as I said he would be. You will go to take back Hlodvir, Einar's brother. He will help you in this. In return, you will help him as he asks you.'

She was right, the man with the pied hair *was* waiting for us. At the end of the crossing, with the *Tranen* lightly manned and Einar Sigurdson alone at the helm, we rowed at dusk into an inlet three hours' march north of Nidaros and beached the ship. On the shore, sitting by a fire built of driftwood with a flame that burned clear, like amber, and gave no smoke, was the man I had seen in my mother's fire. He stood as we beached the boat. Close up, he was as tall as me and his hair was as black, but with the white flash at the temples, as mine has now. His face was lean and there were scars on his cheeks, balanced one side for the other. None of that, in itself, was what set him apart. More, it was the way he stood and the stillness he held with him such as my mother holds with her and the sense that here is someone who walks with the gods. It was the first time I had met a man of power. It was, in fact, the first time I had met anyone of power who was not my mother. I stepped forward out of the surf and waved. He left his fire and came down to the water line to greet us.

'Welcome, hound of the hearth.' It was the second time I had heard that name. 'You made good time.'

'We had the gods behind us.' I looked past him to the dark beyond the fire and the two figures sitting quiet beside it. I was not expecting company. 'You are not alone?'

'No.' He turned and gestured. The first man rose and came to join us. Behind me, men reached for their weapons. The newcomer was, if anything, built bigger than the Saxon. In his favour was the fact that his hair reached to his shoulders and was braided for battle and he wore the Hammer at his chest, not the cross of the Christians. In that moment, I would say he was as unhappy to see us as we were to see him. His face was florid and not from the heat of the fire. 'You promised me an army, Kelda. Not a bare handful of men.' We were a half-hundred, which is more than a handful, but we were not an army by any means.

The lean man stretched a palm to him and the stillness flowed from it. 'Sometimes a handful can achieve more than an army,' he said. 'And it is only one man who must die.'

Weapons moved from their sheaths. Einar stepped forward and the three-quarter moon shone on his blade. 'We are here to take back my brother. We kill who stops us. If none get in the way, none will die.'

The witch-man smiled in the way my mother smiles at the cat. 'Einar Sigurdson, do you think that if you take back your brother tonight and Olaf Trygvason lives, the Orkneys will be a safe place to hide?'

Einar watched him. We had thought of that. Olaf Trygvason was not kind to those who angered him. Any man might die in battle, we knew it and were not afraid. None of us wished to die on a cross or a wheel and we had word that a man could be made to live for three days if the Christ-wolf set his mind to it. Nevertheless, my mother had said that we would take Hlodvir safely and that Orkney would not be assaulted. We trusted her words. Einar turned to me. In this, I have his trust also. 'Arne?'

I looked to the giant standing between me and the fire and knew where I had seen his double before. 'You are Eirik, son of Hakon who was earl of Norway. Am I right?'

The blond man said nothing which was his right. It was said that he was in Sweden. Olaf Trygvason had spent a fortune on envoys to Sweden in an attempt to buy his life. If he was taken alive in Norway, three days would be the start of his dying. He looked at me and the truth was in his eyes. Eyvind Kelda let us talk that way in silence and then he gestured again to the fire and the second man came to join us and any need for talking was done. Einar's blade slammed home in its sheath.

'Hlodvir! How are you here?' He was right, it was his brother. A small, lean, neat, darker version of Einar with hair cut in the Norwegian style. Einar grasped him by the shoulders. 'Are you well?'

'I am. I will be better when I see the hall at Orphir but I am well enough now.' His voice was not as clear as it had been when he was younger. As he moved in the firelight, it could be seen that he was tired and not well fed and more than a little drunk. Above all of that, he had three years not fighting and it showed. I asked again the question Einar had put to him: 'How are you here, Hlodvir?'

'I was at Nidaros,' he said. 'The king is not there. He has gone inland to Magnus Grenske's farm. I stayed in Nidarholm with the lower half of the court. Eyvind Kelda and the earlson came in disguise and freed me as the moon rose this evening.' He looked to each of the men he had just mentioned. When neither spoke, he said: 'If I am not back by morning, my loss will be noted.'

And so that was it. My mother had said we would do for Eyvind Kelda that which he asked of us and we had listened and nodded and assumed something small. We had not considered that he might want us to take the throne for the next king of Norway. I forget, even now, that when my mother says something will happen, she is not giving an order, but stating the truth – and that she does not deal in small things. We stood on the beach with the men at our back and said nothing. We had Hlodvir and we could have sailed but there was none who believed we could face the entire fleet of

120

Norway and live. On the other hand, there were few who believed that a half-hundred of men could take the kingship and give it to the earl-son. In time, Einar looked to the two men who flanked his brother. He said: 'You know a way this can be done?'

The witch-man raised both his hands and gestured back towards his fire. 'Shall we sit?' he said.

We sat for an hour, maybe slightly less, by the fire on the beach. A bare five minutes of that was spent deciding *if* we would do it. The rest was devoted to how. It was not complicated, the best plans never are. As in all cases where a smaller force assaults a larger one, we had the advantage of surprise, of the dark and of not having spent half the night and all of the week before it drinking ourselves to a stupor. We also had the advantage of being in the open while the Christ-wolf and all his men were sleeping in a wooden farmhouse in the height of midsummer when wood burns like dried grass. It is an easy way to kill and has little valour in it but we were not there for honour or glory, we were there for vengeance and to put a man on the throne and we intended to live to see it happen.

At the end it was settled. Twelve men stayed with the *Tranen* to guard her from seaward attack. The rest of us picked up our weapons and gathered in three groups ready to follow the witch-man, the earl and Einar's brother for the hour's march inland.

I watched Einar and Eirik leaving at the head of the first group. Whatever their misgivings, they had put them aside and they walked together as if they had been born from the same womb. They suited one another and they knew it; each a big man with an earldom as his birthright who knew what it was to lead men in battle. This is the thing that makes bonds between countries that last for a lifetime and don't fall apart at the first offer of men or money or land. I touched my

Hammer and gave a prayer that it would last. Hlodvir took the middle group. He was not fit for battle but he would not have it said that, on the night of his rescue, he stayed with the ship, and he knew the way to the steading which was as necessary as a good fighting arm.

I walked with the third group and took the rear guard as was my right. Eyvind Kelda chose to walk beside me.

'Are you well, son of the she-hound?' I had not then heard my mother so named. In another man's mouth, it would have been an insult for which one of us would have died. In the far north, where he comes from, the hound is a man's closest companion and the protector of all he values. The knowledge of that kept my hand from my axe.

I nodded. 'I am well.'

'Einar Sigurdson is a good man,' he said. 'He thinks well.' Listening to him was like watching knife blades glide over ice; everything slid in harmony and was beautiful but it was things he did not say that hung in the air around him. I watched them now and waited for him to speak.

'You think it cannot be done,' I said, when he had walked beside me for a while in silence.

He smiled thinly. 'I know it cannot be done the way he thinks it,' he said.

He had just spent an hour helping Einar and Eirik to plan otherwise. Still, I believed him. I said: 'Then how?'

His eyes looked into mine. They were black and things moved through them like flames from his driftwood fire. 'What did you bring me from your mother?' he asked.

A catskin pouch of the kind in which she keeps her sacred things hung from my belt. I had forgotten, to be honest, that I carried it. I unhooked it now and passed it to the witch-man who weighed it before he opened it. He was pleased with what lay inside.

'Good.' He put his hand to my arm. 'Then when we reach

the clearing at the Grenske steading, tell Einar to hold his men and let us work first. He will take it better from you than from me.'

In that, as in most things, he spoke only half the truth. Einar took it from me as he might have taken a hive full of bees. He would not have taken it from the witch-man at all. Like most of us, he was able to turn a blind eye to the mist that had enshrouded us and let us walk through the night in security. It was something else entirely to be asked to stand in silence under a three-quarter moon within bowshot of his sworn enemy and do nothing. That the men did so when Einar asked it is testament to his leadership and the honour in which they hold him. That he asked it of them at all was his gift to me. Eirik Hakonson who owed nothing to anybody would have killed all three of us had it not been that we were too close to the farmhouse to risk the noise. What changed him was when Eyvind led us through the trees to within sight of the steading to show us more clearly what we faced.

I lay beside the earl-son with my face buried in pine loam beneath the shadows of the first rank of trees and saw the light of the moon reflected back at us from the wood of the farmhouse as it would be from a polished blade. Wood doesn't shine like that, not unless it's been under water. To push the point home, the wind backed round and the earthen smell of sodden timber blew back at us on the breeze. Eirik cursed in the name of every one of the gods and when he was done he drew a knife faster than any could have stopped him and held it to Eyvind Kelda's throat.

'He has soaked it, witch-man. He knows we are coming and he has soaked it so that it cannot burn. You will die before I do. I promise you that.'

Kelda smiled his cat-smile and kept his neck still. 'I will die before you do anyway,' he said, 'but not tonight.' He pushed the blade hand away. 'The king is not stupid; these things should not surprise you. Remember it for later when you are in his place – better to sleep damp and have the serfs hunting far abroad for firewood than to die cooked in your own bed.'

'So how do we do it? You would have me call him out and fight him single-handed?'

'Not unless you want to die before the gods would take you, no.' He turned and slid back along the way we had come. For a lank man, there was little enough to hear of his passing. Back at the men, he had us sit. 'You wanted fire,' he said. 'I will give it to you. Have your men place their timber as you planned. Call me as the dog fox barks when it is done.'

It is astonishing, sometimes, what men will do if they trust enough. Each of us had gathered and cut timber along the way. A half-hundred minus twelve with two extra is fifty men, fully laden. It is enough to burn down the best of houses but still some of those who placed theirs earliest went back into the forest for more. We worked quickly and in silence and if there were dogs in there, they were as drunk as their masters. At the end of it, brushwood and bigger timber piled three feet high around the full circuit of the farmhouse with deeper, denser piles at the doors and windows. It was not the driest of wood and the farmhouse itself ran with water as the sails of my father's ship had run before we set fire to it. Given pitch and sheep fat and goose oil, we might have fired it alone but we had none of those things and nor, as far as I could tell, had Eyvind Kelda. We stepped back and gathered at the wood's edge and Eirik Hakonson, smiling as a man smiles at his own death knell, made the bark of a dog fox to its vixen.

The witch-man joined us in seconds. The earl-son said nothing, simply nodded once to the man and once to the steading. Einar was less restrained. 'We have done our part,' he said. 'We are waiting for you to do yours.'

'Good.' He looked past Einar to where I was standing with

the earl-son. 'We will need nine fire arrows,' he said. Nine. Thrice three. Everyone noted that, no one said it.

I knelt to find the steel and tinder. A shadow fell across my hand. The witch-man tapped me on the shoulder. 'Not you,' he said. 'I need you with me.'

I had not expected that. I had my axe at my side and my mind half set for battle. Staring at him, I felt the smooth grip of the haft. 'I know nothing of magic.'

'I know.' He didn't smile then. 'But you are the son of your mother. It is not possible to do this without.'

I might still have refused but Einar stepped back and knelt beside me. 'I have tinder,' he said. 'We will make the arrows and light them. Go with the witch.' I had no choice. I went.

He led me round the back, into the shadow where the moonlight lit least. We stood in black silence. I could smell fresh-cut wood and soaked timber and the smell of wet cat from the skin my mother had sent him. The witch-man kept his hand on my shoulder and put his mouth close to my ear. 'How well can you recall your mother?' he asked. I shrugged. We were too close to the enemy to risk speaking. Still, he nodded as if I had answered.

'Think of her now. Think of her fire as you last saw it with her sitting beside it.'

The hairs rose at the back of my head. I am used to my mother speaking like that, not other men. He shifted his grip to my arm and moved me forwards, sunwise around the back of the building. He spoke to me in a language I did not understand and I heard the voice of my mother inside my head. She said: *Welcome home*, in a way that made me want to weep. I held the image of her and nodded to the witch-man. He had his eyes shut. I saw the skin alongside them crease.

We walked very slowly side by side, he closer to the walls, me closer to the edge of the clearing. At the beginning, all I could hear was the sound of our feet on the packed earth and it sounded like a host gearing up for battle and there was no way the Christ-wolf and his men would not hear it and wake. Soon, with his grip on my arm and the sound of his voice speaking nonsense in one ear and my mother speaking clearly in the other, I let go of the fear of discovery and found myself a child again at my mother's hearth with the flames burning gold and then blue and then red. The cat came in from the rain, dripping wet, and sat at her fire to dry itself, growling low in its throat as they do when the hunt has been good. Gradually, as we came round into the moon, the stink of wet cat became less than it had been and I could smell clean fur and dry wool and hear the voice of my mother singing the songs of her childhood about hearth-fires and their burning. Later, a man told me we walked round three times. I only remember it as once. Whichever it was, we returned to the place we had come from and I felt the grip grow less on my arm. I was not aware of the pain of it – in battle, one never is – but even now, I could show you the burn marks where the witch-man held me. At the time, I stood in the half-dark under a waning moon and saw a man who had aged ten years stand before me. There was more white at his temples than there had been. If he was a raven when we started our circuit, he was a magpie when we finished. The smooth tan of his face was greyed yellow and his scars stood out white. He laid the empty catskin pouch on a stave of ash that leaned up against the front door of the steading. 'Thank you,' he said, and his voice was thinner, if still as moving. 'Now you can fight.'

There is too much to tell you of the battle that followed. You need to know that the wood burned as if we had dried it in a kiln and the steading with it. We ringed it in steel, one man deep all the way round, two deep at the doors and the windows. Olaf Trygvason was not the first to come out; my guess is that he had drunk more than some of those closest to the door and that perhaps men did not have waking their king as their first thought when they smelled smoke and saw flames and heard the sounds of death all around them. When he did come at last, it was not alone, but with his bondes and his bodyguard around him; twelve men and all sworn to die before him. They held rugs soaked in water around their arms and threw a bucket on the flames by the door as they came. Already the walls were ablaze and the roof timbers were falling so a splash of wet did little to put out the fires, but it made a great deal of smoke and hid at first who was coming. It was Hlodvir, the hostage, who had seen him most recently, who called out the name. I heard his voice as the cry of a gull in the storm of battle.

'Trygvason! There! The red tunic and the helm in the middle of the bondesmen.'

There were four of us fighting together: me and Einar, Eirik Hakonson and Hlodvir. Behind us, Harald and Thorlief Egilson and Skeggi Hoskuldson fought in a three-pointed star. So seven of us faced twelve with the king in the middle. We came together in a curving line, shield and axe together. They had only axes and one sword amongst them and only the king wore a helmet. Four of his bodyguard were known to fight bare-sark for preference. They stood to the fore, axes swinging, and began their death-song. Looking back now, they were not calling on the White Christ. At the time, one does not notice these things. There was one to the left with blond hair so pale it was almost white and a great burn mark down his left arm. I took him first with my throwing axe, a deep wound to the chest, and then followed it up, from the side, with my great-axe. At the other side, an archer took the other. Einar and Eirik Hakonson picked one each and began fighting, which was when the king saw who they were.

If Einar has a voice like a bullhorn, Olaf Trygvason can call on the voice of the thunder-god himself. He raised his

127

head and the noise of it would have carried all the way to Nidaros. '*Treachery!*' he bellowed, which was obvious, and then '*Orkney and Hakonson!*' which, perhaps, was not.

Nobody has ever said that the Christ-wolf could not fight. He took the kingship by force and he held it by force and it was his axe arm men feared most. We were seven facing eight when he threw his helmet at Einar and lifted his great-axe, which was bigger than the Saxon priest's had ever been, and began the howling swing of a true berserker. No man stands before that and expects to live. Skeggi Hoskuldson died in a bright plash of blood as his face caught the full force of the first swing. Later, we identified him by the ring on his arm. Thorlief Egilson and his brother cast axes from either side before Harald died where he stood. Blood flowed from him like running water and behind us, a building made of itself a pyre that burned metal as if it were straw. In all the sounds of screaming men and falling timber, I heard my name.

'Arne! Look to Hakonson!'

It was Einar, fighting for his life on the far side of the group now, killing one of the bondes with the back edge of his sword blade, swinging for another. I looked and saw the three-quarter moon shone clear over his right shoulder and remembered the words of my mother.

'Einar! Move out of the moon!' I screamed it as I have never screamed anything else but I was already too late. The king swung to the sound of his voice saying the name of the one man he feared above all. The great mallet of his axe came down in an arc that started up at the height of the moon and finished at the ground and passed through the chest of Einar Sigurdson, my brother-in-life, on the way. I heard his voice saying my name, choked off halfway, and I saw the pain of the wound fill his eyes and pass out again. I was not sane then.

'*Einar!*' I caught up the blade of a bare-sark and threw it wide. A man moved on my right. Ahead of me, the killing axe,

128

fresh with red blood and bone, swung back in its arc. I hurled all that I had forward in to meet it and struck with my axe in a back-handed stroke for the helmetless head, for the bright gold hair, for the black eyes of the Christ-wolf who had killed my soul-friend – and saw them all showered in red before a fist punched in and tore the breath from my throat and the life from my heart and left me falling through eternity to a floor that wasn't there.

I came round in the light of dawn with a man leaning over me. It was Eirik Hakonson, earl-son, now king of all Norway. He was stripped to the waist with great burn marks over the skin of his chest and his shoulders and the hair burnt all away from his back. His face was red and white in patches and a purpled bruise swelled his upper lip.

'Einar?' I asked.

He shook his head. 'I'm sorry.'

I lay back and closed my eyes. 'He died well,' said the voice of the man who was now king of Norway. I let the noise of it wash over me. It made no dent in my loss.

'You, on the other hand, will be well again when your ribs have healed. You were lucky; he only caught you with the haft.' A hand gripped my forearm. I opened my eyes. Eirik Hakonson's eyes shone in the space above me and there was a warmth in them I had not seen before. He said: 'If you can stand, I would show you Einar before he goes to the gods.'

I could stand. I could also walk and look around me and recognise the living and count the bodies of the dead. 'Eyvind?' I asked.

'He lives. And Hlodvir. Orkney will have its earl when Sigurd goes.'

'It will not be the same.'

'No. It will not be the same.'

We came to the pyre. It was bigger than my father's although

129

it was on land and not at sea. We had no boat to spare and Eirik was not prepared to start asking for things until he had secured himself in the kingship. Still, they had given Einar everything a warrior could ask for. He lay in peace on his shield in full armour with his sword on his chest and his axe at his side and they had gathered as much wood for this one man as we had gathered to burn the entire steading. There was a reason for that. When I looked further, I saw that it was a pyre for two. Or, perhaps, there was one and then a smaller one behind it. I looked at Eirik.

'Trygvason.' He spoke it as a minor curse; a small withered thing of no consequence. Then he tapped my shoulder. 'Come. You killed him. You should see it.'

They had done him no honour. He lay naked on bare wood with no armour and no weapons. I am told this is how the Christians would have it but I doubt if it was done with that in mind. He was burned far more badly than any of the living. His skin was blistered all along one shoulder, turning to black at the elbow as if he had tried to force his way through the fire at another point before he came to the door. The wound on his head was a good one: clean and sharp and it bit deep, like my father's. He was only the fourth man I had killed.

Eirik Hakonson leaned on the side of the pyre. 'Einar told me of your fight with the Saxon,' he said. 'If you ever feel you want to leave Orkney, there will be a place for you in Norway. I will need a bodyguard of men who can kill with weapons they do not favour as well as with those that they do.'

I nodded. It was not a time to think of such things. The king reached forward and traced the wound on the Christ-wolf's head.

'They say you favour your left hand for the killing stroke,' he said. His eyes as much as his voice made it a question. They were blue, to match the dawn sky, and very bright.

'Yes.' I was thinking of Einar, of how I would tell his father.

130

Of my mother and her warnings and the reasons why I had not listened as I should.

'And the Saxon favoured his right?'

That was said as a question but was not. I brought my mind back to where I was standing. Eirik Hakonson smiled, and, for a moment, he looked very like the witch-man.

I said nothing. It occurred to me that I had not sworn fealty and that the dead man was still, technically, my king. Thus, amongst other things, I was guilty of treason. The living man was watching me. 'Eyvind Kelda tells me that your father had the sweet-water sickness, that he was already going blind and that it pained him to walk. Is this true?'

One does not lie to one's future king. 'Yes,' I said. 'It is true.'

'It is also true, I believe,' he said, absently, 'that a blow delivered by the left hand from in front would look exactly the same as one delivered by the right hand from behind.'

I had need of water. My lips were parched to leather. I licked them and they stayed that way. Eirik Hakonson reached to his belt and gave me his water-skin. I drank and felt no better. He took it back and drank himself. His eyes searched the sky beyond my shoulder, watching the clouds to see if they were different now that he was no longer the hunted son of a murdered earl. I might have spoken then but he put out a hand to stop me.

'I knew of your mother,' he said. 'She warned my father of his death in time for him to send me to Sweden. I have given thanks nightly to the all-father that she spoke when she did. All through the time when the Christ-wolf was killing in the name of his false god, I have prayed to her memory that something might be sent to stand in his way.'

His eyes were really very blue. They came back to mine. 'A man who lives for the true gods might choose to make of himself a sacrifice so that the people might find their way

131

again. This has always been so. Even the Christians have their sacrifice, albeit in their case it is the son who dies and not the father. Still, I would say that the principle is the same.' His face was different now; a judge and a judgement in one. There are some crimes greater than treason. I watched his right hand as it lay on his axe and waited for it to move. He said: 'Did Einar know?'

It was his voice that told me what I needed to know. I looked at my death and saw it walk past me into the morning sun. 'No,' I said. 'No one else knows.'

'Good. It is best kept that way.' He stood and gave me the water-skin again. We began to walk away from the pyre and I saw that the entire half-hundred of men, such as were still alive, were standing on the far side, waiting for us to finish. The king nodded to Eyvind Kelda who nodded back and did not smile. As we passed Einar's body, the king said: 'I will come to Orkney myself to thank your mother in person when there is time to do so. In the meantime, you can tell her from me that I will make certain your father did not die in vain.'

Historical Notes

With the exception of Arne Thoreson, his father and mother, the characters from this story are all taken from the Saga of Olaf Trygvason and, as such, are as close to being historically accurate as any other characters of the time. Certainly, it appears to be true that Olaf Trygvason was king of Norway in the closing years of the first millennium and he did, unquestionably, convert Orkney by force (and by dint of taking the earl's son hostage) and go on to convert the whole of Norway in like manner. He was killed, finally, in a truly epic sea battle by Eirik Hakonson with the (very limited) aid of the Swedish and Danish fleets. That story in itself deserves retelling but it is more of an act of extraordinary valour than a crime and this is not its place. Instead, I have given Eirik his victory six months early so that he can undo the work done by Trygvason and render northern Europe free of the blight of Christianity for the next thousand years (one can always dream).

In the smaller parts, the ship the Crane (*Tranen*) was Olaf Trygvason's own flagship and was the largest long-ship ever seen in northern waters at that period in history. Eyvind Kelda was a Norse 'witch' of Finnish or Lapp descent who was, in fact, tortured to death by Trygvason for failing to accept Christian baptism. I have thus, in my parallel universe, given him a part in the victory as some small recompense for his pain. The priest Thangbrand the Saxon was, indeed, sent to bring Christianity to Iceland, did kill the skald who lampooned him (plus two other men) and did return to Norway with his task unfulfilled. There is no record of his having been to Orkney and so his conflict with Arne is my invention.

Finally as a minor note of historical detail, you should know that the Norse counted in great-hundreds. One great-hundred = 120, thus a half-hundred men is sixty by our reckoning.

The Shoulder-Blade of a Ram

Edward Marston

Wales, 1188

U ntil I witnessed the phenomenon with my own eyes, I
    would never have believed that a murder could be solved
by means of the shoulder-blade of a ram. The right shoulder-
blade, to be exact. It happened when we reached Haverfordwest.

Baldwin, Archbishop of Canterbury, a man respected for
his learning and piety, was travelling around Wales in the
service of the Cross, endeavouring to recruit solders for a
Crusade. I, Gerald de Barri, more usually known as Giraldus
Cambrensis, was privileged to be his companion on this holy
journey. In Haverfordwest, the Archbishop first gave a sermon
and then the word of God was preached with some eloquence
by the Archdeacon of St David's, whose name adorns this
story; in short, by me. A great crowd of people assembled,
soldiers and civilians. Many found it little short of miraculous
that when I preached first in Latin, then in French, those who
could not understand a word of either language were just as
moved to tears as others. I was duly touched.

That evening, over an excellent meal, we heard more about
the Flemings.

'They're dreadful people,' complained our host, the ancient
but waspish Owain ap Madog. 'Wild, arrogant and hostile.'

'Yet several of them pledged themselves to join the
Crusade,' I noted. 'That must surely be evidence of Christian
impulse.'

'Evidence of their warlike spirits, that is all.'

'I thought that they were affected by my preaching.'

'Flemings kill for the sake of killing, Archdeacon.'

'The same has been said of the Welsh,' suggested Baldwin.

Even archbishops make foolish comments at times. Owain and I ignored him.

Having been born and brought up in Pembrokeshire, I was aware of the enmity between the indigenous Welsh inhabitants and the Flemish colonists who had been thrust upon the area by the edicts of Henry I, king of the English. The two races remained in a state of perpetual conflict, each inflicting outrages upon the other with deplorable regularity. Honesty compels me to admit that Flemings are not wholly reprehensible. Highly skilled in the wool trade, they are ready to work hard and to face danger by land or sea in pursuit of their commercial ends. Though they have turned their hand to the ploughshare, however, it still reaches too easily for the sword.

'Then there is this nonsense about the shoulder-bone of a ram,' said Owain, plucking at the food lodged in his silver beard. 'They claim to have powers of divination. Flemings boil the right shoulder-blades of rams. Instead of roasting them, they strip off all the meat and, by examining the little indents and protuberances, can foretell the future or reveal the secrets of events long past.' He gave a cynical snort. 'Or so they say. I think it's just one more idle boast.'

'Why the right shoulder-blade?' asked Baldwin, sipping his wine as if receiving Communion. 'Would not the left serve just as well?'

'Yes,' said Owain sourly. 'And so would the head and the horns, Archbishop. They could use any part of the beast to justify their monstrous claim. Nobody can foretell the future or conjure up the past.' He turned to me. 'Can they, Archdeacon?'

I was too intrigued by the notion to dismiss it out of hand.

Long experience had taught me that anything is possible on Welsh soil. Even when it is settled by foreigners. Owain wanted me to agree with him. Baldwin awaited my answer. I was circumspect.

'I would like to put this claim to the test,' I said, nodding sagely.

The murder gave me the opportunity to do just that.

The crime occurred that same night. While her husband was away on business, a woman called Margaret was strangled to death in her own bed. When the body was discovered by a maidservant, the whole town was thrown into a tumult of fear and indignation. Baldwin wanted to ride on to Pembroke to continue our work but I persuaded him to linger until the full facts of the murder were known. In the event, the personal interest that I took in the affair turned out to be crucial and I am not being immodest when I claim some of the credit for unmasking the killer and bringing him to justice.

Margaret was a popular member of the community. The wife of a successful merchant, she was a kind, friendly woman who gathered good opinions from all who met her. It was difficult to see what possible motive lay behind her foul murder. She was a handsome lady, by all accounts, and generous to a fault. Nobody was more devout or more loving towards her husband. I spoke to several people who knew her and they all agreed on one thing. Only a madman would slaughter such a domestic saint.

The victim's husband, Richard, returned to find his household in disarray. He was horrified to learn that his wife had been strangled and was at first inconsolable with grief. When he finally mastered his anguish, he was overcome by feelings of revenge. He drew his dagger and swore a terrible oath. Fortunately, I was on hand to calm him down and to offer practical guidance.

'I can understand this surging anger,' I said, gently.

'Can you?' he growled.

'Yes, my friend. But you will need more than blind fury to catch the vile rogue responsible for this heinous crime. You will need a cool head. I share your sorrow and long for retribution.'

'It is no business of yours, Archdeacon Gerald.'

'It is the business of every man to hunt down a ruthless killer.'

'Leave him to me,' warned Richard. 'This quarry is all mine.'

'Let me direct your steps, good sir.'

'How can you do that?'

It took me a long time but I eventually convinced him that the very fact that I was a stranger told in my favour. I viewed everything from the outside. I could be objective and dispassionate. Lacking any acquaintance with the dead woman, I was not caught up in a welter of emotions. Richard looked at me with a mixture of respect and caution.

'What do you advise?' he asked.

'First,' I said, 'I would like to question everyone in the household.'

'Why?'

'All the doors were locked last night yet the killer somehow entered and left the building without being seen or heard. If,' I added, reasonably, 'that is what happened.'

'What other explanation is there?'

'That the killer is a member of your own household.'

'Never!' he exclaimed. 'My servants loved their mistress. None of them would dare to lift a finger against her. I can vouch for them. We keep three men and four women beneath our roof. The women would not have the strength to commit such a crime and one of the men is so old that he can be discounted as well. Of the other two, I have the highest

140

opinion. Tried and trusted fellows with every cause to worship my wife.'

'I would still like to speak to them all,' I persisted.

'A waste of time, Archdeacon!'

'I might garner vital information.'

'Far too slowly. I want that villain run to ground now.'

'Then there may be a quicker way to identify him, my friend. I hear that your people have gifts of divination. Seek out the best of them. Kill a ram from your own flock and present the right shoulder-blade for examination. Will that content you?'

A strange look came into his eye as he listened to my counsel. He was patently surprised that a man of the Church should offer such advice, wondering if I really believed in the stories about divination or if I was subtly mocking the Flemings' habit of resorting to the shoulder-blade of an animal for critical information.

'It shall be done,' he said at length. 'Thank you, Archdeacon.'

'I would still like to talk to your servants.'

'It may not be necessary.'

Richard moved swiftly into action. One of the rams was selected from his flock and he insisted on slaughtering the creature himself, standing over the cook while the man cut out the right shoulder-blade before boiling it in a pot of hot water. I was not allowed to be present in the kitchen but I did accompany Richard when he hastened across to a house on the edge of the town. It was there that we found the person most accomplished in the arts of divination by means of animal bone. Her name was Adela.

I was astonished to see how relatively young she was, barely thirty years old in my estimation, a soulful widow whose beauty was marked by clear indications of suffering yet who had an air of distant wisdom about her. Could this pale woman really have magical powers? I doubted it. Adela was highly sympathetic towards Richard and offered her condolences time and again. Anxious to help him, however, she was very reluctant to become involved in the case, fearing that any mistake on her part might lead to the arrest and execution of an innocent man. Richard pleaded with her until she finally consented to use her skills on his behalf.

'Do not expect too much,' she said, diffidently.

'Everyone knows your reputation,' argued Richard.

'I have never been asked to solve such a hideous crime before.'

'Then this is a unique moment,' I observed, always delighted to see an important precedent established. 'Find the killer and you will do the whole community a service.'

'I will try, Archdeacon Gerald.'

'It will be some murderous Welshman,' asserted Richard. 'I know it.'

'Let us see,' she murmured.

Taking the shoulder-blade from him, she held it in the palm of one hand so that she could use the fingertips of the other to explore every inch of it. I was fascinated. All that I could see was a shoulder-blade picked clean of meat and gristle, yet it obviously had a series of invisible markings that could be read and interpreted by someone with the gifts of a seer. Adela clearly had such gifts. I watched her face closely. Eyes shut to aid her concentration, she worked her way deftly over the shoulder-blade until her fingers came into contact with something that caused her to stiffen. She sat up with a start.

'What is wrong?' I wondered.

'Nothing,' she said, opening her eyes.

'You've found him, haven't you?' pressed Richard. 'What's his name?'

'Truly, I don't know.'

'Tell me,' he demanded. 'I must avenge my wife.'

Adela was torn between willingness to help and a lack of faith in her own abilities. She licked her lips and took a deep breath before reporting her findings.

'The killer was a strong young man who hated the Flemings,' she said.

'A Welshman!' shouted Richard.

'He cannot speak his name nor hear your denunciation of him.'

Richard's jaw tightened and his eyes blazed. Before I could stop him, he charged out of the room as fast as he could go. I turned to Adela for elucidation.

'He has recognised the man,' she explained.

'One of the servants?'

'Not exactly, Archdeacon.'

'Then who is the fellow?'

'A poor, wretched deaf and dumb creature with no more sense than the ram whose shoulder-blade helped to identify him.' Her voice hardened. 'Yet he is capable of a bloody crime and must pay for it.'

'You saw all that with your fingers?' I said.

'Everything but his name.'

'An extraordinary gift!'

'I'm pleased to put it to such a valuable use,' she said with a wan smile. 'Most of the people who come to me simply want to know the sex of an unborn child or to hear a comforting prophecy about their futures. I have now helped to catch a murderer.'

'You and the shoulder-blade of a ram.'

'Yes, Archdeacon.'

'If you've finished with it, I'd like to inspect it myself.' She was hesitant. I smiled quietly and held out my hand. 'May I?'

The villain's name was Hywel and he was lucky that the sheriff arrived in time to save his life or, at least, to postpone his death until legal process had been observed. Hywel was a thickset man in his twenties whose disabilities made him a figure of fun in the locality. He earned his keep by doing mundane chores on a farm a few miles away from the town. When Richard caught up with him, Hywel was working in a field, sublimely unaware of the presence of an enraged man who was brandishing a sword. It is probable that the incensed husband would have slain him on the spot had not the sheriff and his men turned up providentially, having been told of the crime and having trailed Richard. Less inclined to accept the judgement of a ram's shoulder-blade, the sheriff nevertheless arrested Hywel and placed him under lock and key while an investigation was conducted.

It soon yielded results. Hywel, it transpired, was a kinsman of the old servant in Richard's household and – without the permission of the master – was sometimes admitted to the house in the dead of night to sleep in comfort for a change. Under questioning, the old man confessed that he had let Hywel into the building the previous night to escape the storm that was brewing. Customarily, the deaf and dumb Welshman slept in the stables with the other animals on the farm. The old man, Iestyn by name, took pity on him. Richard, by contrast, was quite pitiless in his questioning.

'So you are an accomplice in this murder!' he roared.

'No, sir,' pleaded Iestyn. 'I'm no killer. Nor is Hywel.'

'You sneaked him into the house.'

'But that is all I did.'

'Is it?' said Richard. 'Are you sure you didn't help him to strangle my wife?'

The old man wept bitterly. 'I'd never do that, sir. I adored and respected my mistress. You know that. You trusted me.

Have I ever given you cause to doubt that trust, sir? Tell me. Have I?'

'Not until now.'

'Hywel slept beside me all night. I swear it.'

'Planning the murder.'

'No!'

'Yes, you Welsh cur!'

'How could I plan anything with someone who can neither speak nor hear?'

'You acted on instinct. Two evil men, consumed by hate.'

'But I loved your wife, sir!'

Richard's blow caught him across the face and sent him reeling. The sheriff had heard enough. The old man was dragged off to join Hywel in a dungeon. When he had calmed down, Richard was able to suggest motive for the crime. Soft-hearted as she was by nature, his wife had accepted that Iestyn was too frail to be kept much longer in their service. She had told him that he must leave within the month. The old man must have used Hywel to get his revenge on her, confident that, if caught, his kinsman would have no voice to incriminate him.

Impressed by the speed and the manner in which the murder was solved, I was troubled by lingering doubts. When I was allowed to examine the two hapless Welshman, I found no malice or violence in them. The one was far too dim-witted to know what he was doing and the other too loyal to harbour any feelings of revenge. Instead of confiding my worries to the sheriff, I repaired to the home of Owain ap Madog, where Baldwin awaited me with growing impatience. I related the events of the day without embellishment. To his credit, the Archbishop sat enthralled, but Owain was sceptical. Not only was he furious that the murder was laid so hastily at the feet of two of his compatriots, he had grave misgivings about the part that Adela had played in the whole affair.

'It was a wild guess,' he contended. 'She plucked Hywel's name out of the air.'

'But she didn't give him a name,' I reminded him. 'She merely said that the killer had been deaf and dumb. That led Richard to the malefactor. The shoulder-blade somehow yielded up the information required.'

'Remarkable!' said Baldwin.

'Trickery!' countered Owain.

'But I was there,' I said, producing the shoulder-blade from my satchel. 'I saw the lady tease out the secrets locked away in this bone. Do not ask me how part of a dead ram can divulge the identity of a killer but it did. I witnessed it.'

'God must have been acting through the lady,' decided Baldwin, never one to acknowledge powers from a source other than heaven. 'This Adela was inspired by the wonder of the Almighty.'

Owain took the shoulder-blade from my grasp and scrutinised it carefully.

'Inspired or misled?' he asked.

'What do you mean?' I said.

'Where did this shoulder-blade come from, Archdeacon?'

'A ram in the flock owned by Richard himself.'

'Who killed the beast?'

'He did. Then he stood over the cook while the shoulder-blade was boiled and cleaned.' Owain held the object up to the light and stroked it. 'What is wrong?'

'I smell a rat.'

'But you're holding part of a ram,' said Baldwin.

'No, I'm not, Archbishop. And neither was the lady.'

'What are you telling us?' I said, suspecting what his answer might be.

Owain savoured his moment. 'If this came from a ram,' he announced, waving the shoulder-blade before us, 'then it was

146

a most peculiar beast. It might deceive most people because the two are so alike but it would never deceive me. I'm a true Welshman, remember, brought up among goats. As a boy, I tended, killed and ate them on occasion. I also carved the bones of sheep and goats. That teaches you a lot about both animals. I'd stake my life on the fact that this is the shoulder-blade of a goat and not of a ram.'

Baldwin was mystified. 'Then why did this Richard slaughter a beast from his flock? A wool merchant can surely tell the difference between a ram and a goat?'

My mind was racing. A ram had indeed been killed and the cook had extracted and prepared the shoulder-blade, but there was no proof that it was then presented to Adela for inspection. Could a clever switch have occurred? The lurking doubts that had assailed me now began to take on a more definite shape. Perhaps I had not witnessed an act of divination, after all. I rose to my feet and headed for the door.

'Where are you going?' bleated Baldwin.

'To solve a crime.'

'But the villains have already been arrested.'

'On false evidence, Archbishop.'

I have never liked the practice of eavesdropping because it smacks of nosiness but there are times when it is unavoidable. Sensing that the true facts of the case had yet to come to light, I made my way discreetly back to Adela's house and approached by means of the garden at the rear. I concealed myself in the bushes and kept the lady herself under surveillance through the open shutters. Adela was tripping happily around her parlour, singing to herself and glowing with anticipatory pleasure. The rather sombre young woman who had been so reluctant to examine the shoulder-blade at first was now a spirited creature who was almost luxuriating in her sins. I did not have long to wait. A horse approached at a steady canter and the rider brought it to a halt outside the stable. I caught only a glimpse of him as he rushed into the house but I recognised him instantly.

Richard had also undergone a transformation. The demented husband was now an urgent lover, racing to claim his prize, so supremely confident of the success of his plan that he did not pause to think that he might be giving himself away. When they came face to face, he and Adela embraced like the conspirators they were. I had seen enough. As I scurried off to summon the sheriff, I worked out why and how the crime must have been committed. Richard was a strong, virile man who needed more sensual excitement than a God-fearing wife like Margaret could provide. Evidently, the widowed Adela supplied that excitement and relished it in turn. The only way that they could be together was to rid themselves of the obstruction posed by Margaret and arrange for someone else to bear the blame for her death.

My guess was that Richard knew only too well that his aged servant took pity on his deaf and dumb kinsman and that the time when Iestyn would most probably let Hywel into the house was during his master's absence. It was a cunning gamble. Pretending to be away on business, Richard instead let himself into the house with his key, strangled a wife who would have made no protest when she saw her husband unexpectedly entering the bedchamber, then fled into the night. The rage that he kindled on the following day was an effective cloak for his own wickedness. Other details that I had gleaned now fell neatly into place. With a skill born of years of practice and with an insight into human depravity culled from a life of random ubiquity, I solved a cruel murder without resort to the shoulder-blade of any animal.

The sheriff took a long time to accept the inexorable logic of my theory.

'Richard?' he said, shaking his head. 'A murderer? What does he stand to gain?'

'Adela,' I replied.

'She is a rich widow, it is true, and very beautiful. But so was Margaret. Indeed, she had even more private wealth than Adela.' He paused as a secondary motive came into view. 'Lust and gain? They are strong enough temptations for any man. Richard would be set for life if he were to inherit his wife's wealth and merge it with the money left to Adela by her late husband.' He was persuaded. 'And you say that you saw the pair of them together, Archdeacon?'

'Meeting up to celebrate their triumph.'

'Hardly the action of a grieving man.'

'Approach the house with stealth, my lord sheriff. I fancy that you may even take them *in flagrante*. Would that be proof enough for you?'

'It most certainly would.'

We stayed in Haverfordwest long enough to see the arrest of the two accomplices and the release of Iestyn and his kinsman. Richard tried to bluff his way out of the situation but Adela broke down under interrogation and confessed all. She had genuine powers of divination and would have been impelled to make a true prophecy had the correct shoulder-blade been put in her hands. That was why the substitution was made and false information given. I allowed myself the rare pleasure of receiving unstinting congratulations from all sides. It is not often given to me to be in a position to wield the sword of justice to such effect. As we took our leave of our host, I was gracious enough to acknowledge his crucial contribution.

'Your help was quite invaluable, Owain.'

'I'm always happy to imprison a couple of lying Flemings,' he said with a chuckle. 'Especially when two innocent Welshman are set free into the bargain.'

'You were magnificent,' complimented Baldwin. 'Who else could tell the shoulder-blade of a ram and that of a goat apart? I praise God that such rare knowledge could be put to such a critical use.'

'It serves as symbol of the whole sorry business,' I opined.

'What does?'

'The difference between sheep and goats, Archbishop.'

'I do not follow you, Gerald.'

'Nor more do I,' added Owain.

'It is simple,' I explained. 'Richard was a wool merchant who was married to a submissive lamb of a woman. But he could never be entirely happy among the sheep of this world. He was a man of goatish inclination and sought out a woman as red-blooded and rampant as himself. According to the sheriff,' I confided, enjoying the opportunity to scandalise Baldwin, 'that libidinous pair were caught in the very act of adultery, their naked bodies so entwined that they had to be prised forcibly apart.'

'Saints preserve us!' gasped Baldwin.

'Flemings are born lechers!' commented Owain.

'The lady brought about her own downfall,' I concluded. 'The sheriff tells me that, when they burst into the bedchamber, Adela was holding her lover's shoulders. Deception came full circle. For the second time in one day, a scheming woman had her hand on the right shoulder-blade of a goat that was pretending to be a ram. As well she could not foretell the future from that bogus shoulder-blade or she would have known that the sheriff was coming.'

I swear that Archbishop Baldwin came perilously close to laughter.

Flyting, Fighting

Clayton Emery

England, 1192

'I didn't want to dance with her, but she clung like a leech!'

'Ah, so you had to prop her bottom with both hands?'

'No! I – I don't know what I did.'

'*I* do. You acted like a perfect pig!'

Robin Hood stifled a groan. His head throbbed, his stomach churned, his ears rang, his vision blurred. Worse, Marian yammered like a woodpecker to drill his wooden head full of holes. Even the late spring sun hounded him, searing his eyes as he stumbled along the forest path. 'It was – quite a dance.'

'You outstepped St Vitus, you vulgar swine!' Marian was dressed like her husband in a green shirt and deerhide tunic and soft hat sporting a pheasant feather. Like her husband, she wore a quiver and an Irish knife and carried her longbow ready in her left hand. 'You clutched that saucy tart as tight as any tankard!'

'Folks give me drinks. 'S rude to deny 'em.'

'Such chivalry! My mother warned me not to marry an outlaw!'

' 'N' the one time she was right, you didn't listen.'

'Take my soul! Now you'd defame my mother?'

'No! *Ow*, my head! I— what the hell?'

The trail intersected another wending east–west. Eastward lay the Greenwood, but Robin blocked Marian from stepping. Dropping to one knee, and gurgling inside, he squinted through a headache at the muddy track.

He studied the track for a number of yards. Twice he put his hand alongside a footprint, then laid his head to peer sideways. He measured the length of strides against his bow, then traced a small scuffed print.

Rising, he pronounced, 'The king's foresters have made off with a girl.'

Arms crossed, Marian said, 'What?'

'Look. Poison Hugh has a crippled toe that turns out. He's head forester. These other two must be foresters, because their stride glides like ours. This'n must be Osborn because it's his bailiwick and he's big. They drag a girl against her will. Her feet are tiny and toed-in in doghide slippers. See how she stumbles? Here she dug in her toes but got yanked along, likely bound by the wrists. Why else would a girl travel with loutish foresters except by force?'

Marian looked at the jumbled tracks of men and deer marring the mud, then snorted. 'You made that up.'

'Made it up?' Robin's jaw dropped. He spread his hands at the trail. 'It's plain as a page of Scripture!'

Marian gazed at treetops. 'I suppose it might rain.'

'I – I disbelieve this! You doubt my word?' Robin trotted a dozen feet down the trail and pointed. 'Look! She planted both feet and went to her knees, but here she's dragged again.'

Marian turned a beech leaf to study its underside. 'Be time to pick mugwort soon.'

Robin Hood pinched the edge of a footprint to find it still sharp-cut, not yet crumbling. He pressed a calloused thumb and watched dampness recede. 'An hour agone. Let's get after them.' Eyes on the trail, bow bobbing in his left hand, Robin Hood trotted.

Skipping, Marian caught up. 'If you think this excuses your boorish behaviour, you're dead wrong.'

Thumping along, skull throbbing, Robin snapped, 'I've half a mind to let these kidnappers keep the girl just to spite you.'

'So?' Marian sniffed. 'If a helpless girl is abused, what matter? What's the suffering of one more woman in this man's world?'

'It's men suffer the vexations of women. Ask Adam.'

'Ywis! Blame Eve! " 'Twas her done it, Lord! She made me eat of the fruit! I never had a thought for myself, nor will I shoulder the blame, so help me Almighty God!" '

Bile bubbled in Robin's throat, but he refused to slow. 'You concede there *is* a girl in distress?'

'I concede no such thing,' Marian retorted.

Robin suddenly halted. 'She's gone.'

Marian piffed.

'No. Someone's hoisted her on his shoulder. Osborn, probably. His tracks deepen and shamble. She must be a handful.' Moving on, Robin nodded. 'Here she is. Too much trouble to lug. I hope she doesn't resist too long. They might find it easier to knock her on the head.' He resumed trotting.

'That's men for you.' Marian puffed alongside. 'Cruel. Unkind. Liars, cheaters, *gropers*.'

'I wonder if this girl gives them an earful like some I could name. I wonder if she was at the wedding. Everyone in Nottinghamshire was there. If she left early—'

'For a secret rendezvous with a dashing outlaw?'

'Eh? No! I just wonder if—'

'If she exists? Likely you hope't so. Dozens of girls fell over their feet to dance with you.'

'Is that knavery?' Robin jog-trotted, watching the trail but the woods too, as always, for oddities or ambush. 'You circled young men laughing gay as a lark.'

'Would you have me pine under some arbour? A weeping willow, mourning unloved and unattended?'

Robin paused as the tracks swerved towards brush. 'She broke away. But they caught her again.' The outlaw swiped at a bush and found a long hair, held it against the sky, then a tree trunk. 'She's blonde.'

Raven-tressed Marian sniffed. 'Surprise.'

Watching his wife, Robin Hood ran the hair through his mouth. Tasting, he mused, 'She's . . . fourteen, this high, blue-eyed, dressed in red . . . Her name is Mary.'

Marian frowned under dark brows. 'You are *such* a liar. An evil, low, lying blackhearted *dog*.'

'A goodly gazehound, let's hope.' Robin trotted. 'Come, before they hurt her.'

Panting alongside, Marian groused, 'Behold who speaks of hurting! I can't believe I married you. I should have bid the huntsman set the hounds on you when first you sniffed round my door!'

'Wouldn't w-work.' Robin belched thunderously and gasped, but felt better. 'Dogs like me.'

'Foul. Like likes like. I should have had my brothers thrash you!'

'When I was sneaking in,' Robin laughed, 'or sneaking out at dawn?'

'Don't you besmirch *me*, you malken trash!' Marian's dark eyes smouldered as her hair bounced around her shoulders. 'I never let you stay the night! And I never shall again!'

'As I recall, your brothers begged me on bended knee to take you off their hands.'

'They did not!'

'Picklepuss, they called you. Shrew-tongue. Hammer-fist, too.'

'You lie! They'd never slander me! They daren't!'

'I told them, "I don't understand. Marian, my sweet poppet? She's gentle as a milch cow and tender as a lily!" Oh, Lord, they laughed to split their spleens! I thought they'd never stand erect again. They offered me the Rushcliffe wapentake to marry you because it's the farthermost fief and they reckoned to only suffer you at Christmastide.'

'Lies, lies, lies.'

'Did you really push Galliard out of a window? And set

Marshall's clothes on fire? And lock Sidney in the tower?'

'I'll kill them,' Marian growled. 'As God is my judge, I'll make them suffer.'

'Marry them off. That'll do it.' Robin Hood stopped abruptly. 'No hope. An hour'r more ahead. They could harm the girl grievously before we catch them. If we catch them.'

'If there's a girl.'

'Yes, if.' Robin scanned the forest. 'Advise me . . .'

'Why think?' snapped Marian. 'Why not indulge your basest instincts? Just do what you will, heedless of consequence. Such you've always done. Why change now?'

Stroking his beard, Robin mapped trails in his mind. 'Too true. Plunging into marriage has been the ruin of a good woman. The poor creature's wasted the prime of her life on an undeserving cad . . .'

'God wot't. A woman's a fool to marry.'

'Hmm? Softly now . . . If Osborn drags the girl but not the other two, 'haps only Osborn has designs on her . . . Yes, we'll essay. Come, Marian.'

Leaving the trail, bearing south, Robin cut cross-country. Nimbly he and Marian dodged beech and oak trees, then startled a herd of fallow deer dappled yellow and white. Marian panted, 'Where do we go?'

'Osborn has a croft in Elmsley. I doubt he'd take her there. Even a forester can't drag a girl about like a baulky calf. But there's a hut near the old iron mines at Black Hill. We'll diverge to the path to Brown's Covert and cut their trail.'

'And if we don't?' asked Marian.

'I'm proved wrong and you can gloat. And an innocent girl suffers. Any road, it wasn't my idea.'

'What wasn't?'

'To marry. I had no say. Ever since I could walk I tripped over this skinny girl with dark hair who'd tell me, "We're going to be married, Robert Locksley." Crass to take advantage

157

of an eight-year-old. Still, it saved me seeking a betrothal.'

'Lackaday. You needs practise for your next wife.'

'Never. I'll abstain. I'll take the cowl and tend sheep.'

'Much like the women you prefer. Fluffy and brainless and clinging for protection.' In falsetto, Marian warbled, ' "Ooh, Master Robin, you're so powerful strong you crush me like a rose blossom!" '

'Better the blossom than the thorns,' muttered the husband. 'And I can think of a few rosy buds I've nipped that delighted the gardener.'

'Don't be crude.'

They saved their breath for running. The short cut was short only because it vaulted hills, and they chugged upslope around ash trees towering like columns in a cathedral. Before long Robin raised his hand. They skipped across open heath, then crept through a scatter of silver birches on to a narrow trail of polished roots and rocks. Frustrated by lack of sign, Robin dashed along the path until he found a muddy wallow. Rising, he waved Marian behind a cuckoo oak, an ancient hollow trunk stuffed with saplings.

'They haven't passed,' whispered Marian. 'Even I see that.'

'Never yet.' Crouching in the scrub, Robin Hood slipped off his quiver and laid it on top of his bow, as did Marian. He plied his Irish knife to cut and whittle a sapling. Too, he pointed with his knife to green shoots. 'Adder's Tongue. Good omen.'

Marian puffed and watched. 'You'd attack three foresters with just a club?'

'What fear I to die if my Marian rejects me?' Robin's only sign of anxiety was to whittle the club obsessively. 'Pray you're lucky and I'm killed. Men love to comfort a widow.'

'Likely you'll fly off the handle and flounder. Besides all your other faults, you've a filthy temper.'

'I can't indulge it today. We needs get the girl back.'

'I remember that fair where that boor manhandled me. You

158

half killed the man. It took the entire Merry Men to pull you off. A horrid display!'

'Good thing I'm the only one in the family with a temper.'

'Jape. Mock me.' The Vixen of Sherwood tsked. 'Why didn't I see your cruel streak? Why was I blind? What did I that God punished me with a vindictive vengeful louse for a husband?'

'Serves you well for not taking the veil. Decent women dedicate their chaste bodies to God, not bawdy pleasures. Do you want a stick?'

'Dare you tell me how to fight?'

'Never. You wouldn't listen anyway.'

'Ro-bert Lock-sley—'

'Hark!'

Silently they waited, hearing only their breathing. Then a small cry like a kitten's. The tramp of heavy feet. A girl whined and sobbed. A man growled. Creeping, without touching, Robin Hood peered through leaves. Came three foresters in brown with the king's arrow stitched on breast or hat. They wore quivers and weapon-knives, and one man carried two bows. Poison Hugh was unshaven and jowly and red-eyed. A second forester Robin didn't know. Osborn was a big brute dragging by rawhide thongs on her wrists a skinny girl in a bright gown and kirtle now tattered.

The Fox of Sherwood drew his long Irish knife and tucked it alongside the club in his fist. He hissed, 'Make noise as if all the Merry Men. Here we go!

'*Yahhhh!* Have at them, me hearties! John, Scarlet, kill them all!'

Just past, the foresters had their backs turned. Surprise was complete as Robin and Marian leaped out roaring like lions and swinging weapons.

The unknown forester bolted headlong. Poison Hugh fumbled his bow to draw his sax-knife. Osborn whirled the wrong way and tangled with the bound girl. Robin Hood walloped Osborn's knee so he crashed to earth. Marian charged Poison Hugh with her long keen blade laid along her forearm. As Hugh shrank back, Marian slashed the villain's sleeve and tunic straight across. Blood welled. Hugh shrieked and stumbled.

With both felons down, Robin Hood chucked the club, snipped the girl's thongs an inch above Osborn's fingers, caught her arm, and half pitched her at the scrub. Snatching up quivers and bows, making sure Marian followed, he gasped, 'Run like the wind!'

Hard they pelted past trees and through bracken, not letting up until they were half a mile from the path. Only then did Robin collapse to his knees. And laugh and laugh, sobbing for breath. Marian crumpled too, gasping and giggling. 'Benedictee! Did you see – their faces? Lord – we showed them! Oh, dear – oh, dear, what's your name?'

Still in the grip of terror, the girl hiccuped, 'M-M-Mary.'

Robin Hood hooted. Marian tried to glare, but rubbed her nose and smiled. 'A lucky guess. Don't fret, honey, we'll see you safe.'

'God's fish and teeth!' gasped Robin. 'That'll teach those foresters to cross you, Marian! You half-dressed Poison Hugh like a prize pricket! Oh, you're wonderful! The most boon companion a man could want! Come to my arms, turtledove!'

'Ooh, you're so aggravating! You really are impossible!' But Marian scuffled on her knees into her husband's embrace. Passionately they kissed, though their noses ran and they lacked breath. Coming up for air, Robin squeezed Marian so hard she grunted.

'See, Marian?' laughed Robin. 'You're the only woman I could desire. And so beautiful when you're angry. Far more stunning and exciting than any scrawny minx from Clipstone.'

'What?' Marian shoved free of her husband's clinch. Dark eyes hot, she snarled, 'You still think of *her*? And dare compare her to *me*? You swine! You cur! You lowly stinking *toad*! . . .'

The Trebuchet Murder

Susanna Gregory

Ely Hall at the University of Cambridge, 1380

Brother Edmund set down his pen and used both hands to rub his aching back. As Prior Richard's secretary, it was Edmund's duty to make notes on the meeting currently taking place in Richard's chamber. The meeting comprised a trio of eager young men and Richard himself, and had been going on all morning. Edmund was tired of writing down questions and answers, his eyes stung from the smoking candle, and his shoulders were cramped from hunching over his work. The clerk glared at the three young men, as though they were personally responsible for his discomfort.

The young men in question had applied to Ely Hall in the hope of being appointed its next Professor of Theology. A month before, old Brother Henry had choked on his dinner and died, leaving his colleagues not only shocked by the suddenness of his death, but a teacher short in the middle of term. Therefore, Prior Richard, Ely Hall's warden, was obliged to find a replacement as quickly as possible.

Ely Hall was the college at the University of Cambridge where the Benedictine Order sent its most promising students, and Edmund knew that Richard was taking his responsibilities very seriously: it would not do to appoint the wrong man. The grey-haired but still energetic prior grilled the young hopefuls relentlessly, probing the quickness of their minds and their ability to grasp complex arguments under pressure. The candidates looked as exhausted by the interrogation as Edmund felt, but the clerk knew that Richard was conscientious, and that he was simply working hard to ensure the college he loved appointed the best man.

The prior paused, leaning back in his chair to allow the three men to draw breath and collect their thoughts. Taking the opportunity to stand and flex his sore shoulders, Edmund studied the candidates as they sat uneasily on the hard wooden bench in front of him.

First, there was Brother Luke, a slightly balding fellow in his late twenties, who already had the soft, dissipated appearance resulting from too many good dinners. His face was dominated by protuberant blue eyes, and his manner was gentle and almost diffident. Luke had penned two short essays on creationism that had been favourably received by his fellow academics, but Edmund was more impressed that the Archbishop of Canterbury had written to Richard personally, to say that Luke showed great promise as a scholar and should be given the chance to prove himself at Ely Hall.

The second candidate was a Frenchman, Brother Jean, whose books were well known, even by undergraduates. His long, awkward limbs and large, bony hands made him seem ungainly, an appearance accentuated by the fact that the Benedictine habit he wore was rather too small for him. It was also the blackest garment that Edmund had ever seen – he supposed Jean had ordered it re-dyed especially for his interview, but that the dyer had done a poor job. At breakfast that morning, Jean had revealed a wry sense of humour that Edmund found amusing. The clerk hoped Richard would choose Jean over the other two.

Finally, there was Brother Bravin, who sniffed constantly and was always wiping his long, dripping nose on a piece of linen. Despite his unprepossessing appearance, Bravin preened like a peacock. He was fastidiously clean, and his immaculate habit fitted him perfectly, a stark contrast to Jean's. As far as Edmund could tell, Bravin had no qualifications at all that rendered him suitable for the post. He had written nothing of note, and his replies to Richard's probing questions were hesitant and superficial. And there was the letter of recommendation he had brought with him from his abbot, in which the latter praised Bravin's genius and worth. Edmund regularly corresponded with the abbot over business matters and knew very well that the signature at the bottom of Bravin's testimonial had been forged: it was obvious that Bravin had written the glowing letter himself.

Richard did not allow them respite for long, and was soon back to his questioning. But eventually, when Edmund was so tired and stiff from writing that his whole body seemed to burn with fatigue, Richard indicated that the ordeal was over, and summoned a lay brother to conduct the three candidates to the refectory for some much-needed refreshment. When they had gone, Richard slumped in his chair and rubbed his eyes. His normally neat hair was awry, and he looked weary and dispirited. Flexing stiff fingers, Edmund poured him some wine.

'I wish Brother Henry had not choked on those oysters,' the prior said, as he took a substantial swallow from the goblet. 'Then I would not be in this predicament.'

Edmund was surprised that Richard should consider appointing a new master as a 'predicament'.

'But Henry was old and was no longer a good teacher. His death has provided you with an opportunity to hire a younger, better man. And what a choice! Jean is already famous for his excellent scholarship, while Luke comes recommended by the Archbishop of Canterbury himself. Either one will be an asset to Ely Hall.'

Richard gave a smile that was without humour. 'True. But I am obliged to offer the position to Bravin.'

Edmund's jaw dropped in horror. 'But why? He is no scholar, and, as I told you last night, I am sure he forged that letter from his abbot.'

Richard's smile became a grimace. 'Bravin may not be scholarly, but he is cunning. He went to wealthy Catherine Deschalers, who provides Ely Hall with much of its funding, and ingratiated himself with her. We are obliged to take her wishes into consideration.'

'Then tell her Bravin would not be good for Ely Hall,' said Edmund, failing to see why Richard should listen to the demands of the forceful but often misguided Catherine. Everyone knew she changed her mind more rapidly and frequently than the direction of the wind, and Edmund was sure she could be persuaded to accept Jean or Luke instead. 'She will want what is best for the institution that costs her so much money each year. Tell her Bravin is a fraud.'

'I tried,' said Richard wearily. 'But Bravin anticipated me. He had already spun her some tale about an illness that left his abbot without the use of his right hand, hence the difference in the signatures that you observed.'

'Then we will have to rely on Brother Thomas to help us,' said Edmund, thinking fast.

'Thomas is the bishop's agent, and the bishop will not want a man like Bravin appointed. I dislike Thomas because he is greedy and ambitious, but even *he* would not approve of a forger elected to Ely Hall.'

Richard finished his wine, then held out his goblet to be refilled. 'Again, Bravin anticipated me. He promised Thomas preferential treatment for any students he sent to Ely Hall, and even intimated that he would make such students' examinations easier, to ensure their success.'

Edmund was shocked. 'But we are a reputable institution. We do not want accusations of favouritism and cheating levelled at us!'

166

Richard laid a comforting hand on Edmund's shoulder, then walked to the window. Edmund followed him, and they stood side by side to gaze into the Market Square below. It was a fine spring day. The sky was blue, dotted with bright white clouds, and the market was alive with activity as vendors shouted the prices of their wares: chickens, cloth, wine, goats, bread and ribbons.

'You are right, Edmund,' said Richard softly. 'But my hands are bound by Catherine and her money, and by Thomas and his influence with the bishop. Bravin will be our next Professor of Theology.'

Edmund continued to gaze out of the window. Suddenly, the colours of the market did not seem so vibrant, and the warmth went out of the dancing sunlight. It was a poor world, he thought, when worthy men like Luke and Jean were thwarted by liars and frauds like Bravin, and good, upright men like Richard were powerless to prevent it from happening.

The following day, thick grey clouds covered the sky, promising rain. Edmund attended church, then walked home in a gloomy frame of mind, thinking about the machinations of Bravin and the damage his appointment would do to Ely Hall.

As he approached the college, he saw Prior Richard talking with two people. He recognised the bald head and the false smile of Thomas, the bishop's man, while the other person was the wealthy Catherine Deschalers. Catherine was a thin, big-boned woman, whose fortune allowed her to indulge her taste for bright clothes; that day she wore a scarlet cloak edged with ermine.

'The decision is made,' Thomas announced as Edmund drew closer. 'We think Bravin is the best candidate. You will draw up the appropriate deeds appointing him today, and we will tell him the good news when they are ready.'

'On what grounds do you choose Bravin?' demanded

Edmund, ignoring the warning glance shot at him by Richard for his impertinence. 'Jean is a brilliant scholar, while Luke comes recommended by the Archbishop of Canterbury. How can Bravin compare to them?'

'He is our choice,' replied Thomas sharply. 'He has also promised to favour any students I send him. The bishop will like that, I am sure.'

'And I think he will make a better professor than the others,' added Catherine. 'He has also promised to teach me to read – something you have never offered to do.'

Before Edmund could say he would teach her himself if she would reconsider her decision, she had raised the hem of her skirts above the muck of the High Street and flounced away. He watched her go, a tall, pinched woman wrapped in her billowing scarlet cloak. He opened his mouth to plead with Thomas, but fell silent when the door opened and the three candidates emerged. He hated seeing the nervous anticipation on the faces of Luke and Jean, and felt a surge of contempt when he saw the secretive smile that played around the corners of Bravin's mouth, as if the man already knew he had won. Bravin dabbed his ever-dipping nose fussily, and addressed Richard.

'You promised to show us around Cambridge this morning, Father. I would like to see the town that may become my home.'

'I have a headache,' said Richard sharply. Edmund knew the prior never suffered from headaches, and realised that he simply could not bear to spend time with the gloating Bravin and the two men who were to be disappointed.

'And I am rather busy for walking today,' said Thomas. He smiled at Bravin. 'But visit me later, and I will answer any questions you might have.'

Edmund saw Luke and Jean draw their own conclusions from that exchange. It was obvious that some arrangement had been made between Bravin and the bishop's man, and

Jean and Luke were too intelligent not to guess what. Luke's rounded features broke into a worried frown, while Jean pursed his lips in disapproval.

'When might we expect a decision about the appointment?' he asked coolly. 'Today?'

Thomas nodded. 'Later today.'

'Good,' said Luke with a wan smile. 'The waiting is the hardest part. But it would be worth the anxiety if I were successful: a post like this would give me the opportunity to write something truly worthwhile.'

'I prefer teaching,' said Jean, almost wistfully. 'There is something noble about taking a new mind, then opening it to the wonders of learning.'

Bravin regarded him in supercilious amusement. 'Anyone with any sense would delegate teaching to his senior students, thus leaving him time to do what interests him. That is what all the other masters do.'

'Not all,' said Edmund, nettled by his attitude. 'Prior Richard does his own teaching.'

'Prior Richard will soon retire,' said Bravin carelessly. 'And then Ely Hall will be under the control of younger, abler men who will change it for the better.'

Edmund was appalled by Bravin's brazen confidence, and was not pleased when Richard issued a curt order that Edmund should show the visitors the sights of Cambridge.

'We have heard a lot about the colleges, and would like to see them for ourselves,' said Luke shyly, when Edmund hesitated, no more happy with the prospect of Bravin's company than Richard had been.

'And the libraries,' added Jean eagerly. 'We would like to see the libraries.'

'I would rather see the taverns,' said Bravin drolly. 'I imagine that is where most of the important business is conducted.'

'Show them the libraries, Edmund,' said Richard, giving Bravin a glance of disapproval as he walked away.

Reluctantly, Edmund led Bravin, Luke and Jean along the High Street, pointing out the grand edifices that formed Cambridge's powerful colleges. King's Hall was large and magnificent, Michaelhouse small and elite, Gonville shabby and sprawling. Among them were the religious foundations, and friars belonging to the Dominican, Franciscan, Gilbertine and Carmelite orders scurried along the dirty streets as they went to and from their lectures. Pardoners and tradesmen mingled among them, along with the rough soldiers who prevented the unruly scholars from fighting with the equally quarrelsome townsfolk.

Eventually, Edmund's tour led them to the castle, which dominated the northern part of the town. By then, the day had grown greyer, as if it were matching Edmund's mood. The window shutters of the nearby houses were closed against the gloomy weather, and the only thing that moved under the bleak shadow of the fortress was a stray dog. Tucked below one of the sturdy curtain walls were the remains of a wooden contraption, forlorn and neglected.

'What is that?' asked Bravin, immediately interested in the heavy stone weights and the complex mess of ropes, pulleys and struts.

'A trebuchet,' replied Edmund curtly. 'It is an instrument of war, and not something to pique the interest of scholars – especially Benedictines, who have forsworn the bearing of arms.'

'Nothing should be beyond the interest of a scholar,' lectured Bravin pompously, running his hands over the lethal structure in a way that indicated he considered weapons more appealing than the libraries they had visited. 'Tell me how it works.'

Edmund sighed irritably, reluctant to spend longer in the company of the odious Bravin than was absolutely necessary. 'A trebuchet has a long pivoted arm. As you can see, there is a basket of stones (the counterweight) at the short end, and a sling at the long end. To fire it, you fill the sling with missiles—'

'What kind of missiles?' demanded Bravin, fascinated.

'Anything,' replied Jean before Edmund could answer, indicating that his learning had not been restricted to theology. 'During a siege, a trebuchet can hurl stones at walls, or fling dead animals and burning pitch into castles.'

'Really?' asked Bravin keenly. 'How does the mechanism fire?'

'The weight of the stones at the short end makes the long arm fly through the air, discharging the sling's contents,' answered Luke, not to be outdone by Jean. 'It is actually just a big catapult.'

Edmund frowned in puzzlement. 'Why do you two know so much about weapons?'

'I was a soldier before I took the cowl,' explained Jean.

'And, as an eldest son, I was taught such things before I relinquished my birthright to my younger brother,' said Luke. 'I understand how weapons work, but have no desire to see them in action. Spilt blood is something I find repellent; in fact, it makes me swoon.' He blushed suddenly, and looked as if he wished he had not made such a confession to people he barely knew.

'Even a monk should not be so squeamish,' said Bravin disdainfully, studying the old machine. 'I am not.'

Edmund had long since tired of Bravin's offensive company, and longed to return to the warm fire in Richard's chamber and be about his normal duties. The prior allowed him a good deal of freedom, but even so, there was a limit to the amount of time the secretary could spend with visitors when there was work to be done – and it would take him several hours to draft the document that would make Bravin's appointment legal.

'Be careful with that machine,' he said, as he left them to explore the rest of the town for themselves. 'It is unstable and should have been dismantled years ago.'

'It is an interesting monument,' contradicted Bravin. 'It should not be hauled away and consigned to some peasant's fire. It should remain here to be an object of interest for visitors.'

This began a spirited debate among the trio, and Edmund left them to it, retracing his steps along the High Street until he reached Ely Hall. Shortly after he arrived, it began to rain. Thatched roofs and plaster-fronted buildings turned dark and dirty in the deluge, and the leaves of trees shuddered and quivered as raindrops pattered on to them. Huge puddles formed across the muddy morass that was the High Street, and people scurried around them, anxious to complete their business and return to their homes. Edmund was glad to be indoors.

He spent the rest of the morning working on Bravin's letter of appointment. At noon, Thomas arrived to inform him that Catherine had been unable to restrain her pleasure regarding Bravin's success. She lived near the trebuchet, and had spotted Bravin inspecting it with Jean and Luke. She had hurried outside to tell Bravin of his good fortune. It was a tactless, inappropriate way of making the decision public, but typical of Catherine.

'I assume Bravin accepted the offer?' asked Edmund, hoping that he had not.

'He did,' replied Thomas. A sudden harshness in his voice caused Edmund to glance at him in surprise. 'And he had even prepared a little speech laying out his conditions. He delivered it there and then, by the trebuchet.'

'Conditions?' asked Edmund, puzzled. 'What do you mean?'

'I mean that he has given his future duties some thought. I would not have recommended him had I known he would immediately demand more pay and a bigger room.'

Edmund might have told the bishop's man that such behaviour was only to be expected from a character like Bravin, but he held his tongue and Thomas left. A few moments later, Prior Richard returned from visiting some parishioners, wet and out of sorts. While Edmund mulled wine, he mentioned Catherine's indiscretion in telling Bravin the 'good' news.

'I know,' said Richard with a sigh. 'I happened to see them when I was out. I guessed from her gestures and their reactions – Bravin's satisfaction and the others' dismay – that she had been unable to restrain herself.'

'It is unfortunate,' said Edmund. 'I was still hoping she would see Bravin is unworthy, so we could have Jean instead.'

Richard shook his head slowly. 'It is too late. We are stuck with Bravin now.'

A little later, in the early afternoon, a lay brother burst into the chamber. Richard's silver brows drew together in annoyance at this lack of manners.

'Father Prior!' the man gasped. 'Bravin is dead.'

'Dead?' asked Richard, startled.

'He was playing with the trebuchet when it collapsed and crushed him.'

'So, we will not have a charlatan as our Professor of Theology after all,' remarked Edmund, as he followed his prior out into the rain.

Bravin was indeed dead. The trebuchet's counterweight had been held in place with a badly rotted rope, and it appeared that Bravin's tampering had been the last straw: it had snapped, depositing the heavy basket of stones cleanly on Bravin's head. His skull had been squashed flat, although the one feature that had somehow survived the accident was the long nose with its reddened end. It dripped even in death, as rain pattered on to it and then slid into the bloodstained grass below.

'I told him to be careful,' said Edmund, gazing dispassionately at the mess. 'The machinery is old and dangerous; he should not have displayed such a morbid interest in it.'

'Who found him?' asked Richard, crossing himself as he regarded Bravin with the compassion Edmund would have expected from a gentle man like the prior.

A scruffy soldier stepped forward. 'Me. I often check the trebuchet to make sure vagrants are not hiding in it – it is a popular place for them to shelter when it rains.'

'What happened?' asked Richard. 'Did you witness the accident yourself?'

The soldier shook his head. 'Bravin was alone, as far as I know, and all the shutters of the nearby houses are closed against the bad weather, so I doubt anyone saw it happen. But we all know the trebuchet is unstable: it is an accident just waiting for a curious and careless man.'

Richard sketched a brief benediction at the corpse and instructed Edmund to remain with it while he returned to Ely Hall to summon pall-bearers. Edmund knelt in the mud, trying to ignore the chilly rivulets of rain that ran down his neck as he muttered his prayers. It was not long before his colleagues arrived, bringing a crude stretcher and a sheet with which to cover the body. Edmund watched them struggle to free the corpse from its grisly position, then lift the virtually headless Bravin on to the stretcher. It was an ugly sight, and Edmund turned away, sickened.

As they walked along the High Street, one of Bravin's arms flopped out to trail lifelessly along the ground. Edmund stooped to ease it under the sheet again, but as he did so, he noted that the hands were filthy, and that under the dirt were moon-shaped crescents of blood. Since Bravin has been so fastidious, it was odd his hands should be muddy. Curious, Edmund told the pall-bearers to stop and looked more closely.

It was clear to Edmund that Bravin had clawed at something or someone before he died. Since the load that landed on Bravin's head would have killed him instantly, Edmund could only suppose that such a struggle had happened before that – in which case, Bravin's death might not have been an accident after all. Edmund rubbed his chin thoughtfully. Who had fought with Bravin and why? The obvious answer was that it was Luke or Jean, angry because Bravin had inveigled himself into the post with his sly charm.

Leaving the others to carry Bravin to the church, Edmund walked back to the trebuchet and inspected it more closely. The ancient rope that had supported the counterweight had clean bright ends, indicating that they had been cut rather than had frayed, and the wet grass was more damaged than it should have been from a few people inspecting Bravin's remains. It seemed to Edmund that a fight had taken place, which had resulted in the ground's being churned. As he knelt to look at the rope again, something glinting in the grass caught his eye: it was a knife with a blade that was spotted with blood. Thoughtfully, Edmund put it in his scrip and walked to the church.

When he arrived, candles had been lit, filling the gloomy interior with a soft golden light. His colleagues had removed Bravin's wet habit, and were preparing to dress the body in a shroud. Edmund asked them to wait, then inspected the corpse for further signs of violence.

He found them in the shape of some small cuts in the middle of Bravin's back. At first, he thought they were injuries suffered when the trebuchet had collapsed, but then he matched the tiny triangular indentations to the blade of the knife he had found. There were also some red marks on Bravin's neck, and muddy patches at knee-height on his habit. While his

175

colleagues listened in horror, Edmund told them what he had deduced: someone had seized Bravin from behind, which accounted for the red marks around his neck; Bravin had struggled and scratched his assailant, and it was therefore the killer's blood that formed the rings under Bravin's fingernails; and the muddy hands and knees indicated that Bravin had been shoved forward on the ground, leaving the killer to slash the rope that held the counterweight. Death occurred when the stones landed on his head.

One monk suggested a different scenario: that Bravin had been held at knifepoint first, then had escaped to struggle and the rope sliced by accident. Edmund shook his head, pointing out that Bravin had muddied his hands *after* he had scratched his assailant – the blood would not have been under his nails if they were already filled with dirt.

He left the monks preparing Bravin for his burial, and went to tell Richard about his discoveries. The gentle prior was predictably appalled.

'I do not believe you,' he said in a hushed voice. 'Bravin must have bloodied his nails when he tried to claw his way from under the trebuchet.'

'He was killed instantly,' Edmund pointed out. 'His head was crushed almost flat.'

'Then these so-called knife injuries occurred earlier – before he came to Cambridge.'

Edmund shook his head. 'They are fresh wounds.'

Richard shuddered. 'This is dreadful. We must tell the sheriff.'

Edmund disagreed. 'We do not want the townsfolk accusing us of harbouring a murderer in our midst: there will be a riot. And we do not want that drunken sot of a proctor – the University's law and order officer – investigating, either. I will do it.'

'You?' asked Richard, startled. 'Why you?'

'Because I will be discreet, and I will not harm Ely Hall's reputation,' replied Edmund. 'And anyway, we only have two possible culprits. It will not be too difficult to decide whether Luke or Jean is the guilty party.'

'What makes you think it is either?' asked Richard.

'Because they are the ones who were wronged by Bravin's underhand tactics. Both are more deserving than Bravin, and they know it. Anger and frustration has led one of them to have his revenge.'

'Then you had better solve this mystery quickly, Edmund,' said Richard softly. 'Because with Bravin dead, we will appoint Luke or Jean in his place, and I do not want a murderer teaching my students.'

Edmund left Prior Richard and went to find Jean and Luke. Virtually all Ely Hall's students were lingering in the church to stare at the corpse of the man who had almost been appointed to teach them. Among the onlookers was Jean, who stared dispassionately at the sheeted figure. Edmund noticed that the rain had caused the black in his newly dyed habit to run, and that his bony hands were deeply stained with it. Jean saw that Edmund had observed the marks, and scrubbed self-consciously at them. Edmund thought the Frenchman should have paid more and had the garment dyed properly: it would have been cheaper in the long run.

'Bravin should not have shown such a perverse fascination with instruments of death,' said Jean harshly, to hide his embarrassment. 'God did not want such a man teaching his novices.'

'There is nothing to suggest his death was God's work,' replied Edmund. 'Indeed, all the signs suggest he was murdered.' He regarded Jean intently, trying to determine his reaction to such a statement. But the Frenchman merely nodded.

'Bravin was not a pleasant person.'

'Where were you when he met his death?' asked Edmund bluntly.

Jean did not seem surprised by the question. 'I was sitting alone in this church. I was disappointed by the decision to appoint him rather than me, and I wanted solitude.'

'Were you disappointed enough to kill him?' asked Edmund.

Jean gave a half-smile. 'Yes, I was, but I did not do it. Look elsewhere for your murderer, Edmund. But do it quickly. I leave Cambridge at dawn tomorrow.'

There was no more to be said, so Edmund looked around for Luke. However, Luke was not among the spectators in the church. Edmund walked outside, and saw the portly monk perched on an ancient tombstone, oblivious of the drizzle that still fell. Luke's hands were unsteady, and his face was pale and wan.

'You are the only Benedictine not gawking at Bravin's mortal remains,' said Edmund, wondering why the man looked so ill. Was it his guilty conscience? 'Why such a lack of curiosity? It is not every day you can view a man killed by such bizarre means.'

'I have already told you that the sight of blood makes me weak-headed,' replied Luke. 'I could not look on such a sight without swooning; I feel sick even thinking about the manner of his death.'

'He was murdered,' said Edmund in a soft voice. 'It seems someone did not want him to become our new theologian.'

Luke nodded slowly. 'I can see why. Catherine and Thomas clearly realised their mistake after appointing the man. You should have seen their faces when Bravin made his little speech accepting the post.'

'They were pleased with their choice,' said Edmund. 'They wanted him.'

'They were not pleased,' contradicted Luke. 'Bravin immediately declared he would show no favouritism to any students Thomas might send him, and then claimed he would be too busy to teach Catherine to read. After all they did to secure his appointment, I am not surprised one of them ordered him killed.'

'You think Thomas or Catherine killed him?' asked Edmund, startled by this new information. Thomas had mentioned Bravin's speech, but he had failed to indicate that the contents had been personally objectionable.

Luke sighed. 'You think that either Jean or I made an end of him. I confess, I would have enjoyed doing so. The man was one of the most unpleasant people I have ever met, but I would not have chosen a way that involved such a spillage of blood.'

'Then where were you at the time of his murder?' asked Edmund, not sure what to believe.

'Walking alone by the river. I was disgusted that Ely Hall had chosen Bravin, and wanted to be alone. No one saw me, and I cannot prove I had no hand in his death. You will just have to believe me. But I recommend you look to Catherine or Thomas for your culprit. There is nothing so dangerous as a powerful person who finds he – or she – has been cheated.'

Edmund walked away, his head bowed in thought. Whom should he believe? Jean and Luke had good reason to want Bravin dead, and both had demonstrated a knowledge of the trebuchet and its workings: either would have known which rope to cut to ensure Bravin was killed. And neither man had an alibi for the crucial time. Was Luke exaggerating his dislike of blood? Was he pale because he had killed a man, not because he had an aversion to the sight and thought of violence? Why did Jean plan to leave Cambridge so soon? Was he merely leaving a place that had disappointed him, or

179

was he fleeing the scene of his crime before justice could be done?

And what about Luke's claim – that Catherine and Thomas's favoured candidate had already turned against them and had no intention of giving them what they thought they were owed? Had one of them killed him? Edmund decided there was only one way to find out, and walked briskly along the High Street to Catherine's house.

When Edmund was admitted to Catherine's solar – a pleasant chamber on the upper floor with glass windows and a merrily crackling fire in the hearth – he found Thomas already there, comfortably seated on a cushioned bench near the fire. Prior Richard was there, too, giving them the grim details that Edmund had uncovered regarding the manner of Bravin's death.

'It is a pity so many people know Bravin was murdered,' Thomas was saying. 'It would have been best for everyone if we could have buried him quickly and claimed he had a fatal seizure when given the good news.'

'It would have been wrong to hide such a wicked crime,' said Richard sternly. 'Edmund is already hunting for the killer, although I confess I am not optimistic about his chances of success. I have questioned the people who live near the trebuchet whether they saw or heard anything, but they all claim the rain had driven them indoors with the shutters fastened.'

'So no one witnessed anything?' asked Edmund, disappointed. 'What about you, Catherine? Did you hear anything? Your house is very close to the scene of the murder.'

'I can tell you nothing,' she replied. 'I saw Bravin with the two other candidates at the trebuchet this morning, and I desperately wanted to tell him of his success. With Thomas at my heels, I rushed out to tell him, but saw no killers lurking.'

'You should have waited before you gave him the news,' admonished Thomas. 'Then we might have learned what kind of man he was before we made our final decision.'

'So I see, with hindsight,' retorted Catherine irritably. 'But before his little speech, I thought him a charming man. However, as soon as he learned of his success, he showed his true colours.'

'He made it clear he would renege on the promises he made us,' explained Thomas, turning to Richard and Edmund. 'We would have remonstrated with him, but it started to rain, and we had no wish to be wet as well as insulted. We left him admiring the trebuchet with Jean and Luke.'

'And that was the last you saw of him?' asked Edmund.

'Yes,' snapped Catherine. 'Why? Do you think we killed him?'

'The killer chose a good place for his crime,' said Thomas, ignoring her outburst. 'He selected a lonely spot on a bleak day when most people were indoors. He is a clever man.'

'Or woman,' said Edmund.

'I confess to loathing the man after his nasty words,' said Catherine, 'but I did not kill him.'

'How long was it after his speech that Bravin was killed?' asked Edmund, wondering whether Catherine had time to recruit a killer – an easy feat given the number of mercenaries who haunted the town – or whether her temper had led her to kill him herself. She was a large woman, bigger than Bravin, and certainly strong enough to fight and overpower him.

'Almost immediately,' replied Thomas. He saw Edmund's eyebrows rise questioningly, and hastened to explain how he knew such a thing. 'At least, I imagine so. It was not long after we left Bravin that we heard the soldier raise the alarm when he found the body.'

Was Thomas telling the truth? Edmund wondered. Or had he and Catherine gone together to kill Bravin? Had Thomas fought with Bravin until Catherine had drawn the knife? He looked at Thomas's cloak, carefully folded across the bench. He saw it was damp, but could not tell how long the dampness had been there. As he left the solar, he surreptitiously took a fold of Catherine's distinctive scarlet cloak between his finger and thumb, and had one answer at least. He walked back to Ely Hall with his head bowed in thought.

He had four suspects for the murder. Luke and Jean wanted Bravin dead because they thought they should be Professor of Theology. Meanwhile, Thomas and Catherine were certainly capable of despatching a man who had crossed them. Edmund rubbed his temples tiredly. Unless someone confessed, he suspected there was no hope of ever solving the crime. And if he were unsuccessful, it was possible that a murderer would come to live at Ely Hall, or that a murderer would play a major role in the way it was run. Neither possibility was attractive to Edmund. He took a deep breath, and began to review all his evidence again, piece by piece, until he began to detect a pattern.

Before he made his thoughts public, Edmund needed to revisit Bravin's corpse in the church, and he wanted to ask a few questions of the people who lived near the trebuchet. Ignoring the objections of the monks who were keeping vigil by Bravin's remains, he inspected the hands and arms closely. Then he visited the houses, hoping that Richard may have missed someone, and that there might yet be a witness to the events that took place at the trebuchet that day.

By the time he had his answers, it was dusk, and vendors desperate to sell the last of their wares before nightfall jostled and pushed him as he returned to Ely Hall. He was so engrossed in his thoughts that he barely noticed them. He barely noticed Thomas, either, and had walked right past the bishop's man before he heard the insistent greeting. Thomas was buying a pie from a baker, reaching out to inspect them before he made his purchase.

'I was saying that this has worked out rather well,' said Thomas loudly, apparently offended at being ignored by a mere secretary. As he stretched out one hand to pass a coin to the baker, his wide sleeve fell away, giving Edmund the opportunity to inspect his arm. The clerk smiled to himself: Thomas was not as clever as he imagined. 'Bravin's behaviour made it clear that we were wrong to have chosen him. Now he is dead, we can have Luke or Jean.'

'We told you not to appoint him,' said Edmund. 'He was a cheat, who wrote his own testimonial and forged the signature of his abbot. How could you have considered such a man in the first place?'

'We only had your word that the signature was false,' said Thomas stiffly, unwilling to shoulder too much blame for the near-disaster. 'To begin with, he seemed an amiable man who would prove to be exactly what we wanted.'

'A puppet,' said Edmund harshly. 'Just like poor Brother Henry, his predecessor.'

'Yes,' said Thomas bluntly, eating his pie. 'It is a pity those oysters killed Henry. He was an excellent man to approach for favours.' He inclined his head and went on his way, leaving Edmund staring after him thoughtfully.

Much later that night, when most of Ely Hall's residents were sleeping, Edmund sat with Richard in the prior's office. They held goblets of mulled wine in their hands, and their feet were stretched towards the fire as they sat in companionable silence.

'So, how have you fared in tracing our killer?' asked Richard, staring into the yellow flames that leaped in the hearth.

'I know his identity, and I know how he committed the crime,' replied Edmund evenly.

Richard stared at him in astonishment. 'Who? How?'

'The killer grabbed Bravin around the neck, then drew a knife. The culprit has scratches on his arms, where Bravin struck out with his nails.'

'We all saw the blood on Bravin's fingers,' mused Richard. 'He must have fought hard.'

'Like a cat,' agreed Edmund. 'But he was subdued when the killer produced a knife. Then the killer pushed him towards the trebuchet, prodding him in the back with the blade. When Bravin was below the trebuchet, the killer shoved him forward, so that he fell on his hands and knees, which became muddy. Finally, the killer cut the rope that held the counterweight. Death was instant.'

'I suppose that is one mercy,' said Richard. 'He did not suffer. So, who is the killer? Luke or Jean?'

'I was obliged to add two more suspects to my list,' said Edmund, declining to reveal his conclusions before he had outlined his reasoning. 'Thomas and Catherine also had cause to want Bravin dead.'

'Thomas and Catherine are the killers?' asked Richard, appalled. 'But that cannot be true! I have known them for years! You have made some dreadful error in your investigation.'

'The killer could not have been Jean. He had dyed his habit for his interview, but the rain made the cheap dye leak: Jean's hands were covered in the stuff, and had the killer been him, then some dye would have been present on Bravin's body. This afternoon, I inspected Bravin's corpse very carefully, but there was nothing: Jean is innocent.'

'Luke, then?' asked Richard. 'He did it.'

'Luke has a strong aversion to blood. I thought he had feigned it, so that we would not suspect him, but he confessed to his weakness *before* Catherine had told Bravin of his success. That means he had admitted to his weak stomach *before* he had a motive to kill Bravin.'

'Perhaps he anticipated Bravin's victory, and was already plotting his murder,' suggested Richard. 'He may be lying about this fear of blood.'

Edmund disagreed. 'He was white and shaking when I found him outside the church, because even the thought of Bravin's crushed head made him sick. But more revealing is the fact that his weakness forced him to give up his inheritance, because he knew he could not protect his estates by fighting. I imagine that was why he became a monk. His fear of blood is real enough: it was responsible for the loss of his birthright.'

Richard sipped his wine. 'So you are left with Thomas and Catherine. But Thomas is a confidant of the bishop, while Catherine is . . . well, a woman.'

'I felt Catherine's cloak – that horrible scarlet thing – when I visited her this afternoon. It started to rain after Bravin made his speech but before he died. If she had killed him, her cloak would have been wet. It was quite dry.'

'Thomas, then?' asked Richard.

'Thomas's cloak was damp, but he had walked to Ely Hall to inform me that Catherine had told Bravin the "good" news, and then returned to Catherine's house – in the rain. I expected his cloak to be wet. However, I saw his arms when he reached out to buy a pie in the High Street. There were no scratches on them, and so I concluded he was innocent, too.'

'Who, then?' cried Richard, exasperated. 'I do not like playing these guessing games.'

'You do not need to guess the killer's identity,' said Edmund softly. 'You already know it. You murdered Bravin.'

'Me?' asked Richard, startled. 'How in God's name did you arrive at that conclusion?'

'Several reasons. The killer was a man who visited the houses near the trebuchet to ensure there were no witnesses to his crime – as you did. You were lucky there were none, or you

185

would have been obliged to kill again, to hide the first murder.'

'This is outrageous,' said Richard, shaking his head.

'You arrived here drenched and unsettled just after Bravin was killed – I saw you myself. You said you had been visiting parishioners, and I had assumed it was Bravin's appointment that was distressing you. But it was the fact that you had murdered Bravin that rendered you quiet and thoughtful. And you were soaked.'

'So?' asked Richard. 'It was raining. What do you expect?'

'You were wet because you had killed Bravin under the trebuchet, not because you were visiting parishioners in their warm, dry homes.'

'This is not evidence,' warned Richard. 'It is conjecture.'

'You sent *me* to show the three candidates around the town, because you said you had a headache. We both know you never suffer from headaches. It was a ploy to delay my writing of the documents that Bravin was to sign – you wanted him dead before anything was made legal.'

'Again, conjecture. Not evidence.'

Edmund ignored the interruption. 'Therefore, I deduce that you had decided to kill him *before* Catherine told him of his success and he made his speech – an incident you told me you witnessed, incidentally, and which forced you to act sooner. You went to some trouble to ensure that the death looked like an accident, and I suspect your horror was genuine when I told you it was murder.'

'This is all gross speculation . . .'

'You also personally questioned the soldier who found Bravin's body, to ascertain that he had seen or heard nothing to incriminate you,' Edmund went on relentlessly. 'You must have been relieved to learn that he had not.'

'This is not evidence,' said Richard again. 'You can prove nothing.'

Edmund reached out and pulled up the sleeve of Richard's

186

habit, revealing numerous angry scratches on the prior's forearms. 'But this is evidence,' he said softly. 'This is where Bravin fought you. You are a gentle man. Why did you kill him?'

'Because I love Ely Hall,' replied Richard simply, no longer denying his guilt. 'I did not want a charlatan teaching the novices in my care. Can you blame me?'

'No,' said Edmund. 'But you should have let me do it. I would not have left a trail of clues as you did.'

'You are much better at murder than me,' agreed Richard ruefully. 'When poor Henry ate those bad oysters, no one considered for a moment that you had deliberately poisoned them.'

Edmund sighed. 'But I did not kill Thomas and Catherine's puppet merely so that they could appoint another in Henry's place. I hope there is never a next time, but if there is, you should leave the killing to me.'

Richard smiled wanly at his secretary, then changed the subject. 'So, shall we have Luke or Jean as our new professor?'

'Jean, I think,' replied Edmund, sipping his wine. 'We do not want a protégé of the Archbishop of Canterbury here to tell tales of monks murdered by their priors. I hope Catherine and Thomas have learned from their experiences and will fall in with our plans this time.'

Richard nodded. 'They will. Now, why did you say Luke could not have been the killer?' he asked, settling back in his chair and staring at the fire. 'Is there any reason why *he* should not hang as Bravin's killer?'

'No reason at all,' said Edmund, raising his goblet in a comradely salute to his prior.

Id Quod Clarum . . .*

Paul Doherty

Oxford, 1441

*That Which is Obvious

William Bradshaw truly considered himself the greatest scholar in Oxford. He was a man full of his own importance who carried his head, as one wit put it, 'as if it was a sacred relic before whom all should bow'. On the feast of St Leo the Great, Bradshaw swept into the schools of Oxford to deliver his third lecture of the week on the existence of God. Bradshaw knew nothing but Oxford. He had taken his degrees in Philosophy, Logic, Theology, Canon Law and Medicine. Much patronised by the great and the good, Bradshaw saw himself as an oracle who could put the fear of God into scholars as well as those heretics who, in the year of Our Lord 1441, dared to argue against the teachings of Holy Mother Church. Bradshaw was a portly, pretentious man with bright black eyes in a florid, fleshy face. His sharp nose cut the air like a scythe as he stood at the lectern and prepared to deliver his lecture. He made sure his heavy, ermine-edged gown hung properly and played for a while with the ring on the little finger of his right hand. The scholars sat hushed before him. They always made sure that they were dressed in their correct gowns, hair properly tonsured. No one dared wear baldric or belt, carry a knife or do anything which might bring them to the attention of this sharp-eyed Master of Oxford, this Professor of Divinity who, despite all his learning and self-proclaimed wisdom, had only a short while to live.

The scholars watched Bradshaw walk up and down the dais, immersed in his own thoughts like a priest preparing to celebrate Mass. This lecture was famous and Bradshaw had all the tools of his trade ready. A jug of wine, the enamelled cup, his books and scrolls. So, if challenged, Bradshaw could refer not only to the Scriptures but the teaching of the Fathers. A bell sounded, and the doors of the hall were formally closed by Tynbroke the servitor, assisted by Simon the pot boy. Bradshaw stared wearily round this stark, sparse building. Everything was in order. Candles, in their brass holdings attached to the wall, had been lit, and because it was not yet Easter the braziers also had been fired, strewn with herbs and wheeled to stand in each corner of the room. Bradshaw was preparing. His eagle eyes surveyed the shiny-eyed scholars sitting on benches before him. In particular, six scholars from his own college, Woodcock Hall, whom he'd ordered to attend on him every hour of the day as punishment for breaking divers regulations and statutes. Bradshaw called them his 'retinue of recalcitrants': Stokes who had been unchaste with a tailor's wife, Marchow who'd baptised a cat and practised witchcraft, Gregory who had brought a prostitute into the hall. Kendrick for losing his book, Kiffle for neglecting his studies to play cards with wandering chapmen. Finally, Master Haycock who, contrary to regulations, had kept a ferret, a weasel and a sparrowhawk in their chamber at Woodcock Hall. Punishment for these woebegone clerks was to attend Master Bradshaw wherever he went in Oxford, whatever lecture he delivered, whatever disputation he became involved in. If he went to dine with other Fellows, they, ragged-arsed and red-faced, would have to sit by the door. If he consulted manuscripts in the library they had to squat on the cold flagstones outside. Their punishment was to last at least till the end of the Hilary term and, if Master Bradshaw so decided, perhaps even into Trinity.

Bradshaw surveyed the 'recalcitrants' with his beady eyes. He smirked. They looked crestfallen enough. Whether they liked it or not, by the time he had finished with them they would be either proper scholars, well schooled in debate and more assiduous in their studies, or no longer at Oxford. Bradshaw tipped the bare lectern: he prided himself that he could deliver a lecture without notes.

'Scholars, gentlemen,' he began. 'I welcome you to this morning's lecture. Instead of confusing your addled pates and blunted wits with the finer philosophical points of Plato or Aristotle, before I clear the mists which shroud the teaching of the great Aquinas, I want to bring to your attention a central truth.' He paused for effect. 'And what is this truth? It is divided into two parts.' Bradshaw warmed to his theme. 'First, that which is obvious may not be real. Second, that which is real may not be truthful.'

Bradshaw could tell from the perplexed looks of the scholars that he had truly confused them with this conundrum. He paused and, crossing to the table, poured himself a goblet of wine which he slurped noisily. The claret sweetened his mouth and wetted his dry throat. He returned to the lectern. His lectures were the talk of Oxford, or so he thought, laced with his little idiosyncrasies and personal foibles. Bradshaw ignored the complaints, always muttered and hushed of course, that he was more interested in complicated philosophy and logic than in making issues clear for all to understand. He grasped the side of the lectern.

'Let me give you an example. A woman dropped a coin in a beggar's bowl. The woman was the beggar's sister but the beggar was not the woman's brother.' Bradshaw paused. 'Tell me, you collective luminaries of the great University of Oxford, how are they related?'

His question was greeted by a deafening silence. Bradshaw smiled and nodded and held up a finger.

'Remember what I said? That which is obvious may not be real: that which is real may not be the truth. You have reached the logical conclusion in the problem I have posed, that the beggar is a man. However, I did not say that. I simply said the beggar was a beggar. In fact, the beggar is a woman and so the two are sisters. You made the mistake,' Bradshaw concluded, 'of believing that it was obvious I was talking about a woman and a man. The reality was that I was talking about two women. Whether the story is true or not . . .' Bradshaw waved a hand and allowed his words to hang like holy incense in the air.

The scholars shuffled their feet. Some of them would have loved to have challenged Bradshaw but that was very dangerous. One day they would have to take their examinations in the Bachelor of Arts. They'd come to this very hall, the centre of the schools, and stand for four days arguing three questions of logic and philosophy against all comers. If anyone upset Bradshaw, he would make a point, being a vicious man, of turning up himself to challenge the hapless scholar and reduce him to embarrassed silence.

'Matters are made even worse,' Bradshaw leaned against the lectern to ease the pain in his belly, 'because each of us has a different perception of what is obvious, of what is real, of what is truthful. I ask three of my "retinue" to step forward.' He gestured at the recalcitrants sitting on the front bench. 'Come on! Come on!'

Red-haired, sallow-faced Stokes, the thin, gangling Gregory and the tubby, anxious-faced Haycock got to their feet and shuffled forward. Bradshaw walked to the table. He once again filled the goblet with wine and drank from it deeply.

'Fine wine.'

Bradshaw smacked his lips, then, like a priest giving Communion, he forced each of the students standing before the dais to take a drink. He held the goblet to their lips and made all three take a generous swig before withdrawing the empty cup and wiping it with the edge of his gown. A man who loved his claret was Master Bradshaw, the best Bordeaux, thick and red. The smile faded from his face. He glared down at the three still standing there.

'Tell me now,' he bellowed. 'We have shared the same loving cup.' Bradshaw smirked at his sarcastic witticism. 'Can any of you great scholars tell me what wine it is?'

'Bordeaux,' Stokes their leader retorted.

'Very good!' Bradshaw mocked. 'And what part of Bordeaux, the city or the fields?'

All three stared speechlessly back.

'And what year? Can you tell me that?'

Again silence.

'I have made an important point.'

Bradshaw clicked his fingers as a sign that the recalcitrants should return to their bench.

'I and members of my "retinue" all agree that the wine we have drunk is the best Bordeaux. Only I know the vineyard and the year of its vintage. Truth therefore is not only objective but subjective. I wish you to remember this advice as we turn to the great question posed by Aquinas in his *Summa Theologiae* about the existence of God. If I could prove the existence of God,' Bradshaw smacked his lips and steadied himself against the lectern: the pains in his belly were now acute, 'it would mean that either there is no God or I am God.' Bradshaw stared quickly round the hall. 'And why is that? Because I, a man limited in my faculties, cannot prove that which is infinite and eternal. Some heretics claim the existence of God is similar to a mathematical problem. It can be stated, analysed and resolved, but that is too obvious. It is not real and it is certainly not the truth. I can only say that the existence of God is above human reason but not against it. I must make that argument obvious, real and truthful. But . . . oh Lord . . .'

Bradshaw paused. The scholars noticed how he gripped the

side of the lectern, staring down at them, all colour drained from his florid face. He looked pallid and haggard, his eyes larger. He was having difficulty speaking and kept opening and closing his mouth. An eerie, choked gargling came from his throat. He pressed his body against the lectern, eyeballs popping, then staggered back, his hands clutching his stomach. He was gagging as if he wanted to retch or vomit. Scholars, alarmed, jumped to their feet and hastened forward, including the six recalcitrants, though they clustered together. Bradshaw staggered to the end of the dais. He gave a low cry and sprawled flat on his face. He turned, arms and legs jerking. The uproar spread. Tynbroke, servant to the schools, came hurrying in, followed by his pot boy Simon. Scholars were on the dais, surrounding Bradshaw. A few, who boasted how they knew a little physic, tried to loosen the tight buttons of the white chemise beneath his brocaded gown. By the time they had succeeded, Bradshaw lay still, eyes staring, face twisted into the rictus of death. His lips, still purple from the wine, hung gaping, a white trickle of saliva coursing down his shaven chin. The scholars drew back, making way for Tynbroke. The servant knelt and pressed his fingers against Bradshaw's throat. He then felt for the bloodbeat in his wrist. He shook his head and covered the dead man's mouth with his hand and, taking it away, looked at the copper bands on his fingers.

'There's no pulse. There's no breath,' Tynbroke declared, getting to his feet; his tired, grey eyes surveyed the assembled scholars. 'Sirs, Master Bradshaw was in good humour and health. I think he's been poisoned.'

All eyes turned to the wine jug and cup still standing on the table. A few stared accusingly at Bradshaw's 'retinue of recalcitrants', the six students who had to follow him every-where. They stood on the dais, still clustered together. Stokes, their leader, glared defiantly back.

'Master Bradshaw may be poisoned,' he declared, 'but we

had nothing to do with it. We are not guilty.'

Tynbroke pointed to the wine cup and jug. 'They must not be moved or tampered with. You' – he pointed at Simon the pot boy – 'will sit at that table and guard that wine until the Proctor arrives.'

He glanced towards the small vesting chamber where Bradshaw had broken his fast before starting his lecture, and pushed his way through the throng. The door to the chamber was locked. He felt for the key on the chain attached to his belt, unlocked the door and pushed it open. The wood-panelled room inside was dark and shadow-filled, but the light pouring on to the table from the window high in the wall showed the remains of a white manchet loaf, a small pot of butter, a knife and pewter pot of honey, specially bought from Osney Abbey for Master Bradshaw. The candle on the table had been snuffed out. Tynbroke walked carefully and, stooping down, sniffed the butter, honey and bread but could detect nothing remarkable. He left the chamber, locked it and put the key back on the chain round his belt. Liveried tipstaffs now guarded the doors leading out of the hall. Tynbroke went and stood on the dais, one hand on the lectern.

'Well?' a scholar shouted. 'What are you going to do? Keep us here all day? Master Bradshaw may be dead but we don't want to join him due to starvation!'

Tynbroke scratched his white, straggling hair, his face even more worried than usual. He glanced at Simon the pot boy, who gazed blankly back.

'Well,' another scholar called, 'Bradshaw, that old bag of wind, is dead. I want to go to the Boar's Head and toast his memory.'

More laughter. The scholars were growing restless. The tipstaffs on the door looked agitated, grasping their poles: they didn't relish a fight if Tynbroke decided the scholars should remain.

'Very well,' Tynbroke declared. 'All of you can leave. Except Master Stokes and his companions. They will stay here.'

'It's only right,' a scholar shouted from the back. 'I mean, we went nowhere near Master Bradshaw or his wine.'

Stokes looked as if he was going to disagree. He pushed his long red hair back and glowered at Tynbroke. Gregory whispered in his ear. Stokes shrugged; he and his companions sat on the bench. Tynbroke heaved a sigh of relief. He just hoped the tipstaff despatched to the Proctor's office had delivered his message quickly.

Master Henry Rossiter, Proctor of the King's University of Oxford, slipped through the doorway of the main hall of the schools. He paused and stared around. Rossiter always disliked this building, its bleak, whitewashed stone walls, the soaring black beams, the lack of any ornamentation; how it was always cold even during the summer weeks. It also brought back memories of his own tiresome disputations, the long, hard struggle to win, by debate, both his Bachelor's and his Master's degrees. Now? Well, now it was different. Rossiter tapped the dagger which hung in its brocaded scabbard and hitched his cloak closer over his shoulders. A tall, sallow-faced, dark-haired man, the Proctor had a reputation for being sharp-eyed and keen-witted: a clerk who could have entered the royal chancery but was now employed by the University to maintain order amongst its scholars, to liaise with the town and to act as a coroner when a mysterious death occurred.

Rossiter walked and acted like a soldier. In fact he had served with the king's army in France, where he had shown both skill and fortitude and won the patronage of no less a person than the Regent John, Duke of Bedford, who had recommended him for this post at the University. Rossiter scratched at a cut on his face. As usual the light in this hall was poor but he could make out Tynbroke sitting on the dais and six scholars squatting like naughty schoolboys on the bench before him. Rossiter stepped out of the shadows. Tynbroke leaped to his feet.

'Oh, thank God, sir! Thank God!'

Rossiter walked alowly up between the benches. In the far corner, Bradshaw's corpse lay stretched out on a trestle table.

'I . . . I did that,' Tynbroke explained, following his gaze. 'I took a sheet from the stores.'

Rossiter stared around. Master Bradshaw's books and papers still lay on the table, beside the jug and cup. Underneath the table Rossiter glimpsed a small metal cage holding the stiffening corpse of a rat.

'You've done well, Tynbroke. Master Bradshaw was giving a lecture here this morning?'

'On the existence of God, sir.'

'Well, he'll know all about that now, won't he?' Rossiter replied, provoking subdued laughter from the scholars seated on the bench. The Proctor glared at them.

'You will not speak. You will not move. You will not laugh unless I tell you to.'

'You have no right to detain us.'

Rossiter walked across and stared down into the scholar's narrow, green eyes. 'You must be Stokes, leader of these merry men from Woodcock Hall? Now listen, Master Stokes: Bradshaw had reason to discipline you and you hated him. I know that he made you follow him about everywhere because your case was referred to my office.'

Rossiter gripped the scholar's shoulder and felt a spurt of compassion. Stokes was thin and bony. The Proctor could tell from the scholar's face that he was hungry, even famished.

'I know this caused ridicule,' Rossiter continued. 'That you murmured against it. You, therefore, are suspects under the law. You have a choice. You may submit to me and the jurisdiction of the University of Oxford, or I can hand you over to the sheriff, who will be only too delighted to incarcerate six scholars in the Bocardo gaol.'

Stokes's eyes fell away.

'So, which is it?' Rossiter pushed a gauntleted hand under Stokes's chin, forcing his head back. 'So, do Master Stokes and his merry men agree to co-operate or shall I call the town bailiffs?'

'You know the answer,' Stokes grated.

'Good!' Rossiter stepped back. 'Whatever happens, if you are guilty,' he waggled a finger at all six scholars, 'you'll hang, scholars of Oxford or not. The only comfort I can give is that, if you came under the jurisdiction of the sheriff, death would not be so quick. According to the law, the punishment for poisoning a master is to be burnt alive.' He stared at the row of pallid faces. 'Have you ever seen a man burnt alive? The flesh crackle and bubble, his eyes turn to water?' Rossiter quietly regretted his threats but he had no choice. 'Good,' he murmured. 'Now, Master Tynbroke. Let me see the corpse.'

The servant led him across to the table and pulled back the sheet. Bradshaw's cadaver was an ugly sight. His belly had already swollen, his face had turned a liverish hue; those staring eyes, that gaping mouth. Rossiter quickly sniffed at the corpse's lips and detected wine and something a little more acrid. He undid the jerkin and the shirt beneath, loosening the points and pulling down the hose.

'Are you a physician?' Master Tynbroke whispered.

'I have studied physic,' Rossiter replied. 'I know a little about poisons and potions. I would wager a pound to a pound that Master Bradshaw drank, or ate, some toxic substance: the juice of henbane or belladonna. Notice the liverish shade to the face, these dark blotches on the belly, now swollen and full of noxious gas. I suggest, Master Tynbroke, to avoid any further unpleasantness, Bradshaw's corpse should be removed to a death house as soon as possible.'

Tynbroke scurried away to fetch the tipstaffs. Rossiter examined the corpse once more, staring at the popping eyes, the hardness of the muscles of the face. He forced open the mouth: the tongue was swollen and very dark, similar in colour to the liverish blotches which covered the torso from crotch to throat.

Rossiter walked across to the lavarium placed in the hall for the lecturers. He washed his hands, dried them and stared across at the corpse. He had known Bradshaw and disliked him intensely. A true bully boy, pompous and arrogant, with a spiteful tongue and a malicious mind. A man trained in the games of logic, he could appear devastating in argument but, in turn, hid behind conundrums and puzzles. A commentator rather than a philosopher, but – Rossiter threw the napkin over the outstretched arm of the lavarium – still a master of the University. According to all evidence, he had been cruelly murdered. Rossiter waited until Tynbroke returned with the tipstaffs: these brought a makeshift stretcher and roughly tossed the cadaver on to it.

'Where shall we take it?' one of them asked, jingling the pennies in his purse.

Rossiter smiled and walked across. He gave the leading tipstaff a coin.

'To the old leper hospital across Magdalen Bridge. Say Master Rossiter sent it. It's to be cleaned and dressed for burial. The Congregation will decide when and where burial is to take place. But, for the moment,' Rossiter waved a hand, 'get it out of my sight!'

Muttering and cursing under their breath, the tipstaffs carried their grisly burden out of the hall. Tynbroke saw them out and hastily returned.

'Master Bradshaw was murdered?'

'Oh yes.' Rossiter smiled with his eyes. 'And I strongly

suspect, Tynbroke, that his assassin is still in this hall.'

The servant's eyes widened. 'You are sure of that, Master Rossiter?'

'As I am that the sun rose this morning and will set this evening.' He pointed across at the 'retinue of recalcitrants'. 'Those are my suspects. Yet I must be honest, Master Tynbroke, so are you.'

The servant paled and swallowed hard.

'But . . .'

'It's possible,' Rossiter whispered. 'However, don't be anxious, Master Tynbroke. You have nothing to fear for the moment. Let us give our assembled scholars a lecture.'

Rossiter and Tynbroke moved back to the small dais. Stokes and the rest still sat on the bench. Dressed in their shabby black robes, with long, straggling hair, they reminded Rossiter of a line of crows on the branch of a tree. They all looked discomfited, shuffling their feet, muttering to each other. Stokes was certainly the leader. His companions were thin-faced with spotty complexions: young men, who ate little and badly, they lived, hand-to-mouth, enduring a poverty a friar would find onerous.

'Are we to stay here all day?' Dark-haired Gregory, scraping a stain off his gown with his thumbnail, glowered at Rossiter. 'We haven't even been given time to relieve ourselves.'

'You may do that now,' Rossiter replied.

Tynbroke led the students out of the hall to the jakes erected in a small, overgrown garden at the back of the schools. During their absence Rossiter crouched and stared at the stiffening corpse of the large, fat rat.

'I hate rats,' the Proctor whispered. He felt his stomach clench at the sight of the brown, bloated body, the long, wet tail, the snout and its half-open mouth revealing strong yellowing teeth.

'I hate rats too!' Simon the pot boy stood beside him.

'Master Tynbroke gave it some of that wine,' the boy chattered on. 'Sir, it went backwards and forwards in that cage like a ball on a string. It shivered, sickened and died.'

Rossiter nodded, got to his feet and picked up both cup and jug. He smelt the fragrance of the claret and something else, slightly bitter. Why wouldn't Bradshaw have smelt that? he wondered. Or did it take time for the poisonous flavour to make itself known?

'They are all here now, Master Rossiter.'

The 'retinue of recalcitrants' returned to their bench. They looked more composed. Rossiter wondered if they had used the opportunity to discuss matters.

'The lecture I am going to give,' the Proctor leaned against the lectern, 'is short and pithy. Master Bradshaw, Professor of Divinity at the University of Oxford, has been foully murdered. The wine in that jug and the cup is certainly poisoned. I suspect the noxious substance used was the juice of henbane, belladonna or foxglove which can be collected in Christchurch Meadows or bought from any of the many apothecaries who plague this town.'

He glanced at Master Tynbroke who sat on the bench opposite the scholars, Simon the pot boy behind him. 'You brought the rat?'

'I did, sir.' Tynbroke's mouth parted in a gap-toothed smile. 'There's also no shortage of them in Oxford.'

'No, there isn't,' Rossiter replied. 'Of every variety.'

'Are you saying, sir, that we poisoned Bradshaw?' Stokes got to his feet and swaggered forward.

'*Pax vobiscum*,' Rossiter replied. Peace be with you.

'And with you,' Stokes retorted. 'But how can we have peace if we are accused of murder?'

'Cicero said, "Cui bono?" Who profits?'

'Come, come, Master Rossiter, you are the Proctor. Your reputation goes before you like a banner. You know the tittle-tattle of the taverns, halls, cookshops and eating-houses. Bradshaw was a viper in human flesh, arrogant and malicious: he was a friend to none and a bad enemy to all who offended him!'

'Out of your own mouth,' Rossiter retorted, 'comes the truth! You, Master Stokes, not to mention Marchow, Gregory, Kendrick, Kiffle and Haycock, all felt the brunt of Master Bradshaw's discipline.'

'Malice,' Gregory shouted.

'Malice, sir?'

'Yes, sir, malice.'

Marchow got up and came to stand beside Stokes. He pushed his black hair away from his face, his eyes glittering. Rossiter noticed how his high cheekbones were deeply pitted. If ever a man hated Bradshaw, Rossiter thought, you did.

'Sit down!'

Stokes and Marchow obeyed. The Proctor stepped off the dais, sat on the edge and studied the scholars. Their like could be seen in any street or tavern of Oxford: poor, threadbare, ill-fed, but with a passion for learning and a desire to better themselves. The younger sons of younger sons with noble names and empty pockets.

'Tell me about Master Bradshaw.'

'What we know, you know,' Stokes declared.

'No, you tell me,' Rossiter insisted. 'Oh, Master Tynbroke, have the doors to the hall locked and guarded. More candles should be lit: this is going to be one of my longest afternoons in the schools.' Rossiter stared at each of the recalcitrants. 'An important debate is going to take place about life and death.'

He waited for Tynbroke to obey. The servant came back and sat opposite the Proctor.

What if I am wrong? Rossiter thought. Bradshaw was as arrogant as any lord. Did his haughty ways and petty cruelties break his servant's patience? Tynbroke held his gaze: his only signs of nervousness were the licking of lips and the way he gripped the bench on either side of him.

'We are alone now, Master Rossiter,' Stokes jibed. 'We await your questions.'

'You have one already. Tell me about Bradshaw.'

'We are all scholars of Woodcock Hall,' Stokes began. 'We are in the third year of our studies. Some of us come from south of the Trent, others from shires to the north. We share a chamber, victuals, clothing, bedding, ink and pens.' He gestured at his companions. 'We know each other better than some husbands do their wives.'

'But not in the carnal sense,' Gregory intervened, causing a ripple of laughter.

'We are poor as church mice,' Stokes continued. 'Sometimes we beg and, aye, I confess, sometimes we steal to fill our bellies. Bradshaw was Master of Woodcock Hall, as well as Professor of Divinity. He had his own chambers with Turkey carpets on the walls and floors. Beeswax candles, sweet-scented braziers, an open bed, featherdown mattress and coverlets any lord would envy. He ate brawn and mustard, capon, quinces, pastries and custards. He had tuns of Gascony wine and there was always bread available, freshly baked that day.'

'And you hated him?'

'He was a fat flea which lived high on the hog,' Stokes replied. 'He was worse than any imp of Satan when it came to us. He made our lives worse than that of any soul suffering in Purgatory. He would raid our chamber, catch us coming in late, and the more he squeezed us the more we protested. And the more we protested the more he punished.'

'And?' Rossiter asked.

'A month ago, around Candlemas, he summoned us individually up to his lodgings. If he'd had his way, he'd have birched us.'

'But you had broken the statutes of Woodcock Hall?' Rossiter demanded.

'Oh, for the love of God and all His saints!' Marchow shouted.

'You in particular, sir! Were you not accused of baptising a cat and practising witchcraft? That's heresy!'

'No, sir, that was drunkenness: a silly, ill-judged jest.'

'And you, Stokes? Were you not unchaste with a tailor's wife?'

'She was kind to me: her husband was Bradshaw's creature. False allegations were laid.'

Rossiter kept his face impassive. He had come across such cruelty before. Men like Bradshaw who loved to exercise power.

'And you, Kendrick, you lost a book?'

The soft-faced, dreamy-eyed scholar shook his head. 'I think it was stolen, sir. I believe Master Bradshaw did it himself. Such venom was common.'

'And Haycock?' Rossiter turned to the ashen-faced bean-pole of a young man who sat on the end of the bench, head down, hands in his lap. 'You kept a ferret and a weasel?'

'They were my pets,' the young man muttered, not raising his head. 'Bradshaw seized them and had them destroyed.'

'So?' said Rossiter. 'You are saying Bradshaw was a liar?'

'He was the father of liars,' Stokes declared.

'Is that why you killed him?'

'We did not murder Bradshaw. There is no evidence.' Stokes's voice was steady, matter-of-fact.

'You forget . . .' Marchow pointed to the wine.

'Hush now, we'll come to that.' Rossiter made a cutting movement with his hand. 'Let's develop the story. For the last month Bradshaw punished you by making you follow him round Oxford?'

'That's right,' Stokes replied. 'From matins to compline. We rose, washed, dressed and waited outside Bradshaw's chamber. We would then have to follow him to this college or that hall, to the schools or a tavern. We sat like Lazarus outside the door of Dives. Two nights ago Bradshaw attended a meeting with other Fellows in a special chamber at the Boar's Head. We were forced to sit on the stairs, our bellies clenched and empty, as roast beef, boiled chicken, vegetables and pies, pastries and other delicacies were brought up the stairs for Bradshaw and the other pigs who feasted with him.'

'Why didn't you appeal against such cruelty?' Rossiter asked.

Stokes laughed and shook his head.

'He treated us like fools,' Gregory declared. 'Even when he went to the jakes to relieve himself. We were forced to stay outside and listen to him fart and strain like the devil's own trumpeter.'

'So, we come to the events of today.' Rossiter tapped his foot.

'As usual,' said Stokes, 'Master Bradshaw rose like a lord and dressed. We followed him through the lanes of Oxford to the schools.'

'Did he force you to carry anything?'

'His saddlebags, that's all.'

'And who carried them?'

Stokes pointed at Haycock. 'He chose Haycock because he was the weakest. He liked to see him stumble.'

'And so you came here?' Rossiter turned to the schools servant. 'Had Master Bradshaw eaten this morning?'

'No, sir.'

'And why is that?'

'It was the custom.' Tynbroke gestured to the small vesting chamber at the back of the hall. 'Bradshaw – I mean, Master Bradshaw – always arrived about a quarter of an hour before the lecture would begin: when the hour candle had almost reached the tenth ring.'

'That was his custom?' Rossiter asked. 'And this morning?'

Tynbroke shrugged. 'Master Bradshaw arrived with what he called his "retinue". I unlocked the door to the vesting chamber. I had prepared what Master Bradshaw had demanded: a white manchet loaf, freshly baked this morning; a small bowl of butter and a jar of honey from Osney Abbey, a delicacy Bradshaw loved. He claimed it soothed both his humours and his throat before he spoke.'

'And you prepared all these, Master Tynbroke?'

'Yes, sir. I put them on a board and placed them on the table in the vesting room and locked the door until Master Bradshaw arrived.'

'Was there anything else?'

'Oh yes.' Tynbroke pointed to the jug of wine. 'I drew that from the stores together with Bradshaw's favourite cup, the one he always demanded.'

'So.' Rossiter got to his feet and stretched. 'Bradshaw enters the vesting room.' He glanced at Stokes. 'And where did his retinue sit?'

'As usual, outside.'

'Did Bradshaw keep the door open?'

'Of course.' Marchow sneered. 'He liked us to see him eat and drink like the pig he was.'

'And how much did he eat?'

Marchow shrugged. 'Half the loaf, smeared with butter and honey. He also drank a goblet of wine.'

'And when he had finished?'

'He came into the hall, telling Haycock to fetch his panniers. Tynbroke brought the wine jug and goblet and put them on the table whilst Bradshaw laid out his books and manuscripts.'

Rossiter looked at Tynbroke who nodded his agreement. 'By that time other scholars were arriving, pouring through the door.'

'And what happened to the vesting chamber?' Rossiter demanded.

'I locked it immediately,' Tynbroke replied.

'And so no one has been in there since?'

'Only myself, sir. Only I have the key.'

'Did anything untoward happen there?'

'Not that I remember,' Tynbroke replied. 'I did hear Master Bradshaw shouting soon after he arrived.'

'That was my fault,' said Haycock. 'I followed him into the vesting chamber and was clumsy with Bradshaw's saddlebags. He cursed and struck me.' Haycock shrugged. 'I scuttled away as fast as I could to join my companions.'

'Then Bradshaw began his lecture?'

'You could call it that,' Stokes scoffed. 'It was supposed to be on the existence of God: about what is obvious, what is real and what is true. It was really devoted to showing how clever Bradshaw was.'

'So you'd heard this lecture before?'

'Oh, of course. The six of us knew it by heart. Bradshaw was a rote teacher like a monkey performing the same tricks.'

'Where and when did you poison the wine?' Rossiter demanded suddenly.

'But we didn't poison it,' Stokes replied. 'Why should we? Three of us would have to drink it.'

'I beg your pardon?' For the first time since he had arrived the Proctor showed his surprise. Stokes grinned mischievously. Tynbroke moved restlessly on his bench.

'Ask Master Tynbroke. Ask the scholars who came here,' said Marchow triumphantly. 'Bradshaw loved to point us out, bring us to the attention of other scholars. In talking about reality he always invited some of us forward to share a cup of wine.'

'And he did that today?'

'Of course.'

'Show me what happened.'

Stokes, Gregory and Haycock got to their feet and came to the edge of the dais as Rossiter picked up the cup.

'Bradshaw drank from it,' Stokes explained, 'then gave it to each of us in turn.'

'Did he drink again after you?'

'No,' Gregory declared. 'A hall full of scholars will bear witness to that.'

'As will I,' Tynbroke declared.

Rossiter stared across the hall. At first the solution to this mystery had appeared so simple. Now?

'How do we know you drank the wine?' he asked abruptly.

'Because Bradshaw made sure we did. He thrust the cup to our lips,' said Stokes. 'He liked to pour the wine down our throats. He hoped it would make us splutter and cough. He knew we hadn't eaten. Such wine sits heavy on an empty stomach. On a number of occasions some of us were sick, a petty cruelty by our Master of Divinity.'

Rossiter hid his consternation. If Bradshaw drank the wine and gave it to these three scholars . . . ?

'Did you know in advance whom he'd invite forward?'

Stokes shook his head. Rossiter stared down at the floor. Perhaps the poison was such that a mouthful of wine wouldn't do any harm? Yet, even so, it would be very dangerous. He glanced up. Stokes's face was impassive.

'So, let me understand this.' The Proctor turned and pointed to the vesting chamber. 'You, Master Tynbroke, prepared wine, bread, butter and honey for our late but, perhaps, not lamented Master of Divinity. You put it in that room?'

'Yes, sir, and immediately locked the door. True, there's a window, but the alleyway beyond is wet and muddy, and such a forced entry would be obvious.'

'So,' Rossiter decided, 'no one broke in to poison the victuals. Now this morning, Master Bradshaw arrives with what he calls his "retinue of recalcitrants". You unlock that chamber. Bradshaw goes in, whereupon he breaks his fast and drinks some wine?'

Tynbroke agreed.

'And who carried the wine to the podium?'

'I did.' Tynbroke stretched his neck like a chicken swallowing hard, provoking a snigger from Marchow.

Rossiter pointed to the table. 'The wine is placed there. It's well known that Bradshaw will drink during his lecture and offer some to his "recalcitrants". So Bradshaw would hardly poison it but neither would they, eh, Master Tynbroke?'

'And nor did I!'

'Why is that?'

'Because I drank from it as well.'

Rossiter stared in surprise.

'I always did, before the lecture began. Master Bradshaw insisted that I take a drink both before and after. I think the custom originated—'

'Ah yes, I know,' Rossiter interrupted. There had been a famous case some years earlier when an irate servant, in similar circumstances, had placed a sleeping draught in a lecturer's jug of wine.

'I saw him do it.' Simon the pot boy spoke up. 'I saw Master Tynbroke take a full mouthful of wine and place the cup and jug on the table. Neither he nor I went anywhere near it afterwards.'

Rossiter walked up and down the dais. The line of scholars sat, heads down. Rossiter stopped and stared at the jug and cup. Bradshaw, he thought, had drunk that wine in the vesting chamber: he had suffered no ill effects. Tynbroke had brought it out here. He had drunk and suffered no ill effects. Three of the scholars had been forced to drink and suffered no mishap, yet the jug and cup were definitely poisoned. So, how was it done? Tynbroke had been watched by Simon whilst Bradshaw had held the cup when the three scholars had drunk from it. Very clever, very subtle!

'Master Tynbroke,' he declared, 'I wish to inspect the vesting chamber. You, sirs,' he pointed to Stokes and the rest, 'will stay until I call you.'

Tynbroke went over and unlocked the chamber. He led Rossiter inside. It was really no more than a long rectangle, a table down the centre, a chair at the top, benches either side. A squat tallow candle in its brass holder stood in the centre of the table. The walls were wood-panelled halfway up. The corners were shadow-filled. Behind the chair, high in the wall, was a large window, shutters open. Rossiter went and sat on the chair.

'Has this bread, honey and butter been tainted?'

Tynbroke shook his head. 'It's what I served Master Bradshaw this morning.'

Rossiter examined it: what was left of the bread was whole and sweet, the butter rather soft, the honey delicious. Rossiter could detect no trace in taste or smell of anything amiss.

'Summon our scholars here!'

Stokes and the rest came and stood in the doorway.

'Is that where you were whilst Bradshaw was eating?'

'No,' said Stokes. 'Bradshaw made us sit like beggars at the entrance.'

'And you never came in here?'

'I did,' Haycock declared. He pointed to the far corner behind Rossiter. 'I went over and placed Bradshaw's panniers there: that's where he liked them, well away from so-called thieves like us. He always inspected them closely to make sure the straps and buckles had not been tampered with.'

'And is that when he shouted at you?'

'I stumbled as I came in here. The panniers were heavy; they slipped as I put them down. Bradshaw struck me on the

212

head and pushed me away to join the rest.' Haycock shrugged. 'The cruel hog often did that.'

'We sat and watched him snout in his trough,' Stokes added. 'Then he swept out to the podium. Tynbroke and the pot boy picked up the wine and locked the chamber whilst we dutifully trotted after Bradshaw.'

'And there was nothing else?'

'Nothing!'

Rossiter waved them away and ordered Tynbroke to close the door. For a while he sat in silence. He could not fathom this mystery or perceive any solution. The wine had been tasted by others with no adverse effects. Yet, after the lecture, the wine was clearly poisoned. No other source of poison could be found. The bread, butter and honey were untainted and Bradshaw didn't put anything else into his mouth. The Proctor sighed, got to his feet and went back into the hall.

'Master Tynbroke? You knew Bradshaw? Would he carry sweetmeats upon his person?'

'One of my tipstaffs went through his pockets and purse: there was no trace of any food. You are correct, sir, Master Bradshaw was most particular about what he ate or drank. Indeed, he only put to his mouth the best wine, honey and butter. Master Bradshaw was a most particular man.'

Rossiter glanced at the scholars who remained seated on the bench. Bradshaw was, the Proctor reflected, not a man to take anything from these and eat it. Rossiter felt sorry for the 'recalcitrants': Bradshaw had been a cruel, vicious man. He would not be missed. He would not be mourned. In a sense his death was a form of justice.

'Master Rossiter.' Stokes got to his feet. 'You have no reason to detain us. Not a shred of evidence points to our having a hand in Bradshaw's death. We disliked him but so did many others. True, he drank poison. Perhaps he intended to kill us?

A silly jape gone wrong? Perhaps you should report that to the Chancellor?'

Rossiter rocked backwards and forwards on his heels. If the truth be known, he thought, he had little stomach for this matter. The six 'recalcitrants' were poor scholars provoked and punished beyond all measure. He believed they were responsible for Bradshaw's death, yet Stokes was correct: he had no proof to lay against them. However, Rossiter would love to know the truth. Of course, there was always Tynbroke. The servant was now standing on the far side of the dais, holding the pot boy's hand. But why should Tynbroke kill Bradshaw? With what motive, and how? Tynbroke also drank the wine whilst the victuals in the retiring chamber were untainted.

'Master Tynbroke.' He walked towards the servant. 'When Bradshaw left the vesting chamber, did you lock it immediately?'

'Yes, I did, and the scholars saw me!'

A chorus of agreement greeted his words. Rossiter returned to the dais. For a long time he stood and stared down at the jug.

'Master Tynbroke, I want these removed, their contents thrown into the sewer. They are to be carefully scrubbed and cleaned in boiling water. You may then go about your duties.'

'And us?' Stokes asked.

'You will remain.' Rossiter raised a hand to quell their protests. 'Stokes, please follow me.'

They returned to the vesting chamber. Rossiter took a tinder and lit the candle. He asked Stokes to close the door and gestured at the bench, seating himself in the chair at the head of the table. He grasped the manchet loaf, liberally smeared it with butter and honey, cut it in two and offered it to Stokes. The scholar ate both pieces hungrily. When he had finished, Rossiter fished into his purse, took out two silver coins and placed them on the table.

'What's that for?' Stokes asked. 'Master Proctor, you don't expect me to betray my friends?'

'I am not asking you to betray anyone, Master Stokes. You are a scholar at Oxford. You and I know that you had a hand in Bradshaw's death, but' – he raised a finger – 'I admit, and I will put this in writing, there isn't one shred of evidence against you. Now, look.' Rossiter leaned forward. 'God forgive me, Stokes, but Master Bradshaw will not be missed. He was arrogant and vicious, a man who provoked scholars and inflicted petty cruelties upon them. God knows how long he would have persecuted you.'

Stokes remained impassive.

'But I wonder, Master Stokes, if you could create a possible hypothesis? After all, we are in the schools of Oxford.'

'A hypothesis, sir?'

'Perhaps you could theorise on what might have happened. If I like your hypothesis, if it's worthy of an Oxford scholar, you may pick up these silver pieces and rejoin your companions: neither you nor they will ever be troubled again.'

'And if I don't agree?'

'I shall pocket my silver coins and you'll be allowed to go, but I can give no guarantee for the future, either over this matter or anything else.'

Stokes made as if to rise.

'No, you can't consult with your companions. We have no witnesses here, Master Stokes. That protects you. It also protects me.'

'I have your solemn word?'

Rossiter nodded. Stokes picked up some crumbs and chewed them slowly. When he had finished, he wiped his fingers on his tunic and clasped his hands as if in prayer.

'It might be said,' he began, 'though without any evidence,' he smiled at Rossiter, 'that we were responsible for Bradshaw's death. He was a vicious, spiteful brute who would have punished us until we either broke and left, or did something worse so he'd have us arraigned before the congregation. I was also fearful for Haycock, whom Bradshaw always singled out for special punishment. Haycock might have done something stupid. He, indeed all of us, might have ended our days on the gallows near the city gates.'

'Oh, I know the motive,' Rossiter said quietly.

'Let us say, *causa disputandi*' – for sake of argument – 'that another group of scholars was being punished in a similar vein by Master Bradshaw. He led them hither and thither till they learned all about his habits, mannerisms and customs. For instance, that when he came down to the schools he always came to a room like this, where he would drink wine and scoff bread and honey to his heart's content. Let us say, Master Rossiter, that the leader of these students, keen of wit and determined to avenge himself and escape from such punishment, managed to purchase, with his precious coins, a small sack of poison – powder, henbane or belladonna. Perhaps not from some city apothecary but elsewhere. Let us say that, on one particular morning, this scholar rose very early and bought a fresh manchet loaf.'

Rossiter smiled. The bread was now gone. He stared at the empty board. 'Continue, Master Stokes.'

'Let us say this scholar, using his dagger, carefully powdered this bread with poison, which being also white in colour could not be detected. He then carried it secretly beneath his cloak. Bradshaw arrives in a chamber like this. A scholar carries his panniers. He deliberately stumbles and falls, distracting Bradshaw. For a short while our Professor of Divinity turns his back. The other scholars are blocking the door so no one in the hall can see in.'

'The other scholars were party to this?'

'Of course, bound by great oaths of secrecy to be of one mind and soul.'

'So, while Bradshaw's back is turned, one white loaf is exchanged for another.' Rossiter whistled softly under his breath. 'Very subtle. One manchet loaf looks very like another. The bread has a tangy taste, whilst the honey will offset any acrid flavour. It would only take a few seconds for the loaves to be exchanged. Bradshaw turns back, sends the stumbling scholar out of the room to sit with the rest and eats his own death. What then, Master Stokes?'

'Bradshaw the pig has now eaten his fill, though some of the loaf, as usual, remains for when he's finished his lecture. He gets to his feet and summons his slave forward to pick up the panniers. He punches and pushes him.' Stokes rose and walked to the door. 'Unbeknown to him, the leader of this coven has slipped into the chamber to hide behind the open door, here in the corner.' He opened the door and pulled it back so it completely concealed him.

'Very good, Master Stokes. Close the door before the others come across.'

Stokes re-took his seat and continued his hypothesis.

'Bradshaw is full of himself. He is the great lecturer going towards the dais. The slave stumbles behind him with his saddlebags. The rest follow. Indeed, they have been following Bradshaw for weeks. He doesn't realise their leader is missing. If he does, they can make some excuse that he was taken short and had to hurry to the jakes.'

'And Tynbroke locks the door.'

'Oh, yes. The bread, the butter and the honey must be left for Master Bradshaw when he returns. Inside the room the scholar changes the bread. He measures the cut and replaces like with like. He removes all crumbs and uses the chair to clamber up to the window. He ensures the alleyway is deserted and drops through. Back in the chamber the bread board holds a wholesome and untainted loaf, or what is left of it. The scholar cleans the knife, gets rid of any trace of the poisoned bread and mixes with the throng of students now entering the schools. He takes his seat with his companions. The lecture begins. As Bradshaw speaks the poison works. He goes through all his mummery and makes three of his prisoners drink the wine.'

'Which, of course, is untainted?'

'Bradshaw collapses. Everyone throngs around. In the confusion the scholar sprinkles the rest of the poison into the jug and the cup.'

Rossiter leaned back in the chair and stared at Stokes. 'It is all feasible, it's all possible.'

Stokes pointed a finger. 'But I have your word? And it's only a hypothesis.' Stokes smiled. 'There is no real evidence: not even members of the group knew precisely what their leader did. He did it for them as well as himself. Bradshaw was intent on destroying them all.'

'You have my word,' Rossiter declared. 'You may go.'

Stokes got to his feet. He leaned over the table, his face only a few inches from the Proctor's.

'In a way, Master Rossiter, Bradshaw learned his own lesson before he died. *Id quod clarum non sit existens. Id quod existens non sit verum.*' That which is obvious may not be real, and that which is real may not be the truth.

And, pocketing the coins, Master Stokes left.

Pie Powder

John Hall

Northern England, 1452

C lement frowned. 'I know it's a court at fairs and so on, but why "pie powder"?'

Martin Byrd, in his mid-twenties, handsome by some standards, looked at his servant. 'An old legal term from the French, *pied poudré*, meaning "dusty feet", because those attending have walked miles to get there. It's time to go,' he added, and led the way to the town hall, where the Court of Pie Powder, to which Martin was the clerk, would be held.

It was summer, 1452, and events over the past few years had affected Martin. Political unrest made all men suspicious, and highly placed men particularly so. Only after several months' enforced idleness in London had Martin obtained this post in a northern town where a midsummer fair was being held.

The town's mayor, a Master Hoskiss, a rotund little gentleman, was already at the town hall, and Sir George Maryon, chairman of the bench, arrived soon after, as did Lord Edmund, commander of the local garrison. Edmund's responsibilities extended over almost half the shire, so he was happy to leave the running of the court to Sir George; indeed, Edmund stayed only a short while before excusing himself. Martin was kept busy all day, though Clement – as usual – soon grew weary of the proceedings and disappeared.

Before dinner that evening, Clement announced his

intention of visiting the fair, to see what was happening. He was gone a surprisingly short time before he burst into the room he shared with Martin. 'Here's a thing, Master Byrd! It's a head.' When Martin frowned, Clement added, 'Like you have on your shoulders, unless the law catches up with you. A showman, and he has this talking head. It tells your fortune.'

Martin stood up. 'I do enjoy a good fair,' he said. And he was soon following Clement through the crowded fairground.

Most of the town had turned out, as it seemed. The fair was the only chance most folk had to buy the goods they needed; and for those too poor to buy, there was plenty to look at.

A sudden roaring noise, and a long flame shooting past him, made Martin jump. He turned to see a cheerful man, a fire-eater, wave at him as yet another flame shot from the fellow's mouth. 'Sorry, master,' the man said, laughing. He produced a sword, and began to swallow it.

'Master Byrd?' Clement frowned. 'We'll miss the next performance if you stand there much longer, to say nothing of being roasted alive.'

Martin followed Clement through the crowds to a modest tent of coarse cloth. A curtain hung across the front of the tent, and in front of the curtain stood a young lad, about ten years old. He shouted at the top of his youthful voice: 'Come along, gentle folk and commoners alike! See the great Dr Sylvester and the marvel of the age, the head of the famous Egyptian emperor, Rameses!'

He pulled back the curtain, to reveal what was evidently a table covered with a cloth in the same red and gold material as the lad himself wore. This cloth reached right down to the ground, hiding the actual table, and on the cloth stood a curious contraption. The base of this thing was a short pillar, on top of which was the carved head of a man, with a very striking appearance. The head was gilded, but the gilt had been

222

knocked off here and there to show that the thing was made of wood.

A man, evidently that 'Dr Sylvester' whom the lad had mentioned, now appeared from the dark interior of the tent. He was an imposing figure, clad in a cloak of the same red and gold cloth that decorated the table and the youthful assistant, and he wore a curious high cylinder-shaped hat on his head. A striking profile and a long black beard helped make him an impressive, and perhaps even a sinister, figure, and the crowd, which had not been slow to give the lad the benefit of its observations and opinions, grew silent as he came forward and bowed low.

'Ladies and gentlemen.' His voice was a deep bass, not at all loud, but commanding. 'You will, I know, have heard of the great emperor of ancient Egypt, the pharaoh Rameses, who enslaved the Israelites and married Queen Cleopatra, the most beautiful woman who ever lived. Is that not so, good sir?' he asked Martin suddenly.

'I have read some mention of this Rameses in Livy, or mayhap it was in Plutarch,' said Martin reluctantly. 'Though as to the historical accuracy of those conquests, of whatever sort, that you mention, I can hardly speak with authority.'

'Well expressed, young master. Perhaps I err in attributing too extensive a catalogue of achievements to him,' said Sylvester magnanimously. 'Still, that is by the way.' He gestured at the head upon the table. 'This is, some say, Rameses' own head, preserved by the alchemical arts of Egypt; some say that it is a mystic device of his invention. But still, man or machine, it will tell your fortune. Come, anything will satisfy Rameses, a silver penny as well as a gold noble.' Sylvester produced a short stave or wand, half an ell in length, and bound round with strips of cloth in the usual red and gold. 'You, good sir,' Sylvester said to Clement. 'Shall we see your fate?' Before Clement could answer, Sylvester tapped the head

223

with his wand and said, 'Speak, O Rameses!'

As the wand struck the top of the head, the hinged jaw moved slowly down and then up, down again and up again, so that the mouth on the thing seemed to open and close in a stiff, jerky fashion, whilst a curious deep voice emerged from it. 'You will find a fine, lusty wife,' said the voice. 'Mind you,' it added, 'I cannot say whose wife it may be!'

Clement was the first to laugh at this. 'It's true enough,' he admitted freely. 'But you could tell that just by looking at me,' he added under his breath. To Martin, he said, 'Well, master?'

'It is impressive, I allow,' said Martin. 'Some mechanical device, as I take it, moves the jaw, some concealed spring.'

'And the voice, master?'

'I can answer that,' said a big man who stood nearby. He had clearly been drinking and his tone was openly sceptical. 'It's that lad,' he went on, 'hiding under that cloth that's over the table.' The crowd seemed sympathetic to this point of view.

Sylvester smiled. 'In that case, we had best remove the cloth and see if he's lurking under there,' he said. He twitched the cloth aside, to show that there was nothing beneath the table. The crowd gasped, and, impressed by this little performance, now began to take more of an interest in Sylvester. One by one they came forward to ask their questions; there was no gold offered, and little silver, but there were several small copper coins laid on the table before the head, along with a wheaten loaf and a slab of cheese.

The questions were mostly of a commonplace nature, and so too, Martin thought, were the answers. A young woman who asked how to choose between two suitors was advised to follow her heart, but to be prepared for disappointment if it led her astray: unbiased enough, as Martin whispered to Clement, but hardly helpful to the girl. And the rest were similarly non-committal answers.

That is, until the crowd had begun to thin out somewhat. Then the head – without being asked any question by anyone – suddenly let out a growl and said, 'You there, Will Glover! Have a care, Will!'

Such onlookers as remained, Martin and Clement among them, turned to see who was being addressed. A middle-aged man, tall, and clothed considerably better than the average, was obviously the one addressed, for unlike the rest of the crowd his face showed not puzzlement but anger. He pushed his way forward and stared, first at Sylvester, then at the figure of 'Rameses'. 'What nonsense is this, then?'

The head went on, 'Will Glover, your treacheries are known. Make haste to repent, lest you be struck down by the avenging hand!' The tone of the voice had changed, grown harsh, the bantering note now entirely vanished.

There was an awkward silence, then Glover cursed fluently for a moment, turned on his heel, shoved aside a curious spectator, and strode off into the crowd. Sylvester bowed hurriedly to those remaining, and went inside the tent.

Martin and Clement, after a moment's hesitation and some lively discussion as to just what had happened, and what it may have meant, set off back through the fair, seeking their dinner. They were staying with the local justice, Mr Moss, whose kitchen was above reproach.

Martin remained at the table, talking, for some time after the meal, and when he retired to the room he shared with Clement he found his servant already in bed. Before Martin could make his own preparations, there was a tap at the door. Clement, the blankets round him, glanced reproachfully at Martin, who opened the door.

One of Mr Moss's servants stood there, a piece of paper held in his hand. 'Letter for you, sir,' he told Martin, handing it over.

'For me? Are you sure? Who left it?'

'Didn't know him, sir. He said it was for "the handsome young chap as is clerk to the justices", begging your pardon, sir.' And the servant bowed and left.

Martin looked closely at the letter. There was no superscription, but it was sealed with wax, and there was a device embossed in the seal, evidently made with a signet ring. 'I don't recognise the crest,' he told Clement.

'I suppose you could always read it?' Clement yawned, and turned over.

'Hmm.' Martin broke the seal, and smoothed out the paper. 'Let's see.' The writing was spidery, cramped, and he had to screw up his eyes to see it. 'Now. "Sir, I take you for a man of" – something – "having seen you advise their honours in the court this morning. And a good king's man as I trust all to be, though some are otherwise. Should it please you to know what will be of value for the knowing, and touching closely upon the business of the court, be at the lone oak near the town bridge at midnight tonight, and you shall learn that which will be of" – something else illegible there – "and worth ten pounds to any man. If you mistrust me, bring your servant." What d'you make of that?'

Clement was at first inclined to dismiss the note as an ill-timed jest, and especially the suggestion to 'bring your servant', but Martin insisted, and they were soon headed for the spot mentioned, along with two of Lord Edmund's men, lest it be a trap of some sort. Edmund's men knew the lone oak, which they said rather shamefacedly was noted locally as a trysting place for lovers, and they were there ten minutes after leaving Mr Moss's house.

Martin had no means of knowing the exact time, but it seemed as if they waited all night. Soon after they arrived at the spot the abbey bell sounded lauds, and Martin looked eagerly for the writer of the odd letter, but all was quiet. Some ten minutes later, and he asked if this was the right place, to be told by the men-at-arms that there was nowhere else remotely answering the description. After what must have been another half-hour, the two men-at-arms began to reiterate this information unbidden, and then to grumble less subtly. Ten minutes more, and Clement made some very pointed, and barely polite, remarks as to the necessity of wasting further time. Over by the fairground some late reveller must have lit a bonfire, and looking at the cheerful red glow that lit the sky only made the night seem more chilly by contrast. Another ten minutes, and Martin too had had enough. With mumbled apologies he dismissed the two soldiers, who set off at a fast pace for their beds, and he and Clement followed at a more leisurely pace.

Martin was now inclined to share Clement's earlier view that the note was a hoax; but early next morning he was woken by Sir George himself, with the news that the burnt and blackened body of Will Glover had been found at the edge of the fairground.

'Who identified him?' asked Sir George, looking with some distaste at the canvas sacking that covered the body. 'Wouldn't have thought anyone would know the poor devil, even his own mother.'

'His apprentice, sir,' said Tom Constable, nodding at a young man with a decidedly greenish look to him. 'Glover wore a distinctive ring, and had a gap in his teeth – there.'

Sir George asked, 'Very well, so the next question must be, how did this Glover die?'

The town's old apothecary, Roberts, who had been called to examine the body, looked up with an evil grin. 'I should have said that was fairly obvious, my lord, in view of the state of the body. The man was burned to death.'

'No, sir,' said Martin. 'You will note that there has not been any fire here apart from that which caused the scorching of the body.'

Roberts looked at him, frowning. 'I fear I cannot well follow you, sir.'

'The flesh is burnt, true enough, but there is no heap of ash such as you would expect if there had been a funeral pyre lit underneath him to consume the body,' Martin pointed out.

Roberts studied the ground closely. 'True enough. Only a small fire, then, for the skin alone is burned, the corpse itself more or less intact.' He lifted the body carefully. 'No, there is no sign of any ash at all. Well then, perhaps the body was burned elsewhere, and then moved here?'

'No, for the grass round about is all scorched,' said Martin. 'The explanation must be that the burning body ignited the grass.'

Roberts's frown deepened. 'But how could the body be burned without some kindling underneath it?'

Martin shook his head. One of the constable's men mumbled something.

'Well, man?' demanded Sir George.

'Beg your pardon, your honour, but there's talk.'

'Talk? What sort of talk? What the devil d'you mean?'

The man shrugged. 'Witchcraft, my lord. 'Tis said the death was foretold.'

'Oh, is—'

Martin interrupted, 'Your pardon, Sir George, but it's true. In part, at least. Clement and I were there.' And he told Sir George of 'Dr Sylvester', and 'Rameses'.

'Right,' said Sir George, when Martin was done. 'The first thing is to get hold of this "Sylvester", or whatever he calls himself. The second thing is to determine, if we can, just how this fellow met his death. How the body comes to be burned in this odd fashion, without any obvious cause.'

Roberts looked up from the body. 'I rather think the

explanation may be a prosaic one,' he said. 'Just take another look, young sir. Or, rather, a sniff. Tell me what that curious odour might be? Not the burnt smell,' he added, as Martin seemed reluctant, 'but something else, something additional, as it were.'

Martin, dubious, sniffed the air round the body. There was indeed a curious smell, one he almost recognised but could not put a name to. 'I know that,' he told Roberts. 'I forget the name, but it's one of the ingredients of Greek fire, if I'm not mistaken.' He frowned. 'Although I'm sure I've smelled it somewhere only recently.'

'Naphtha! To be sure, naphtha!' Old Mr Roberts straightened up, rubbing his hands in delight. When Sir George and the others looked blank, he added, 'Naphtha is a mineral oil, sirs, much used for torches for illumination.'

'Ah. Burns briskly, does it? Must do, if it's used in torches and what have you.' Sir George scratched his head. 'So, the man was doused with this naphtha of yours, and then someone set light to him? That right?'

'That seems to account for the state of the body, sir,' agreed Roberts. 'And for the lack of any ash from what we might call an external agency; and for the scorching of the grass. Yes, that's it exactly.' He looked at Martin, who nodded agreement.

'And what was this Glover doing while all this was going on? You'd expect a man to fight, wouldn't you?' demanded Sir George. 'He must have been tapped on the head first, I take it?'

Roberts bent over the body again, his hands running over the skull. 'Ahah! More than tapped, your honour. Here,' he told Martin. 'Put your hand just there.'

Martin gingerly did as he was bidden, to feel the bone move beneath his fingers. He turned the body over, nodded. 'A violent blow, or perhaps more than one. You can feel it, and indeed just see it, under the burnt flesh.'

Sir George grimaced. 'Killed with a blow to the head, then the body soaked in this naphtha stuff and set on fire. Nothing too supernatural about that. And where would I find some of this stuff?' was Sir George's next question.

'Naphtha, sir? I have no doubt that Lord Edmund would have some, at the castle,' said Roberts. 'As I say, it's much used for torches.'

'But my lord can hardly have had anything to do with this business,' said Sir George, sceptically.

'Perhaps not, Sir George,' said Martin. 'But my lord is not the only man at the castle.'

'No, I suppose not. Anyone else have a stock of this naphtha?'

Martin, who had recollected where he thought he had smelled naphtha recently, said, 'There's a fellow here at the fair, swallows swords and eats fire. I fancy I could smell it in his vicinity yesterday evening. Probably uses it in his act.'

Sir George nodded at one of the constable's men. 'Find this fellow, Sylvester, would you, and bring him to us?' As the man left, he told the others, 'And we'll see this fire-eater. That might be more like it. Here at the fair, that's where the answer lies. But why burn the body, whoever may have killed him? If he were killed first by a blow to the head, the burning is superfluous.'

Martin frowned. 'Perhaps the murderer did in fact mean to hide his victim's identity, to make our task the more difficult?'

Sir George nodded. 'That, or perhaps to make the death seem more mysterious? Perhaps the murderer heard the threat to Glover just as you did, Martin, and tried to make it look as if some unearthly hand had indeed struck him down, to obscure things, make it that much harder for us to solve the puzzle.'

'There is a further point about this man Glover.' Martin produced the curious letter that had taken him on his fruitless errand the previous night. 'This was sent to me last night.

230

Although I had my doubts as to its authenticity, I duly went to the appointed place, but no one turned up. I thought it some elaborate hoax.'

Sir George squinted at the spidery handwriting. 'What makes you think it has any bearing on Glover's death?'

Martin turned the letter over and showed Sir George the wax seal. 'It was sealed with his ring,' he explained. 'I noticed the device just now. And last night I saw what I thought was a bonfire, but which must have been—' He broke off.

'You're quite right, Martin. He was on his way to see you, with some mysterious news or other, and someone killed him, to prevent him talking to you!' Sir George frowned. 'But why you, Martin? No offence, my boy, but why did he not come to me, or Lord Edmund?'

'It may have been a delicate matter, Sir George. Not the sort of thing he wanted known officially, so to speak.'

'Hmm.' Sir George turned to Glover's apprentice, who had recovered somewhat. 'What can you tell us about your master's business dealings?'

The apprentice hesitated a long moment, as it seemed to Martin, before saying, 'Only that the business was prosperous, sir.'

'Who inherits it now?'

'Mistress Glover, sir. His wife – widow.'

'Is she here at the fair?'

The apprentice shook his head. 'No, sir, she dislikes travel.' His face clouded. 'I trust she will keep the business going, or I'll be in a poor way.'

Sir George took Martin's arm and steered him out of earshot of the apprentice. 'What d'you think, Martin? Has this fellow anything to do with Glover's death?'

'I don't see what he would gain, Sir George.'

'No, I suppose not. But there's the widow. Perhaps she's seduced the youngster, got him to kill her husband, with the

231

promise of marriage later? That way, the lad here wouldn't be suspected, for he's apparently nothing to gain, while the widow can't be suspected because she's back home!'

'It would cover it, Sir George. But then why should he burn the body? Though he did seem hesitant just now?'

'Ah, you saw that?' Sir George turned to the apprentice. 'Come, now, the truth! What can you tell us of this? Had Master Glover any enemies, or any particular friends, here in the town?'

'Enemies, sir?' Once more it seemed to Martin that an odd look came over the youth's face.

'He had enemies, then?' asked Martin quickly.

The youth hesitated. 'He'd had words with Master Norland.'

'And who might Master Norland be?' asked Sir George.

'He's a merchant, sir. Deals in spices and the like. His booth's down yonder.'

'Anything more?'

The youth said sullenly, 'I must say that Master Glover seemed to have more money than I could rightly account for from the business.'

'And how d'you think he came by his money? Dishonestly?'

'Oh, no, sir! Never.'

'Well, then, let us consider last night. Did you see or hear him leave your lodgings?'

The apprentice nodded. 'Just before lauds.'

'And did he say where he was going?'

Another pause.

'Come along, boy,' urged Sir George.

The apprentice said, 'Well, then, I took it he was meeting a lady, sir.'

'Did he? I mean, was he in the habit of meeting ladies? Given to intrigues?' said Martin.

'He was a manly man, sir,' said the apprentice.

'And his wife back home?' asked Sir George.

232

The apprentice shrugged. 'It was his way, sir.'

Martin asked, 'A regular occurrence?'

The apprentice nodded, silently.

It was Martin's turn to steer Sir George to one side. 'We may not know exactly who killed Glover,' he said, 'but he seems the sort of man who gets himself killed.'

'You're right, by heaven. A womaniser, adulterer, very likely involved in some shady business dealings. Almost too many possibilities, don't you think?'

'I agree, Sir George. However, since we don't have Sylvester in our custody, and we do know that Glover had quarrelled with this man Norland, I suggest he's next on our list.'

Norland was a tall man with a sullen face. He stood before his stall, which was covered with boxes and bags of pepper, ginger, and more exotic spices. 'Glover was not exactly a friend, my lord,' he said in answer to Sir George's question. 'But I stand to suffer by his death, none the less.'

'How's that?'

'He owed me money, sir. Nothing written down, so I've no claim against his estate, but still he'd borrowed almost fifty pounds from me.'

Sir George whistled. 'And that's why you quarrelled with him?'

Norland nodded. 'I asked for what was mine, and he repeated that he'd get the money before the fair ended.'

'Repeated? You'd asked before?'

'I spoke to him as soon as I arrived here, and again yesterday. He claimed he would find the money, or some small part of it at any rate, before the fair closed.' Norland added, 'Now I've no chance of getting my money back, have I? I can sympathise with whoever killed him, mind, he wasn't a likeable man, but I could wish they'd waited until he repaid me!'

Sir George grunted, and led the way back to Sylvester's tent. 'He'd no reason to kill Glover, had he?' he asked. 'You don't kill the goose before it's laid the golden egg, when all's said and done.'

'Unless he knew he wouldn't be repaid,' said Martin, 'and meant to make an example of the debtor?'

'Hmm.' Sir George nodded. 'Well, it looks as if the constable's man has found Sylvester.'

'Your pardon, Sir George,' said Martin, 'but that's the other man, the fire-eater.'

The fire-eater, who had given his name as Dickon, was a middle-aged man, short and dark. He had a worried look on his face, perhaps natural in the circumstances. 'Aye,' he said heavily, 'aye. I knew the treacherous bastard right enough.'

'I take it he was not a particular friend of yours?' asked Clement. 'I'm sharp like that, you know. Pick things up quickly.'

'I had a brother, see? He was a good lad, but easily led, and he had some fancy ideas. Well, he got in with the wrong crowd. To be plain, he was one of Jack Cade's men.'

Martin nodded. The king, Henry VI, was ineffectual as a ruler, and real power was in the hands of a succession of men who were pretty uniformly detested by the ordinary people. In 1450 a forty-thousand strong band of rebels led by Jack Cade, self-styled 'Captain of Kent', had taken over London for three days, and executed Lord Say, one of the king's favourites. When the rebellion failed because of internal dissent among the rebels, Cade attempted to flee, and was killed.

'And then for good measure, what does my brother do but fall in with the other lot,' Dickon went on.

'The Yorkists, you mean?'

Dickon nodded. Richard, Duke of York, had what some thought a better claim to the throne than had the king, and there were stirrings of unrest. Unrest which some predicted would lead to bloody civil war, and soon at that. 'They arrested him, didn't they? My brother, I mean,' said Dickon. 'Hanged him, too. Treason, they said.'

'And what had Glover to do with that?'

'He betrayed him, didn't he? Told them where he was, what he'd been up to, everything about him.'

'Have you any proof of that?' asked Martin.

'Not proof that would stand up in your court, sirs. But I know well enough who it was that gave him away.'

Sir George cleared his throat. 'I'm sorry your brother was hanged, of course. But if he rebelled, if he was plotting against the king, he must surely have realised that there was danger in it?'

Dickon nodded. 'If he'd been killed along with Cade, or been taken in the act of rebellion and hanged, that would've been fair enough. Part of the game, as you might say. But to be taken in your own home, your own bed, on the say-so of some lousy Judas? I don't call that right, master, say what you will.'

'Well, let's move on,' said Sir George. 'Do you use naphtha in your act?'

Dickon looked surprised at the question, but nodded.

'Show me.'

Dickon led the way to a shabby cart, and indicated a stoneware jar stopped with rags. 'Half full, sir.'

Sir George picked the jar up, frowned, and removed the rag stopper. 'It's empty!'

Dickon swore, took the jar, and examined it. 'I'll swear it was full last night, my lord.'

'I'm not satisfied at all,' said Sir George. 'You disliked Glover, you had a supply of naphtha—'

'Beg pardon, sir,' said Tom Constable, hesitantly. 'But if you're thinking it was Dickon, you're wrong. When the bell

235

rang lauds, Dickon was in the lock-up at the Guildhall. Drunk and disorderly,' he added. 'I picked him up myself, just before compline.'

'Well, the law's the law,' said Dickon, recovering himself enough to grin, 'and I suppose that you'll be all for it, being part of it, as it were. And if a man steals, or kills, and he's taken by the sheriff or the constable, that's fair enough. But this hole and corner business, this betrayal for money, that's different.'

Martin said, 'It may be unsavoury, I agree. But—'

'Oh, there was more,' said Dickon. 'This Glover, he was – what can I call it? A Paul Pry, a man who liked to shove his finger into every pie. More than his finger, too, if you must know, as many of the married men with pretty young wives can tell you.'

'Oh?' said Clement, sitting up, his interest piqued by a topic close to his own heart. 'Men at the fair, was it?'

'Right here in the town, by what I heard.'

'Any names?'

Dickon shook his head. 'But that was the sort of man he was, Glover. Always after another man's money, or another man's wife, or just looking into another man's business.'

'And you would say that more than one man had cause to hate him?'

'I'd say that right enough, master.'

'But you don't know any of their names?' asked Clement again, a note of scepticism in his voice.

Dickon stared at him. 'Let's say I don't choose to know their names,' he said significantly.

Sir George seemed disposed to pursue this, but Tom Constable interrupted, saying, 'My man's here, sir, with the other one – that Dr Sylvester.'

'Simple clockwork, sirs,' said Sylvester, gesturing at the wooden head, 'just as you may see at Salisbury, and also at

Wells.' He pressed a catch, and the head slid open. Inside was a series of springs and wheels, one of the wheels being larger than the rest and having a curious shape. 'And the weights you see there move the wheel, the wheel drives the shaft upwards, which in turn moves the jaw down, opening the mouth. Now, when the shaft slips off the cam on the wheel, the spring – there – forces the jaw back up, and closes the mouth.'

'Here, though, what about the voice?' said Clement suddenly. 'You haven't told us how that is produced.'

'Haven't I?' The question came not from Sylvester, but from the head, causing Clement to step back suddenly and heavily on Martin's toes.

Sylvester laughed. 'It's another trick, your honours,' he said. 'Part of my act from the very start, before ever I bought old Rameses here. I used to make my voice come from a tree, or a dog, or pig, anything – to impress the country folk. But then I acquired the head here, and never looked back.'

'Very well,' said Sir George, 'that explains the head and what have you. The next thing is, what do you know of the murdered man, Glover?'

'Nothing, your honour,' said Sylvester emphatically. 'That is to say, I knew him by sight, we'd met at fairs and the like, as is only natural with us both being in that line, as you might say, travelling about the country.'

'Then why run away when you heard it was Glover who'd been killed?' asked Martin.

'Well, after that business last night . . .' and Sylvester left the rest unsaid.

Martin said, 'You mean because you – or Rameses – had threatened him? You thought you would come under suspicion?'

Sylvester nodded.

Sir George said, 'But you must have had some reason for threatening him in the first place?' And when Sylvester stared at the floor, Sir George went on, 'Here, Clement, put this fellow to the question.'

'Sir George?'

'Torture him, man. Find out what he knows.'

Sylvester held up a hand. 'I'll tell you the truth, Sir George. I was paid to say what I said, and that's the truth of it.'

'Paid? By whom?'

'I had finished my show, the night before last, and had gone into the town, to take a mug of ale. I had all but reached the alehouse when a man stopped me. I thought it was some footpad and made ready to run, when he says something like, "Would you like to earn a shilling?" He takes me on one side, and he tells me to threaten Glover, tell him that his crimes are known, and he'd better watch out. And that's just what I did.'

'And who was he?'

Sylvester hesitated. 'It was the mayor, sir. Master Hoskiss.'

'It's true,' said Hoskiss, with a groan. 'I was the one who paid this "Sylvester", as he calls himself, to threaten Glover. And I must say he did a remarkably good job of it, too,' he added, cheering up slightly. He recalled himself, and went on, 'But I assure you – I swear to you – I had nothing at all to do with Glover's murder.'

'Why the devil did you want to threaten him in the first place, though?' asked Sir George.

'If you must know, I found out that this Glover had been carrying on with my wife,' said Hoskiss between clenched teeth. 'But the threat was all; why should I kill him? Had I wanted to do that, I should not have threatened him.'

Sir George took Martin aside. 'Do you believe him?'

Martin considered the rotund and unheroic figure of the mayor. 'I cannot see him harming a big man like Glover.'

'I agree. Still, he knew something about him. What else does he know? Master Hoskiss,' he said in a louder tone, 'this

Glover – did you know anything of his business dealings?'

'I knew he was a damned scoundrel,' said Hoskiss bluntly. 'He'd been involved in some land dispute with Lord Edmund, for example. Of course, Edmund wouldn't stand any nonsense . . .'

'Oh, that business!' Edmund laughed out loud. 'Not a dispute as such, I assure you. There was a disputed inheritance, and I naturally took the place over. Then this rogue Glover came forward with some spurious claim, which he abandoned very rapidly once he saw how matters lay.'

'This Glover seems to have had a finger in a good many pies.' Sir George made it sound almost like a question, and looked at Edmund.

'That was how it seemed to me,' said Edmund drily. 'At the time of the dispute, I mean. I made some inquiries, found that this Glover was known as a man who had an eye to the main chance. Not a popular man, or that was the impression I formed,' he added.

Martin asked, 'My lord, since there had been bad blood between you and Glover, might he have felt awkward about approaching you with information?'

Edmund frowned. 'As to what?'

'Oh, the political situation, say.'

Another frown, 'It may be that he would feel disinclined to come to me. And to be plain, I have heard whispers, rumours that there is some unrest in the wind. Though when is there not?' He rubbed his chin, and repeated, half to himself, 'Unrest, if not outright rebellion.'

Sir George said, 'There is another possibility. Not civil unrest, but crime. That perhaps makes more sense, given Martin's connection with the court. But what crime could be worth ten pounds?'

'Well,' said Edmund, 'there's only one thing in the town

that might attract the attention of a thief, and perhaps be worth the sort of sum you've mentioned.' He shook his head. 'No. No, that's out of the question.'

'But what is it?' asked the others all together.

'Why, our crown.'

'The crown dates from before the time of Duke William,' said Hoskiss, as they crouched in the darkness of the Guildhall. 'Nobody knows who the king was, some say an Edward, some a Henry, some an unpronounceable old English name. Nor does anyone know how the crown came here, in the town, for this was never a royal capital as far as we know. But here it was, and it became part of our liberties and our prerogatives. William himself is said to have sanctioned our keeping it, and his successors have confirmed that privilege.' He fell silent, as there was a muffled but distinct sound nearby.

Sir George hissed in Martin's ear, 'There's three or four of them, so we're evenly matched. They're down in the cellar where the crown was, and ought to be discovering that it isn't there any longer just about now.' The crown had been moved secretly to Edmund's castle, earlier that day.

In fact they were obliged to wait a further half-hour before there was any sign of movement. Martin's eyes were more accustomed to the darkness now, and he could just make out a couple of shadowy figures moving along the corridor towards them. He heard one of the men make some bitter and scabrous remark about wasting time and labour, then the near-silence was broken by Sir George shouting, 'Now!' and then Martin more or less lost track of events. He did know that someone hit him in the face, hard; Martin never found out just who it was, but Clement's later boastful claim that he 'gave one of the rogues a bloody nose' seemed to Martin to be highly suggestive.

The blow knocked him to the ground, and for a while he

could not think of taking any active part in the struggle. As he was more or less recovering his wits, someone tripped over his legs, and landed heavily on top of him. Martin grabbed whoever it was, and was rewarded by hearing Clement's voice raised in reproof. 'Get off, clod!' hissed Martin, throwing his servant aside and clambering to his feet.

For a moment he stood there confused, for it was pitch dark. Someone struck flint and tinder, and Martin saw that the constable's men had taken the intruders. Martin recognised only their leader. It was Dickon, the fire-eater.

Dickon shook his head. 'I expect I'll hang for the theft, or the attempt,' he said, 'but not the murder! Why, I wouldn't let Glover near enough for him to know about it. As for my lads here, I suppose they'll hang with me; but none of them would betray me.'

Sir George snorted, 'Hang you will. So why not tell the truth?'

'Sir George, I think he is telling the truth,' said Martin. 'If I might have a private word with you?'

Standing outside Sylvester's tent, Martin said, 'Dickon and his companions had heard talk of this crown at the fair, tales of how valuable it was, and how it was locked away and never brought into the light of day. They probably only believed about half of those tales, but decided to have a look at the Guildhall anyway, see just how easy it might be to break in there.'

'That's why Dickon had himself arrested,' said Clement. 'To get a closer look inside the Guildhall.'

'But he didn't kill Glover,' Martin told Sylvester, casually.

'No?'

'No. You did.'

Sylvester laughed. 'Proof? You have proof of this nonsense?'

241

Martin said, almost absent-mindedly, 'It was the way the warning was given to Glover that made me suspicious. It was so direct, so first-hand. When you told me you had been paid, I still couldn't see why there was so much venom in it. A man doesn't get personally involved, not for money and nothing more.'

'Proof?' asked Sylvester again.

'Oh, I've no proof. Not of the murder. But there's the other matter – the prediction of Glover's death. There are plenty of witnesses, and any ecclesiastical court would burn you for witchcraft for that.'

Sylvester turned a sickly green. 'Wait, wait!' he said, as the constable's men started towards him. 'Better hang than burn! Very well, I did kill him.'

'Why?'

'My sympathies do not exactly lie with the king,' said Sylvester. 'Travelling round the country as I do, it's a simple matter to take a message from here to there, to help those I'm working for. Glover got wind of it, and he planned to betray me, but I got to him first. As simple as that. Are we ready?'

Cold Comfort

Catherine Aird

Scotland, 1563

S heriff Macmillan hadn't at first heard the sound of the approaching bagpipes but the hall-boy at Drummondreach had. Upon the instant the lad uncurled himself from the rush-strewn floor and reached for his own set of pipes, listening intently the while. He began to pump up the bag under his arm even as he scrambled to his feet, making ready to carry out his duty of first identifying and then heralding any new arrivals at the policies of Rhuaraidh Macmillan, sheriff of Fearnshire.

Cocking his ear in the direction of the distant pipes, the boy echoed his response with the preliminary notes of a lament. That sound, though, brought the sheriff to the entrance hall of his dwelling-place quickly enough even though the other bagpipe players were still a mile or more away.

'They're playing "The Fearnshire Lament", my lord,' said the boy, his own acute hearing demonstrating one of the many advantages of youth to the older man. 'I ken it well.'

'Aye,' said the sheriff crisply. 'I hear it quite clearly myself now.'

Rhuaraidh Macmillan stepped back more than a little thoughtfully while the hall-boy took up the bagpipes' chanter again and made to answer those heard from afar but as yet still unseen. The playing of that melancholy tune carried its own sad significance to the sheriff. It meant not only that those coming near approached in sorrow rather than in anger but that a man was untimely dead somewhere nearby and within his jurisdiction.

It meant more than just dead, of course.

That particular Lament told both Sheriff Macmillan and the hall-boy at Drummondreach that the death being announced by the playing of the dirge was of a known clansman. It was not some enemy or stranger of no consequence who was being thus sung. It told rather that a man had died from within the tight little circle which comprised the close-knit aristocracy of the Fearnshire clans.

'Who'll it be this time?' he pondered aloud. The sheriff's writ ran among clansmen all tied by generations of auld alliances and ancient fealties. Rumour had it that the new queen in Edinburgh – she who had lately come over from France – had referred to them as unruly tribes but that was not to understand their allegiances to the land and its people, both of which had been established in these northern parts for time out of mind.

'I think I can see them now, my lord,' said the boy.

And it must be said, the sheriff admitted fairly to himself, there were men around, too, who were locked together by equally ancient enmities. Memories in the Highlands were long and unforgiving. Perhaps this was what Her Majesty at Holyroodhouse had been told . . .

Perhaps, too, it was different over in France.

'There's three of them, my lord,' announced the hall-boy, peering out.

Sometimes, of course, the sheriff reminded himself as he scanned the horizon, the enmities were still red and raw, just like the scars on Murdo Ross's face. These were still livid from an altercation at Hogmanay with Black Ian – Ian Tulloch – of Eileanach. The man had drawn his dirk at Murdo Ross – kinsman and friend – over the delicate matter of which of the pair should at the turn of the year first-foot a certain young lady at Achnagarron . . . and Ian Tulloch hadn't been seen at Eileanch or anywhere else in Fearnshire from that day to this.

The pipes were calling to each other now like urgent vixens . . .

Moreover – and this was where the sheriff's responsibilities came in – that Lament also meant that the death was of a Fearnshire man who should not have died: that is to say he – whoever he was – had not died in his bed of a sore sickness or old age.

Thus, according to the old custom of the country, it therefore followed ineluctably that the sheriff of Fearnshire had duly to be told, and that he then had a duty to inquire, to inspect, to pronounce and – if it were then proved that the death had been unlawfully at the hand of another – to punish. What happened in France might well be different but this was Scotland and as far as Rhuaraidh Macmillan himself was concerned this was how things were going to stay, new queen or not.

The drone of the other pipes could be heard quite clearly now and soon a little gaggle of men hove into view hurrying down over the brae.

The hall-boy, keener-eyed of the two, took his lips off the chanter long enough to say, 'Angus Mackintosh of Balblair, my lord, and a Mackenzie . . .'

'Colin of that Ilk,' observed the sheriff without enthusiasm. The man was a troublemaker.

'And Merkland of Culbokie, Younger,' said the hall-boy, resuming his pipes.

Rhuaraidh Macmillan advanced towards the threshold and waited for the men to reach him, sniffing the air as he did so. It was a little warmer today and not before time. Spring, he decided, must really have come to the Highlands at long, long last – and that after one of the darkest, coldest winters in living memory. It was the same each year, though, he conceded to himself. He had always begun to doubt the return of warmer weather when suddenly, like the midges, it was upon them.

The drone of the pipes died away as the three visitors drew near. Colin Mackenzie stood forward as self-appointed spokesman, while Angus Mackintosh and young Hugh Merkland kept a pace or two behind him.

'We've found Black Ian,' announced the man Mackenzie breathlessly. 'Ian Tulloch.'

'Dead,' added Hugh Merkland.

'Long dead,' supplemented Angus Mackintosh.

'And Murdo Ross is away over to the west,' said Mackenzie, adding meaningfully, 'today.'

'Just as soon as he heard Black Ian had been found,' chimed in Angus.

Colin Mackenzie said, 'You'll no' have forgotten, sheriff, that it was Ian Tulloch that struck Murdo Ross.'

'I remember,' said the sheriff shortly. Striking any man was bad, striking a relative or friend much worse. Doing it with a weapon in the hand was never likely to be forgotten, still less forgiven. Even worse was the crime of following a man to his own dwelling-place and assaulting him there – otherwise known as hamesucken. And that was what Ian Tulloch had done.

'Murdo Ross was off like the de'il himself was chasing him,' contributed Hugh Merkland, 'as soon as he was told the news.'

'Perhaps the devil was chasing him,' said Mackintosh insouciantly. 'How can any man tell what Satan looks like?'

Merkland ignored this and went on eagerly, 'Will we be going after him for you, sheriff?'

'You will not,' said Rhuaraidh Macmillan firmly. 'You will be first telling me where you found Black Ian dead.'

'In a barn at Eileanach.'

'More bothy than barn,' put in Angus Mackintosh.

Merkland said, 'The men were taking the sheep up to the hills for the summer.'

Sheriff Macmillan nodded. The annual movement of the

sheep to the higher ground was a late spring ritual in Fearnshire. The French had a special word for it – *transhumance*; not that the new queen would be likely to know about it for all her regal French connections. Summer pasture for sheep would not be one of the concerns of her world . . . She had others, though, from all accounts. Mostly to do with the heart, he had heard.

'. . . and when they got up there the drovers tried to open up the place as usual but they couldna get in,' Merkland was saying.

'How did you know he was dead?' asked the sheriff.

There was a pause, while Mackenzie shifted from foot to foot. 'He was hanging from a beam.'

'We saw him through the cracks in the wood,' vouchsafed Colin Mackenzie. 'We couldna get in either, you see.'

'Dead long since with a bang-rape round his neck,' supplied Angus Mackintosh.

'Someone must have been after the hay,' said the sheriff. A bang-rape was a rope with a noose used by thieves for carrying off corn or hay. It would do fine for hanging a man, too.

'Maybe so, sheriff, but they didn't steal what hay was there,' said Angus Mackintosh. 'It's still strewn about in the bothy.'

'Ian's axe is there, too,' said Mackenzie. 'It's standing against the wall.'

'Nobody could get in to take it, you see,' contributed Hugh Merkland. 'The door was barred on the inside.' He waved a hand. 'It still is.'

'So why then did Murdo Ross go away to the west when he heard?' asked the sheriff, not unreasonably. For a man to take his own life in these parts was rare enough but a man who had harmed friend and family might well feel that he should. 'If the door had been barred on the inside by Ian Tulloch . . .'

Anyone, sighed the sheriff, who had reached man's estate could have told Black Ian that remorse was the most difficult

249

– in fact, the only intolerable – emotion with which to live.

There was an uncomfortable pause and an uneasy shuffling of feet as it became apparent that not one of the three wished to answer his question about Murdo Ross.

'Well?' demanded Rhuaraidh Macmillan.

Eventually Colin Mackenzie said uneasily, 'We couldna see anything there, sheriff, that Black Ian could have been standing on . . . before . . .'

'Nothing at all,' said Merkland.

'Not a thing.' Mackintosh of Balblair endorsed this. 'We looked.'

'Whoever had put him there must have taken it away with them,' said Hugh Merkland, adding, 'whatever it was.'

'I see,' said the sheriff.

'Now shall we go after Murdo Ross for you, sheriff?' said Merkland impatiently. 'He'll be well away by now.'

'No,' said Rhuaraidh Macmillan at once. 'You'll come with me back to Eileanach. First I must see the body.' Now *super visum corporis* was a phrase Her new Majesty at Edinburgh, a daughter of Mary of Guise or not, would surely understand. They said she was good at the Latin as well as at the French. It was her lack of comprehension of the Gaelic, indeed of nearly all matters Scottish, that was the worry . . .

Mounted on his palfrey, his clerk riding a little behind him, the sheriff led the party out towards the broad strath above which lay Ian Tulloch's lands. The journey took time. The bothy was far away up in the hills, alongside the route of one of the old coffin roads over to a clan burial ground, and already halfway to the west as it was.

His mount stumbled and slipped from time to time as it tried to pick its way over the bare stony track towards the rough building. What was possible for men on foot and hardy sheep was not so easy for a horse. Spring might have come to the lower-lying ground but higher up winter had only just left.

Rhuaraidh Macmillan could see that even higher there was still snow and ice lying on the side of the ben. On a north-facing hillside both could linger all summer.

'There, sheriff,' pointed Colin Mackenzie. 'You see yon bothy over there?'

'Aye,' agreed Macmillan, automatically noting that any footprints in the snow leading to the building were long gone. And so were any footprints in the snow leading away ... Equally, any marks made by footprints on the ground since the thaw would have been overlaid by those made more recently by men and sheep.

'Look, sheriff, through this gap here ...' Colin Mackenzie already had his eye to a crack in the door.

Rhuaraidh Macmillan reluctantly brought his horse to a standstill on the track. There would be those – and plenty – who would hold that Murdo Ross had been well within his rights in exacting his revenge on Ian Tulloch – if he had, that is – for raising his weapon against Murdo in anger let alone in jealousy; who would insist for all time that Black Ian had only received his just deserts for an attack on a life-long friend – to say nothing of one with blood-ties.

That, however, was not the law and the law must be served above anger and jealousy. This applied in Fearnshire if not any longer in Holyroodhouse in Edinburgh. Aye, there was the rub. Rhuaraidh Macmillan straightened himself up in the saddle. The difference was that he himself was responsible for the upholding of law and order in Fearnshire. Who exactly it was who was responsible for law and order and not anger and jealousy triumphing at the Scottish court today was not for him to say ...

The sheriff dismounted and, too, bent his eye – albeit unwillingly – to the crack in the wooden door of the bothy.

What the three men had told him was true. Swinging from a high beam without handholds to reach it was a body. That it

251

was of Ian Tulloch he was in no doubt. 'Black' might have been how the man had been known in his lifetime: it was assuredly an accurate description of how he now looked many weeks after his death.

The sheriff's gaze travelled down from the suspended body to the floor. What the men had told him about that was true, too. There was nothing at all there which Black Ian could have climbed on to and kicked aside to drop to his death. All that was visible was a large damp puddle on the floor, surely greater by far than could have come from the body above. He put his shoulder to the door of the bothy and found as the others had done that the entrance was still firmly barred against them.

'Shall we batter the door down, sheriff?' asked Hugh Merkland, always a man of action rather than thought.

'No,' said Rhuaraidh Macmillan sternly. 'Wait you all over there while I take a look around.'

He walked slowly and carefully round the outside of the bothy. Ramshackle it might be but it was still proof against the elements and animals. Deer would not have been able to get in there any more than the four men could. The primitive building had never boasted windows or a chimney.

'Murdo Ross'll be away over the hills by nightfall,' murmured Merkland restively. 'We'll no' catch him now.'

'And Black Ian didn't have any other enemies,' said Colin Mackenzie with emphasis. 'None at all.'

'Och, one enemy's enough for any man,' put in Angus Mackintosh of Balblair, stroking his chin sagely. 'Isn't it, now?'

'Black Ian was his own worst enemy,' said the sheriff, stepping back to examine the roof. 'He didn't need others. You all know that.'

'Aye, that's true,' conceded Colin Mackenzie, nodding. 'The man should never have taken cold steel to a kinsman right

252

enough . . . What is it that you're seeing on the roof, sheriff?'

'Nothing,' replied that official with perfect truth. 'It's quite sound.'

'It would need to be up here,' observed Angus Mackintosh, looking round the bleak countryside. 'If the wind had once got under it, yon roof would be away up over Beinn nan Eun in no time at all.'

'Or down in the loch,' said Merkland.

Colin Mackenzie pointed down the hill. 'It's a wonder Black Ian didn't just jump into Loch Bealach Culaidh there – if he had a mind to make away with himself, that is.'

'It's hard to drown if you're a swimmer,' remarked the sheriff.

'It's hard to hang yourself from a high beam without having anything to hold on to or stand on to get you there,' said Hugh Merkland. 'I still think we should be away after Murdo Ross.'

'No,' said the sheriff quietly. 'Tell me, is that Ian Tulloch's own axe I saw in there?'

'It is,' said Mackenzie.

'Ah . . .'

'Man,' exploded Merkland, 'you dinna need an axe to hang yoursel'.'

'Ian Tulloch did,' murmured the sheriff.

'But . . .' Merkland's eyebrows came together in a ferocious frown.

'He couldn't have done what he did without an axe,' said the sheriff. 'Or something like it.'

'But it's rope you need to hang yoursel',' protested Colin Mackenzie. 'We all know that.'

'Mind you,' said Ruaraidh Macmillan, 'I'm not saying that Black Ian didn't need the rope as well as his axe.'

'But . . .' Hugh Merkland began his objection in turn.

The sheriff said, 'He needed the rope afterwards.'

'Afterwards?' echoed Merkland.

253

'After he had used the axe . . .'

'But . . .' began Colin Mackenzie.

'. . . and the rope together,' said the sheriff.

'I still don't understand,' said Colin Mackenzie.

'Neither did Murdo Ross,' said the sheriff, 'and that's why he's away to the west in such a hurry.' Rhuaraidh Macmillan gave the door of the bothy another great shake. 'It's barred right enough and by my reckoning it was Ian Tulloch himself that put the bar on the inside there.'

'And, so,' demanded Colin Mackenzie truculently, 'how did he get himself high enough to hang himself from that beam without anything to stand on?'

'Ah,' said the sheriff neatly, 'he did have something to stand on.'

'But there's nothing there,' said Colin Mackenzie. 'Nothing at all.'

'There's nothing there now,' said the sheriff patiently. 'There was something there that he could stand on at the time.'

'That's taken itself away?' growled Colin Mackenzie derisively.

'In a manner of speaking, yes,' replied the sheriff. 'But it was brought there by Ian Tulloch himself using the bang-rape and his axe.'

Colin Mackenzie drew himself up and said with dignity, 'I'm thinking that you are for making fools of us, sheriff.'

'Is it the Little People we're going to have to thank for killing Black Ian, then?' chimed in Hugh Merkland scornfully.

Angus Mackintosh asked instead, 'What is there, then, sheriff, that Black Ian could have brought here with an axe and a noose that's gone away on its own after he used it?'

'A block of ice,' said Rhuaraidh Macmillan, pointing to where some still lay unmelted further up the hillside. 'Now will you be away all of you and find Murdo Ross and tell him to come back?'

A Gift to the Bridegroom

Judith Cook

London, 1594

Dr Simon Forman sat in the handsome study of his Lambeth house, which doubled as a consulting room, and wished he had never been born. As he had on many previous occasions, he again swore to give up drink and women. What had begun as a pleasant cup of wine in the Anchor Inn with his actor friend, Thomas Pope, had turned into a long-drawn-out evening with half a dozen other players from the Rose Theatre who had somehow persuaded him, after Tom had gone home to his wife and bed, to accompany them to a house of ill-repute in Seething Lane. Here he had drunk even more wine, of a quality fit only for pickling herrings, after which the rest of the night passed in a haze. At dawn he had been shaken awake by a dark-haired whore demanding two shillings for her services, which he had paid with some reluctance since he was unable to recall if she deserved such an extravagant sum or even if he had availed himself of her at all.

Now, with a head feeling as if it were bound in ever-tightening bands of iron, he was faced with having to dispense medicine and advice to a steady stream of those seeking his services, most of whom were needing linctuses, balsams and such for the usual crop of rheums and chest conditions exacerbated by a wet, cold February. His housekeeper, Anna, had just shown in the last patient, a woman carrying a howling child with an abscess which required lancing, when a man pushed past, thrust the woman aside and planted himself in front of Simon's desk.

'So you're Dr Forman?' he demanded.

'I am,' replied Simon, looking up at him, 'and as you will see, sir, I am busy with a patient so if you'll show rather more courtesy and sit outside in my hall, I'll attend to you as soon as I can.'

His unwelcome visitor was expensively dressed and looked to be in his forties while his face, though still handsome, showed all the signs of over-indulgence. At this present instant it was dark with temper. 'Do you know who I am?' he bellowed. When Simon showed no sign of wanting to find out, he continued regardless. 'My name is Broughton, Sir Arthur Broughton, knight baronet.' Simon still said nothing. 'Does it mean nothing to you? The fortune I made on my last venture to the Indies has made me one of the most talked-about men in London as well as the richest. The queen herself conferred my baronetcy on me.'

Simon stood up. The child was now hiccuping as the mother tried to soothe it. 'Then you will have no problem finding another doctor, Sir Arthur. Indeed I wonder why you bothered to seek out so undistinguished a practitioner as myself. Now, if you will leave us I will get on with the business in hand and lance this child's abscess.'

To his surprise, Sir Arthur hesitated. 'Very well then,' he barked. 'I'll wait outside. But please to remember I am an extremely busy man.'

The abscess lanced, the wound treated with a salve and the child given a sweetmeat for his bravery, Simon showed the woman to his door and was somewhat surprised to discover Sir Arthur was still there. Simon held the door open, ushered him in and offered him a chair. 'Now, sir, what can I do for you?'

The answer surprised him. 'It's not for myself that I am seeking advice. It's for my wife.'

'Is the lady here too, then?' enquired Simon.

'She is not. She's at home at our country house near Chelsea.'

'And the problem?'

'She is weakly. Always whining at me. Worst of all, so far she has not given me an heir in spite of my constant efforts. Only one girl and the rest but shifts,' he added, using the old word for a miscarriage. 'Also, I have fears that she is becoming demented.'

Simon was at a loss. 'So how can I help in this matter?'

'I need some medicine that will strengthen her. I have the services of an excellent apothecary nearby but she refuses to take any of his draughts any more. Says they make her worse. Indeed she has gone so far as to claim they are poisoned. I told you I fear she's running mad.' He stood up and began to pace about. 'She's of a good family with some influence but little money. It seemed an ideal match since I have wealth and they can assist in my preferment: I'm am ambitious man and would climb higher. All Jennifer has given me is a girl and I must have a boy to inherit my estates, preferably more than one.'

'If I could ensure you or anyone else a son and heir,' remarked Simon with some irony, 'I'd be richer by far than you are. I'm not sure I wouldn't be the richest man in the realm. If you have come to me for a draught to bring this about then I must disappoint you. As to the shifts . . . that, unhappily, is all too common and I have little advice to offer other than she take the greatest care.'

'But you can't surely refuse to give me a strengthening remedy,' returned Sir Arthur. 'If you package it and seal it, then at least she might be prepared to take it, coming as it does from a physician.'

'I will give you such a draught,' Simon told him, 'but in order to do so I must see your wife myself so that I can judge both the cause of the weakness and the best course of treatment. If she is too poorly to come to me, then I am quite happy to visit her. It seems you can afford it!'

The knight prepared to take his leave. 'Very well. Will tomorrow suit you?' Simon informed him that it would. 'There's one more thing ... are you, by any chance, able to obtain candied sea holly?'

'Eringo?' said Simon in some surprise. 'From what you claim I would hardly think you in need of a powerful aphrodisiac.'

Sir Arthur smiled. 'In other circumstances it might be interesting to experiment with it. But I was rather thinking of my wife. Since her last mishap she has refused me any congress with her. Such a sweetmeat might well change her mind.'

'I have no experience whatsoever of its effects on women,' said Simon, showing him firmly towards the outside door. 'It might even be dangerous. As matters stand, I would suggest you allow your wife to regain her health and strength and then let nature take its course.'

The weather had improved somewhat the next day as Simon rode across London Bridge, accompanied by his man John Bradedge. He had taken him and his pregnant Dutch wife in after finding them sitting destitute by the roadside after John had been discharged from the army in the Low Countries. He now wondered how ever he would manage without Anna's splendid housekeeping and as for John, he had repaid Simon by saving his life during one of what he described as 'the doctor's mad ventures'.

Sir Arthur's country house was a substantial timbered mansion, set in parkland close to the Thames. Building work was going on to add a new wing. The inside also spoke loudly of wealth, with fine tapestries on the walls, carved sideboards laden with silver and hosts of busy servants. Sir Arthur greeted Simon himself and showed him at once to the chamber where his wife lay on a daybed. Simon looked at the lady with no little

260

surprise as for some reason he had imagined an unattractive, pallid invalid near to Sir Arthur's age; pale, she was, but Sir Arthur had given no hint that she was both young and beautiful.

He looked at his wife with irritation. 'Well, Jennifer, since you won't take either my advice or that of the apothecary, I've brought Dr Forman here from Lambeth to see you. Perhaps he'll be able to get you off your sickbed, rid your mind of your mad fancies and give me a boy into the bargain.'

'I'd like to speak to your wife alone, Sir Arthur,' said Simon, seeing her expression. 'That is, accompanied by her maid, of course. Women often confide health matters to their doctors that they prefer not to discuss even with their husbands.'

She smiled. 'Thank you, Dr Forman. Call Mary, will you, Arthur?'

He did as she asked, looking far from pleased. 'I'll leave you then,' he told them, as a plump, middle-aged woman appeared. 'I trust I'll find it's been worth the time and money.'

Simon sat beside the couch on which his patient lay, took her pulse, then asked her to tell him how she had been brought to her present condition.

'I wasn't always as you see me,' she replied. 'Indeed, I had quite robust health and a deal more spirit'. She sighed. 'Our daughter Alice was born just nine months after our wedding day, since when I have lost four other babies, well before birth. Scarcely have I had time to recover before Arthur is demanding I try again and each time I become weaker.'

'That she has, poor lamb,' broke in the maid. 'He's no more thought than a beast and it's not as if he hadn't interests elsewhere.'

'That'll do, Mary,' declared Lady Jennifer. 'He has insisted too that I be bled regularly though heaven knows in the circumstances it hardly seems necessary even though I know you doctors swear by it.'

'Not me,' Simon assured her, 'particularly in a case like

261

yours. Now, I also understand you are refusing medicines.'

'Not all medicines. Just the potions made up by my husband's apothecary, a man who's little better than his creature. They have made me vomit, given me stomach pains and, on occasion, made me confused in my mind. Now Arthur is saying I am mad and if my fancies continue then I will have to be confined in a dark room. You see, Dr Forman, and I beg you not to let my husband know I've spoken to you of this, I fear I'm being poisoned. Like his first wife.' Seeing his startled face, she added, 'I wager he's not told you this is his second marriage?'

'No,' replied Simon, thoughtfully, 'no, he did not.' He turned to the maid. 'Do you know anything of this?'

'Only what I've heard since my lady and I came here. The other one was rich, that was the basis of his fortune. She was a good bit older than him but he seemed happy enough at first, once he'd got his hands on her money. Two years after the wedding she'd a stillborn child, a year later another; after that nothing. Then, of a sudden she was struck ill. There was talk at the time about how such a big, robust woman just wasted away.'

'As have I these last months,' Lady Jennifer added.

Simon had to admit to himself that at the very least it seemed a strange coincidence but said, bracingly, 'Well, now, let's see what we can do to make you feel better. I've brought various herbs and suchlike with me and to set your mind at rest I will mix you a medicine here in your presence so that you know exactly what I am giving you. I will also come back in a week and see how you are mending.' He turned to the maid. 'In the meantime make sure she doesn't take anything of the apothecary's making. I'm not saying that there is something in his remedies which shouldn't be there – it could be no more than the fact that the particular draughts he made up for her do not suit her present condition. As to the more immediate problem of your husband's desire for a child, Lady Jennifer, I will try my best to persuade him that he has far more chance of an heir if he leaves you time to recover properly.'

'What are you giving me?' she asked as he produced a tiny balance from his bag and began weighing out various aromatic dried leaves.

'Sweet herbs – borage, fumitory, hyssop, rosemary and winter savory.' He took a bottle from the bag. 'This is a distillation of cloves, figs, saffron and white sugar simmered in white wine.' Carefully, he took pinches of the herbs and put them in the bottle, then shook it. 'Take a small spoonful three times a day, without fail. You'll find it quite agreeable. You must also take regular sustaining nourishment if you are to grow strong: a thick potage of meat and parsley is good for the heart, as is warm milk with brandy. As soon as you feel fit, then take some gentle exercise.' He sighed. 'I fear convincing your husband that he should care for you better will be a harder task. He went so far as to suggest you should be given some eringo.'

'What is that?' she enquired.

'Sea holly. It's been much vaunted of late as a powerful aphrodisiac, though I am by no means sure it works other than by suggestion. But I have never heard of its being prescribed for women.'

'Sea holly? That's the prickly stuff with a pretty blue flower that grows on beaches, isn't it?' she returned. 'It must be diffi-cult to collect. But the leaves are sharp. How are they used?'

'It's the root that is used, not the leaves. It looks rather like a very big parsnip. It is cooked and then candied with sugar. It's now in such demand that it is being grown in fields in the eastern counties and so is quite easy to come by.'

After watching Jennifer take the first dose of his medicine, Simon bade her farewell and went in search of her husband. Sir Arthur listened to his report on his wife's condition with growing impatience. 'Very well,' he growled, at length, 'I'll give you a fortnight to see if she improves and stops prattling on about poison. As to leaving her be in other ways, she's my wife and has her duties and I'm her husband and have my rights.'

'Indeed you have,' Simon agreed, 'but there seems little point in impregnating her while she is still so weak that she cannot carry.' He paused. 'I understand your first wife had similar trouble.'

'Maud was older,' he barked, 'and an heir less likely. I can't see what that has to do with anything.'

'Only that she, too, appears to have wasted away and could not give you a child. Might it not be possible that the fault lies in you rather than the women?'

'Are you doubting my virility?' roared Sir Arthur.

'Not at all,' Simon reassured him, 'but recall, if you will, the problems faced by the queen's late father, Henry VIII. He had six wives and, from them all, but two girls and a sickly boy.' Also the French pox, he thought to himself, but did not say.

'Do you think he is trying to rid himself of her?' asked John as the two men rode back together towards the city.

'I'm not sure,' Simon admitted. 'I believe he's capable of it and it strikes a cold chill when you hear what happened to wife number one. But then the lady is very weak and childbirth and shifts often put strange fancies into women's heads. Certainly she is far from well and needs care and nourishment.'

'While you were with the lady, I was well entertained in the kitchen,' his servant informed him. 'They say Sir Arthur's eyes are already looking elsewhere, that he frequently visits a stout young widow who lives not far away who gave her late husband two healthy lads and is related to the Cecils to boot. I would think it well the present lady watches her back.'

'You make him sound like a villain from the playhouse,' laughed Tom Pope when Simon had finished telling him of the beautiful invalid in Chelsea, 'with a closet full of the skeletons of past wives. How does he do it? Do they kiss poisoned pictures or the skulls of past lovers? Or is the potion secreted in a ring? As you know, these are regular tools of the trade in drama but rarely, I imagine, in real life!'

'Possibly it does sound a trifle far-fetched,' agreed Simon. 'But the symptoms suffered by wife two do sound, from what we heard, very similar to those of wife one. Just suppose he *is* poisoning them. One wonders how many wives he could get through, each one bringing him money and position, before folk found it a trifle odd.'

Tom shook his head. 'I imagine there would eventually be a shortage of women prepared to take the risk. What was it the Princess of France wrote to old King Harry? That she'd be happy to become his wife except for the fact that she had only the one neck! But surely if this lady provides him with his heir, then she should be safe.'

'I'm beginning to wonder if she or any other can give him a living son. You talk of the late king and as it happens I drew Broughton's attention to the fact that even with six wives, he had only one son who survived birth and him dead at sixteen years old. Though I would not say it outside these four walls, I am as certain as I can be that none of King Henry's wives were at fault, not even poor Queen Catherine who bore him seven or eight stillborn or sickly children. It was the king himself who was to blame, for contracting the pox.'

Riding up the drive to the Broughtons' Chelsea house a week later he was pleasantly surprised to find Lady Jennifer taking a turn outside on the terrace. She greeted him with a smile. Though still thin and somewhat wasted, she certainly looked a great deal better and her face now was full of life. She was dressed in a fine gown of plum-coloured velvet which went well with her black hair. Such hair colour, matched with blue eyes, was most striking and Simon wondered if she had Irish or Scottish blood in her.

'You will take wine with me, Dr Forman?' she enquired as they went indoors. 'As you see, your remedy has proved effective. And I have done as I was told and taken much nourishing broth and other good food. Mary guards my medicine bottle like a dragon to see no one comes near it and I have refused all the preparations from the apothecary on the grounds that you have warned me against taking anything other than what you have prescribed for fear of one draught acting against the other.'

'Sir Arthur is pleased, then?' He looked around as he spoke.

'You can speak freely. He isn't here. He has gone over to Morpeth Hall, a-wooing, I imagine. Well, if I leave this sad world soon, Millie Raynsford will fast console him and she has proved she can breed boys.'

Simon let this pass. 'Surely he is pleased with your progress?'

She shrugged. 'He's tired of me, and of my still refusing him my bed. He keeps on telling me what I already know: that he is one of eight born scarce a year apart, yet his mother suffered no ill from it. Indeed, she's still alive and close to eighty.'

After he had drunk his wine, he felt her pulse again, looked at her eyes and felt her forehead. 'The fever certainly has gone but you need more flesh on you. Since you stopped taking the apothecary's brews, you have had no more strange symptoms?'

She shook her head. 'No pains or sickness. Tell me truly, do you think me mad? Suffering from delusions? You can see how much better I am for refusing the medicines Arthur gave me. Why should that be if they were not poisoned?'

'They might simply have disagreed with you. Surely if there had been poison in them, we would not be sitting here discussing it.'

She was unconvinced. 'Could it not be that he was feeding it to me little by little so that it would look as if my illness was entirely due to my miscarrying?' A shadow crossed her face. 'I am still fearful he will contrive to have me put away as a madwoman, after which it would be quite easy for him to be rid of me for good.' She leaned forward and clutched his arm. 'Promise me, Dr Forman – Simon – that if you hear of such a thing you will come here at once and demand to see me. Or, indeed, if you learn I am suddenly again at death's door.'

He reassured her as best he could. 'I promise I will do what I can. Send for me if you are worried and I will come at once. As to poison, if you are still worried then the remedy is in your own hands: do not take any other medicines.'

'But supposing he put it into my food,' she persisted, 'what might he use that I should look for?'

Sweet Jesu, thought Simon, perhaps she really is becoming demented, but possibly it was best to humour her. 'There are many poisons, some from base metals, others from plants such as monkshood and digitalis. Monkshood would have a hot taste, which you would surely notice unless the food were very highly spiced. Digitalis is more easily disguised, especially in sweet foods. I prescribe it in small quantities to slow down a racing heart but in larger amounts it will slow the heart for good! Truly, though, Lady Jennifer, I beg you will put such morbid thoughts out of your mind and concentrate on becoming well again.'

She still seemed dissatisfied but her next remark surprised him. 'It is months since I went to the playhouse. If I continue feeling better, then I am determined Mary and I shall go to town to see a play. Arthur isn't interested and is out so much either about his business affairs or flirting with Mistress Raynsford that there should be no hindrance.'

'If you can give me warning of that too, then I will be most happy to escort you,' Simon told her. 'I hear Burbage is to play the part of crookbacked King Richard again at the Curtain next month. You should see that. It is a mighty performance.'

He was so busy over the next little while that he was unable to give the matter much further thought, for as the cases of winter sickness diminished, so visits from those seeking horoscope castings increased, merchant venturers requiring forecasts as to how their forthcoming argosies would fare, seamen's wives wanting to know if their husbands would survive a voyage. Young husbands enquired if their brides were likely to be faithful to them, older married men if their wives still were, while giggling girls, in twos and threes, demanded to know if they would find the lover of their dreams. Better weather meant more performances at the playhouses and he was also much patronised by players wanting one of his special draughts for the voice. Then, one morning, a note was delivered to him from Lady Jennifer to say that she and Mary would be attending the forthcoming performance of *Richard III* at the Curtain and had been recommended to the White Hart as a suitably respectable establishment in which two ladies might take midday dinner. Would he care to join them? If so, as the performance was due to begin at two o'clock, perhaps he could meet them at noon? There was no need for a reply. If he did not arrive then she would understand he had more pressing matters in hand.

He found the two women snug in a private room. The change in Lady Jennifer was remarkable and he noticed with satisfaction that she ate her pigeon pie with relish and chattered in a lively way as they made their way to the theatre. The performance of Burbage in the role of King Richard was, as he had promised her, an event to remember. By the time they left the theatre it was dark, indeed the last acts had been played by the light of torches, giving an even more eerie atmosphere to the appearance of the ghosts to the king before the battle of Bosworth Field.

'It was just as you said it would be,' Lady Jennifer told

him, her face aglow. 'What a monster!'

'Aye,' Mary agreed, 'and the way he wooed that Lady Anne, right across her husband's coffin. Then treated her so shamefully that she died.'

Lady Jennifer shuddered. 'And would have married again before she was scarce coffined. She had her revenge from the grave, however, when her ghost visited him before the battle and pronounced: "Despair and die!" '

Simon enquired if they were proposing to return to Chelsea that night, but it seemed they were not. Anticipating how late the performance would end, they had arranged to remain at the inn until the morning, uneasy at the prospect of travelling into the country with only the driver of the carriage for protection.

'Do you need any more medicine?' he asked Jennifer as he took his leave.

'I will take another phial with me, if I may,' she told him, 'though my strength is returning by the day.'

'Then I'll deliver it to you in the morning,' Simon assured her, 'along with a tonic that I also prescribe which might assist your recovery further.'

The next morning he arrived at the inn with the phials of medicine. It was Mary who came down to him. Her ladyship had been tired after her first expedition outside for such a long time, she said, but she sent her kind regards, thanked him most sincerely for all he had done for her and for escorting them to the play and had given Mary sufficient money to cover the cost of the medicines and his trouble. The maid then handed him five guineas; Lady Jennifer had indeed been generous.

'I am delighted to see her looking so much better,' said Simon. 'I do believe most of the trouble was caused by her having conceived too frequently. I don't really think she was poisoned, do you?'

Mary looked thoughtful. 'She was ever wilful, as I know,

269

for I was her nurse. And playacting! She could take her place beside that Master Burbage, were women allowed to take to the stage. I think you're probably right, though; the apothecary's draughts did disagree with her. But whether she really believed she was being poisoned or pretended so to further annoy Sir Arthur, your guess is as good as mine.'

It was to be months before he was involved with the Broughtons again, months which had taken him to the wild Borders of Scotland on a mission which had nearly cost him his life. It took some time for him to discover all that had happened in his absence and when he finally came to sift through the letters and messages left for him, he found a note from Lady Jennifer asking him to attend on her when it was convenient.

'I trust we're going to find the lady fully restored to health,' he declared to John as once again they took the road to Chelsea. 'Possibly even some months forward with child if she continued to gain in strength.'

The shock, when it came, therefore, was all the greater. It was obvious that some festive event was due to take place for there were garlands in the large hall into which he was shown and much activity among the servants. He sent in his name and asked first, out of courtesy, to speak to Sir Arthur. A few minutes later the steward appeared and told him that the master would be with him shortly.

'Please do not trouble him if he's busy,' said Simon, looking round at the decorated hall. 'I see you are in the midst of some entertainment or other, and it's Lady Broughton I've come to see.'

The man's face showed blank astonishment. 'You have not heard, then?'

'I've heard nothing,' Simon told him. 'I've but recently returned from Scotland and only now discovered her letter asking me to call on her. I trust she is still well?'

'Lady Jennifer sadly died nearly three months back,' the steward informed him with a grave face. 'The – er – festivities you mention are for the master. He is about to marry again.'

Simon's blood ran cold. 'She's *dead*? Lady Jennifer is actually dead? But when I last saw her she was vastly improved.'

At this point Sir Arthur came into the hall. 'I am sorry you have come such a long way to hear such news, Dr Forman.' Compared to his behaviour before, the baronet was certainly in a more amenable frame of mind. He motioned Simon into a fine sitting room, offered him a chair and poured him a glass of claret. 'Yes, poor Jennifer, she died some three months back. I imagine you, like many more, look askance at my marrying again so soon. But Mistress Raynsford and I are . . . old friends and little Alice needs a mother.'

Simon still found the news hard to take in. 'So tell me, Sir Arthur, what ailed Lady Broughton? Did she miscarry again and this time bleed to death? Or did she suffer once more from stomach pains and sickness?'

'It was neither,' Sir Arthur declared. 'It was the plague.'

'But there's been so little pestilence this year,' said Simon, puzzled.

'She had gone into Kent to visit her cousin, Lady Elizabeth Fellows. It is thought the disease was brought into Dover by ship. Its onset and progress was so quick that by the time the message saying she was mortally sick reached me, and I had taken horse to ride to her, she was dead and buried. You, above all, know how fast this has to be done in such cases.'

'And her maid, Mary? Did she take the sickness too?'

Sir Arthur frowned. 'I'm told not. I was somewhat surprised to discover that she left Lady Elizabeth immediately after my wife's funeral and we have seen nothing of her here since. But then, she had known Jennifer since childhood and so perhaps

271

was too prostrated with grief to return. But be assured, Dr Forman, all was well between Jennifer and me when she left for Kent and on her deathbed she wrote the sweetest of letters declaring that I must marry again. She even went so far as to send me this,' he picked up a small package, 'which must only be opened on my wedding night. See for yourself,' and he took a letter from the table and handed it to Simon.

' "Dearest Arthur," ' Simon read, ' "I fear I have made a poor wife to you with my sickness and lack of ability to give you the son you so badly want. Now, my doctor here tells me that you will not be troubled with me long, for he fears I have the pestilence. My most ardent wish is that you remarry and I hope and trust that your new wife will give you not only comfort and support but also a brace of fine boys. I send a small token of my love – a gift to the bridegroom, to be opened on your wedding night. Your loving wife, Jennifer." '

'Do you know what it is?' asked Simon.

Sir Arthur shook his head. 'I have done as she asked and I will not open it until tomorrow night.'

The news of Sir Arthur's acute sickness the morning after his wedding was brought to Simon by a sweating groom. 'He is attended by his own physician but begs that you should come as well.' Simon took horse at once and both men rode out to Chelsea as fast as was practicable, but they were too late. Sir Arthur was already dead, his new wife howling beside the bed.

'What brought this about?' Simon asked the doctor who was trying to comfort her. 'I saw him but two days ago and he was in perfect health.'

The physician shook his head. 'It is a mystery to me also. I understand the wedding went off well; Sir Arthur ate and drank plentifully but not to excess. The couple were bedded, as is customary, and he was in high good spirits. Then, in the night, he was taken sick, complaining of numbness in the limbs and difficulty with breathing. When I arrived I found his pulse very slow and eventually the heart ceased altogether.'

The third – and last – Lady Broughton had little to add. Yes, they had been bedded and then Arthur remembered the gift from his late wife. The wrapping removed, it turned out to be an exquisitely carved cedarwood box inside which was a whitish sweetmeat, smothered in sugar. 'He laughed when he saw it. "Good for Jennifer!" he said. He told me it was candied sea holly and he'd been told it provoked venery (though I swear he needed little provoking), and also made strong semen for the procreation of children. And now he's gone – and me but two days married!' At least, thought Simon, as he left her sobbing noisily, she would be well compensated with only herself and Alice to inherit Broughton's vast estates.

He rode home, his mind in turmoil. Was it chance or had Jennifer Broughton, like Queen Anne in the play, cursed her husband from the grave? Had she, out of revenge, sent him poisoned sea holly? Most uneasy in his mind, a few days later he rode down to Kent and introduced himself to Lady Elizabeth Fellows in her fine house in a village near Canterbury, explaining how Lady Broughton had been his patient and how sad he was to hear of her death. 'Nursing her here, you must have been fearful the disease would spread to your family.'

'As matters turned out, we were not called upon to do so, for which the Lord be thanked,' Lady Elizabeth told him. 'She and Mary had gone to Dover to meet with an old friend and were to remain overnight. We took little heed when she did not return the next day, then a groom came from an inn with the terrible news. She had died within hours of the onset of the plague.' She became tearful. 'I could not even bid her a proper farewell, for her coffin was already nailed down for fear of infection. At least we saw to it that she was buried with all the proper rites. Her grave is nearby in the churchyard. Would you like to see it?'

A cool autumn breeze was blowing as they made their way to the small church. It was a fine, sunny day and all around the trees were turning to gold and bronze. A simple headstone marked the spot where Jennifer Broughton, aged twenty-five, wife of Sir Arthur Broughton, baronet, and mother of Alice, had been laid to rest.

'We told Mary she was most welcome to stay with us, but she said she preferred not. She was devoted to Jennifer but took her death with great fortitude.'

'And there were no more cases of plague in this part of Kent?' enquired Simon, somewhat surprised.

'No,' replied Elizabeth, 'we were fortunate. It seems that a single sailor brought it with him and passed it on to his whore, poor girl. She had no such fine burial but was tumbled post haste into some pauper's grave.'

Simon declined her offer to dine with the family and stood for some time looking at the legend on the simple headstone. An awful notion had crept into his mind. How easy it was to get to France from Dover if one wished to leave England in a hurry ... He looked at the mound again. Surely not ... He shook his head, shrugged and went to find his horse. What he needed to set him right was a pleasant supper and some good wine in a fine inn. He would simply refuse to conjecture any more as to just who might really be in the coffin under the green mound in the churchyard.

A Matter of Flesh and Blood

Gavin Newman

Stratford-upon-Avon, 1602

Hidden, fearful eyes monitored the progress of the rider in the gathering dusk. Past the chapel, through the deserted market, a tall figure hunched in the saddle of a sweat-streaked black stallion. Pallid cadaverous features stark in the shadow of his wide-brimmed hat, deep sunken eyes that flicked from side to side, missing nothing.

In spite of the heat, he wore a long black coat and open breeches. The horse slowed, maybe sensing that they had finally reached their destination and there would be a stable with a bucket of water to slake its thirst. Its tail flicked continually at a swarm of flies; there were flies everywhere, as if they anticipated a feast on gently swinging corpses, remembering this horseman from a previous visit and knowing what would follow.

'*The witchfinder is here.*' A whisper that came from behind windows and doors in unison; seemed to hang in the stillness of a sultry summer evening.

A scavenging cur slunk down the deserted street, tail curled between its legs. It, too, scented death in the air.

There was silence except for the steady clip-clop of the horse's hooves.

Constable Symes stood watching from the gaol steps, a bulky figure clad in an embroidered scarlet coat which matched his canions and nether socks. His florid face seemed to have paled, though it might have been a trick of the fading light. He licked his thick lips; even he was ill at ease.

The approaching horseman reined in before him, head uplifted, those gimlet eyes fixing him with a cold stare.

'You have the wench, constable?' The thin lips scarcely seemed to move, the words crackling like a thunderstorm over the distant Welcombe Hills.

'Aye, sir.' Symes's voice trembled. 'She is in the cell, awaiting you.'

'Take me to her.' The witchfinder dismounted with surprising agility, straightened up, tall and terrible to behold in the encroaching night.

Elida, none knew her family name, was no more than sixteen or seventeen years of age, a scrawny figure in ragged filthy clothing, cowering in a corner of the ill-lit, stinking cell. Washed and better dressed, her straggling hair trimmed, she would have been attractive to the opposite sex. She whimpered softly.

'A witch!' Luke Jeffries, the witchfinder, let out his pent-up breath as he pronounced judgement. 'One of many, undoubtedly, a coven who steal babes to sacrifice to their master, Lucifer. And when they have done with their vile ritual, they roast and feast on the infant flesh, believing that it will give them immortality.' He gave a harsh laugh. 'That fallacy I will soon dispel as a warning to others who might follow them into cannibalism. Wench,' he thrust his face close to Elida's, 'tell me the names of these other witches. In return, your death shall be quick, hanged instead of burned!'

The girl gasped her terror aloud. 'Sire, I am no witch. I know no witches. My baby was stolen, I have not seen her since. Please, find my baby.'

'You will talk before you die.' Jeffries glanced at the various implements that had been laid out on a bench opposite, the constable having anticipated his needs. A pair of calipers that could grip and extract fingernails, a thumbscrew that was operated with a minimum of effort to effect maximum pain, tinderboxes and tapers to singe living flesh or burn off body hair. And a cylindrical length of iron with vicious spikes for use on stubborn females when all the other means had failed to produce the required information.

'Give me names and the end will be easier for you.' He threw her rotting dress up around her waist, noted how she pressed her thighs tightly together, terrified that the ultimate means of torture would be used, whatever she said or did not say.

'Will you be needing me further, sir?' Symes had stepped back a pace, hoped that his trembling lips would go unnoticed in the shadows beyond the single, flickering candle.

'As you wish, constable,' Jeffries answered without diverting his gaze from the shaking prisoner. 'I need no help, but you may stay and watch if you wish.'

'I must patrol the town.' The excuse sounded hollow. 'My deputy is not due for another hour.'

As Symes stepped out into the street, Elida's first scream followed him. She would give names to the witchfinder, undoubtedly. The usual ones, the gypsies who camped in the forest; the moonmen, that travelling bunch of thieves who had arrived only last week. Whoever she named, her fate was certain, hanged on the outskirts of town along with other innocent victims of the witchfinder's purge.

All the same, there was no denying that infants had disappeared and that there was a resurgence of witchcraft throughout Warwickshire. Neither could it be disputed that gypsies were inherent takers of small children. Cannibalism was just supposition.

Symes increased his pace away from the gaolhouse until he could no longer hear the screams.

Stratford to Warwick was an arduous ride in one day, especially in the heat of summer. Guy Kent was grateful when his route

279

took him through woodlands where the overhanging boughs provided welcome shade. But woods were a dangerous place for a lone traveller, harbouring footpads who lay in wait for the unwary. His hand was never far from the pistol thrust into the belt around his waist.

An observer might have mistaken Kent for a bowman, clad in dark green, his headgear matching velvet with a narrow brim. His doublet and tight-fitting canions accentuated his slender stature and his bright yellow socks were in dazzling contrast to the rest of his attire.

His fair lovelock belied his thirty years, as did his choice to go clean shaven when most men of his age sported a beard with pride. He had given a solemn vow to his lover, Diana Hawker, that, upon her consent to marriage, he would snip off his locks and allow his facial hair to grow unchecked.

His clean-cut features and clear blue eyes had a look of naivety about them, a youthfulness which he used to his advantage. Those who did not know him underestimated him, dismissed him at a glance. Sometimes they were careless with their talk within earshot of him. Kent's boyishness was his forte.

Which was why Richard ap Cynon, Lord Lieutenant of Warwickshire, had chosen him for a role which was not officially listed within the appointments of his local government. Corruption was rife within his own administration and only one who moved and worked unsuspected within it could expose that cancer. He overlooked the fact that Kent's breath sometimes smelled of tobacco. Every man was entitled to one small vice. Richard ap Cynon's was of a liquid nature.

Richard ap Cynon's long dark hair, groomed to perfection, swirled as he turned to look out of the window across the rolling parkland. His fine lace-edged coat, his height and poise, his pointed beard, gave a swashbuckling impression. His age was indeterminable. Kent thought that the other was barely a year or two older than himself. A hard but fair man, you either liked or disliked him; there was no room for compromise.

There was a lengthy silence, an uncomfortable one. Then the Lord Lieutenant spoke, still staring out of the window. 'It is a bad business, Kent. Witchcraft has always existed, but not . . . cannibalism, if the stories are true. I doubt that the girl was anything more than an innocent victim of the witchfinder's latest purge, her infant taken for some vile sacrifice. That, in itself, is bad enough, but now . . .' He paused, still did not turn to face his visitor. 'Luke Jeffries himself is missing, presumed murdered by those he sought. Have you no ideas?'

'Not yet, sire,' Kent answered. 'I came straightway when I received your summons. The witchfinder's horse was found grazing on the edge of the forest.'

'Perhaps his horse threw him, and he lies injured or dead in the woods.' Richard ap Cynon's tone was unconvincing.

'The constable organised a search. Jeffries was not found.'

'And what of the gypsies? And those infernal moonmen?'

'Gone, sir. Their camps are deserted. They have fled, probably north to Staffordshire or beyond.'

'It is a bad business.' The Lord Lieutenant turned round and there was no mistaking the anxiety on his handsome features. 'Other witchfinders will come, from London and the cities, probably with a troop of soldiers. The purge will be like no other we have known, the blameless will hang from trees in the forest, the air will be filled with the stench of burned bodies. It would seem that those who kidnapped and indulged in satanism have taken Luke Jeffries for their victim this time. The vile perpetrators of this crime must be found, Kent, before a host of innocents become scapegoats. The purge will not just be to eradicate supposed witches in the area, it will be a quest for revenge. Even I cannot stop it. You understand, Kent?'

'I understand.' Guy Kent nodded. 'I shall leave no stone unturned, my lord. I shall hunt the murderers down as I have done others, my task made that much easier by the fact that none know I am commissioned by yourself.'

'I wish you luck, Kent.' Richard ap Cynon's stoic expression gave way to a fleeting smile, a nod of encouragement.

If Kent could not find the murderers, then nobody could.

Guy Kent began his search early the next morning at the place where the witchfinder's horse had been found grazing on the edge of the forest. It was the logical starting point, for this matter demanded attention to every detail even in the wake of the previous methodical search. Symes was a good constable but, outside keeping law and order within the town, his powers of perception were somewhat limited.

The ground was hard and dry after a month of drought, no hoofprints visible. Kent's keen eyes noted where the brown stalky grass had been nibbled by the horse. Apart from that, there was nothing which might lead him to the fate of Luke Jeffries.

Elida's body hung from a gallows on the outskirts of town; Kent had skirted it, not even glancing in that direction, the raucous cawing of crows as they pecked the flesh a reminder of what would happen to others if the matter was not resolved soon.

Kent rode slowly into the forest, scrutinising every yard of the narrow, winding track. He saw nothing untoward, could well be wasting his time.

His ears picked up a furious grunting ahead of him. That would be Jeremy's pigs. Kent almost made a detour, for doubtless Symes would have questioned Jeremy the pigman. Nevertheless, it was worth ensuring that Jeremy knew nothing. Negative answers were a necessary means of elimination in any inquiry.

The track led to a clearing of a few acres, once the home of a charcoal burner, but on the latter's death Jeremy had moved in. A tumbledown stone hovel stood at the far end. Adjoining it was an enclosure, constructed of felled trees, where the pigs were housed.

Kent glimpsed the pigman in the doorway of his home, a stocky figure clad in ragged hessian clothing, with squat features and thinning long grey hair.

Guy Kent experienced a pang of pity for the other. Once Jeremy had looked after himself, wore clothing that was regularly washed, and there had been a sprightliness in his step. Now he was unwashed and bowed his head, rarely acknowledging passers-by, one who bore no interest in life other than tending his herd of pigs.

The change was due to the death of his wife, a pretty peasant girl who had died in childbirth two winters ago. Jeremy's grief would probably shorten his lifespan and maybe he would welcome death.

'Good day to you, Jeremy.' Guy Kent dismounted by the pig enclosure, cast a glance inside and almost recoiled at the sight which greeted him.

A sow had given birth to a litter, probably only the day before. They squealed and milled around her as she fought in vain to drive off half a dozen adult porkers which were fighting over the lifeless body of a piglet. One of the attackers succeeded in grabbing it, dragged it away, and vicious bloodied tusks stabbed into a gaping wound in the tiny corpse. A strip of flesh was torn free; the other pigs homed in on the feast, squealing their delight. The enraged sow decided that discretion was best and kept her distance, shielding the rest of her litter from the ferocious onslaught.

Jeremy watched expressionlessly, not so much as lifting his head to look at Kent.

'A nasty business,' Kent remarked, leaning on the timber wall alongside the pigman.

'Better than wasting it,' Jeremy grunted. 'Saves burying it, and at least they will eat well today.'

'You have no doubt heard that the witchfinder is missing, Jeremy?'

'I heard.'

'Unless we find out what happened to him, the consequences will be dire. Perhaps even for you.'

'I do not care.' The pigman was still staring fixedly at the pigs, which had succeeded in tearing the stillborn into two halves. Others had come grunting and squealing in search of a share. The sow had accepted the fate of her offspring and had retired to a corner to let her litter suckle.

'Did you not see any sign of the witchfinder when he rode into the forest?'

'Aye, he stopped off here but I could not help him. Then he rode off to look for the gypsies and the moonmen, for surely it was one of them who have been stealing children. Maybe they killed him, buried his corpse in the forest where nobody will find it. Or he was killed by a footpad. Who knows? I do not.'

All the flesh was gone from the tiny body. Now strong teeth crunched on frail bones. A timid sow was even licking the bloodstains on the churned-up, foul-smelling ground.

'Then I will be on my way.' There was nothing to be gained by lingering here. Time was running out and the pigman was best left to his grief, for nobody could change that. 'I'll bid you good day, then, Jeremy.'

Guy Kent next visited the site of the recent Romany camp. He examined the dead ashes of a cooking fire, delved amongst them and found some bones. They came from a badger. There was nothing to denote whether Luke Jeffries had been here or not, alive or dead.

Kent rode on and eventually came upon a clearing which had undoubtedly, until very recently, been occupied by the moonmen. Again he sifted through the ashes of a cooking fire and studied the bones which he found. Chicken bones this time, the remnants of poultry thefts for which the itinerant band of thieves were well known.

He searched the surrounding undergrowth, but there was no sign of any freshly turned earth where a corpse might have been buried.

Eventually he emerged from the forest and looked westward to where the setting sun was starting to dip behind the Welcombe Hills.

Tomorrow he would continue his search. Just where, right now, he did not know.

Stratford rumour had it that Guy Kent was the 'eyes and ears of the Lord Lieutenant', a spy in their midst who would inform upon them for the slightest misdemeanour, and thus he was not welcome in some circles. Which was why he chose to visit Diana Hawker after darkness had fallen, for he had no wish to have this distrust focused upon her, too. Perhaps, when she finally consented to marry him, they would move on elsewhere, possibly as far away as Warwick.

In the meantime he would indulge briefly in the pleasures she had to offer before continuing his search at first light.

Diana was the daughter of a Staffordshire landowner. Some years before, an outbreak of plague had wiped out the family with the exception of herself and her brother. Not wishing to remain in the family home with the latter and his new bride, she had accepted a generous payment from him and headed south into the county of Warwick.

With the money she had purchased a neat thatched cottage at Newbold, with an acre of land adjacent to an oak wood. From late childhood she had shown an interest in herbal remedies, much to the chagrin of the local physicians, and so she had cultivated her land, grown herbs, and already built up a reputation for preparing various medicines.

'Any luck?' Diana had her back towards Kent as he entered the cottage, her slim figure bent over a chopping board as she prepared a herb salad for supper. An appetising aroma came from an iron pot suspended over a fire in the grate.

'No,' he sighed, lowering his weary frame into a chair. 'I have found nothing which might solve the mystery of the disappearance of Luke Jeffries. Time is running out, I fear. Within days a deputation from London will be scouring the town and its outskirts, dragging out innocent people who will either hang or burn after a sham trial.'

His brow furrowed, his gaze concentrated on that shapely slim body which would lie with his own tonight. And for how many more nights? Perhaps he should take Diana to a place of safety before it was too late.

'How can you be certain that kidnapped babies are being used for cannibalistic satanic rituals?' She put a platter of sharp-scented greenery in the centre of the table.

'What else would infants be taken for? Eight within the last six months, all stolen from their cradles and never heard of again. The gypsies might kidnap the odd child but not that many, they would be too conspicuous. And an innocent girl has just paid the price for having her newborn baby stolen. Elida's body is hanging at the other end of town, pecked by the crows and magpies until it is unrecognisable for what it was.'

'Ugh!' Diana shuddered. 'Maybe, though, there is some kind of cannibal cult in the area, nothing to do with satanism, just people who like to feed on the flesh of their own kind.'

'That is how it seems right now.' Kent moved across to the table. 'I cannot say I have much sympathy for Luke Jeffries, though, if they have eaten him, too. May they choke on his rancid flesh! But others will take his place, and before too long, I fear.'

'Roasted rabbit, tonight. There was one in the snare I keep set by the rocket patch.'

'So long as it is not pork,' he laughed, then grimaced. 'I was by Jeremy's this morning. A piglet had died and the others ate it, crunched up the bones. They even licked the spilled blood off the ground. Disgusting creatures! It has put me off pork for a long time to come.'

'Pigs are the ultimate omnivores.' Diana lifted the rabbit

286

out of the pot, began slicing the meat off the bones. 'They will eat just about anything. Now, let's forget about Jeffries. Tomorrow is another day and you cannot go looking for him in the dark.'

In spite of his fatigue and a long session of love-making, sleep eluded Guy Kent. In his mind he kept turning over the possibilities; the gypsies or the moonmen were unlikely and just too obvious a solution. Satanic rituals involving cannibalism were a possibility not to be totally ruled out.

He dozed. Slept a little. Then, just before dawn broke, he awoke with a start. He sat upright in bed, knew that at least he had to be sure. Elimination was an important factor in arriving at the truth.

He dressed quickly and quietly, listened to Diana's rhythmic breathing. There was no reason to disturb her; it could well be a fool's errand. It was something she had said that had slumbered in his brain, then aroused him from his own fitful sleep.

Outside, he saddled the bay and headed back towards town, branching off towards the forest. The sky was beginning to pale. He might just be in time, for if he was wrong, then he needed to be away before his presence was detected.

He tethered his mount to a tree and moved forward into the large clearing. Everywhere was silent except for a faint twittering from roosting birds as the grey light of dawn crept across the forest.

Jeremy would still be sleeping; he was probably not an early riser. So far, so good. The pigs in the enclosure were huddled in a corner, with the exception of the sow who had slept apart from the others for the protection of her litter.

A boar grunted sleepily as Kent straddled the timber wall and lowered himself down on to the other side. The bracken litter rustled beneath his feet.

He stood there waiting. Another few minutes and the light

would be good enough for him to see. If there was anything there for him to see.

He dropped to his knees, began parting the dead fronds with his hands, sifting, searching. No, it could not be. It was a fanciful figment of his imagination, born of the night hours.

The big boar stood up, grunted disapprovingly. Human intruders were not welcome in his domain. Only Jeremy the pigman, because he brought them food. Food was all that mattered to the pigs.

Kent's probing fingers worked faster, moving litter, looking beneath it. All he found was soil and stones rooted up by the animals.

Until his fingers touched something that was soft and smooth. He held it up to the dawn sky, gasped his triumph aloud. A ragged piece of torn material, black in colour.

The boar was advancing slowly, grunting loudly now. The other pigs were up on their feet watching, small eyes glinting angrily.

Guy Kent began to back away slowly, knowing better than to run. That boar would have an amazing turn of speed for its size. Watching it, backing all the time, he dared not look behind him. He could not be far from the enclosure wall; a quick leap would take him to safety.

Somehow he sensed the danger behind him whilst still occupied with the one that was closing in. His sideways leap was quick, but not quite quick enough to dodge the cudgel that would almost certainly have smashed his skull. Instead, the blow caught him on the shoulder, flung him to the ground.

Dazed, he looked into the open jaws of the big boar, saw the true size of its tusks.

'You will die here, Guy Kent!' Jeremy sat astride the wall, a heavy willow staff clutched in his fist. Gone was the vacant expression, replaced by one of sheer malevolence. 'You will die because you came back. They will never find you, not so much as a gnawed bone. Like the witchfinder. And the babies.'

'Except that there is always a trace if you look hard enough, Jeremy.' Kent was easing the pistol from his belt. 'You piled the litter deep so that anything which might remain would be hidden from prying eyes. It would have been better if you had not, and instead removed and burned it yourself, for the bracken hid *this*!'

'What is it?'

'A piece torn from the witchfinder's coat, Jeremy. Evidence enough to send you to the gallows and spare a lot of innocent people.'

'Give it to me!'

'No. If you want it, come and get it. But tell me, why did you steal the babies and feed them to the pigs?'

'I hate infants. One took my beloved wife from me. The others have paid the price for that. And,' he hesitated, 'it was food for the pigs when I could not afford to buy grain. Then the witchfinder came and, like you, he guessed the truth. But he was not quick enough to save his skull from being crushed. Then I fed him to the pigs. Now, I shall kill you and the pigs will feast again.'

The boar was motionless, watching as Jeremy lowered his stocky body down into the enclosure, crouching, cudgel raised, ready to strike.

Kent's right arm hung limply. The pain was excruciating. He knew that he was no match for the pigman's brute strength fuelled by his madness. The boar snorted angrily.

Guy cocked the pistol, transferred it to his left hand. 'Stay where you are, Jeremy!'

The other gave a roar of rage and launched himself forward, stave upraised for a bone-splintering blow. Guy Kent fired, saw Jeremy stagger, the weapon falling from the pigman's hand as his shoulder shattered.

'I want you alive, Jeremy,' Kent shouted.

The enraged boar charged with amazing speed from a standing start. Kent hurled himself to one side, felt the animal brush against him. There was no way he could escape its ferocious jaws now.

He hit the ground, lay there waiting to feel himself gored by tusks, his limbs crushed and the flesh ripped from them. But the maddened beast ignored him as it scented fresh human blood, pinned its master to the ground, seized his limp arm and tore at it.

The pigman's screams brought the rest of the herd on the run, grunting their hunger, the sow with her litter bringing up the rear, all converging upon the fallen human. Jeremy's screams rent the dawn air as his other limbs were seized, his ragged clothing ripping as stabbing tusks sought out tender flesh.

Kent struggled to his feet, staggered across to the wall, flung himself at it and somehow scrambled to safety.

He did not look back, he did not want to see. As Diana had said last night, 'Pigs will eat anything.' Jeremy was but another feed to them. Soon they would be crunching his stripped bones, lapping at the blood which stained the ground. This time, though, there would be nobody to remove the remnants of any shredded clothing and bury it to hide the evidence.

Kent tucked the piece of cloth from the witchfinder's coat into his pocket. It was evidence enough. His only regret was that he would be unable to hand the murderer over to the authorities.

Would those who came to avenge Luke Jeffries's death accept that the witchfinder's killer had paid the full penalty, a death worse than the gallows? Or would they seek a living scapegoat to torture and execute?

Kent climbed into the saddle and headed out of the forest, turning north towards the Warwick road. The Lord Lieutenant must be informed forthwith, in the hope that Richard ap Cynon would be able to use his influence to appease those who rode in search of vengeance.

Spellbound

Carol Anne Davis

Hungary, 1610

I was fifteen when my beloved sister Marika was stolen from me. Marika, as comely a child as exists in all of Hungary, was a tender twelve. We were in service on the Csejthes' farm, with two days out of seven without bread or wages, yet still she danced to the pipes and saw all that was good in everything.

The Count stood for all that was bad – as did his servants. They fell upon her as she dug for sweet roots in the forest and took her back to his mist-clad castle, high upon a limestone hill. Many girls climbed that hill as unmarried kitchen maids and seamstresses but fewer came out. And sometimes a weary traveller would smile with one eye and weep with the other as he told of piteous cries near the castle which could have been a maiden screaming or the force of the wind through the thick black pines.

The Count had a heart as black as his charcoal beard. It was said that he would thrust all the purity from a girl then take his whip to her as if she were the wildest of horses. Then he'd cover her body and wrap his great hands with renewed *kegyellen* (cruelty) around her throat. Distraught, I wrung my own little hands as I stared into a fragment of looking glass whilst beseeching the spirits to save my sole blood relative, and I clutched the golden amulet our long-dead mother had given me.

Mama had also given me her talent with the magic arts and I had Nature's cleansing leaves and purging milks at my disposal. But I would need a strong elixir to break down the walls that held my sister captive, a forceful spell to bring her back to our straw bed in the barn.

I had a little time for the Count was away fighting the infidel Turks in a bloody battle – but he was due back at the castle soon and would be thirsting for virginal blood to celebrate his wins.

Meanwhile, my Marika was between stones – locked alone in a room – adjacent to the Count's bedchamber. My friend, Ibronik, who laundered at the castle, saw her there and offered words of comfort through the feeding hatch in the door. She said that Marika had everything that a girl could need apart from a prayer book and her dear sister's love. Yes, my darling would have a week of the most golden grain, the finest hams and stoutest chitterlings, until the Count ravished and scourged her and threw her lifeless body to the wolves.

Ibronik was giving her favours to a different kind of wolf, one of the castle's henchmen. I begged her to steal his keys to free my only living relative but my friend wept that the very herbs and flowers told tales around the castle and, truly, she dared not help. Much as she cared for us, she had seen the execution of many traitors, crushed-limb-and-pyre-led deaths.

Alone with my fears, I spoke many cloud-conjuring incantations. I was still reciting a cure when word reached me that the Count was on his way back to his homeland with unnatural lusts on his mind.

Alchemists and cabbalists wait and watch, but my Marika's peril bade me act swiftly. Creeping out as soon as the farmer and his wife were abed – if I lived, I would take my beating for it afterwards – I packed some ash cake, a cabbage and a water bottle, then I walked for a night and a day and part of a second evening to reach the Count's accursed camp.

The scent of stale blood on swords, guard dogs on watch and men without conscience at last told me I was nearing the end of my journey. With trembling fingers I removed my clothing and used the forest plants to darken my hair before bathing my haunches in the stream.

It was vital that none of the camp followers recognise me when I returned – if I lived to return – to service at the Csejthes' farmstead. With this survival in mind, I also spread plant compressions on myself to cloak my true visage, making my lips as red as berries and my eyes as dark as the midnight sky. I even dripped juices all over my shy nakedness so that my very essence changed.

When I had altered my creation as much as a poor girl could, I put my cord-strung amulet between my breasts so that it was hidden from the sight of the greedy. Mother had promised in her death throes that it was more than a golden bauble; that it possessed a strength that would get me through the most difficult times.

My most difficult time was drawing near. I put on my skirts again and crept towards the outskirts of the camp, causing some of the white dogs to start barking darkly. The soldiers on guard soon espied me and I was surrounded by laughing, jeering men who tore at my bodice and my one good sheepskin cape.

I screamed as loudly as I could, and my cries brought the Count before my sight. He ordered them to bring me to his quarters. 'Am I your first?' he asked, probing with his battleworn fingers at my maidenliness.

'Yes, sir,' I lied, knowing that my mother's tinctures had formed a sealant inside my body that made it seem as if I had never lain with a man.

He took me then, and it was worse than the two men who had taken me in the forest when I was thirteen summers. I screamed inside but outwardly kept my counsel, knowing that this mustn't happen to a virgin child. 'Whore, you fail to please,' he shouted, all glittering eyes and lustful panting, and he picked up his riding crop and brought it down again and again on my cringing flesh. '*Usd, usd, jobban,*' I heard him whisper to himself, as if his right arm needed telling to beat harder. 'Don't drown my fair straw with your peasant blood,' he roared finally, throwing down the leather whip and fastening his teeth upon my heaving breast. He licked and lapped then grabbed roughly at my throat, and a wickedness as boundless as the sea flowed from him. I gasped out every spell that Mama had ever told me, and he fell into a very sound sleep.

An hour before daylight I tiptoed out of the camp and went to the stream and changed back to my usual countenance. Then, God speed, I ran as fast as I could, resting under dog-rose bushes whenever demons cast away my strength. Eventually I got back to the farmhouse where I told them I'd been stolen and scourged by a band of gypsies, that I'd been made to collect wood for them to charcoal and had only just escaped. Refusing me bread, the farmer gave me a beating which awakened the Count's cruel whip marks, then I limped back to the many chores that had my name on them. All I could do now was wait.

For one full day nothing happened at the castle – and then there was an uproar. Ecclesiastical and council men were everywhere, lamenting the death of the Count and wondering who would take his place. 'You can surely possess yourself of that key now,' I said to my friend Ibronik, 'as there's no Count to berate you.' And she slid the crucial key from her hench-man's belt and set my frightened Marika free.

Though I rained many kisses on my sister's head, I never told how I earned her precious freedom. Sometimes I wonder if our dead mother knows. I'm sure that she would have done the same thing.

The sleeping herbs I'd anointed my body with were designed

296

to take effect as soon as the Count licked my flesh. If he hadn't tongued at my blood I planned to pull his open mouth against my skin, in the way I'd seen Mother do to men who wanted more than the cures she was selling. But, with Marika trapped back home in his buttressed castle, the Count's sleep would not be enough. It was then that I turned to the amulet Mother had given me and I used its hard strength as never before . . .

Herbs and spells have their uses and doubtless the witches of the day would say that the Turks had hexed him. But the true source of the Count's death lay in the amulet I pushed deep into his throat to steal his breath.

But Poor Men Pay for All

Mat Coward

West Country, Britain, 1647

'**A** matter for the sheriff, surely?'

'Dead,' said Hopton.

'Dead?' said Woodward.

Hopton nodded. 'Resulting from the late public differences.'

'I see,' said Woodward. He and Hopton had been on different sides, at least nominally, of the war between Parliament and the king. Both had survived; both hoped to prosper, now that peace and normality seemed to be returning to the realm. 'The sheriff was too old to take the field, surely?'

'Died in the castle.'

'Ah,' said Woodward. So the sheriff had been a king's man, killed during the Roundheads' siege, and subsequent ruination, of that local landmark. It was so hard to keep track; the market town in which lawyer Woodward and publican Hopton did their business had, like so many in the West Country, changed hands often during the past five years. So too, in many cases, had the loyalties of the local merchants and professional men. 'The constable, then.'

'Dead,' said Hopton.

'Oh, really, Hopton – is *everyone* in this town dead, except us two?' As soon as he'd said it, Woodward regretted it. In 1642, Hopton had three sons; today he had none. 'Forgive me, my friend, I forgot myself. It's just that, well, what with the . . .'

'Late public differences.'

'. . . late public differences, quite so, and the famine *arising* from the late public differences, it is hard to see how a town built on trade might ever recover.' He put a hand up to stroke his beard and then remembered he was shaven. 'Was the constable in the castle, too?'

Hopton shook his head. 'He died of an appointment.'

'An appointment?'

Hopton nodded. 'With a rope.'

'Ah.' That placed the constable's affiliations, then. The only hangings in this town had been carried out by Royalists. 'What of the squire? I don't believe *he's* dead. Unless of surfeit; not of rope, musket or famine, for sure.'

'He's alive,' Hopton allowed.

'Then perhaps—'

'Hasn't set foot outside his library since Naseby. Says if he does, clothworkers will use his books to wipe their arses on.'

'Why on earth should he believe that?' No, that was a silly question. People would believe anything these days. Woodward sighed. 'I begin to suspect, sir, that if I were to list every man of rank within a day's ride, you would declare each of them in turn to be dead. Is that not so?'

'Dead or fled,' Hopton agreed. 'Meanwhile, a corpse still lies upon the floor of my inn.'

Woodward sighed again. 'I suppose you'd better show me,' he said.

The Angel had been a travellers' inn for hundreds of years, and was renowned for the strength of its dark, sweet beer. Lately, it had been used as quarters by Parliamentary forces, and then by king's men, and then by Parliament again. For now, with the talk all of settlement and compromise, the Angel was back to being merely a pub.

'Did they give you much trouble, the soldiers?' Woodward

302

asked, as he and Hopton walked over the bridge in the crisp winter sun. He had spent most of the troubled years in quieter parts; explaining, since his recent return, that *My occasions did not allow me to be much here*.

'The hairy ones, a bit. Not the Puritans.'

Woodward nodded. This seemed to be the story almost everywhere. The Saints of the New Model Army – General Cromwell's fearsome military machine – were not, as their forefathers had so often been, pressed unwilling into the service of a great lord. Rather, they were serious of purpose and enthusiastic in manner, since they believed themselves to be doing God's work – fighting for nothing less than the salvation of England. More importantly, in Woodward's view, they were fighting not for a master, but for themselves. Thus, in battle and away from it, they behaved with a degree of unity and discipline unprecedented in English experience.

'That's him,' Hopton said, rather unnecessarily, pointing at the body on the floor of his backmost room.

Woodward, careful not to drag his clothing in the pool of congealed blood that surrounded the dead man, squatted and observed. A knife protruded from the corpse's belly. 'Quite a young fellow. Twenty-five or so, I'd say. Somewhere, a mother is weeping.' He straightened up, his knees cracking loudly as he did so. He was not shaped for crouching, but for lawyering. 'The first thing is to discover the poor boy's name.'

'He is Adam Pretty. I am his younger brother, Edward Pretty.'

Woodward looked at the newcomer's long nose, deep-set eyes, and down-turned mouth; and from them, to the corpse. Yes, there was a resemblance. So, too, in the thin, light hair, which on both brothers was rudely chopped in the Puritan style. 'I am sorry for your sadness,' he said, and after holding his gaze a moment, almost in challenge, Pretty nodded, once. 'I am Benjamin Woodward, a lawyer of this town, and I suppose you have met Mr Hopton, landlord of the Angel. I do not think I know you, sir; you are not from here?'

'From Bath. We were returning home, and broke our journey here last night.'

'Returning from where, sir, if I might ask?'

This time, there was no mistaking the challenge in the young man's eyes. 'From Putney, Lawyer Woodward.'

'I see,' said Woodward. He had hoped that this bloody matter would prove to be a simple case of cuckoldry revenged, or of resentment unleashed by ale. Perhaps it still would . . . but all the same. *Putney*.

'You were there for the debates?' said Hopton.

'We were, landlord.'

'Ah,' said Woodward. This was looking worse every moment. 'You attended the debates in, might I ask, what particular capacity?'

At this, Pretty laughed for a moment; and then, finding himself laughing, wept for a moment more.

Benjamin Woodward had never lost a loved one – nor ever owned one to lose – but he had seen grief before, and was not a cold man. 'Forgive me, Mr Pretty, these questions can wait. Mr Hopton – might we not move to your private rooms?'

'We might.'

'And, since I doubt any of us has yet eaten this morning, would it be possible to find there bread and ale?'

After a moment, Hopton replied: 'Possible.'

'And if *possible*, my friend, might it be *probable*?' Since the landlord still made no move, he added, 'It would, of course, be my honour to pay for same.'

Hopton nodded. 'Come, then,' he said, and led the way across the alley towards his kitchen. None of the three men looked back at the blood, or the knife, or the dead man on the Angel's floor.

* * *

'To answer your question, Mr Woodward,' said Pretty, as they ate, 'concerning my *particular capacity*. Neither my brother Adam nor I had the honour of being elected to represent our regiment as Agitators. That was what you wished to know, I think? We attended at Putney merely as onlookers.'

'Onlookers?' said Hopton. 'While the grandees determined your fate?'

'While the grandees *discussed* the future of the kingdom with our representers,' Pretty corrected him. 'For as the Romans said, "That which concerns all ought to be debated by all." '

Hopton snorted, and drank his beer.

'And that being done,' said Woodward, 'you and your brother were returning to the west, following the ending of the—'

'The ending of all our dreams of liberty,' Pretty interrupted. 'Following the unconstitutional disbandment of the army. Following the treachery at Putney. Following the murderous villainy of the new tyrant, Cromwell. Following the—'

'Following the late public differences,' said Woodward, firmly. He had been a lawyer for many years, and knew well the force of words. 'You paused here at the Angel, to be refreshed from your travels. And whilst here, several men, including Adam, fell into a discussion in Mr Hopton's backmost room, which in its topics continued that which lately had taken place at Putney. I have that correctly? And you, sir, were also present during these conversations?'

Pretty hesitated before answering. 'Yes. I was there.'

'And this discussion became . . . heated? Is that so?'

Pretty said nothing.

'Mr Pretty, may I ask you – and I ask only because I must, you understand – of what party were you and your brother?'

'Levellers,' said Hopton, delivering the words as if it were a mouthful of phlegm.

305

Woodward ignored him, and looked only at Pretty. 'Sir?'

'Your friend has it.'

'Thank you, sir. Now, this discussion; how many took part?'

'Five,' said Hopton. 'This one, his brother, three others.'

Woodward swallowed his irritation at the innkeeper's interruptions. 'These others, Mr Pretty. They were known to you?'

Again, Pretty's answer was slow in coming. 'Men of the regiment,' he said eventually.

'Fellow soldiers, then. Good. Now, Mr Pretty, I beg you to understand that this matter of parties is of no import to me. A man's opinions are between him and his God. But to comprehend the death of your brother, I must take note of all insignificant details. You understand? It is my training in the law that makes me this way. These three others – were they of the Leveller persuasion, also?'

Pretty chewed slowly. *Chewing food or thoughts?* Woodward wondered.

'By their words, I took them for supporters of the Presbyterians.'

'I see. Well, now, we are all on the same side, are we not?' Woodward looked purposefully at Hopton. 'The *victorious* side, by God's grace.' Hopton grunted – which was, Woodward supposed, at least better than snorting. 'The discussion between you and Adam on one side of the table, and these good Presbyterian gentlemen on the other – it continued for an hour or so?'

Again, the thoughtful pause. *There is something he wants to tell me, but won't,* Woodward thought. *Or something he doesn't want to tell me, but in the end must.*

'The discussion was continuing when I left the room,' said Pretty.

'Ah. You left the room?'

'I was weary. I went in search of sleep.'

'You had taken a room here at the Angel?'

'I slept in the stable. With the horses.'

'Of course – simplicity and modesty in all things. Most commendable.' *But sufficient to damn you as a niggard in the innkeeper's eyes*, thought Woodward. 'So the first you knew of the tragedy that had befallen your family . . . ?'

'This morning when I awoke, Adam was not alongside me in the stable.' Pretty looked at Hopton. 'He was upon your floor, landlord, stabbed to death.'

'These three Presbyterian soldiers,' said Woodward. 'I think it necessary we speak to them now. If they are still to be found.'

'In their rooms,' said Hopton.

'Still asleep?' said Woodward, a little surprised that Parliamentary soldiers of any party should lie abed so late.

'Asleep or awake, in their rooms is where they'll be.' Hopton produced from his sleeve a bunch of keys. 'I locked them in, see.'

'Through the windows,' said Hopton, by way of explanation when he returned some minutes later accompanied by but one Presbyterian soldier. 'That's that settled, then, is it not? Clearly, the two who have flown are guilty, and this one who stayed isn't.'

The 'one who stayed', a solidly built man of perhaps thirty-five, his head half bald and his skin walnut-brown, gave his name as William Church, and asked: 'What is this talk of guilt? And why was the door to my room locked during the night? Is this an inn or a prison?'

Woodward showed coin to Hopton, which the landlord correctly interpreted as a suggestion that food and drink be fetched for Mr Church. 'Sir, forgive us, I beg of you, these irregularities. Ours is a hospitable town, and I trust you will return to it in happier times, but for now I must tell you that a

307

horrible thing has occurred, and that is that this gentleman's brother has been done to death. Murdered, that is.'

Church stared at Pretty. 'Murdered? Your gentle brother, that was with us last night?'

'The same one.'

Church's heavy eyebrows achieved union, as his face screwed up in thought. 'And the two other men that were also present?'

'Gone,' said Woodward. 'Flown, though it was thought they were caged.'

'Flown,' said Church, to himself; and then, evidently remembering his niceties, he added: 'Mr Pretty, I am most sympathetic that you have suffered such a loss as this.'

Pretty nodded acknowledgement. Hopton returned with Church's meal, and as the soldier made a somewhat distracted start on it, Woodward told Church his name and profession. 'When you have recovered from your shock, sir, I shall ask you to tell me all you know of your two companions from last night, so that I may pass that information to the magistrates.'

'Of course,' said Church. 'Though I knew them but slightly.'

'That seems to be the end of the matter,' said Hopton.

'It does,' said the lawyer, but his tone was uncertain, even if that uncertainty was only noticeable to his own ears. 'Tell me something of this Leveller creed of yours, Mr Pretty, for I would attain a right understanding of it. It's said that you would give all a voice in the choosing of Parliament-men. Is that so?'

'Certainly, sir, for as Colonel Rainborough said at Putney, the poorest he that is in England has a life to live as the greatest he. Meaning that the man who has forty shillings a year has no greater right to representation than has any other free Englishman.'

'*Any* Englishman?' said Hopton. 'Any man at all, that has a breath and being?'

'Indeed, sir. All men who retain their birthright should be electors, equally.'

'It is true what they say, then,' said Hopton, horror mingling with disbelief in his voice. 'You would destroy all distinctions of degrees between men?'

Through a mouthful of bread, Church said, 'More than that, sir. Mr Pretty and his friends would abolish property itself.'

At this, Hopton could only splutter. Even Woodward, who had heard such things said before, felt a little sick. Both men noticed that Pretty did not trouble to deny the accusation.

'Mr Pretty's belief,' Church continued, 'is that every man has a *natural right*, given him by God, to choose who shall govern him. Is this not so, sir?'

'It is self-evident, sir,' said Pretty.

'Then, sir, you must also say that by the same law of nature, which surely states that a man must have sustenance rather than starve, then any man has a right to take my food, my clothes, my house, my crops. He may take what he pleases, for I have only as much *natural* claim upon those things as he has. And then, sir, we shall be animals, and we shall have anarchy.'

Pretty shook his head in obvious irritation. 'Not so, sir, for you seem to forget the law of God, which is above the law of nature. The law of God forbids us theft and murder and adultery. But there is no law of God that sets one man above another in the matter of who shall govern.' He turned to Woodward. 'I suppose that men began to choose representatives when there were too many for all to speak directly. But if we were to start a government today, for the first time, would we say that only the man who has forty shillings a year might have a voice? It is unthinkable!'

Before the lawyer could reply, if such was his intention, Church spoke, his voice urgent. 'The granting of an equal voice to every man *must* lead to the ending of property, for how can it not? for the representation of those who have nothing must certainly exceed that of those who have much—'

Pretty struck his fist on the table. 'Please God that it should!'

Church's fists tightened, and he took a deep breath before replying. 'Yet that was not your brother's view, Mr Pretty.'

Pretty's face froze. 'My brother's view . . . no. Adam argued that, on the contrary, an equitable parliament is the *guarantor* of the rights of property, for it gives to all a material interest in the ease of the kingdom. If I own a bakery, I might fear the starving man, but I need not fear my neighbour who has a full belly.'

'You would do away with *property*?' said Hopton, his face grimacing with perplexity.

The frustrated grinding of Pretty's teeth was audible around the room. 'With this talk of property, we are much deviated from the question, which is only this: may a man be bound by any law that he has not consented to? Nor any of his ancestors, betwixt him and Adam, did ever give consent to? Governance can be by the people's consent alone.'

Woodward turned to Church. 'But your party of Presbyterians, sir, do not favour this view?'

'That all electors should be equal, yes. But that those equals should be drawn from amongst them that have a *settled* and *permanent* interest in England, which is to say—'

'Which is to say,' cried Pretty, half rising from his chair, 'that all men are equal, only some are more equal than others!'

An angry silence fell. Pretty and Church busily avoided looking at each other. Hopton continued to mutter to himself. Woodward sat quietly, deep in troubled thoughts. After a while, he spoke. 'Then, gentlemen, I wonder: what is to become of the king?'

'We shall have a king of a new kind, sir,' said Church. 'A king may be in any form. He can be hereditary or elected, he

310

can enjoy absolute power or limited power—'

'Only superstition makes us desire a king of any shape!' Pretty interrupted.

'Divine law commands us to honour our fathers and mothers, though we have not a choice in who they are,' said Church. 'This principle can extend.'

'But we should honour them only if they are righteous. We have one true King – that is Christ – and we do not need another, except that we do not trust ourselves to govern ourselves. We have been vassals since the Conquest, and now we are ready to regain our freedoms.'

'The king is tamed,' Church began, but was again interrupted.

'You speak of restoration, but you have not the courage to call it by its name!'

'It is not *restoration*, Mr Pretty, to say to a man, you had two strong legs, and you used them for kicking the arses of your children, and so from now on your legs will be bound.'

'We suffer now under arbitrary government,' Pretty shouted. 'As the law stands, a king may do what he wishes, soever, and no lawyer or sheriff may call him to account.'

'Which is why, sir, if you will only hear me—'

'There can be no compromise with tyranny! I would have you know that I interrupt you with great reluctance, and with only love in my heart,' said Pretty, flecks of spit gathering on his lips, 'but surely you must see that if the king is restored, then he is our lawful ruler; if he is our lawful ruler, then we have been, these years, in mutinous rebellion against him—'

'To which he will sign an Act of Indemnity.'

'How *can* he, if he be our lawful ruler, sign such an act? If we are traitors to lawful authority, then we must hang. And, sir – you say the king's legs are to be bound, so that he can no longer kick at the arses of children. I say, if he is king again, then he may order his legs *unbound*, and who can say he must not?'

'Then you say, Mr Pretty,' Woodward asked, 'that the king must be tried?'

'*Try* the king?' Hopton gasped.

Church held his head in his hands, as if against a headache. 'We cannot put the king on trial, sir, for this very reason – that he is the king! And we are all vowed to—'

'But if a pilot steers his ship towards the rocks,' said Pretty, 'then the man that takes his command away from his is breaking his vow. Yet who will call such a man a vow-breaker, and not a life-saver? I am not bound to assist that which tends to my own destruction, no matter what engagements I have made.'

'It is said by the lawyers – is this not so, Lawyer Woodward? – that a man may not injure himself voluntarily. So that if man enters into a vow—'

'As always, we go round in circles! A vow has no meaning, if the man who made it was not free to refuse it. We have been bereaved of our liberties as Englishmen by the king, and if we do not act we shall be so bereaved by Parliament in its turn, and by the rich men who rule in Parliament. We shall be a nation of pismires.'

Both soldiers were standing now, facing each other across the table. Woodward was getting quite a crick in his neck from looking up at them.

'Mr Pretty,' Church said, 'in a loving spirit, I would urge you, look at the truth of our situation! The people turn against the army, because of the demands made upon the realm by this war, because of the famine it has caused—'

'They shall turn against it more, Mr Church, when they discover that they have been cozened.'

'Cozened, you say?' asked Woodward. 'How so?'

'If the king is restored, then we shall have found little fruit of our labours. Do you not think it were a sad and miserable condition, that we have suffered all this time for nothing?'

'For *nothing*?' Church was so furious, he had taken to pacing. 'I shall but humbly take the boldness to put you in mind of one thing: the king is forced to negotiate with us! That is hardly *nothing*.'

'Negotiation! With sweetness in my heart for you, sir, and in search only of the justness of the thing, I tell you – the sword alone may sometimes serve for the recovery of stolen rights; you may read that truth in your bible.'

'But what is won by the sword may be lost similarly. If we allow the king to divide us now, Presbyterian against Independent, he will conquer us. If we dispute, we are lost.'

'I cannot agree, sir. God gave us reason that we might use it.'

For his part, Woodward thought the Presbyterian had a point. No doubt, Charles would happily side with one party against the other, for as long as it took to ensure the destruction of both.

'In any case,' Pretty continued, 'it is too late to talk of not disputing. You know as I do that Cromwell has already begun arresting Levellers. That is what your liberty is worth, sir!'

Enough, thought Woodward; he had seen what he needed to see. He would stop the debate now, before it produced yet more bloodshed. 'Gentlemen, your standing and shouting is giving me an inconvenience. I would beg you to sit.' Both men – apparently surprised to find themselves standing – obediently sat. 'I must ask you both to remain here a little longer. I have the need to perform a small amount of clear thinking, after which I shall return, and then, I believe, the matter of Adam Pretty's death can be settled.'

Church frowned. 'I had thought that matter already settled, Mr Woodward?'

'Perhaps, perhaps not. While I am gone, I would suggest

that you spend the time in prayer. Mr Hopton, no doubt, will see to your temporal needs.'

'He would abolish *property* and *try* the king,' Hopton mumbled, his eyes fixed on, or through, the table top.

As Woodward stood to take his leave, Edward Pretty asked him softly: 'And you, sir? For what will you pray? Wisdom, or revelation?'

The lawyer smiled. 'I fear I am not a greatly prayerful man, Mr Pretty. It seems safer not to bring myself to God's attention unnecessarily. No, while you gentlemen are at your prayers, I go in search of an onion.'

'An onion?'

'For the bowels, sir,' said Woodward. 'For the bowels. A man must shit well before he may reason well.'

'When a thing is done,' he told them an hour and a half later, his mind clear now, and his bowels likewise, 'it is done for a reason. Or, if not done for a reason, then done out of madness. Either way, it is sense, you will agree, that if we can excavate the *will* behind a particular act, then we shall also expose the actor.'

'Thought we'd done so,' said Hopton, apparently recovered from his earlier shocks – with the aid of strong drink, if his breath were any guide. 'The two flown Presbyterians.'

'Ah, yes,' said the lawyer. 'Five men were debating in your backmost room. As we have seen for ourselves this afternoon, these are dialogues of a kind to bring the flush to a man's cheeks. One man, Edward Pretty, went to bed, leaving four men.'

'Not so, sir. I was the first to retire.'

'Indeed, Mr Church? I beg your pardon. I had understood that Mr Pretty was the first.'

'I did not say so,' said Pretty.

A successful lawyer's mind is a net, from which little

escapes. And Benjamin Woodward was a successful lawyer, if not a wholly successful man. After a moment's recollection, he said: 'No more you did, sir. It was I mistook your meaning. So, then; William Church leaves, and four remain. Some time later, Edward Pretty leaves, and three remain.'

'And the two,' said Hopton, impatiently, 'do for the one. We know all this.'

'Both of them do for him?'

The landlord waved the question aside. 'One of them does him, and both flee. What does it matter? We have their names, they will be taken eventually.'

'Yet why did they not flee upon the instant? Instead, it seems, they murdered poor Adam, then went calmly to bed.'

'Perhaps,' Church offered, 'they acted calm so as to prevent suspicion.'

'What, and then escaped through their windows in the morning?'

'They found themselves locked in,' Hopton suggested, 'thus knew they were discovered, and so fled. This were no mystery.'

'Ah, perhaps. But I ask myself also, what was it about poor Adam that drove these men into a killing rage?'

'His many opinions,' Hopton insisted. 'Concerning the abolition of property.'

'Your brother, Mr Pretty, was a man of strong opinions, strongly spoken?'

'He was as other men,' Pretty replied.

'Mr Church; you found him argumentative?'

'Not overly so.'

'No indeed, this I gathered from your remarks earlier. That Adam Pretty held milder views than his brother, and expressed them more mildly, too.' Church looked at Pretty; neither spoke. 'An unlikely man, perhaps, to be killed during an argument.'

'You believe,' said Hopton, 'that his killers had some other reason?'

'Possibly. Mr Church – can you think of any reason?'

Church could. 'King's men, seeking to cause disunity within the army. If those men last night were secretly Royalist agents—'

'Or,' said Woodward, gently, 'agents of General Cromwell, hunting down Levellers? Mr Pretty, you say nothing, but surely you would not put such villainy past one who you say is a dictator?'

For a long moment, Pretty stared hard at Church. But when he spoke, it was with a shrug. 'I suppose not.'

'We have only Mr Church's own word for his whereabouts at the time of the deed,' said Woodward. As Church began to protest, he added: 'And the same can be said of Mr Pretty.' Pretty, the lawyer noticed, did not protest. He seemed quite sunk in silent thought. 'But in any case, if the murder were plotted, then the plotters made a rough job of it. Though we must also admit that if it were done in a moment's madness, then it were done very quietly. Neither Mr Hopton, nor any of his customers, were alarmed by the noise of an angry struggle. Neither case seems to fit our facts.'

'Yet it must have been one or the other,' said Hopton. 'Either plotting, or ire.'

'Yes, my friend, you are right. It was ire of a sort. Was it not, my boy?' He reached across and laid a hand – a consoling, not an arresting, hand – on Edward Pretty's shoulder.

Pretty bowed his head for a moment, and closed his eyes. Then he said: 'Of a sort, Lawyer Woodward.'

Church fell to his knees. Not in a faint, Woodward decided, but in prayer. Hopton poured ale from a jug, drank it, and did not offer the jug to his guests.

'Before you say more, Edward, I would caution you of this: that I have no proof of anything I have supposed, other than what may come out of your own mouth. No man is obliged to place his own neck in the noose.'

'You are a kind man, Mr Woodward, but I have told you one lie today, and I will not tell you any more. I killed my brother.'

Hopton was on his feet. 'That is a confession, witnessed by us three. I'll ride to fetch the magistrate. Woodward, you can hold the murderer till morning?'

'He offers no threat to me. Take Mr Church with you; two will make better time than one.'

When Church had been retrieved from his piety, and he and the innkeeper had left, Woodward poured two mugs of beer, and Pretty told his story.

'As you have seen, that man Church and I could not so much as wish each other a good morning without heat entering our words. The other three – well, they talked, too, but with less passion. They tried to turn the conversation to gentler matters, but Church and I were unwilling, or unable, to follow their lead. In the end, it was Church who retired to bed first, as he told you.'

'While you, without quite lying, managed to give the impression that you had retired earliest of all.'

'I lied only when I said that the discussion continued after I had left. Only one lie, but it is the one for which God shall damn me.'

'From the start, I noticed your reluctance to say untruths, and that it caused you to hesitate often in your speech. You are not trained as a lawyer, I suppose?'

'No, sir. I was an ostler, before the . . .'

'Before the late public—'

'Before the war, Mr Woodward.'

Woodward gave a small, formal bow of concession. 'The war, Edward. Quite so. Now, Mr Church retired . . . ?'

Pretty rubbed at his scalp with his knuckles. 'I see now that he did so in order to avoid conflict, that he was guided by God

317

in that action. But at the time, it seemed to me that he offered insult, by withdrawing from a conversation that I was not yet done with.'

'You went after him?'

'Not immediately. I stewed for a minute or so. But then, yes, I stood and cried, "Damn the man!" Forgive me, Mr Woodward, I am not usually a blasphemer.'

'I don't doubt it.'

'I stood, and found that my knife was in my hand.'

'I do not believe you would have harmed Mr Church.'

Pretty spread his hands. 'I trust I should not have. I think I meant only to remonstrate with him. But that is just as wicked! A man who truly loves Christ does not yield to rage, no matter the provocation.'

He does after five years of war, thought Woodward, who had learned in his career at law that men returned from fighting were often subject to uncontrollable rages, though they might previously have been of the mildest character.

'I made for the door, and Adam . . . he was my elder and only brother, Mr Woodward, and sworn to protect me from harm. And had done so, through so many years and across so many miles. And now, only a day from home . . .'

'Drink had been taken,' said Woodward. 'You were all perhaps a little unsteady on your feet.'

Pretty nodded. 'That is how it was. Adam went to take the knife from me, speaking softly, saying, "*Quiet now, brother.*" I made to pass him, but he wouldn't yield. I pushed at him, he held my arm as he fell, and as we landed, the knife entered his belly. He died in my arms. The two Presbyterians, terrified beyond their wits, went white as snow. "We have seen nothing," one of them said, and both fled.'

'Hopton came upon you like that?'

'He did, some minutes later, puzzled by the silence, perhaps. I told him there had been an accident, which was the truth, and he ordered me to my bed, and to say nothing.'

It was not hard for Woodward to imagine Hopton's feelings, for his own might have been similar. *Stay uninvolved and stay alive* had been the motto of many men, throughout those years of tumult. It might be that Hopton truly believed the Presbyterians guilty, and had truly believed that all three were in their rooms when he locked their doors. Or it might be otherwise.

'Why did you not confess your part in the matter? It was an accident, after all. And I see that you loved your brother, and are not a man of criminal character.'

'We were closer in love than in beliefs. We had often quarrelled, at Putney. And before. And since. Adam was a true Leveller in the matter of representation, and of the fate of the king, but we differed concerning property.'

'Is it such a big difference?'

'Sir, I believe it is all the difference in the world. The difference between bondage deferred, and liberty secured. While some are rich and some poor, none may be free.'

'You feared then that some might think you capable of killing Adam in a rage born of debate?'

'That, sir, but even more another thing. You see, I have a mother.'

And with that, Woodward felt he understood all. The smallest reason imaginable, in days when every action seemed pregnant with great motives; that a boy could not face the shame of having his mother learn that she had lost one son, by the hand of the other.

The lawyer stood, and gripped the soldier's forearm most urgently. 'Ride now, Edward! I will not give you away. To Ireland with you, or France! You cannot put your trust in the law, we both know that – it is as the song says: *Rich men in the tavern roar, but poor men pay for all.* Flee now, in the name of God, and your mother shall have at least one surviving child!'

But Pretty only took the lawyer's hand, and held it firm, and made no move to rise from his chair. 'The poorest he must have a voice, and all must be bound equally by the laws of the kingdom. Those are my beliefs. I forgot them, but only for a while. Sit with me, Benjamin Woodward, if you have the time, and we shall wait out the hours together.'

In melancholy, Woodward sat, unable to ignore the new and angry knowledge in his heart, that the one man truly responsible for Adam Pretty's death would never pay at all. Whatever fate might befall Charles Stuart, one thing was for certain: England would never find the courage to hang a king. A nation of pismires, indeed.

A Poisoned Chalice

John Sherwood

Britain, 1666

'**I**t doesn't make sense. It's crazy.'

'So is a lot of what happened in the seventeenth century,' said Miss Barton primly.

'Not as crazy as this. According to his tablet in the church Philip Beauclerk "dyed on ye 20th day of Feby 1666". But here he is signing his will in 1669 and leaving his estate to his wife and, to show that he was not only alive but virile, to his infant son.'

Miss Barton cocked her head at him, like an inquisitive bird. 'I had no idea a will existed. Where did you find it?'

'In a hoard of paper that came from the muniment room at Pelling Place. When the Fortescues sold up, everything went into the county archive.'

'Goodness, Mr Burke, what was Philip Beauclerk's will doing in the Fortescues' muniment room? They and the Beauclerks have been mortal enemies for generations.'

'I know. That's another thing that's crazy.'

'You're taking your research for this assignment very seriously.'

'Unfortunately I have to.'

This was only too true. Neil Burke was taking an extra year at Cambridge to do a doctorate. He had stayed at home to finish his thesis while his family holidayed abroad. In a reckless moment he had agreed to write the script for a pageant about the history of the village. Too late he had discovered that the village had no history, or rather that what history it had was sharply controversial. The village green was unmentionable because of a bitter quarrel between supporters and opponents of a plan to turn it into a car park with a public lavatory at one corner. There had also been trouble about removing an inconveniently placed mounting block outside the Red Lion. Even the village hall was taboo. Someone's grandfather had been suspected of embezzling its funds, and the family concerned had not forgotten or forgiven. Neil had spent desperate weeks ransacking obscure historical sources in search of something innocuous to write about.

Miss Barton was the secretary of the local history society. She had been detailed to act as his historical adviser. So far her advice had consisted entirely of helping him to find his way through extensive minefields of no-no subject matter.

According to her the muddle over the date of Philip's death was in a heavily mined area. 'The colonel won't like you researching into his ancestors' behaviour,' she said with a mad little giggle. 'Having Philip's will in the Fortescues' muniment room amounts to a personal affront. If they hadn't sold up and gone to Australia he'd still be snapping at their heels.'

Colonel Beauclerk was a short red-faced man whose conversation consisted of sharp barking noises uttered from beneath a military moustache. From its imposing Queen Anne headquarters at Brooke Hall his family had presided over the village from time immemorial and expected it to do what it was told. In these democratic days that did not always happen. But on this occasion he was footing most of the bill for the expenses of the pageant, so he had to be handled with care.

Accordingly, he was the first person Neil had contacted in his search for pageant subject matter.

'Quite right to come to me,' said the colonel. 'The village are a dull lot, no history here apart from our family's. Plenty of that, though. Take for instance Sir Robert Beauclerk. Seventeenth century. The great Sir Robert. A real bigwig, Secretary of State under Charles II. Here, take a dekko at this. Put together by my grandmother. You'll find all you need in there.'

'This' was a memoir of Beauclerk family history written by Olivia Beauclerk and privately printed in 1926. She had little to say about the origins of the family, which were evidently obscure. The first Beauclerk to make a mark was the great Sir Robert. He was Olivia's pride and joy, and she spent pages listing the high offices of state that he had held. But unfortunately the scene of his triumphs had been London. They could hardly be dwelt on at great length to pad out the village pageant.

Surely he must have done something on his home ground that one could write about? Neil ransacked the records in the county archives, but found only dry-as-dust wills. With a heavy heart he began trying to concoct something about the affairs of a fourteenth-century nun who had done nothing much to distinguish herself. A fable about a wishing well that had dried up under the Regency yielded even thinner pageant fodder. After another blank day of research in the county record office, he wandered, not expecting to find anything useful, into the town's picture gallery. There he struck lucky. Facing him on the wall was a full-length portrait of a rather handsome man, described on the label as Philip Beauclerk. And across the bottom of the canvas was the information: *Aetatis suae XLVII*.

So Philip Beauclerk had sat for his portrait when he was forty-seven. When was he born? Olivia's memoir was in his briefcase.

According to the family tree in her appendix he had been born in 1622. Relying on the memorial tablet in the church, she gave 1666 as the year of his death, when he would have been 44. Here, then, was confirmation that he had, surprisingly, signed his will three years after his death.

Pageant or no pageant this had to be investigated.

The curator of the gallery was glad to find someone interested. 'Ah yes, the John Hayls. Rather a fine piece of work; we're lucky to have it.'

'He was a well-known painter, then?'

'He was a minor follower of Vandyke and a competitor of Lely's. A court painter, really. It was unusual for him to take on a mere country gentleman.'

'Expensive, would he be?'

'Well, he charged Pepys fourteen pounds, a lot of money in those days, for painting a portrait of his wife.'

'And the inscription, giving the sitter's age. Was that unusual?'

'Rather old-fashioned, perhaps. Why do you ask?'

'There seems to be some doubt about the date of his death.'

The curator smiled. 'Ah. Several researchers have been puzzled by this, but the family put us right about it. The sitter wasn't the Philip Beauclerk you're thinking of, but a cousin of the same name. There were Beauclerks all over the south of England, and this Philip was a member of the Devon branch who settled in these parts.'

'Why did he do that?'

'It's not very clear. He seems to have started as a tenant of the local Beauclerks and bettered himself.'

'He must have, if he could afford a court painter's prices. Where did the portrait come from?'

'We acquired it from the Fortescues at the same time as the contents of their muniment room.'

'Really? What was it doing there?'

'He married one of the Fortescue daughters.'

In a thoughtful mood he reported his find to Miss Barton. 'So we've got two Beauclerks mixed up with the Fortescues.

That's a bit much for me to swallow.'

'Coincidences do happen, Mr Burke.'

'How do we find out about this cousin from Devon?'

She considered. 'We could ask their county archivist about him. If anyone knows, he should.'

While they waited for the reply from Devon, Neil concocted a gloomy sequence for the pageant about the ravages of the Black Death in the neighbourhood. He was putting the finishing touches to it when Miss Barton came to report the result of their enquiry. 'According to Devon there were three seventeenth-century Philip Beauclerks in that branch of the family. One died under James I, and another was much too old to fit the bill. But the third would do. He was born in 1622 as well.'

'Good. If there were three Philips in Devon it was enough to create confusion in people's minds if someone decided to conjure up a fourth.'

'Who would want to do that?'

Neil looked again at Olivia's family tree. 'There's this younger brother of our Philip's. Gervase.'

'Yes, Mr Burke. The colonel traces his descent from Gervase's line of the family.'

'Then Gervase, not Philip, must have inherited their father's money. Why? Oh, look here! The great Sir Robert died in April 1666. And Philip died two months earlier, in February '66. Another coincidence. They really are piling up.'

'I don't quite see what you're suggesting.'

'We've got Philip apparently dying just in time to miss inheriting Sir Robert's millions. His younger brother collars the lot.'

Miss Barton looked at him severely. 'Mr Burke, you're not suggesting that Gervase killed him in order to secure the inheritance?'

'Not quite. Gervase must have employed an incompetent

327

contract killer, or a dishonest one. He told Gervase that the job had been done. So Gervase put up a memorial tablet in the church, then found to his dismay that Philip wasn't late lamented after all. So he invents cousin Philip from Devon, so that the real Philip can conform to his memorial tablet and remain firmly dead.'

Miss Barton had been a schoolmistress. She gave Neil a withering look, as if at an insubordinate pupil. 'Mr Burke, you're letting your imagination run away with you.'

'I still think Philip survived his alleged death date, and the cousin from Devon is a figment of Gervase's imagination, to account for his failure to be dead.'

'But people in the village would see through the deception at once. They'd know what Philip looked like.'

'Not necessarily.' He flipped through Olivia's pamphlet again. 'Yes, here we are. "Little is known about Sir Robert's elder son, Philip, a seafaring man who spent most of his life abroad." There, you see? The village won't have seen much of him. Not enough to spot the imposture.'

Miss Barton's frown deepened. 'There's an easy way of settling this. We must have a look at the Beauclerk Cup.'

'A sporting trophy, is it?'

'No, a chalice. Part of the Communion plate belonging to the church. I've always understood it was presented to the parish by Gervase or one of his descendants. It's heavily engraved with coats of arms, and if they're Gervase's arms it settles the matter.'

'Why?'

'Philip's would have been different. If it was he, not the Devon cousin, who married a Fortescue, hers would be on the right of the shield, not Gervase's wife's.'

'By all means let's look, Miss Barton. Philip left a silver cup and cover to the church in his will. I've got this right, haven't I? If the Cup has Beauclerk quarterings on the left and a lot of Fortescue quarterings on the right, it would mean that it was our Philip who married into the Fortescue family.'

'I suppose so, yes,' she admitted grudgingly.

'Then by all means let's look at this chalice. Is it kept in the vestry?'

'Oh dear me no, it's far too valuable, they couldn't afford the insurance. It's at the bank, but the secretary to the Parochial Church Council can give us permission to see it.'

Next morning they were sitting in a basement room at the bank with the Beauclerk Cup in front if them. It was beautiful, standing almost a foot tall, with a heavily ornamented cover. Wasting no time on admiring it, Miss Barton peered at the coat of arms engraved on it, then sat back, aghast. 'Oh, Mr Burke, I do apologise. These are the Beauclerk arms, crossed with the Fortescues'. I was quite wrong, and you were right. Oh dear, this upsets everything. Philip was alive, disguised as the Devon cousin.'

'But he behaved very oddly, didn't he? He jumps up out of his grave, like Giselle in the ballet. But instead of saying "Hey, I'm alive, give me my share of Father's money", he keeps his mouth shut and lies low and masquerades as the cousin. Why?'

'Why indeed?' murmured Miss Barton, deeply shaken.

'He's scattering clues around, isn't he? He has the date put in large letters on his portrait, to show that he was alive after 1666. He gives a chalice to the church, to show that he isn't the cousin from Devon.'

'But he doesn't come out with the truth.'

'Could it be some kind of tease?' Neil suggested. 'He keeps Gervase on tenterhooks with these hints, but Gervase has a hold on him of some sort, so he has to go along with the Devon fantasy.' He thought for a moment. 'What if he's under a cloud, and liable to be arrested if he's identified?'

Miss Barton treated him to another of her bird-like glances.

329

'I think we should look again at what Olivia Beauclerk says about him.'

'Little is known,' they read, 'about Sir Robert's elder son, Philip, a seafaring man who spent most of his life abroad. He had much to do with the Dutch, and was an unofficial naval adviser to Sir William Temple, who acted as King Charles's negotiator with the States General.'

'That's the government of the United Provinces of the Low Countries,' Miss Barton interjected.

They read on.

'He also had commercial interests in Holland,' wrote Olivia, 'but there is no proof of suggestions that he engaged in the export of slaves from the Gambia to supply labour to the plantations in the American colonies. He died in the far east, while engaged in an attempt to break the Dutch monopoly of the lucrative trade with the Spice Islands.'

'The Spice Islands means Indonesia,' said Miss Barton. 'Conveniently far away, if you want to pretend that someone's dead when they're not. Records can easily get muddled at that distance.'

'Olivia doesn't think much of him, does she? The vague connection with Temple makes him look respectable, but there's also that nasty hint about the slave trade. He must have blotted his copybook somehow.'

'Treason?' suggested Miss Barton.

'Could that be it?'

'Well, it was a very confused period in Anglo-Dutch relations. A lot of double dealing must have gone on, because Charles couldn't make up his mind whether to back the Dutch against France or ally himself with France against the Dutch. Philip would have committed treason if he sided with the Dutch while Charles was in one of his anti-Dutch moods and making war on them as an ally of Louis XIV.'

Neil nodded. 'That would explain why his memorial tablet

was so tight-lipped about his career. When it was put up his treason would have been fresh in people's minds. Centuries later, Olivia can say what she likes about him without fear of contradiction.' He thought for a moment. 'Why put a tablet up at all? Why not keep quiet about the whole disgraceful episode?'

'No, Mr Burke. If Gervase wanted to inherit, he had to establish firmly that Philip was dead. A memorial tablet is a very solid argument.'

They were sunk in deep thought when a not very politely worded note arrived from the colonel: he wished to see Neil immediately.

Neil duly presented himself at the Beauclerks' imposing Queen Anne headquarters, where an unsmiling manservant ushered him into the presence. Sitting at his desk, the colonel took no notice of him, and did not invite him to sit, but pretended to be busy with some papers.

Faced with these signs of extreme displeasure, Neil waited for an invitation to sit down. Not having received one for over five minutes, he took matters into his own hands and perched on a hard chair some way from the colonel's desk.

Eventually the colonel looked up. The look turned into a glare when he saw Neil sitting. 'Ha!' he said in a grimly offended tone. Sharp barking noises from beneath the moustache suggested that some further utterance was to be expected, but none came.

'You wanted to see me, sir?'

'Yes. Understand from the secretary to the PCC that you've been interesting yourself in the Beauclerk Cup.'

'I had a look at it, yes.'

'Didn't occur to you, did it, to ask my permission first?'

'Well, no. I understood it was the property of the church.'

'It is. Quite right, in a sense. But it's part of our family history. What's more, I pay for the insurance on it. Quite a lot.'

'Even when it's in the custody of the bank?'

'That's not the point. Thinking of showing it around the place, were you? In this pageant?'

'No, sir.'

'Look here. There'll be a four-figure bill for the pageant's expenses. I'm picking it up. No way will I shell out for the insurance on the Cup so that you can parade it round the village.'

'There's no question of that, I assure you. It never entered our minds.'

The colonel looked taken aback and his bark became sheepish. 'Then why go and gape at it at the bank, eh?'

'I'd never seen it,' said Neil, taking defensive action. 'Miss Barton was telling me how beautiful it was, and she arranged for me to have a look at it.'

The colonel shot him a penetrating glance. 'Ha! Take my advice, young man. Concentrate on getting this pageant off the ground. No point in getting caught up in sidelines.'

Neil reported back to Miss Barton in a thoughtful mood. 'He knows. I'm sure he does.'

'Knows?'

'Well, he barks nervously whenever anyone goes near the Beauclerk Cup. It's kept in the bank incommunicado, so that no one can see the Beauclerk arms crossed with the Fortescues' and realise what that means. And the barking means that he knows what Gervase and Philip got up to.'

'But we don't,' said Miss Barton in an aggrieved tone.

There was a long, thoughtful silence.

'Let's start,' said Neil, 'by asking ourselves about Philip's will. He left an estate which included four farms and a lot of woodland. Was he making his wife's family bankroll him?'

Miss Barton frowned. 'Let me have another look at that will.'

She studied it carefully, and pored over an old map of the village. 'No, he didn't get any land from the Fortescues.

332

All he left came from the Beauclerk estate.'

'Could he have bought the land with Fortescue money? His wife's dowry, for instance.'

'Oh no, Mr Burke. That was valuable land. A younger daughter's dowry would have been a drop in the bucket by comparison.'

'So Gervase is buying Philip off? In other words, we're back at blackmail. But who's blackmailing who? They've both got grounds. Gervase can denounce Philip for committing treason and not being dead, and Philip can denounce Gervase for mounting an unsuccessful attempt to murder him.'

'What the cold war strategists used to call a balance of terror,' said Miss Barton.

'Rather an unequal balance, don't you think? With a charge of treason on one side and an unconfirmed story about a failed murder attempt on the other. Philip would have been in a much stronger position if he'd said who he was and accused Gervase of attempted murder, instead of masquerading as the cousin from Devon.'

'We don't know how strong the evidence was against him.'

Neil digested this, then passed on to another aspect of the puzzle. 'The Fortescues are keeping very quiet about all these goings-on. Why?'

'They've got their daughter's interests to consider, Mr Burke. What happens to her if Philip is disgraced?'

'True, but I think there's more to it than that. The embarrassingly dated portrait of Philip was in their possession. They kept his will. It looks as if they were a party to the tease.'

Suddenly Miss Barton looked like a bird that has spotted a juicy worm. 'Talking of teases,' she said, 'I've just been reminded of something. Have you ever been inside Pond Cottage?'

'That half-timbered house by the church? No.'

'About five years ago a young couple bought it and started

to do it up. They were rather antiquarian minded, and wanted to restore it as far as possible to its original state. They thought there was some kind of painting under the distemper on the sitting room wall, and decided to strip it and see. They were right, there was a frieze all round the top of the wall, consisting of wreaths of holly and ivy, with some lettering mixed up with it. The lettering was almost obliterated, but there were versions of the inscription on all three inside walls, and after comparing them they and their experts decided that it probably read "Et tu, Beauclerk".'

'Echoing Caesar's remark "You too, Brutus" when he found that Brutus was among his assassins.'

'That didn't make sense. Gervase Beauclerk hadn't assassinated anyone.'

'But he'd tried to,' said Neil.

'Yes. It looked like what you describe as a "tease" by the Fortescues. Pond Cottage had always belonged to them, it was listed as one of the lots offered for sale when the estate was broken up in 1927. But the Fortescues were happily farming in Australia and had lost their appetite for quarrelling, so the colonel had the field to himself. Stung to the quick by the slur on his ancestors' honour, he waded in, puffed up with family pride. He brought in experts of his own, who decided that the half-obliterated inscription almost certainly read "Exultate", an exclamation of Christmas joy which admittedly fitted in better with the Yuletide garlands of holly and ivy than hints of murder. The young couple who were doing the place up were quite happy to fall in with his wishes, and the inscription read "Exultate" when the mural was, not very sensitively, restored or rather repainted.'

' "Exultate" may have been right,' said Neil. 'Anyway, it doesn't get us any further.'

They had come to a dead end, and the pageant called urgently for attention. He had discovered a bare mention in the county archive of a visit to the village by King Edward III, though it gave no indication of what purpose he had in mind. Drawing heavily on his imagination, he began to build this up into a pageant episode.

Miss Barton, meanwhile, was pursuing some line of research of her own and had surrounded herself with historical tomes. Presently she emerged from behind her barrier of books in a state of great excitement.

'Mr Burke, I think I've got the answer,' she cried, brandishing one of them. 'Listen to this. "In the 17th regnant year of King Charles II an act was passed that all and singular His said Majesty's subjects who from and after the first day of February next ensuing at any time during the continuance of the war with the States of the United Provinces should serve the same States either by land or sea, soldier or mariner . . ." Oh dear, there's a lot more of this, but listen to how it ends up. "The said person should be attainted of high treason and should suffer and forfeit to His said Majesty all his manors, lands and tenements and hereditaments, goods and chattels whatsoever." There, what d'you make of that?'

'Typical of the Stuarts. Charles II was always strapped for cash. Any excuse for pocketing a penny or two was good enough. But how do the dates fit?'

'Perfectly. Charles was a stickler for the monarchical proprieties. He didn't date his reign from his restoration in 1660. He'd reckon he came to the throne when his father was executed in 1649. Seventeen years from then brings us to 1666, with the Dutch fleet blockading the Thames and setting fire to British men of war. Anyone who sided with the Dutch at that moment was obviously guilty of treason.'

'And the great Sir Robert chooses that moment to die. Philip is up to his neck in treason in Holland. If he inherits the estate, Charles collars the lot. Bang goes the Beauclerk inheritance.'

'Exactly, Mr Burke.'

'So the two brothers collaborate to frustrate him. Gervase hasn't committed treason, so he gets a message somehow to Philip: you sham dead. I inherit. You lie low somewhere abroad and we share the proceeds.'

'Yes. But we know now that Philip is an awkward and uncooperative character . . .'

'. . . and he doesn't keep his side of the bargain. Instead of lying low abroad he turns up as bold as brass in the village. So Gervase has to cover up for him by conjuring up the cousin from Devon. And all of them have to keep the secret. Not only the two brothers, the Fortescues have their daughter's interests to consider. They don't want her to be left in poverty because the king had confiscated the whole Beauclerk inheritance.'

They sat back thoughtfully, looking at the story from this new angle.

'When did Philip die?' Miss Barton asked suddenly.

Without thinking, Neil reached for Olivia's memoir.

'It's no use looking at that, Mr Burke. According to Olivia he was already in a watery grave in the far east.'

'Of course, stupid of me. He had to die disguised as the cousin from Devon.'

'Yes. Needless to say, he's not in the churchyard here.'

'They must have buried him somewhere, in a hugger-mugger way. In Devonshire, perhaps?'

'I don't think so. If the Devonshire Beauclerks were asked to dispose of him, they'd have said, "Who is this person? He's not in our family tree." '

'So he must be somewhere round here.'

'Oh botheration,' Miss Barton exclaimed. 'That means we're in for a tedious search.'

Several nearby parishes had kept registers of deaths and burials going back to medieval times. No Beauclerks were to be found in any of them. As a last resort she suggested a long shot.

'We could try Wilton Regis. It's about fifty miles away but a cadet branch of the Fortescues had settled there, and the family could have asked them to oblige.'

Her long shot paid off. In answer to a written enquiry the vicar of Wilton Regis reported that a Philip and Margaret Beauclerk were indeed buried in his churchyard, having died on 26th December 1669. 'Since they died simultaneously,' he added, 'one presumes that they met with an accident, though this is not recorded.'

Miss Barton went pale to the lips. 'An accident? Or—Oh my goodness!'

'Et tu, Beauclerk,' Neil remembered. 'Surrounded by Christmas garlands of holly and ivy. And they died on December 26th!'

'A murder disguised as an accident,' murmured Miss Barton faintly.

'I think so. Gervase was being blackailed into handing over more and more of his estate to Philip, and I think he was probably a rather solemn character who hated being teased. The portrait with Philip's age on it was probably the last straw.'

'Yes, Mr Burke. And now you know the truth, what are you going to do about it?'

What indeed? To suppress what he was sure was the truth went against the grain. But nothing could be proved, it was all conjecture. If he came out with the story the fallout would be devastating. The colonel's terrier-like barks would be amplified into the trumpetings of a wounded elephant. He would have a permanent fit of the sulks and his purse strings would be firmly shut to local good causes. The village would take sides for and against, the ructions would be far worse than the quarrel over the village green. Both factions would round fiercely on Neil for causing so much trouble. They would turn on his family; even his father's medical practice might suffer. Poor Miss Barton would sink under the weight of guilt by association.

'Little is known,' he wrote, 'about Sir Robert's elder son, Philip. A seafaring man, he died in the far east in 1666, while engaged in an attempt to break the Dutch monopoly of the lucrative trade with the Spice Islands . . .'

He was not being paid for his work on the pageant. But if he changed the people's names, he could always sell the true version as a short story.

Miss Unwin's Mistake

H. R. F. Keating

London, 1875

Miss Harriet Unwin, governess, did not make mistakes. Brought up in the workhouse as a nameless orphan, she had always known that, if she was to make any progress in the world, she must do everything that came in her way as faultlessly as could be. Her success in this over the years was not something on which she particularly prided herself, except perhaps on having gained – from a fellow-employee lady's maid – a command of French more euphonious and accurate than that of most of her supposedy well-educated employers.

It was, in fact, this unusual accomplishment that, on what was her last day in the employ of Mr Dorset Merriman, wealthy member of the Worshipful Company of Mercers, led her to giving a final lesson, not in French but in life, to Maria, Mr Merriman's daughter. It was French, however, that brought about her passing on to her pupil a rule she had learnt herself long ago.

'Oh, Maria, Maria,' she had unthinkingly exclaimed as, reading over the last French composition her pupil was ever to write, a letter to a supposed French girl of her own age, she came across a howling error.

'Maria, how could you? Look. *Excusez-moi si j'avais fait un bêtise en orthographe.* And that is exactly what you have done, committed a stupid error in spelling. Haven't I told you more than once that *bêtise* is feminine? Perhaps because

341

gentlemen think silly mistakes are the province of us women? It's *la bêtise*, Maria. *La bêtise*.'

She realised a moment later that she should not perhaps have been quite so vehement. Maria, on the very eve of her sixteenth birthday about to put her hair up and enter the adult world, burst into a fit of weeping.

'Now, now, my dear girl, it is not a matter for tears. What you must learn – and this really will be my last lesson for you – is that if you have made a mistake you have made it. It can be corrected afterwards, of course. But it cannot be taken back. That is something that you, even on the point of attaining what are called the years of discretion, would do well still to take to heart.'

She thought she saw then in Maria's eyes a hint of rebelliousness, a tiny flicker of feeling that her time under a governess's rule had come to an end.

'No,' she said quickly, 'let me tell you how I learnt that lesson, although as it happened I had done nothing that particularly required it. In the family where I was teaching a girl much younger than yourself, the grandmother, a wise old lady, took me aside one day, when she had learnt by chance that I had had my full share of troubles, and said something to me that I have never forgotten. She told me I was always to think, however black events in the past had been, that *they are over and must be accepted*.'

Little did Miss Unwin think, however, that before many weeks had passed those were words she would have full cause to take to heart herself.

The whole trouble began late next evening. Widower Mr Merriman, who as a rule took little interest in his daughter, now apparently feeling that the time had come to make some amends, had arranged for a large dinner party to celebrate her birthday. It would introduce Maria to the world, her hair up in an elaborate arrangement worthy almost of the heiress to a duke. Miss Unwin, no longer properly in Mr Merriman's service, was, on Maria's insistence, present to give any reassurance that might be needed.

Of the assembled guests, almost all of whom were business-men with their diamond-laden wives – Mr Merriman's concerns were not wholly with his daughter – Miss Unwin knew only two of the gentlemen, Maria's cousins, Frederick and Nicholas, frequent visitors to the house. They were some years older than Maria, and had both, in Miss Unwin's eyes, tended to patronise a girl who was not, on Mr Merriman's death, going to become like them decidedly wealthy. It had been long ago made plain that Mr Merriman's large fortune was to be divided equally between the two cousins, who both bore his name and were almost exactly of an age – when Miss Unwin had first seen them one after another she had thought they were brothers – and a respectable sum only was to be left in trust for Maria on her marriage.

Frederick who was a fine figure of British manhood, tall, broad-chested, upright of stance, blue-eyed, with regular features and a fine head of fair hair with a moustache to match, was Miss Unwin's favourite, despite his treating her pupil by and large as he might have done a puppy, a creature to be given a pat or a jocose word every now and again. Nicholas was quite as handsome as his cousin although, a good eight inches shorter, hardly as fine a figure, even if his hair was as fair and his moustache as dashingly masculine. But, moodily dour of temperament and taking even less notice of Maria than his cousin, with all his attentions given to his cantankerous old uncle, he was by no means as high in Miss Unwin's estimation as Frederick.

When all the guests except Mr Merriman's two nephews had left the house Miss Unwin, who had been discussing the evening with Maria as she prepared for bed, found it necessary to go downstairs again. Maria, still much excited half an hour and more after the event, said she would not be able to sleep unless she had a book to read, and the one she had set her heart on had been left somewhere in the drawing room. It was a finely bound copy of one of Honoré de Balzac's novels, a present from a French business acquaintance of her father who had been impressed on a previous visit to the house by the young girl's lack of any heavy English accent in speaking his language. Miss Unwin thought, slightly risqué though the Balzac book might be, its picture of a more adult world than anything Maria had yet come across would be a useful step in her education.

So, candle in hand, she entered the dark and deserted drawing room and looked about. And then, from Mr Merriman's study next door, she heard his voice raised in loud anger.

'By God, young Nicholas, how can you have the temerity to ask me that?'

She knew she should make no effort to hear more. Family business was family business. But she had not yet found the book Maria wanted so badly. And in any case whatever reply Nicholas had made must have been no more than a few muttered words.

But then she did hear words, loudly and clearly spoken, that she regretted at once having become privy to.

'I am sorry, sir, but I must state that I believe Nicholas was doing no wrong in asking you.'

It was Frederick.

How good of him, Miss Unwin thought at once. Frederick could have stayed silent, and let Mr Merriman's wrath fall wholly on his cousin, losing him perhaps a portion of the wealth to come. But, no, Frederick, as she would have expected of him, had unhesitatingly spoken up in the interests of justice.

'You, too, sir. You pup. You pup.'

Mr Merriman's rage was mounting instant by instant. Miss Unwin envisaged him there in the study, standing legs apart in

344

front of the dying fire, his face echoing that of the bewigged bust of his seventeenth-century ancestor, Bishop Merriman, high up on the tall glass-fronted bookcase opposite as he looked down with cold severity on the miscreants below.

But Frederick seemed undeterred by his uncle's anger.

'Sir, no, I must repeat. Nicholas's request, though perhaps relying too much on your indulgence, was reasonable. Indeed, sir, I, too, have been injudicious in my expenditure and could well have requested a similar—'

'You, too? No, this is too much. I'll tell you here and now that I've a mind – no, damn it, more than a mind – to alter my will. The two of you seem to believe it entitles you to rob me left and right. I'll teach you it does not. Yes, by God, I'll leave every penny to little Maria. She's a damn clever girl, and deserves it. Did you hear her prattling away in French this evening to Monsooer Doopain? Yes, she'll never waste the money I've fought to earn. No damn tailor's bills for her. And no gambling debts either. And worse, I dare say. Far worse.'

At this point Miss Unwin – transfixed, she had not even glimpsed the Balzac novel – thought it best to glide swiftly as she could out of the darkened drawing room. She certainly did not want to hear details of whatever vices Nicholas had fallen into, and it seemed as if before long old Mr Merriman would castigate him in yet clearer terms.

The flame of her candle almost blown out in her haste, she ran up the stairs.

But, she thought as she came to Maria's door, do what I will I shall carry away with me from this house tomorrow morning all that was said, and perhaps decided on, in the study tonight.

She found sixteen-year-old Maria, still affected by her two glasses of champagne, by no means ready to sleep.

'Oh, Miss Unwin, how could you come back without my book? When it's in French, too. The French I can read, thanks to you. *La bêtise*, Miss Unwin. *La bêtise*, I won't make that mistake again. Please, can't you go down and have another look? I know I left it on the little table with the silver snuffboxes. But the servants may have tidied it away. Please, go and look. Please.'

So Miss Unwin, somewhat against her better judgement, went downstairs again.

Almost at the stair foot she saw that the door of the study, shut when she had passed it a few minutes earlier, was now partly open.

Let's hope those two young men have left, she thought. I don't want to hear more family secrets than I've heard already.

In the dim light of her candle she looked across the hall to the hatstand, where it was customary for the servants, if late at night they had been sent to bed, to leave the hats and coats of any remaining visitors. She saw only one shining silken hat hanging there.

So only one of the two has left and the other is still there in the study, she thought. No doubt it is Frederick, continuing manfully to plead for his cousin. But what if he fails? What if, because of his intervention, they are both cut out of the will? Maria will be a very rich young woman one day then, unless the old curmudgeon changes it all back again. And I don't think he will. It isn't as if he's a fussy old lady altering her will four times a month. No, if he carries out his intention tomorrow, then my Maria will be a catch indeed in the marriage market. I only hope the man who claims her treats her as he should.

Inside the study all seemed silent.

Miss Unwin moved on down a step. And then, through the wide gap between the inner edge of the heavy half-open door and its jamb, for one half-second an extraordinary sight just caught her eye. The marble head of Bishop Merriman appeared, through the firelit gloom of the study, to be flashing downwards from its perch like some avenging fury.

It was a vision instantly, and horribly, explained.

346

There came a sickening thud as the heavy bust came into contact with some almost solid obstacle. It was accompanied by a single short groan. The groan of a human being mortally struck down.

Afterwards Miss Unwin blamed herself for not having immediately entered the study. But the vision and the fearful sound, coming one after the other, had so stunned her that she had all but fainted, clutching desperately at the stair's ornately carved newel-post.

It was only a short time, a few seconds she thought, perhaps a full minute or more, before she recovered herself. A cold draught sweeping into the hall had revived her. She pulled herself upright, picked up her candle from where it had fallen, still smokily alight, and turned to the wide open front door.

To hear the clatter of boots on the steps, and to catch a glimpse – later she was to wonder whether this had been reality or imagination – of a head of fair hair disappearing, hatless, into the night.

An inspector of police from the Detective Department at Scotland Yard was on the scene within the hour. Standing in the hall, still lit only by her own guttering candle, Miss Unwin, answering his questions, soon acquired for herself a clear notion of what had happened. Mr Merriman had been killed. His head had been caved in by a single blow from the bewigged marble bust of Bishop Merriman. She thought, too, that she knew why it must have happened. She had heard Mr Merriman make it abundantly clear that he was going to alter his will. His two nephews would not, on his decease at some reasonably distant date, share his considerable wealth. Had he been able to go to his solicitors next day, as it was likely he fully intended to do, little sixteen-year-old Maria would have become his sole heir. Motive enough for a hasty and unscrupulous young man to end his life.

If it had been any business of hers, she would have argued that old Mr Merriman had been about to act with undue haste. Yes, both Nicholas and Frederick, by their own overheard admissions, had got badly into debt, which they should not have done. But on the other hand both young men, judging by all she had seen of them during her years in the house, were fundamentally of good character.

So should she tell this inspector of police – he was a pouncing, beady-eyed sort of man – about the dispute she had unwittingly overheard? Or should she not? After all, no one had seen her in the drawing room when Mr Merriman had so forcefully denounced his nephews' tailor's bills, gambling and . . . worse. She might very easily have not been there at all. Or have left the room before that shouting had broken out. Or not have entered till it had quietened down.

What would happen if she did tell what she had heard? She had no doubt that the inspector, with a body of constables, would be round at each of the young men's lodgings long before the night was out. Before the first streaks of dawn one of them would be under arrest. But which of the two had ended that old man's life?

She had assumed, without much reason, that Frederick had been the one staying behind in the study to plead with his uncle. But it need not have been him. It could as easily have been Nicholas, still demanding money to clear his debts. Or, after all, was the person she had half seen running down the steps out of the house as she had begun to recover from her near-fainting fit a mere hallucination? Had it been? She found herself hoping ferociously that somehow it had been, that neither Nicholas nor, even worse, Frederick had killed Mr Merriman. If, in her dazed state, she had imagined that fleeing figure, she would have no obligation to inform the inspector about the words she had heard coming through the wall of Mr Merriman's study.

But, if it was no hallucination . . .

Then a sudden flare of hope sprang up in her. Could the person she had barely seen have been neither Frederick nor Nicholas, but a passing thief? Could the murder have been committed by someone of that sort? Say, the two young men had left together somewhat earlier. And wasn't that likely? They could then, with their minds full of the quarrel that had just taken place, have failed to pull the heavy front door quite closed. That passer-by from the gutter could have seen it standing just a little open. He could have decided to slip inside to see if he could lay his light fingers on any small valuables. He could next have ventured in as far as the study, not noticing in the gloom of the room that its owner was there. Then, seized on, attempting to escape he could have launched out with whatever heavy object was within his reach.

With some eagerness she told the inspector then, not what she had overheard standing silently in the almost completely dark drawing room, but what she thought might have happened.

'You see, Mr Inspector, with the front door standing open, it would have been the greatest of temptations to any light-fingered fellow passing by to try his luck inside. Wouldn't it? Wouldn't you agree with that?'

The inspector gave her a small bleak smile.

'And how, madam, would your light-fingered passer-by have noticed in the darkened hallway here that there was any opportunity to come in and take his pick of objects he could not possibly have seen?'

'I – I don't know, Mr Inspector.'

And then she found the moment had come when she could no longer evade her duty. She drew in a breath and gave her beady-eyed interrogator a full account of what she had heard coming from the study shortly before old Mr Merriman's head had been battered in.

'But,' she concluded hopefully, 'surely this doesn't

necessarily mean that either Mr Nicholas Merriman or Mr Frederick Merriman killed their belov— killed their uncle?'

'Quite right, madam. It means nothing of the sort.'

'Oh, I am so—'

'Until we have some more positive evidence, what you have told me means very little. But, rest assured, we shall investigate. And before too long, I venture to say, we shall get down to the truth of it all.'

And then she realised there was a way in which she could point that investigation in the right direction.

She could tell the inspector, if he would listen, which of the two cousins had been the last in the house. It would be simple. All she had to do was to go over to the hall stand and take down from its hook the one silk hat remaining there. It would belong to whichever nephew it was who had stayed behind after the other had left and had then killed the man who was about to change his will. To either Nicholas or to Frederick.

With unswerving steps she took her candle across to the hatstand. She reached up. She lifted down the glossy hat. She turned it round and peered at the leather band inside.

Whose initials would she find?

Yes. Yes, there they were. *N.D.M.*

Nicholas. Yes, of course, dour, disreputable Nicholas. And not Frederick, the fine fellow who had leaped to the defence of his unamiable cousin. Not him, despite the fear, unexpressed even to herself, that it might have been.

She turned and went back to where the Scotland Yard officer was still standing, pensively staring down at the black-and-white marble squares of the hall floor.

'Mr Inspector,' she said, 'will you look at this?'

Events had moved rapidly from that moment on. Before three months had passed Nicholas Merriman was standing in the dock at the Old Bailey, under the sombre scrutiny of Mr Justice

Forester, the so-called Hanging Judge, accused of the murder of Thomas Merriman, of the Worshipful Company of Mercers, his uncle. And in the witness box Miss Unwin was steadying herself to give, with all the clarity she could, the remainder of her evidence, one small brick in the edifice the prosecution had built up. She must not make even the smallest mistake.

'Miss Unwin, I would now like to take you back,' Counsel for the Defence said, 'to the time shortly after you had found the body of your master so foully done to death.'

'Yes, sir.'

'You showed then to Inspector McWhirter a certain object. Yes?'

'It was a hat. A silk hat.'

'Ah, a silk hat. Now, Miss Unwin, I want you to tell us what it was about that hat which caused you to show it to the Inspector.'

'It was the initials inside it.'

'Ah, yes, the initials. And what made you believe, Miss Unwin, that those initials would be of use to Inspector McWhirter in his investigation?'

Miss Unwin felt a prickle of resentment at the tone of the questions.

'It was because I had reason to believe that the murderer of – of Mr Merriman had fled from the house immediately after his crime without taking his hat.'

'You saw him, as you put it, *fleeing from the scene of his crime*?'

'I saw him,' she replied with some sharpness, 'running down the house steps, and I learned later that Mr Merriman had been killed.'

'Very well. If you choose to put it in that way. But perhaps you could tell us now, in whatever language you care to express yourself, precisely what it was you saw in that hat which you considered to be a vital piece of evidence.'

Miss Unwin paused, took a breath, found no reason not to say what she had to say.

'I saw in the hat the initials *N.D.M.*'

'So you decided that this was the hat belonging to the prisoner here in the dock, Mr Nicholas Dorset Merriman?'

'Yes, sir.'

Defence Counsel rocked a little back on his heels. And smiled.

'Miss Unwin, have you never in the course of your life experienced circumstances where two gentlemen, with heads of much the same dimensions, have happened to take one another's hats? Be careful before you give us one of your impulsive answers, Miss Unwin. Think. Think carefully.'

Miss Unwin stood making a show of careful thought, but all the time resenting those words *one of your impulsive answers*. She had not given a single impulsive answer. She had thought before she had spoken. She had been determined not to make a mistake. And she had not done so.

And, what is more, she thought, although perhaps I was a little impulsive in showing Inspector McWhirter Nicholas Merriman's hat, he was impressed by what I had deduced. And he made it a piece of the case for the prosecution. All right, gentlemen do mistake each other's hats. I know they do. But Mr McWhirter should have thought of that before making the hat part of his case. And it still remains that the person I saw running hatless down the steps was Nicholas. It must have been. And he must have been the murderer. Only a few seconds passed between the moment I heard that terrible sound when the bishop's bust struck poor Mr Merriman's head and the moment I saw that figure racing away down the steps. I am utterly sure of that.

And am I as certain that it truly was Nicholas I saw?

In her mind she brought up again the vivid picture she had had in front of her so many times in the months between

Nicholas's arrest and this day at the Old Bailey.

And then, for the first time, she saw something she had not at all taken into account before. She saw beside the running figure's fair head, right at the foot of the steps, the iron torch-holder that jutted out from the pillar there. It was an object she had seen on hundreds of occasions during her time as Maria Merriman's governess. So she knew exactly how far up from the ground it was. From that she could tell precisely how tall the running figure had been.

And he had not been as short as Nicholas Merriman. He had been as tall as Frederick Merriman. More – she realised now, too – she had proof that it must have been Frederick and not Nicholas who had seized that heavy marble bust to use as a weapon. Better proof, far better proof, than the initials in that one remaining hat, which, yes, could have been left behind in error. No, Bishop Merriman's bust had always stood on top of the tall bookcase in the study, and that was proof of who had used it to kill old Mr Merriman. No one as short as Nicholas could possibly have taken it down. Only Frederick, eight inches the taller, could have reached up that far.

Now that she thought more, she saw at once that, yes, it was clearly possible Frederick was the murderer of his old uncle. After all, he had confessed equally, in the interview she had overheard, to being in debt. And, by implication at least, he had confessed to all the sins the irate old man had accused Nicholas of. It was as much in Frederick's interest to prevent that will's being revoked as it was in Nicholas's. It was ridiculous, just because she had found that tall, upstanding young man the pleasanter of the two, to believe that he could not, like any hothead with drink inside him, have perpetrated that terrible, spur-of-the-moment act.

No. No, she had made a mistake. And an appalling one. It was the idea she had put into Inspector McWhirter's head that had led directly to his arresting Nicholas Merriman, never mind what merely circumstantial evidence he had later added to his case. And as she had made that mistake, it was her plain duty to set matters right.

But how could she? How, standing here in the witness box at the Old Bailey, with the press gallery full of scribbling reporters, with Mr Justice Forester looking at her at this moment as if she were a scuttling beetle that had caught his eye, how could she announce that all she had been saying, with every appearance of conviction, was simply wrong? Very well, the correction of her mistake would be a simple enough matter. But to be seen as having made it . . . That would be to expose herself to the whole crowded courtroom, to the statue-stern judge, to the whole world beyond, as no more than a silly, misguided woman, a maker of mistakes, hardly knowing she had made them.

And she was not that.

Then into her mind there came words she had spoken, three months ago and more, to her then pupil Maria Merriman. Or, rather, words that had been spoken to herself years before by someone she had described to Maria as *a wise old lady*. She heard those words again now, in that old lady's quietly soft voice as she had talked to the young governess about the many miseries in her workhouse past. *They are over and must be accepted.*

She lifted up her head and looked across at Mr Justice Forester, staring down at her as impassively as if she were that still scurrying beetle, or perhaps in the way old Bishop Merriman had looked down at her being taken to task by her employer for some imagined fault.

'My lord,' she said, almost eagerly, 'I regret that I must tell you that in the evidence I have just given I made a grave and almost fatal mistake.'

The Case of the Abominable Wife

June Thomson

London, 1892

'Now here's an extraordinary coincidence!' Holmes exclaimed, briskly folding back the *Daily Telegraph* to a particular page. 'You know, Watson, I might very well write a monograph on it.'

'On the newspaper report?' I asked, looking up from my seat by the fire, for it was a bitterly cold winter's morning.

'No, my dear fellow! On the subject of coincidence. Have you not noticed that one has only to read a word one has never seen before to come across it several times subsequently? Or a book title? Or a name? Of course, there is a perfectly rational explanation for the phenomenon. For some reason one is not fully aware of, one's mind is alerted to that particular word or name or book title and that is why one keeps noticing it. It must be so in this case.

'If you recall, it was only last week when I was going through my tin box of documents that I happened to mention several cases I was associated with before your advent as my biographer. Although at the time I recounted the particulars of the adventure of the Musgrave ritual, I also referred briefly to the case of Ricoletti of the club foot and his abominable wife, did I not?'*

*In 'The Adventure of the Musgrave Ritual', Sherlock Holmes remarks that in his tin document box he has 'a full account of Ricoletti of the club foot and his abominable wife'.

'Yes, I do recall it, Holmes. You said you had a full record of the affair amongst your papers. I remember feeling particularly intrigued and hoped you might one day give me an account of it. But where does the coincidence come in?'

'Here in the *Telegraph*,' Holmes explained. 'Allow me to read the item out loud. It is quite short and was no doubt inserted merely to fill up a space at the bottom of page three. "Mr Luigi Ricoletti, a shopkeeper of Beak Street, was yesterday knocked down and killed by a two-horse delivery van as he was crossing Charing Cross Road. An inquest is to be held." That is the coincidence, Watson! To my knowledge, the name Ricoletti had not crossed my lips for several years and yet I have only to mention his name to you in passing last week for him to pop up again like a jack-in-the-box a few days later!'

'Extraordinary, Holmes!' I agreed. 'Do tell me about him. What was the inquiry you were engaged on which concerned him?'

'I shall satisfy your curiosity later, my dear fellow. First I must send a telegram. On my return, I shall look out the documents and you shall hear a full account of the affair.'

He was gone for about half an hour, and on his return I heard him entering his bedroom. Shortly afterwards, he came into our sitting room dragging behind him a large tin box. Having thrown back the lid, he began to search excitedly among the bundles of documents and other mementoes which the box contained, putting me in mind of a terrier digging out a rat from under a barn. After several moments of energetic activity, he came up with his prize: a large manila envelope inscribed with the words 'The Ricoletti Case', which he passed to me.

On opening it, I discovered several newspaper cuttings clipped together and two photographs, one of a young man on his own. He was in his twenties, dark-haired and very good-looking, but there was a disturbing air of menace about him as he stood, arms folded, staring defiantly at the camera as if to outface it.

The other photograph was of a couple, a man and a woman, the man seated, perhaps on account of one foot which appeared to be crippled. It was encased in a black surgical boot and was turned inwards at an unnatural angle. He was middle-aged and unprepossessing in appearance with a straggly moustache and an expression of craftiness rather than intelligence. In contrast to him, the woman was handsome in a bold, rather intimidating manner and it was as much from this insolent air as from the physical likeness to the young man that I assumed they must be closely related. She stood behind the older man, very upright and domineering, one hand on the back of his chair as if to indicate he was her possession.

I had put the photographs to one side and had begun to read the newspaper cuttings when Holmes interrupted me.

'You may read those later at your leisure, Watson. For the moment, allow me to give you a short résumé of their contents and to acquaint you with the background of the Ricoletti affair as well as the *dramatis personae*.

'It was in the year 1879,* I believe, that Inspector Lestrade of Scotland Yard approached me with a problem. Although I had been in practice for only four years,** I had made quite a

---

*The Musgrave Ritual case, the third inquiry Sherlock Holmes undertook as a professional consulting agent, has been variously dated to 1878, 1879 or 1880 while the written account, 'The Adventure of the Musgrave Ritual', was first published in the *Strand* magazine in May 1893. Assuming the account was written in 1892, the encounter with the Ricolettis must have taken place between 12 or 14 years earlier.
**In 'The Adventure of the Musgrave Ritual', Sherlock Holmes states that it was four years since he had last seen Musgrave, a fellow student of his at St Luke's college. Assuming he set up in private practice soon after arriving in London, he had been a consulting agent for that same period of time.

reputation for myself as a private consulting agent and the police were already in the habit of asking me for help with their more intractable cases. Lestrade's difficulty was this. There had been four garrotting attacks* on respectable citizens over the past six months, one of which resulted in the death of the victim, a man named Prosser, and the authorities were concerned that London was about to suffer a repetition of a spate of similar crimes which had occurred in the early '60s. You may have heard of them. In case you have not or do not recall the details, permit me to refresh your memory. The gang or gangs responsible for them became increasingly bold and in the summer of 1862 two highly respectable citizens, Mr Pilkington MP and Mr Hawkins, the antiquarian, were attacked in the West End. Other attacks were reported elsewhere in the country. It was indeed a very worrying situation although in my opinion the mass hysteria which followed these crimes was largely caused by the sensational reporting in the popular press.

'Lestrade and his superiors were evidently anxious to avoid a similar public outcry by asking for my assistance before matters went too far.

'Now I had made a study of the garrotters of that earlier period as well as their methods and had come to this conclusion. They almost certainly worked as a trio, consisting of a lookout or "crow" who warned them if anyone approached, particularly a policeman; a woman who served as the bait and who first accosted the victim; and the "choker" who attacked the victim from behind while his attention was on the woman and half strangled him using a scarf or his bare hands. While

---

*Parker, a member of Moriarty's gang, who kept watch on 221b Baker Street after Sherlock Holmes's return to London following the Great Hiatus, was said by Holmes to be 'a garrotter by trade, and a remarkable performer on the jews' harp'. Vide: 'The Adventure of the Empty House'.

the attack was going on, the woman searched the man's person, relieving him of his watch and chain, his pocket-book and any other valuables he might have on him in the way of a signet ring or loose money. The trio would then scatter, leaving their victim lying in a semi-conscious state on the ground.

'No one was ever caught. The attack was fast, silent and usually without witnesses, apart from the victim himself who never saw the "choker" or the "crow", only the woman and her only fleetingly, often in a dark alleyway, and was therefore unable to give a full description of the gang.

'However, in the case of these more recent attacks in the '70s, someone had noticed a man hurrying away from the vicinity and described him as middle-aged with a wispy moustache and, what was crucial to my inquiries, as having a decided limp. At that time, I had a very useful contact in the underworld, a retired cat burglar called Billy Marples who, for a modest retainer of five shillings a month, would not only keep me informed of any interesting plans brewing among his criminal confrères but could name and identify suspects for me. So I turned to Billy. Who was likely to work in a gang of three, I asked him, one of whom was a middle-aged man with a limp, the second, another man who was probably younger and stronger than the first, and the third a woman who was also young and handsome?'

'If you are speaking of Mrs Ricoletti, as I assume you are,' I broke in, 'I'm aware she was handsome from the photograph. But I feel that description hardly agrees with that other you applied to her – abominable.'

'Oh, my dear Watson!' Holmes said with a smile. 'There is such a refreshing air of naivety about you! One's outward appearance often has nothing to do with one's inner virtues. The most handsome and charming man I ever encountered, who was unfailingly courteous to women, was hanged for disposing of three of them with arsenic for their insurance money. As a young woman, Mrs Ricoletti was renowned for her beauty, although I cannot vouch for her charms at this present moment. She came from Wapping, one of eleven children born to an Irish coal-heaver, Pat Ryan, all exceedingly good-looking and all in one way or another criminally inclined. Among their number were thieves, blackmailers, pickpockets and rampsmen* whose favourite Saturday evening entertainment was a street brawl, and I speak not just of the men of the family either.

'Kitty Ryan was one of the younger daughters, a bold, black-eyed beauty as you yourself have seen, who went up in the world socially as well as economically by forming a relationship with Luigi Ricoletti who owned a little curio shop in Beak Street, off Charing Cross Road. I do not think the union was ever regularised but she was given the courtesy title of "Mrs Ricoletti" and the pair lived happily enough together even though he was older than she and a cripple, for he had been born with a club foot. He doted on her and she found certain advantages in throwing in her lot with him. Compared with the young men she had known in Wapping, he was comfortably off and was able to support her in a manner to which she was definitely not accustomed, such as a proper bed to sleep in and food placed regularly upon the table.

'By the way, I should add that not all Ricoletti's curios were legitimately acquired and he was long suspected of being a "fence" but the police were never able to catch him with stolen property on the premises.

'He was also very adept at "christening" certain articles such as watches, rings and small pieces of silver by removing any distinguishing marks in the way of initials or monograms,

*A 'rampsman' was a slang term for a street thief who used violence when robbing his victim. The verb was 'to ramp'. The modern equivalent is a mugger.

a skill he employed not only for his own benefit but, for a fee, for other fences as well.

'Once she had moved away from Wapping, Mrs Ricoletti had no further contact with her family apart from one brother, Danny, the youngest of the brood and evidently a favourite of hers. They were very similar in many ways: in features, manners and temperament for, unlike the rest of the Ryan clan, they were ambitious and set their sights further than the nearest taproom. Consequently, Danny moved into the Ricoletti household as a lodger and made himself useful by serving in the shop if need be and collecting or delivering the larger curios on a handcart.

'And so they apparently lived happily together until they came to my notice through Billy Marples. He knew them because of Ricoletti's activities as a fence. Before his retirement as a burglar, Billy used to pass some of his smaller items of booty to Luigi so, when I gave him a description of the trio I was looking for, he recognised them at once.'

'Just a moment, Holmes!' I interjected. 'There is something I do not quite understand. If Kitty Ryan was so comfortably settled as Mrs Ricoletti, why did she risk all by becoming part of a garrotting gang? Or was it Ricoletti who forced her to turn criminal in this way?'

'A good point, my dear fellow. Why indeed? The motives behind human behaviour are often dark and impossible to fathom. However, in the case of Mrs Ricoletti, the answer is quite simple and was certainly not because Ricoletti forced her. The boot was firmly on the other foot. Although I never interviewed her, I think I may speak with some authority about her. To put it quite simply, the lady was bored.'

'Bored?'

'Yes, bored with the humdrum routine of serving behind the counter, preparing meals for her menfolk and shopping in the nearby market. While she might for the first time in her life have a fine Sunday shawl and, so I have been told, even a pianoforte in the little parlour above the premises, she missed the excitement and the violence of her old life in Wapping – the brawling and the fisticuffs in the public houses on Saturday nights.

'I have no idea what put garrotting into her mind although that type of street crime was second nature to some of the Ryan tribe. Two of her brothers were sent to prison for "ramping" and garrotting is, after all, only another form of the same criminal behaviour. The idea may also have occurred to her when trade was slack and funds were low that the occasional stolen watch or the contents of a victim's pocketbook would augment the family coffers. But whatever the reason, I am absolutely convinced that it was she who instigated it and the main motive was not so much the money as the sheer excitement of carrying out the crime and the thrill of having some helpless male victim entirely in her power. I have good reason for saying so, Watson. She was in the habit of taking out her hatpin and, holding it close to the victim's face, threatening to put out his eyes if he showed any resistance.'

'Oh, Holmes, how horrifying!' I exclaimed.

'Exactly, my old friend. Now do you understand why I refer to her as "abominable"? She would have had no trouble in persuading Danny to fall in with her plan. As I have said, they were very alike in many ways and shared, I believe, the same perverted pleasure in inflicting pain on other people. As for Luigi Ricoletti, he was so infatuated by her that, had she asked, he would have walked through fire to please her.

'As soon as Billy Marples identified the trio and gave me their address, I disguised myself as a shabby, out-of-work clerk and took a couple of objects to Ricoletti's shop to sell. To my disappointment, I did not on that occasion see either Mrs Ricoletti or her brother, only the husband who struck me not so much as a ruffian but rather as a weak and greedy man who was easily led.

'After that first encounter, I contrived to rent a front bedroom in one of the houses overlooking Ricoletti's premises and, from its window, was able to watch the comings and goings of the members of the household. Thus I was able to become acquainted with their appearances and their routines.

'Apart from working in the shop and her domestic chores, Mrs Ricoletti and her husband were in the habit of paying twice-weekly visits to the Hare and Hounds, a public house a little further down the street, where they sat in the saloon bar like any other respectable citizens enjoying half a pint of old and mild or a more festive glass of porter. Being a good-looking young man and single, Danny Ryan led a more complex private life although on the surface that, too, was blameless. He was walking out, as they say, with a pretty little milliner called Rosie whom he used to escort on various outings including, as special treats, visits to the West End, especially in the neighbourhoods of theatres and other places of entertainment. Later, I began to suspect an ulterior motive behind these excursions.

'There was no break in their routine for several weeks and I was beginning to wonder if Billy Marples was wrong in pointing the finger at Ryan and the Ricolettis when I noticed a change in their behaviour. That particular Saturday evening, neither of the Ricolettis left the house at their usual time to visit the Hare and Hounds. Instead, they left separately and later than expected, first Ricoletti followed, after an interval of half an hour, by Mrs Ricoletti. Danny had already gone but his departure had not surprised me. I simply assumed he was meeting Rosie a little earlier than usual. But the Ricolettis were another matter and, when I saw the wife slip furtively out of the house alone, I decided to follow her. She was dressed, I noticed, much more modishly than usual in a fetching little hat with a bright pink feather and a very pretty shawl. Guessing her destination was somewhere more fashionable than the Hare and Hounds, I quickly threw an ulster over my shabby attire and, seizing up my stick, I hurried after her.

'She walked as far as Charing Cross Road where she hailed a hansom in which she quickly rattled away in the direction of the West End with me close behind her in another cab. Her destination was the Strand where she alighted and met both her brother and her husband outside the Lyceum theatre,* clearly a prearranged rendezvous. Although it was by now nearly half past eleven, the pavements were still crowded with pleasure-seekers who were strolling about looking for entertainment and with those whose very livelihoods depended on these casual passers-by. I speak, of course, of the pickpockets and thieves and ladies of the night. I had no doubt that Mrs Ricoletti and her accomplices were among these predators looking for a suitable victim.

'It was entirely due to Mrs Ricoletti's charming hat, adorned with the pink plume, in which the hatpin was undoubtedly concealed, that I did not lose her in the crowd. All I had to do was to follow this pretty piece of frippery as it bobbed along among the mass of tall silk hats and bonnets of every hue and description. Close at her heels were Danny and Ricoletti while I was close at theirs. I did not actually see her make her choice but, after about quarter of an hour of parading up and down, I saw her slip out of the crowds into Carting Lane, one of those little side alleys which lead down to the Victoria Embankment, in the company of her intended victim.

'She had chosen well. He was a short, middle-aged man

*In 'The Sign of Four', Miss Mary Morstan, later to become Mrs Watson, received a letter asking her to meet someone outside the Lyceum theatre in order to discover the identity of the unknown correspondent who had sent her six valuable pearls. Sherlock Holmes and Dr Watson accompanied her to the rendezvous.

with a little round paunch, not the type to put up much of a struggle even if he were in a condition to do so, which on this occasion he was decidedly not. He was tipsy in a genial, hail-fellow-well-met manner, very much off his guard with his hands in his pockets and a cigar in his mouth.

'It was quite clear to me that the attack would take place shortly for all the participants had already moved into position with the efficiency of a squad of well-trained troops setting up an ambush. As Mrs Ricoletti went off down the lane arm in arm with her victim, Danny Ryan, a black silk scarf hanging negligently about his neck, turned quickly after them while Luigi Ricoletti limped to his post at the entrance to the lane and, lighting his pipe, proceeded to eye the passers-by with a careful scrutiny.

'I knew I had not a moment to lose. In a few seconds, the victim would be lying senseless, if not dead, on the ground and his attackers would have disappeared. I therefore rushed towards them brandishing my stick and knocking Ricoletti off balance who shouted out a warning to the others as he fell. They immediately scattered, Mrs Ricoletti darting past me back to the safety of the crowds in the Strand, in her flight inadvertently blocking that escape route so that Ryan had no choice but to go forward down the alley towards the river. He was an exceedingly fit young man and ran like a hare so that, for all my best efforts, I could not quite catch up with him and he remained always that elusive three or four yards ahead of me.

'Once we had emerged on to the embankment, he turned left towards Waterloo bridge and, darting up the steps, gained the upper level of the road and public footpath which runs across it to the Lambeth side. Realising that once he gained the far bank, he could go to ground among the back streets round Waterloo station, I put on a further turn of speed, intending to bring him down at the first opportunity. I could see he was tiring for, although he was agile, he lacked staying power. He was aware of this himself and, as we drew near to the centre of the bridge, he glanced back at me over his shoulder.

'I shall never forget the expression on his face. I was within an arm's length of him. A few more seconds and he would be within my grasp. After that, all that lay before him was arrest and the trial for Prosser's murder, culminating in the walk to the scaffold and an ignominious death at the end of a rope. The realisation of this dreadful fate was so clearly stamped on his horror-struck features that it might have been emblazoned there in black letters a foot high.

'I blame myself for what happened next. Knowing his desperation, I should have been prepared but I was not. As my fingers touched his shoulder and flexed themselves in readiness to tighten into a grip, he gave a wriggle like a great fish escaping from a net and sprang up on to the coping of the bridge where he crouched for a second before, with a dreadful cry which I still sometimes hear in the long, dark stretches of the night, he plunged down into the black water below.

'A small crowd quickly gathered and, having sent a cab driver to alert the river police,* I remained on the bridge, straining my eyes to see where he might emerge. Eager though I was to capture him, I was not foolhardy enough to dive in after him.'

'I should think not, Holmes!' I interjected. 'Even if you had not drowned, the water itself could have killed you. God knows what filth it contains.'

'Exactly,' Holmes said grimly.

'So what did you do?'

'What could I do? I waited until a police steam launch

---

*The River Police, or Thames Division of the Metropolitan Police, was first formed in 1798. A police launch was used to chase the *Aurora* in 'The Sign of Four'.

arrived and made an unsuccessful search of the area. Several months later, a body was found washed up at low tide. Although hardly recognisable after its long immersion in the river, Luigi Ricoletti identified it as Danny Ryan's. It was assumed he had been dragged downstream by the current and became trapped under some submerged debris. The case against him was therefore closed.'

'What a shocking way to die!' I exclaimed. 'But, if Ryan was dead, what about the Ricolettis? Were they ever brought to justice?'

'Unfortunately, no. There was no proof, only a strong suspicion, that they had ever been involved in any of the garrotting attacks, including the murder of Prosser, and although I was prepared to give evidence, what exactly had I witnessed? Nothing criminal; only Mrs Ricoletti walking with a man into an alleyway. The most she could have been charged with was soliciting. As for the proposed victim, he said he would not be able to identify her. As he was a married man with a respectable post as clerk in a firm of City brokers, I can understand his reluctance. He ran the risk of losing his wife, his job and his good name. Nor were the police any more fortunate with the earlier victims. Prosser, of course, was dead, another had since died, a third they were unable to trace, and the fourth refused to testify for much the same reason as the City clerk.

'The Ricolettis did not escape entirely without punishment, however. Mrs Ricoletti lost her brother, possibly the only person that flint-hearted beauty had any softer feelings for and, for a time at least, the police kept a close watch on Ricoletti's premises so that his activities as a fence were severely restricted. Occasionally, I, too, visited their shop in various disguises in order to observe them but more out of curiosity than for any other reason. Mrs Ricoletti, I am pleased to report, was a great deal less bold than she had been; in fact, she seemed positively dejected and on the last two occasions she was not behind the counter although I caught a glimpse of her once in the street, bundled up in a shawl and looking greatly aged. In fact, for the last two years, the Ricolettis have withdrawn into themselves and have even abandoned the Hare and Hounds for a much less popular public house, the Blind Beggar in Stack Lane.

'In many ways, it was an unsatisfactory conclusion to the case. I should have much preferred to see the three of them brought to trial, Ryan hanged and the Ricolettis behind bars as they so richly deserved.'

He broke off to ask with apparent inconsequentiality, 'By the way, Watson, you do own a black suit of clothes, do you not?'

'Yes, of course, Holmes,' I replied, a little bewildered by the question.

'An old suit, I trust?'

'Yes, it is a little shabby,' I confessed, even more taken aback. 'Why do you ask?'

But instead of replying to my question, he merely nodded to show his satisfaction and turned his attention back to the *Daily Telegraph*.

The mystery was solved a little later that morning when a telegram arrived in answer to the one he himself had sent earlier. Having read it, he passed it to me. It stated simply: RICOLETTI FUNERAL TO TAKE PLACE AT ST MARYLEBONE CEMETERY* FRIDAY 11 AM STOP MARPLES

From the name, I assumed the sender was none other than Billy Marples, the former cat burglar who in the past had identified the trio of garrotters for Holmes's benefit.

---

*This cemetery is now known as East Finchley cemetery and comes under the jurisdiction of the City of Westminster.

'You see now why I asked if you had a set of dark clothes?' Holmes enquired as I handed the telegram back to him.

'Indeed, Holmes. I assume we shall be attending Ricoletti's funeral?'

'Not quite correct, my dear Watson. We shall certainly be present at the cemetery in time to see the burial take place. But we shall not be mourners; at least, not at that particular interment. Instead, we shall be laying a wreath on the nearby grave of a dear departed relative of ours.'

'But why must the clothes be shabby?' I enquired.

'I do not wish to draw attention to ourselves,' he explained. 'If we arrive in our best attire we shall be too conspicuous. For that reason, we shall both be wearing bowlers, not silk hats. There was something else you wished to ask, my dear fellow? When you clear your throat in that interrogative manner, it is usually a sign that you have another question in mind.'

'Only the reason why we shall be going at all, Holmes,' I said, smiling at his perspicacity. 'Is it really necessary?'

'Not at all, except to satisfy my curiosity. As I have said, I have not had the pleasure of seeing Mrs Ricoletti at close quarters for a considerable time. She appears to be keeping out of the public eye but I imagine she will be present at her husband's funeral.'

As events were to prove, Holmes was incorrect in this supposition. We arrived at St Marylebone cemetery by cab a little before eleven o'clock on the Friday morning, both wearing bowlers and shabby black attire. Holmes also sported a thick brown moustache and carried a wreath of white chrysanthemums and laurel leaves to give the impression we were mourners tending to a family grave near to the ready-dug plot where Ricoletti's coffin would shortly be interred.

As the small funeral procession drew near and Holmes bent down to place the wreath on the tombstone of one Edith Maud Buckmaster, I glanced across at the group which was preceded by the undertaker's men carrying a coffin and followed by three mourners, all of whom were men.

I looked quickly at Holmes but could not tell if he were surprised or disappointed by the absence of Mrs Ricoletti. His expression was inscrutable.

Having laid the wreath, he straightened up and began to walk away so rapidly that I had difficulty in keeping up with him.

'She was not there,' I remarked as we climbed into our hansom which Holmes had instructed to wait for us at the gates.

'I am well aware of that, Watson,' he retorted testily.

'Do you suppose she is ill?'

'That is a possibility. There are also other explanations which I shall make it my business to look into.'

'Such as?'

'At this stage in the game, I am no better informed than you,' was all the reply he would give before lapsing into a moody silence which, from my long association with him, I knew better than to interrupt.

I was therefore left with my own thoughts, in particular those concerning Holmes's use of the word 'game'. In the circumstances, it seemed a curious turn of phrase but one which I was quite sure he had chosen deliberately.

Over the next five days, he made several mysterious excursions in which I was not invited to take part but, as he made no further reference to Mrs Ricoletti during this period, there was no way of telling if they concerned the case or not. Indeed, I was not even sure whether there was any case or if Holmes had decided to draw a line under the whole affair.

On the afternoon of the fifth day, however, he seemed in better spirits.

'Come, Watson! Try these on, there's a good fellow!' he exclaimed, entering the sitting room, an overcoat over one arm and a flat cap such as workmen wear in the other hand.

'Why, Holmes?' I asked, as I put on the garments. They were very shabby but fitted me well enough.

As he stood back to regard me critically, he made no direct reply, except for the comment, 'Your boots are too shiny, Watson. Smear a little ash from the fire over them to dim their brightness. Otherwise, you look quite suitably dressed for an afternoon visit to a certain lady.'

'Lady?' I asked, a little puzzled at first as I failed to make the connection.

'A widowed lady,' he explained gravely.

'Ah, Mrs Ricoletti!' I cried, light dawning at last. 'I thought you had forgotten all about her.'

'Forget her? Never!' came the riposte. 'By the way,' he added, handing me a small package wrapped in brown paper. 'Put this in your pocket and produce it when I ask for it. Also make sure you bring your cab whistle with you.* And do not ask any questions, my dear fellow. All will be made clear very shortly.'

We set off soon afterwards by hansom for Charing Cross Road, Holmes dressed as shabbily as I in an old tweed coat, a flat cap similar to mine and a woollen muffler wound about his throat. The attire was, however, entirely suitable for the neighbourhood which was our destination. The curio shop was in Beak Street, a narrow turning behind the main thoroughfare which was lined with terraces of little brick houses, opening directly on to the pavement. The dingy monotony of their soot-stained façades was broken here and there by small, drab shops, mostly dealers in secondhand goods or cheap groceries. The only touches of colour on that bleak winter's day were the three brass balls hanging outside a

---

*Many Londoners carried a whistle to summon a cab, one blast for a four-wheeler, two for a hansom.

pawnbroker's and the garish red and gold paint of a public house on the corner, the Hare and Hounds.

The curio shop was as dreary-looking as the rest of the street, its one window crammed with a most extraordinary collection of household flotsam and jetsam in the way of cracked china jugs, tarnished brass candlesticks and chipped enamel basins.

The interior of the shop was just as cluttered with so many pieces of furniture, glass cases full of moth-eaten stuffed animals and bundles of old curtains smelling of dust that Holmes and I had difficulty picking our way towards the counter at the far end where a ginger-haired youth, alerted to our arrival by the sound of the bell ringing over the door, had emerged from a back room to attend to us.

It was quite clear from Holmes's opening remark that he had visited the place before.

'You remember me?' he asked the youth, assuming the air and accent of a Cockney costermonger. ' 'Arry 'Iggins as called last Monday. I said I'd come back with the goods to show to Mrs Ricoletti. Like I said, I've dealt with Mr Ricoletti in the past and 'e knows I allus asks a fair price.' In an aside to me but intended to be heard by the youth, he added, 'I only 'eard the other day as Mr Ricoletti's dead, run over by a van. Shockin', ain't it?' Turning back to the youth, he continued, 'Now, if you'd like to fetch Mrs Ricoletti, the three of us, me, 'er and me friend 'ere, Perkins, can strike a bargain over the yack.* Tell 'er it's a fifty-guinea job, no initials or name on it to say 'oo it belongs to, and I'm only asking a finny for it.'*

As the youth disappeared behind the curtain which closed off the back room, Holmes silently indicated the pocket of my coat in which the parcel was stowed away and, taking it out, I

---

*'Yack' is a slang word for a watch while 'finny' is slang for a five-pound note.

held it ready in my hand. A moment later, the curtain was drawn aside and a woman stepped out from behind it.

She was dressed entirely in black, including the shawl about her head and shoulders, and, in comparison with this dark attire, her skin looked ghastly white with the dead pallor of a corpse. In no way could she be described as beautiful. In fact, she had a haggard, unwholesome appearance but I could see vestiges of those bold good looks I had seen in the photograph in the black eyes, the straight dark brows and the structure of the bones beneath the pallid skin.

'Mrs Ricoletti,' Holmes was saying. 'First off, let me give you my condolences on the death of your 'usband. A good man was Luigi; one of the best.'

She accepted these commiserations with a little bow of her head but said nothing.

'And now,' continued Holmes, 'if I may turn to business. My friend Perkins 'as a yack 'e wants to sell. Give the lady the package, Fred. Let 'er see for 'erself the quality of the h'article.'

I handed over the parcel which she started to open, her face beginning to show signs of animation for the first time. While she was thus occupied with unwrapping the brown paper, Holmes suddenly struck with the speed and accuracy of a mongoose attacking a cobra.

Leaning across the counter, he gripped her tightly by one arm, with his other hand seizing the shawl and twisting the fabric tightly beneath her chin so that it served as a garrotte, a fitting means of restraint, I thought, considering the lady's criminal past.

At the same time, he shouted to me over his shoulder, 'Quick, Watson! Go to the door and give three blasts on the whistle!'

I scrambled through the barricades of chairs, chiffoniers and washstands and, having reached the threshold, I blew three

375

loud blasts as Holmes had instructed.

At the summons, the street burst into life as if at the sound of the last trump. Two uniformed police officers, accompanied by Inspector Lestrade in tweeds, came bursting out of the pawnbroker's shop while the driver of a four-wheeler which I had noticed on our arrival standing outside the Hare and Hounds as if waiting for a fare whipped up the horse and brought the cab at a smart canter to the very door of the curio shop.

We tumbled inside to find that, in our absence, Holmes had succeeded in forcing Mrs Ricoletti out from behind the counter and was holding her in a baritsu grip,* her arms tightly pinioned behind her back. She was struggling like a wildcat to be free, those black eyes blazing like hot coals with hatred and fury, her lips drawn back to show her teeth.

Aghast though I was at her appearance, I could not help but feel a little uneasy at Holmes's treatment of her for, despite everything, she still remained a member of the softer sex.

I was therefore considerably taken aback when Lestrade, advancing on her with a pair of handcuffs, commented, 'Well done, Mr Holmes! So you've managed to capture him?'

Him!

Seeing my expression, Holmes said with a smile, 'Yes, my dear fellow, Mrs Ricoletti is none other than Danny Ryan, the lady's brother and the murderer of Mr Prosser.'

'But Holmes!' I began.

He held up a hand.

'Not now, Watson. If you care to take a cab back to Baker Street, I shall accompany Inspector Lestrade to Scotland Yard

---

*'Baritsu' or 'bartitsu' is a Japanese form of self-defence, using hand-holds and techniques of balance. The name is derived from the Japanese word 'bujitsu', meaning 'material arts'. Sherlock Holmes defeated Moriarty at the Reichenbach Falls by using the baritsu method. Vide: 'The Adventure of the Empty House'.

to make a statement. On my return, I shall explain all.'

It was three hours later when Holmes arrived back at our lodgings, having given Lestrade a full account of his part in the affair and seen Ryan charged with murder. In the meantime, I had to try to contain my impatience until I, too, should be granted a similar explanation. As I waited, many questions clamoured in my brain. How had Ryan escaped drowning in the Thames? What had happened to the real Mrs Ricoletti? And how had Holmes determined that Ryan was impersonating her?

On Holmes's return, we drew up our chairs to the fire which I had encouraged into a cheerful blaze and, in its warm and flickering glow, my old friend gave me his account.

'It was by sheer good fortune that Ryan survived that desperate leap into the river from Waterloo bridge,' he began, lighting his pipe and settling back into his chair, his keen, aquiline features taking on the eager look of the ardent story-teller. 'The force of that initial plunge sent him down well below the surface and, while he was under the water, the current carried him along so that, when he finally emerged, he was some distance away. That fact, combined with the darkness of the night and the confusion of lights reflected in the water, made it impossible for me to judge his precise position and I assumed quite wrongly that he had drowned. In fact, he managed to come ashore further downriver between two moored barges. One of the bargees threw him a rope and, when he told them he was escaping from the police, they gave him a change of clothes and let him hide on board until it was prudent for him to leave.

'To be further on the safe side, he went to ground in a lodging-house in Rotherhithe until he felt any police surveillance on the curio shop would be lifted before he returned home. Of course, the Ricolettis were delighted to see him, having assumed he was dead, and, as soon as a suitable body was found washed ashore, Ricoletti claimed it as Ryan's, thereby strengthening the assumption that Ryan was no more.

'I have already explained how alike the Ryan brother and sister were in appearance, a similarity which they themselves were naturally aware of. Knowing that Ryan would have to lie low for fear of being arrested for murder, they decided that on occasions he would dress in his sister's clothes and, wearing a wig and with a shawl about his head, would venture out after dark in Luigi's company to walk about the streets and visit the public houses. As I learned this afternoon, they even went to the music hall together. Meanwhile, as their garrotting days were over, Luigi taught Ryan how to "christen" watches and he made himself useful helping in the little workshop in the back room.

'This situation could have continued indefinitely except for an unforeseen circumstance. Mrs Ricoletti, whose health had been deteriorating, died from a heart attack. This left Ricoletti and Ryan in a quandary. If Ryan was to continue impersonating his sister, what were they to do with her body? They could not let it be known in the neighbourhood that she had died.'

'I wondered about that myself, Holmes,' I put in eagerly. 'How on earth did they manage it?'

'Quite easily, my dear fellow. They pretended Mrs Ricoletti was a sister, a Molly Ryan, who was staying with them temporarily and who had died suddenly of heart seizure. A doctor who had not met the family but was known not to ask too many questions provided he was paid generously was called in and provided a death certificate. After that, they required only the services of a discreet undertaker and Mrs Ricoletti was buried quietly in the same cemetery in which her husband was interred the other day. In fact, I returned there last Tuesday and found her grave. There is a modest headstone inscribed to Molly Ryan with the words 'In Loving

Memory', together with the date of her death which was on 19th February two years ago. It was this, of course, which confirmed my suspicions regarding Ryan's impersonation of his sister.

'The unexpected death of Luigi Ricoletti placed Danny Ryan in a dilemma. If he were to continue running the business, he had either to place himself more in the public eye or employ somebody else to serve behind the counter. The youth we saw today was a temporary stop-gap who had no idea his employer was a man. The so-called Mrs Ricoletti kept very much to herself and spoke only in a whisper as she said she had suffered a throat injury which made talking difficult; an ironic excuse when one considers Ryan's past career as a garrotter. From papers found on the premises, it is clear Ryan intended to sell the business as soon as he could and flee to Ireland with the money where he would have assumed a new identity.'

'Male, I assume,' I asked with a smile.

'Oh, undoubtedly, my dear fellow,' Holmes riposted jocularly. 'I doubt even Ryan, for all his daring, could have maintained the role of the abominable wife indefinitely!'

The Curzon Street Conundrum
A Luther Darke Story

David Stuart Davies

London, 1896

I nspector Edward Thornton leaned forward and gazed out of the tiny window of his office in the upper reaches of Scotland Yard. It was a cold November day and grey swirls of fog wreathed the adjacent rooftops, reducing them to vague silhouettes.

Thornton sighed wearily. Sergeant Grey looked up from the case notes he was scribbling in his crabbed hand. 'It's not that Curzon Street business, is it, sir?'

Thornton replied without moving. 'Of course it is, Grey. There is something not quite right about it.'

'I don't know what you mean. We've got the blighter who did it locked up in the cells. Case solved.'

'We have someone locked up in the cells, but I'm not so sure it's the "blighter who did it". And if Armstrong really is the murderer, we have so little evidence.'

'There was the blood on his coat.'

'Blood on his coat and the knowledge that he was in great debt to the dead man. There's not enough material there to weave a hangman's hood, Grey. A good lawyer would blow those flimsy suppositions away in no time. And besides, I need to know how the crime was committed and how the murderer escaped from a locked room.'

'Then you know what to do. You know where to go. When you've had a real puzzle in the past . . .'

Thornton turned to his sergeant and pulled his thin, pale face into a mournful grimace. 'I know. Darke. I have been trying to put off that inevitability for some time. There is an element of humiliation in seeking his help.'

'Go on, sir. Go and see him. At least it will put your mind at rest.'

Luther Darke poured himself a large whisky and sat back in his chair. As he did so a lithe black cat leaped on to his lap with practised ease, curled up tightly, and began to purr. Absent-mindedly he stroked the contented creature as he stared across at his visitor, his dark brown eyes shining. He raised his glass in a mock toast. 'It is good to see you again, Edward. I am sorry that you will not join me in a drink. However, I am sure it is a wise move. Respectable gentlemen should not drink before noon and then decorum decrees that it should be a sherry aperitif.' He took a gulp of whisky, rolling it around his mouth. 'Whisky is the milk of the gods; sherry is their urine.'

Thornton remained silent. Like an actor waiting for his cue, he knew when it would be his time to speak. This preamble was a variant of the usual extravagant felicitations that he always experienced when he visited Luther Darke.

'To be honest, Edward, I am surprised to see you under my roof once more,' said his host, affably. 'You disagreed with me so strongly in the Baranokov affair – until my theory was proved correct that triplets had been used as a ploy in the theft of the diamonds – that I thought I had lost your friendship for ever.'

Thornton blushed slightly. Partly for being reminded of his failure in the Baranokov case and partly because this strange man referred to him as a friend. He didn't think anyone could get close enough to Darke to become his friend. He was too enigmatic, too self-possessed, too complicated to give himself to straightforward friendship. There was Carla, of course, his lover, but she in her own way was just as mysterious.

Luther Darke was the son of a duke but his father had disowned him at an early age because of his undisciplined and outrageous behaviour. He had been a rebel and hated the arrogance and pomposity of the aristocracy. Although Darke had inherited a considerable amount of money on his father's death, he had passed over the title and the family home to his younger brother. Ducal respectability and responsibility were abhorrent to him. Darke now occupied most of his time in being an artist and was gaining a growing reputation for his work. But even here his energies were erratic. On a whim he would drop his brush halfway through a painting in order to follow up one of his other passions, which were varied and eclectic. He had a fascination for the unexplained and the unknown. He took a great interest in the work of spiritualist mediums and in unsolved crimes. It was his offer of assistance in the Carmichael mystery, when Ralph Carmichael, a foreign office official, his wife and two children, along with their pet spaniel, apparently disappeared into thin air, that brought Inspector Thornton into contact with this unique individual for the first time. Darke helped to solve the case and Thornton had sought his assistance several times since.

Darke took another gulp of whisky. 'Ah, we see the world from different hilltops you and I, Edward. You are the professional, scientific detective with a demand for rationality and feasibility; whereas I am the amateur, an artist, doomed to view things from a different angle and able to see shifting and often unusual perspectives. We are two halves of the perfect whole.' He grinned at his own conceit and his eyes glittered mischievously. He had a broad, mobile saturnine face that possessed a wide, fleshy mouth. Dark, expressive eyebrows topped a pair of soft brown eyes that radiated warmth. His head was framed by a mane of luxurious hazel-coloured hair. He would have been handsome but the crooked nose, broken in one of the many fights he had had at school, robbed him of the classical symmetry of male beauty. He was not handsome, then, but he had a magnetic presence that compelled one to watch his face with fascination as Thornton did. Every conversation was a performance. It was as though he was acting his life.

'So, enough teasing. The Curzon Street murder? Am I right?'

Thornton nodded. 'I am not happy about it.'

'From what I have read in the papers, the case seems a straightforward one. Shipping magnate Laurence Wilberforce is murdered at his Curzon Street mansion – stabbed – and one of the guests in his house at the time was a certain Richard Armstrong, who owed the magnate a considerable amount of money that he could not repay. To make matters worse, I believe that blood was found smeared on the wretched fellow's overcoat. Have I caught the essence of the matter?'

Thornton gave a thin smile. 'You knew I'd come to you.'

'Indeed, I did. I was sure my worthy Thornton would not be taken in by such a simplistic solution. No doubt your superiors are quite content with Armstrong's arrest and cannot wait to see him dangling at the end of a rope.'

'They are indeed, despite the fact that one essential element of the case still remains a mystery.'

'And that is?'

'How the murder was committed.'

Darke laughed. 'Just a minor irritation. Not worth considering, surely? Pull the lever and let's have done with the scoundrel.'

Thornton's sensitive face darkened. There was more truth in Darke's flippant observations than was comfortable.

'I presume that Armstrong has not confessed in some fit of madness?'

386

'On the contrary, he professes his innocence most strongly.'

'So, young friend, we have come to that precious, that essential moment: give me the facts. Give me the minutiae.'

Thornton nodded. 'Do you mind if I walk about while I talk? It will help me recall the details more clearly.'

'The house is yours.'

'This room will do.'

'That's what I like about you, Edward. You are so literal. Pray begin.'

'The murder occurred two nights ago at the Curzon Street mansion of Laurence Wilberforce. There was a small dinner party with six guests, business associates of Wilberforce, some of whom brought their wives.'

'Armstrong's wife was there?'

'He's a widower.'

'Ah. Another avenue closed. Resume.'

'There were Lord and Lady Clarendon, Mr Clive Brownlow, the Member of Parliament for Slough, and his wife Sarah, Jack Stavely, a junior partner in one of Wilberforce's concerns and apparently very much a blue-eyed boy. And Armstrong.'

'And Armstrong.'

'Richard Armstrong who until recently worked for Wilberforce as a designer but left twelve months ago to set up his own business, helped by a generous loan from his old boss. But it was one that he had to pay back within the year.'

'How much?'

'£35,000.'

'A considerable sum.'

'One which he could not repay.'

'You know this for certain?'

'He freely admits it. His business is in great financial difficulties. Only the previous week he had written to Wilberforce asking for more time to settle the debt.'

'And the old boy refused?'

Thornton nodded. 'Apparently Wilberforce was a harsh, unsentimental man in business.'

'And that is seen as a motive for murder. Very well. So what happened?'

'All the guests had arrived but Wilberforce had not shown his face. Mrs Wilberforce, Beatrice, was somewhat annoyed at his non-appearance. Apparently, he had retired upstairs to his dressing room over an hour before and had not been seen since. She sent up their butler, a fellow called Boldwood, to inform him that the guests had arrived. The butler returned some minutes later to say that Wilberforce was not in his dressing room but that the door to his study, a chamber that adjoined the dressing room, was locked and light could be seen at the bottom of the door. Somewhat concerned, Mrs Wilberforce asked Jack Stavely to go upstairs with her to investigate. It was as the butler had said. The study door was not only locked but it was bolted – and bolted from the inside, thus indicating that there was someone within. After knocking on the door for some moments to no avail, it was felt that perhaps Wilberforce had fallen ill and was in no fit state to withdraw the bolt. With Mrs Wilberforce's permission, Jack Stavely broke the door down. And what a tragic sight met their eyes.'

'Describe this tragic sight.'

'Lying on the floor in a pool of his own blood was the master of the house. Near to his body was a long-bladed knife. The man was dead.'

Darke rubbed his hands with glee. 'Fascinating. One assumes he died as a result of being stabbed.'

'There was just one knife wound to the stomach.'

'A pretty puzzle, Edward. How could the murderer leave the room if it was bolted on the inside?'

'Precisely.'

'There is no suggestion that this was an elaborate suicide?'

The policeman shook his head. 'Practically it is possible, I suppose, but it would take tremendous courage to stab oneself in the stomach in such a way. However, I am certain that it was not suicide. Life was very good for Laurence Wilberforce. I've checked both his medical records and his financial situation. He was very healthy in both departments. And besides, suicide was just not Wilberforce's way.'

'Well, let's hear the end of this captivating tale.'

'The Yard was summoned and I was assigned to the case. Before I arrived Jack Stavely discovered one of the visitors' coats smeared with blood. It turned out to belong to Richard Armstrong. Stavely immediately accused Armstrong of the murder. Sergeant Grey had to restrain him from attacking Armstrong. Mrs Wilberforce then showed us a letter to her husband from the suspected man in which veiled threats were made to Wilberforce. He said he needed more time to pay his debts, adding something like, "If you are intent on breaking me on the wheel in this matter, the consequences will be far the worse for you." '

'Nicely phrased. So on these two pieces of evidence – a smear of blood and an angry letter – you arrested Armstrong for the murder of Laurence Wilberforce.'

'I had no alternative. Sometimes one has to do things one doesn't believe in, especially as a public servant. But the more I've considered the matter, the less convinced I am that Armstrong is the guilty party. But I don't know why. I think the key to the whole problem is how the murder was committed.'

'Indeed. My very thought too. Let us go back to this study for a moment. Describe it to me.'

'It is a small room, some ten feet square. There was a fireplace, with a fire burning in the grate. The chimney aperture was too small to allow access.'

'Even for a child?'

Thornton gaped. He hadn't thought of that. 'Even a child,' he said at length.

'Window?'

'There was no window and no ceiling trap. We've had the carpet up and moved the desk and bookcase, which were the only pieces of furniture placed against a wall.'

'So in essence what we have is a sealed box with a door.'

'Yes. And that was bolted from the inside.'

'A very pretty puzzle indeed, Inspector Thornton. I thank you for bringing it to my notice.'

'But can you solve it?'

'Oh, yes. All one needs to do is to view the problem from a different angle.' With great care he lifted the sleeping cat and placed it down on the rug before the fire. It stirred fitfully in its sleep and then, shifting its position slightly, returned to its feline slumbers. 'Sorry, Persephone, my friend,' he murmured gently, 'but I have to leave you now.' Swilling the remainder of his whisky down, he turned to his visitor with enthusiasm. 'What say you, Edward? I think it best if we visit the scene of the crime together, then we can really get to grips with this mystery.'

The two men decided to walk from Darke's town house in Manchester Square to Curzon Street. Although it was only just after noon, the November day was already darkening and the fog that had begun to disperse was thickening once more and cloaking the city in a bleary haze.

'Tell me about Wilberforce's wife, Beatrice,' said Darke, as Thornton fell into step with him. 'Was she very upset when she found her husband?'

'Naturally, she was distressed.'

'But this distress quickly turned to anger.'

'What do you mean?'

'Well, when the blood was discovered on Armstrong's coat,

you said she then produced the letter with the well-phrased threat.'

'Yes.'

'So the lady was able to repress her grief sufficiently to retrieve this missive, one which strengthens the guilt of Armstrong. That suggests that anger rather than grief was governing her actions. What do you know of their marriage?'

'There was very little gossip about it. They have been married for twenty-two years and have no children. It was rumoured that in the early days Laurence Wilberforce was something of a ladies' man, but . . .'

'Age cools the ardour, eh? I met the man once. A cold fish, as I recall. There was no humour or *joie de vivre* in his demeanour.'

'A business man.'

Darke laughed heartily. 'You put your finger on it, Edward. The concerns of profit and loss place a handcuff on your soul.'

'Do you suspect Mrs Wilberforce of the murder?'

'No more than Armstrong, I suppose. In one sense she is the natural beneficiary: she loses a humourless husband and inherits his wealth.'

Edward Thornton fell silent. An image of Beatrice Wilberforce flashed into his mind. A small, slender woman in her late forties with her blonde hair turning grey. Her pale, rather pinched, face had once been girlishly pretty but now it was set ready, eager almost, for old age. Did she have the determination and malevolence to carry out the cold-blooded murder of her husband and then implicate Armstrong?

Thornton's reverie was broken by Darke's announcement: 'Well, my boy, it seems that we have arrived at our destination.'

Sure enough, the two men stood before the Wilberforce mansion in Curzon Street. The lights from the windows shimmered through the moist net of the fog.

'Lay on, Macduff,' cried Darke, pushing the inspector towards the door.

The butler, Boldwood, received the visitors and invited them to wait in the hall while he informed his mistress of their presence. He was a tall, dignified man, prematurely bald, with a naturally melancholic demeanour. As he walked away in a stiff, erect fashion, Darke nudged his companion. 'By the look of his gait, our friend Boldwood was recruited from the ranks – an ex-soldier, sergeant probably – and that scar on his neck suggests that he has seen some action.'

'Is that relevant to the case?'

Darke grinned and shrugged his shoulders in a nonchalant fashion.

Within minutes Boldwood returned. 'Mrs Wilberforce will see you in the drawing room, but I beg you gentlemen to keep your visit as short as possible. My mistress has not yet recovered her strength after her terrible loss.' It was more of an order than a request.

'We shall be as brief as possible,' said Thornton.

'Served in India, did we, Boldwood?' asked Luther Darke.

The butler eyed his interrogator with suspicion. 'I did, sir. 101st Bengal Fusiliers.'

'Good man.'

Boldwood paused for a moment, staring intently into Darke's face with some puzzlement, and then neatly turning on his heel he led them to the drawing room. As he held the door open Darke leaned over and addressed him again. 'I think it would be propitious if you join us, Boldwood, old boy. You can help fill in certain pieces of the puzzle.'

Reluctantly the tall manservant entered the room and positioned himself by the door.

Beatrice Wilberforce rose from the chaise-longue on which she had been reclining to greet her visitors. Her face was gaunt and dark circles ringed her pale blue eyes. She seemed not to notice Boldwood's presence. She looked with some disdain at her two visitors.

'What can I do for you, inspector?' Her voice was weary and distant.

Before Thornton could respond to this request, Darke moved forward and gave a low theatrical bow. 'I am the one you can assist, dear lady. Luther Darke, a seeker of truth.'

The woman seemed somewhat taken aback by this effusive stranger in her drawing room and involuntarily she sat down on the chaise-longue as if she needed it for support.

'I wonder if I can prevail upon you to recount the events on the evening of your husband's passing,' he said, in soft, musical tones.

Beatrice Wilberforce glanced over at Thornton. 'But I have already told the inspector everything I know several times.'

'But you have not told me.'

A flicker of irritation passed across her brow, but it was gone in an instant. 'If . . . if you think it will help.'

'It may save a man's life.'

Mrs Wilberforce seemed puzzled, but she made no comment on Darke's enigmatic claim. In a soft, clear voice, she began to recount the events of the evening when her husband had died. 'We were having a little dinner party – for no special reason. It was just a social occasion.'

'Who drew up the guest list?'

'I did . . . in consultation with my husband, of course.'

'Of course. What was the purpose of inviting Richard Armstrong to this soirée? There was bad blood between him and Mr Wilberforce.'

'It was my idea. The bad blood you refer to was purely a business matter and not personal on my husband's side. Laurence was a strict man of business and he expected – and indeed demanded – others to be so. Sometimes this led him to

393

act in what I suppose may be regarded by some as an unreasonable manner – but he could be reasoned with. I thought that in a relaxed, informal atmosphere some amicable arrangement between Armstrong . . .' Her eyes misted and she clutched the edge of the chaise. It struck Darke that she was dismayed at her own emotions, her own weakness. It wasn't the memory of her husband but the cracks in her own reserve which were causing her distress. 'As it turned out,' she said at length, 'inviting that man to dinner was the worst decision I could have made.'

She reached for a handkerchief but there was none. Darke flashed the cream silk one from his breast jacket pocket and pressed it into her hand. As he did so, his eyes were caught by a mark on the woman's arm.

'At what time did you last see your husband alive?'

'At around six o'clock,' Mrs Wilberforce replied, dabbing her eyes with the handkerchief. 'He said he was going to his study to write some letters and then have a long soak before the party.'

'Were any letters found?' This question Darke addressed to Thornton. The policeman shook his head.

'Who laid out his evening clothes?'

'Boldwood, of course.'

Darke turned to the butler with a quizzical glance.

'That's right, sir.'

'Did you see your master while you attended to this task?'

'No, sir. The study door was closed.'

Darke shut his eyes for a moment and sighed heavily. He raised his hand slightly as if he were reaching out for something. The room fell silent as the others waited for him to return to them. At length his eyes sprang open and, with a ghost of a smile playing about his lips, he resumed his questioning of Mrs Wilberforce. 'Who were the first guests to arrive?'

'I . . . I can't really say for sure, everyone came more or less at the same time. I think Lord and Lady Clarendon were the first.' She grinned briefly. 'I know Jack Stavely was last – and late.' Her grin broadened. 'He's always late.'

'He comes here a great deal?'

Beatrice Wilberforce nodded, her face resuming its pained expression. 'He is a regular visitor.'

'You were cross when your husband did not appear to greet his guests.'

'Yes. I felt sure he had become absorbed with his correspondence and lost track of the time. I asked Boldwood to check on him for me.'

With a wave of the hand, Darke indicated that Boldwood should come closer and join the inner circle. 'Tell me, Sergeant Boldwood, what happened next?'

'I went up to Mr Wilberforce's dressing room. He wasn't there and neither were his evening clothes so I assumed that he had bathed and dressed and was now in his study. I tapped on the door. There was no reply. I tapped again, louder this time in case he had nodded off, and informed him that the guests for the party had arrived. There was still no reply. Then I tried the door. It was locked.'

'Did he often lock it?'

'Never when he was inside the room.'

'What did you do next?'

'I went downstairs to inform Mrs Wilberforce.'

'Were you worried?'

'I . . . I thought that it was strange.'

'And then with Mrs Wilberforce and Jack Stavely you returned to the room and Stavely broke down the study door.'

Boldwood nodded and bowed his head.

'The door was bolted on the inside, Mrs Wilberforce. Is that correct?'

Suddenly the widow's patience snapped and Darke

witnessed the flame of anger that burned inside that soft and timid exterior. 'You know it is! How long is this deluge of questions going on? Why must you put me under this torture yet again? I cannot tell you any more than I have already told you. My husband is dead and all you can do is make me relive that dreadful evening when he died. Have you no tact or manners?'

'Gentlemen, I think it best if you leave,' said Boldwood, taking a pace forward. There was more than a hint of aggression in his demeanour.

Darke grinned back at the butler. 'Distressed though your mistress is, Sergeant Boldwood, I am sure that she is also very concerned that the person who killed her husband is caught and tried for his murder. She would not want to hinder the course of justice.'

'But the police have caught him,' snapped Mrs Wilberforce, the anger still vibrant in her voice. 'Richard Armstrong. Inspector Thornton arrested him.'

'An arrest doth not a conviction make. You seem so very certain that he was your husband's murderer.'

Boldwood took another step nearer to Darke, his eyes blazing, but Beatrice Wilberforce stopped him in his tracks with a spirited glance.

'In order to allow you to recover your equilibrium, Mrs Wilberforce,' said Luther Darke smoothly, 'perhaps you will allow Boldwood to show us your husband's dressing room and study so that we may examine the scene of the crime?'

'Yes.' Her reply was hardy audible. 'As you wish.'

As Boldwood led the two men upstairs, Thornton held his companion back a few steps and whispered in his ear. 'You were rather harsh on the poor woman,' he hissed.

Darke nodded. 'I overstepped the bounds of decency – again. I shall repent. Boldwood, old fellow, pause a moment will you? I just want to apologise for my brutish behaviour towards your mistress. It was unforgivable.'

The butler turned to face Darke; his face was stern. 'I must confess, sir, if it had not been for the thought of disturbing Mrs Wilberforce further, I should have struck you for your insolence.'

'And I should have deserved it. The lady is lucky in having such a chivalrous protector. You have been with her long?'

'Five years.'

'Mr Wilberforce was a good employer?'

'He . . . he was, sir.'

'They were a happy couple? The marriage was a sound one?'

Boldwood's face blanched with anger. 'How dare you! That is none of your damned business. What right have you got to come here . . . ?'

Darke halted this tirade by holding up his hands in a mock surrender. 'There I go again, overstepping the mark. I shall say no more. Pray continue.'

Without a word, the butler carried on up the stairs. Thornton and Darke followed, with the latter giving his companion a huge wink.

At length the two men were shown into the dressing room of the murdered man.

'You can leave us now, Boldwood. Inspector Thornton and I need to inspect these rooms alone. We shall not be too long.'

The butler hesitated by the door.

Thornton gave a polite cough to initiate the servant's departure. 'Thank you, Boldwood. We shall make our own way downstairs.'

With reluctance, Boldwood left the room.

'Now,' said Darke, rubbing his hands, 'show me this magic room.'

Thornton led him to the rear of the dressing room and flung open the study door to reveal a small, dark chamber beyond containing a desk, a chair and a small bookcase. There was a fireplace on the far wall. Thornton switched on the electric light which bathed the study in a suffused amber glow.

Immediately Darke had entered the room he examined the door. 'Was the key to the study found?'

'No,' said Thornton kneeling beside him. 'But it was bolted, too, remember.'

'Oh, indeed, I do remember. This is the poor thing hanging off here.'

'It was damaged when Jack Stavely broke down the door.'

'Mm. He did us a bit of a favour. Look here, Thornton, at these screws: they are new and the bolt is shiny and unmarked. Notice also the portion of wood which had been covered by the bolt before Mr Stavely's boot came into play. It is the same colour as the surrounding wood. There is no differentiation whatsoever.'

'What are you saying?'

'That this bolt is new, very new. Can't have been there for very long. If it had been in place for any length of time, the wood beneath it would be of a different hue. See the screw holes, how white and fresh the wood is. And, my friend, most damning of all . . .'

Darke scooped up a few white specks from the carpet. 'Sawdust,' he explained. 'From the screwholes. It is possible that the bolt was only fixed there on the day of the murder.'

'This is all very well, but I yet fail to see how this throws any fresh light on the identity of the killer or indeed on the way in which the murder was committed.'

'Patience, my friend.' Darke had now moved to the centre of the room and was examining a dark stain on the carpet. 'Wilberforce's blood, I suppose?'

'Yes.'

'Not as large a pool as I had expected, but that fits the

theory which is forming nicely in my mind. I suppose the knife is at Scotland Yard.'

'It is.'

'Describe it to me.'

'It's a long-handled knife. Dull metal with some simple carvings and a longish blade which turned slightly at the end.'

Darke sat at the desk and sketched out a crude drawing. 'Something like that?'

'Why, yes . . .'

Before Thornton could say more, a strident voice called out: 'What the devil is going on here?'

Both men turned to discover a young man standing in the doorway of the study. He was short of stature and had his hands on his hips in an aggressive manner.

'Mr Stavely,' said Thornton.

'Yes, inspector, and you will answer to your superiors for this – barging into Mrs Wilberforce's house and upsetting the lady.'

'News travels fast, eh, Edward?' observed Darke with a flicker of amusement.

'You may do what you wish, Mr Stavely,' said Thornton, approaching the intruder so that he towered over him comfortably. 'But there is no case of "barging" anywhere. We were invited into the house and as a police officer I am carrying out my duties in a murder inquiry. I would hope you have no wish to hinder that inquiry.'

Stavely hesitated. 'But the inquiry is closed. You have the wretch who murdered Laurence.'

Darke joined his friend and placed a hand on his shoulder. 'It is amazing how everyone is so certain that an innocent man who had the misfortune to owe Wilberforce a lot of money is guilty of his murder.'

'And who the hell are you?'

'I, sir, am Abraham attempting to drink from the well of

399

truth. And how did you learn of our visit?'

'I have just arrived. I have called every day since the murder to spend some time with Beatrice . . . Mrs Wilberforce.'

'And Boldwood informed you of my dreadful behaviour.'

'Yes.'

'Well, sir, I have apologised to him and I will apologise to you. Any rudeness on my part was calculated in order to bring this mysterious case to a swift conclusion. I am afraid Boldwood may have been more concerned about what we may find in this room than about our apparent disrespectful ways. I suspect he was hoping that your heroic intervention would put a stop to our scrutiny of this room.'

'What on earth do you mean?'

'Mr Stavely, let us do a deal together. I will tell you some of the matter on the proviso that you help us with a little subterfuge. Is that agreed?'

It was just over thirty minutes later that Thornton and Darke sat in the drawing room with Beatrice Wilberforce and Jack Stavely. Boldwood had just served tea and was about to leave the room when Thornton stopped him. 'You had better remain,' he said. 'What Mr Darke has to say will be of great interest to you.'

'Come, sit down, man,' cried Darke, indicating a seat next to Stavely.

Casting an apprehensive glance at his mistress, he pulled up a chair.

'Mr Darke, you have been mysterious, you have been rude and you have been persuasive. Now pray tell us what this is all about,' said Beatrice Wilberforce.

Luther Darke placed his cup and saucer on the tea trolley and stood facing the small group. 'Murder most foul as in the best it is. Inspector Thornton here sought my assistance because he was far from convinced that the poor devil

400

languishing in the cells at Scotland Yard was the perpetrator of the crime that was committed here a few evenings ago. After hearing the details of the case, I was certain that debtor Armstrong was innocent. It was all too convenient. Anyone capable of carrying out a clever murder in a locked room would not have been careless enough to leave some blood on his outdoor coat. It was a careless embellishment placed there in order to provide a scapegoat. I had my own ideas concerning the method of the murder but I needed to discover a few further details before I could be certain. Now I am certain.' He retrieved his cup and drank some tea as his audience absorbed this information. It was a brave act on his part. He abhorred tea and as a rule it never passed his lips.

'In the detection of crime, sixth sense and guesswork play a valid part in reaching the right conclusion. On very slender evidence, I guessed or at least sensed that the marriage between Laurence and Beatrice Wilberforce was not a completely happy one.' He raised his hand to silence Mrs Wilberforce.

'I do not wish to speak ill of the dead but Laurence Wilberforce was a humourless, cold-hearted bully who could turn nasty even towards someone of whom he once thought kindly. His treatment of Richard Armstrong bears witness of that. As does the bruising on your arm. You have been badly used, my dear.'

The woman said nothing, but stared determinedly ahead of her, avoiding Darke's gaze.

'The bruising gave some foundation to my surmise. Similarly Boldwood's angry reticence when I questioned him concerning the state of the Wilberforce marriage added more grist to my mill. Boldwood revealed himself as a great protector of his mistress. What did you say, sergeant? Something like: "I would have knocked you down for being so impertinent but it would have upset Mrs Wilberforce." Words to that effect. A real Sir Galahad. How difficult it must have been for you, Boldwood, to live and serve in a house where the husband treated his wife miserably and on occasion struck her with some violence. Hard for a man who loved his mistress and wanted to protect her. Here you were, an old military man used to action, used to fighting for what you believed in but unable to do anything about the injustice going on under your nose. But, oh, there are straws – there are straws, apparently insignificant, puny little straws, which yet have, as the proverb has it, the power to break a camel's back.

'On the day of the murder, Wilberforce was in a foul mood. Probably he had seen the guest list and noticed Armstrong's name. He lost his temper and behaved abominably. The bruises that are now fading from his wife's arm were, I am sure, administered on that day. For you Boldwood, late of the 101st Bengal Fusiliers, this was your last straw. You conceived a plan to rid your mistress of this troublesome husband. It was a well-wrought plan indeed.'

Boldwood made to rise, but Thornton, who had manoeuvred his way around the back of the butler's chair, placed both hands on his shoulders and gently pressed him back into his seat.

'I cannot be sure how accurate I am as to the minutiae but I am sure that my broad strokes paint the true picture. Boldwood bought a bolt from the local ironmongers. We found the bag in which it was wrapped and the receipt stuffed in the drawer in his room. I am sorry, Boldwood, but with Mr Stavely's connivance we searched your room just now, while he busied you with other chores. Like many murderers before you, you were confident that you would never be suspected or your room searched. We also discovered the screwdriver you used to fix the bolt on the inside of Wilberforce's study. Then you waited. Waited until your master had dressed for dinner before you entered his dressing room armed with a knife. You told him, no doubt, what a despicable creature he was. How he was a monster ruining the life of one of the finest women you had known. And he, no doubt, laughed at first . . .'

'He did laugh. Until he saw the knife.' Boldwood uttered these words in monotone without a trace of emotion showing on his face. 'And then the coward stopped laughing.'

'You stabbed him once. That was all that was necessary. And then with the knife still lodged in his stomach you pushed him into the study. You stood outside the room uttering curses and threats about how you intended to finish him off. In desperation, he attempted to shut the door on you and you let him. One can but imagine his surprise and delight to find that the door now possessed a bolt. His disordered brain would not question how it got there. For Wilberforce it was a godsend. His desperate hands slammed it home, thus trapping himself within his own tomb.'

Boldwood said nothing but a fevered light illuminated his eyes as, through Darke's narrative, he relived the moment.

Darke continued: 'Although badly wounded, Laurence Wilberforce now thought that he was safe. What he didn't know – what no one knew or suspected – was that the tip of the knife had been tainted with a strong poison which brought about death within five minutes or so. No doubt this deadly brew was one of the prizes that you brought back with you from India, along with the knife. I know of few soldiers who served out there who did not bring back one of those long-handled knives. The bazaars were full of them. "A souvenir, sahib?" '

'Is this all true, Boldwood?' asked Beatrice Wilberforce, her voice no louder than a harsh whisper.

'It is all true,' came the solemn reply.

The woman rose to her feet, her face suddenly flushed with anger. 'You fool, you damned fool,' she screamed. 'Don't you know that whatever Laurence did to me, I loved him. I loved

403

him with all my heart. He was my husband! And now you have taken him away.' She made a mad dash for the servant but Jack Stavely stepped forward and held her back. She sank into his arms sobbing.

Boldwood looked in horror at his mistress. His features blanched at the sudden realisation that he had been both blind and foolish. He turned sharply as if to make for the door.

'Don't bother with that, Boldwood. You will find there are two constables and my assistant Sergeant Grey waiting outside ready to take you to the Yard,' said Edward Thornton, stepping forward and clasping a pair of handcuffs on the man. He had visibly shrunk and his eyes moistened with tears.

'I did it for the best, sir. I did it for m'lady.'

At this reference to her Beatrice Wilberforce pulled away from Jack Stavely. 'Get out of my sight, you devil. I never want to see you again.'

Luther Darke poured himself another large whisky. Thornton clapped his hands over his glass. One large nip was enough for him, but not for his triumphant friend.

'I need this as an antidote to that tea with which I sullied my throat in Curzon Street.' The two men were seated around the fire in Darke's sitting room later that day. Persephone still lay like a wax image, curled in a foetal position, before the grate.

Luther Darke took a gulp from his glass and rolled the liquid around in his mouth before swallowing it slowly, allowing its warmth to burn his throat. He grinned. ' "Gie me ae spark o' Nature's fire, That's a' learning I desire," as Maester Burns has it. Well, Edward, a successful day: solving of a murder and releasing an innocent man.'

'Indeed, but it gave me no pleasure to lock up Boldwood. He is a sad creature whose intentions were for the best.'

'Misplaced affection, passion in Boldwood's case, can drive

a man to behave like the devil. And it was a devilishly ingenious plan. He knew that with the evidence of a stab wound, the pool of blood and the knife, no one would think of poison as the real cause of death. The locked room was also an added subterfuge to fog the truth. A real November crime, eh? Remember, he was virtually making the rules of his murder plan up as he went along. He was determined to muddy the waters as much as possible. If he had not tried to be too clever by smearing Armstrong's coat with blood he might even have got away with it.'

'Because then there would have been no definite suspect and nothing to prompt my unease which sent me running to you.'

'I cannot believe that you came running. With a dignified policeman-like gait, surely.'

Thornton laughed. The whisky was already going to his head. 'I had better be going. There is work still to be done back at the Yard.'

Luther Darke saw Edward Thornton to the door. Thick winter night with its grey coils of fog awaited the inspector beyond the threshold.

'Thank you for your help, Luther. You are an amazing man.'

For a moment, Darke's face grew serious. 'We are all amazing men in our own way, my friend. Come again soon.'

With that the two men shook hands and Thornton walked out into the darkness which soon swallowed him up. Darke returned to his fireside, his cat and his whisky.

Unsettled Scores

Jürgen Ehlers

Hamburg, 27 October 1897

Drizzling rain. The Hanseatic town showed its most unfriendly face. David Lindley shivered with cold. He produced his invitation, and a liveried servant opened the massive oak door. David handed his coat to the cloakroom attendant and entered the hall. A babble of voices. The huge room was crowded. Everybody seemed in high spirits. It had taken fifty-five years to build the new town hall, after the old one was destroyed by the big fire of 1842. Lindley had come from London specifically to attend the opening ceremony. It was his first visit to Hamburg for four years.

A tall, grey-haired gentleman who stood next to the door caught his eye. Senator Heymann, a major participant on various committees of the city's government over the last few decades. David had expected to meet him here. Him and all the others. Heymann approached with a big smile. 'Welcome back to Hamburg, young friend! How glad I am to see you again!'

Lindley felt a slight chill. He forced himself to return the smile. 'I'm also glad to be back in Hamburg,' he replied. He managed to shake hands with the man without visible hesitation.

'See the young chap over there? That's Lindley.' Carstens, the ship owner, pointed with his cigar.

The young man he was talking to looked puzzled. 'Surely you jest. Lindley must be well beyond eighty now.'

'Not William Lindley, of course! I've no idea if he's still alive. No, this is David Lindley, his nephew.'

'Talking to Ballin and Woermann,' the young man observed.

'His company is in the Africa trade, just like yours.'

'Should I worry about that?'

Carstens gave him an appraising glance. Was he really that naive? 'You should worry because he is a Lindley,' he said. 'And because he knows far too much.'

'Welcome to Hamburg!'

'Emmy!' David Lindley spun round. This was the critical moment he had hoped for and feared at the same time. 'What a pleasure to see you again!' His heart was pounding.

'I'm glad, too.' She smiled. If she realised his excitement, she concealed it well.

Silence. What should he say?

Emmy Weusthoff reacted first. 'So, do you like our beautiful new town hall?'

He looked into her eyes. No doubt, she was joking. 'It certainly is quite large,' he conceded.

'It has six rooms more than your Buckingham Palace!'

Well, it wasn't exactly his Buckingham Palace, and he didn't care about the number of rooms it had. 'The architecture might have been a bit more modern,' he suggested. 'And those monumental paintings . . .'

'Ghastly, aren't they? They should have chosen some of our modern artists, don't you think? Eitner, Wohlers, Siebelist. Or the brilliant Arthur Illies!'

'Yes, perhaps.'

She was perfectly aware of the fact that he didn't know any of the names. She had always enjoyed teasing him. But she realised that something completely different occupied his mind right now. 'You look very serious today,' she said.

'You never answered my letter,' he said brusquely. There it was.

Emmy cast down her eyes. 'Mother was against it,' she said.

He gave her a questioning look.

'I cannot leave and go abroad. I'm needed here, Mr Lindley. After my father's death – the company must go on, don't you understand? And Mother is sickly. It would be well beyond her means to run a business such as ours.'

'But couldn't I—'

'Mr Lindley, may I introduce you to my fiancé?'

David had not realised that a young man had approached them holding two glasses of champagne. He gave one to Emmy, then turned to David. 'Heinrich Wagner.' He held out his right hand.

'Lindley, my pleasure,' muttered David. They shook hands. The young man had a strong grip. David scrutinised his opponent, looking for any obvious faults. He found none.

'I've heard a lot about you,' said Wagner. 'And of your famous uncle, of course!'

Lindley could not remember what they talked about for the next quarter of an hour or so. He only knew that it took him all the effort he could muster to smile, nod where appropriate, and now and then add a few remarks to the conversation. After it was over, he asked for two glasses of champagne, and emptied them both in one gulp each under the astonished eyes of the waitress. It did not help. Nor did the big glass of port, which he drank afterwards in small sips. He felt tired and weary of the crowd. He went out on the balcony. It was a clear night. Below him lay the sleeping city. It seemed cold and empty.

'Mr Lindley, may I have a word with you?'

David turned round. He had to concentrate on keeping his

balance. There was Heinrich Wagner again. Emmy was nowhere in sight. 'What's the matter?' David had difficulty in controlling his voice. He knew that he was drunk.

'I'm sorry to bother you, but I would really like to know. What was the cause exactly, when Emmy's father died four years ago?'

'The cholera,' mumbled David. 'The cholera finished him off. Like so many others.'

'Yes, but it wasn't the big epidemic of 1892, only the small second outbreak the year after. Isn't that right?'

'Well, yes, but dead is dead!' David had no idea what the young man was after.

'Hardly more than a hundred people were infected in '93. And one of them was Weusthoff.'

'Certainly.' His demise must have suited a number of people quite well. Weusthoff had been just about to uncover a major political scandal. But it hadn't happened.

'Why Weusthoff, of all people?' insisted Wagner.

'Bad luck,' murmured Lindley.

'Just bad luck?'

'What else?' Why didn't this man stop bothering him? He wanted to go back to his hotel, go to bed, sleep.

'Nonsense!' The senator puffed his cigar. 'The man is completely harmless.' He had observed Lindley getting drunk. Now the guests were starting to leave, and he would have liked to go home, too. But then he had run into Carstens.

'He isn't.' What gave Heymann this excessive self-confidence? He was as much in danger as Carstens himself.

'Listen, this is how I assess the situation: the cholera is no longer an issue. Those who are still alive are thankful that they managed to escape. And the dead won't complain. The filters were under construction, after all, when the epidemic started.'

412

'But twenty years late, Heymann! If the public ever gets to know that! It would still be explosive, politically, if you know what I mean. We could all go down. We all know that William Lindley had urged us to build the filters more than twenty years earlier!'

'Whom do you mean by "we all"? You and me as a matter of fact. Most of the others who governed Hamburg then are dead. And there's no hard evidence any more since I personally burnt that infamous letter from Lindley.'

'But young Lindley is alive and here. And he knows perfectly well what kind of a game we were playing.'

'He knows just a small part. And he'll shy away from using that knowledge to make mischief, politically. He's a business-man. It would harm his interests.'

'And what about the young miss?'

'Engaged, Carstens. She is out of the game.'

'I wonder, I wonder. Why did young Lindley return to Hamburg anyway?'

'As a representative of his company, or so I've heard. The opening of the new town hall is a major event, where any big company would want to be represented.'

Carstens seemed unconvinced. 'Then why does he carry a gun in his luggage?' he asked.

It was late when Lindley reached his hotel. His uncle had stayed in the same place some fifty years before, when the big fire had broken out that had reduced most of the city to rubble and made his uncle famous overnight. With great competence he had intervened in the fire-fighting, ordered the blowing-up of rows of houses to cut breaches in the densely built area. Breaches the fire could not pass. All through the power of his personality, without having any official position. Single-mindedly he had looked on as this very hotel was blown up, including all his personal belongings. He had prevented the

413

rescue of his possessions. Where others lost all, he wanted no special rights for himself. A well-calculated move which assured him the sympathy of the whole population.

At least for a time. Later, after he had developed the sewer system and water supply, when he suggested newer, better plans of improvement, the Hamburg people found out that good advice was not necessarily cheap advice. In the end it got too expensive for the penny-pinching bureaucrats. They dismissed him.

Tonight nobody will blow up the hotel, David thought, as he asked for his key at reception. With heavy steps he ascended the stairs. To his surprise he found the door of his room unlocked. He was sure he had locked it. Cautiously he pushed the door open. The room lay in darkness. David took his lamp and inspected every corner. Nobody there. Perhaps the chambermaid had been in and forgotten to lock up afterwards? Not very likely. David locked the door and turned the key so that it could not be pushed out from the other side. Then he inspected his luggage.

Difficult to tell if the big bag had been searched or not. He should have kept his things more tidily in the first place. At least nothing seemed to be missing. He yawned. Even the heavy revolver was still there. David took it out, checked that it was in working order and put a cartridge in each of its six chambers. Then he placed the gun under his pillow, turned out the light and lay down fully dressed on his bed. He fell asleep immediately.

The hotel breakfast was insubstantial. David gave the two rolls and the small jars of butter, jam and honey a disapproving look.

'*Haben der Herr noch einen Wunsch?*' the waiter asked.

Yes, indeed, David did have a wish. He ordered bacon and eggs with toast. He also asked for a newspaper, only to learn that the Hamburg dailies were not yet out. But a letter had arrived for him. David placed the small envelope next to his plate. *Für Herrn David Lindley* it said in a delicate handwriting. He had no doubt about the author, but what about the message?

David sipped from his cup. The coffee was excellent. David decided to have his breakfast first before opening the letter. Whatever it might offer, new hope or final despair, it would be hard to face on an empty stomach.

The breakfast came. When Lindley had eventually finished it, he opened the envelope. It contained just a short message: 'Could you, please, come over and see me this morning? Emmy.'

David folded his napkin, put it back on the table and ordered a cab.

The big house in Harvestehude seemed unchanged. David would have liked to enter the extensive garden, which he knew stretched down to the Alster lake. He saw the bare trees, which on his last visit had shown their autumn foliage. He pulled the bell. The door opened. David held his breath. He had expected Emmy; instead, he looked into the face of a maid he knew only too well.

'David Lindley,' he said. 'I would like to see Miss Emmy.'

'I know.' Only her eyes revealed that she had recognised him, too. How much hate, he thought, being well aware that from her point of view he fully deserved it.

'Welcome to Harvestehude!' Emmy had appeared. The maid stepped aside, and David went in. 'Come, let us sit in the library!'

She led the well-known way, and he followed. How carefree he had felt here on his last visit! They had talked endlessly about poetry and the arts. But the clocks could not be turned back. And it was a long time ago that he had painted for the last time.

'The maid – wasn't that . . . ?'

Emmy nodded. 'I know, I should have dismissed her immediately, but I couldn't do such a thing. It would have been too harsh and cruel. I mean, after all, she paid dearly for her mistake.'

'That is very honourable of you,' said David. In fact, he would have acted differently. But then, of course, he was not living under this roof. And to his knowledge the girl had no antagonistic feelings towards Emmy. Only against him. After all, he had shot her friend. In self-defence, of course, but it would make no difference to her.

Emmy sensed that David was upset. 'I'm sorry,' she said. 'How careless of me. I should have known.'

'Never mind. Perhaps you should tell me why you wished to see me?'

'Yes, indeed.' Emmy looked at him. 'I want to show you something. But you must promise not to laugh, will you?'

'Promise,' he said.

Emmy put a map on the table. David saw that it was a street plan of Hamburg. 'You know, I've thought a lot about the cholera epidemic. The 1893 outbreak, the one that killed my father, not the big one. I've drawn a map of the known cases. Each cross stands for one reported infection.'

David had to come closer to see the small, pencilled crosses. Most of them clustered in a narrow area that was called Veddel, others were in the port area. In fact, only one cross was in a completely different part of town. Emmy pointed to that cross. 'That is us,' she said.

He nodded.

'David, do you know how cholera spreads?'

Didn't she know? 'Bacteria,' he said. 'They spread through polluted water. That's what happened in September 1893. A hole in the drinking water main let polluted water from the Elbe River enter the water supply system. That's all I know. So

416

the bacteria were distributed through the water pipes.'

'That's what they say. But then we have our own private well here, David. Did you know that?'

No, he didn't. He fell silent.

'Heinrich laughs at me when I bring up the subject. Although he was trained as a doctor himself, he doesn't want to hear anything about it.'

'It certainly sounds fantastic,' David admitted.

Emmy looked at him. 'David, I must know the truth. What really did happen on that terrible day in September four years ago. You're the only witness.'

'But you know it all. There is absolutely nothing that we didn't talk about back and forth after it happened.'

'You talked with my mother, not with me, David.'

She was right. Lindley shrugged. 'There isn't much to tell. Your father had invited me to Hamburg, as you know. I'd brought some of my uncle's papers, which apparently bore evidence that the local government had neglected the water supply system and thus practically caused the disaster of 1892. Almost nine thousand casualties. Your father wanted to exploit this politically. Your mother and you stayed with relatives in Lübeck, if I remember right . . .'

'My grandmother.'

'That night this house was raided. A number of items were stolen, including my uncle's letters. Your father intercepted the raiders. In the resulting fight your father was injured, and I managed to shoot one of the attackers. The others fled.'

'That's all?'

'That's all. Later the police came and asked questions. Oh, yes, and also Carstens and Heymann arrived. They'd heard of the attack on your father.'

'Or known of it?'

Lindley shrugged. 'Possibly. Indeed, right then I'd assumed that it was all their work, and probably made remarks in that

417

direction. But the gentlemen acted very properly and correctly. In fact, Carstens even—' He stopped.

'Yes?' asked Emmy.

'He brought your father a glass of water,' muttered David.

Hugo von Brandenburg, solicitor. He smiled. 'What you're telling me, Mr Lindley, sounds rather fantastic, to be honest. As a lawyer I don't know how to advise you. Of course you might go to the police. And I can assure you that they will hold a thorough investigation. Our German police are very efficient.'

'I see.' Von Brandenburg was the solicitor his company relied on, an expert in commercial law no doubt, but this was a criminal case. But whom else could he ask for advice?

'On the other hand I must tell you that the matter as far as I can see rests entirely on your own statement. If I've understood you correctly, you say that you are the only witness – apart from the accused party.'

David nodded.

'I'm not sure that I would advise you to pursue this matter any further in the circumstances.' The lawyer leaned back in his armchair and looked at David, enquiringly.

'But they must have had help, mustn't they? I mean, how does one get hold of a sample of cholera-infested water?'

'I've not the slightest idea.' The lawyer rose from his chair, indicating that the discussion was over, the case closed. Again, David was too late to press his hand. He found it difficult to readjust to the custom of shaking hands all the time.

'Now we have a problem.'

Mrs Carstens looked at her husband enquiringly.

'I've just received a phone call from von Brandenburg. Of course everything is confidential, but he said enough to suggest that there might be some inconvenience caused by a young Englishman. Lindley, he means.'

His wife put down her spoon. 'An inconvenience?' she asked. 'A serious one?'

He shook his head. 'A minor inconvenience, I would say.' He should not have told her. He loved his wife and had no secrets from her. Well, almost no secrets. But this was beyond her scope. 'I've taken precautions,' he said.

A maid removed the empty plates. Mrs Carstens waited until she finished and had left the room. 'Don't do anything you would regret later,' she said.

Carstens shook his head. He tasted the wine. Delicious. Just the right temperature. It really did pay to have qualified servants. 'Clara,' he said. 'We must do what is necessary for the business. Everything. Even the utmost. No trophies for fairness are awarded in this world. So we must be strong and trust that all will turn out well.'

Clara nodded. 'Yes, dear, we must be strong and trust in God.'

He did not contradict her, but this was not exactly what he meant.

Lindley had finished his discussions with the representatives of the Deutsche Afrika-Linie. Thus the business part of his trip was over. It had proved a complete failure. Woermann did not need any English partner for their African trade operations. They regarded him as a competitor and did not want to strike any deal. Nothing he could do about that. David decided to take a walk along the Alster lake and then go back to the hotel and pack his luggage. He would leave tomorrow. He had booked a cabin on the steamship that would take him back to London in less than two days.

The mail was late that day. Emmy had a brief look at the

419

letters. Regards from Lübeck, from her sick mother, then several business letters and also a large envelope. She cut it open. The answer to her request. It had been done very promptly. It was good to know the right people. She sat down and had a look. She had asked for a list of all the people who might possibly have had official access to the samples of contaminated water in '93. And here it was. It contained more than a hundred names, all in alphabetical order.

Just as she had suspected: none of the names meant anything to her. No, wait. What was that, down there, right at the bottom? That must be a mistake, certainly. But there it stood: Dr Heinrich Wagner allegedly had worked at the Hygienisches Institut from 1892 to 1895. Her Heinrich. Was that the reason why he never wanted to discuss this matter with her? For heaven's sake, did it mean that she was engaged to the man who had murdered her father? Or could she be mistaken?

Only one person could help. Quickly she wrote a few lines, put the letter in an envelope and asked her maid: 'Take this letter please directly to Mr Lindley's hotel!'

'Clever child,' said Carstens.

The girl had brought him the letter. *Mr David Lindley* it said on the envelope. It was unsealed. Carstens took out the letter. The message was brief and clear: 'David! I must see you immediately. There is a new development. Emmy.' Very convenient.

'I will deliver this letter personally,' declared Carstens. He thought about it. There was no method of faking the handwriting, but he might easily add a sketch map with an alleged meeting point and a convenient hour. Perhaps the Hygienisches Institut? He still had the key. Lindley would come alone, naturally, and unsuspecting. He dismissed the maid with a smile.

'You give her nothing?' asked Heymann in surprise.

Carstens shook his head. 'She hates Lindley. That is enough of a motivation.'

'She hates him? Do you know why?'

'Lindley shot her friend, back in '93, during our raid on Weusthoff's house.'

'Voss? He was her gentleman friend? But I would have thought he'd never consider marrying a servant!'

Carstens smiled. 'He didn't tell her that,' he replied.

The building lay completely in darkness. Lindley passed it, and then, after perhaps two hundred yards, asked the driver to stop, paid him and waited until the cab had disappeared. Then he walked back to the tall, grey building. An enamel name plaque next to the entrance told him that this was the right place. *Hygienisches Institut* it said. One of the few scientific institutions Hamburg had. Closed, of course, at this time of the day. What might Emmy have come across? A new witness, some kind of hard evidence? Possibly an internal report of 1893, mentioning the disappearance of some water sample? And where was Emmy, anyway? Lindley looked around. The street lay deserted. Was he too early? He checked his watch. No, in fact, he was a bit late. Could it be that she was inside the building?

David walked up the three granite steps. The main door was unlocked. Once more David looked around. Nobody seemed to be watching. Quickly he went in and pushed the door shut behind him.

The interior of the building was not as dark as it had appeared from the outside. There was light coming from one of the back rooms. Everything was quiet. 'Emmy?' he asked in a low voice. No reply. David tried to make no noise as he proceeded slowly towards the open door. But in vain; the wooden planks creaked under his feet. Once again he stopped.

And again there was nothing to hear. He approached the door and pushed it open more widely.

In front of him lay what seemed to be a scientist's room, the walls lined with bookshelves, on the desk a microscope, some pens, papers and a paraffin lamp. The chair behind the desk was empty. 'Emmy?' Lindley asked again. Then he went in.

'Welcome to my former office!'

David spun round. Wagner must have been standing directly behind the door. He held a revolver in his right hand, the barrel pointing at David. A trap!

'Stop this nonsense,' David said. His voice sounded strange.

'Take a seat, Mr Lindley,' Wagner replied. He seemed totally calm.

David stepped round the table. What should he do? His revolver lay back in his hotel. And even if he had brought it here, he would not have been able to draw it. He had lost.

'You provided the polluted water,' guessed David.

Wagner shrugged. 'That may or may not be so. It doesn't matter to you any more. You will now sit down here, write a farewell letter and then have a bullet put through your head. You don't want to live any longer, with Emmy being out of reach.'

'Nobody would believe that!' he said.

'Yes, they would. You were looking for some deadly poison; this building is obviously full of poison. But then you found this gun and thought otherwise.'

What a ridiculous notion, David wanted to answer, since I have a gun in my luggage at the hotel. But then he realised that this gun looked very familiar. It was his own revolver.

All of a sudden there were footsteps in the corridor, and a voice called: 'Anybody here?' Wagner was distracted for a second. With a sudden movement David brushed the lamp off the desk and dropped to the floor. The shot came instantly.

And missed. The room was plunged into darkness. David rolled sideways, towards Wagner. His opponent strode round the desk and fell over the Englishman. Something clattered on the ground, immediately next to him. The weapon! David groped for it. The second he grasped it he received a heavy blow to the shoulder. He cried out in pain, grabbed the gun and fired upwards. In the flash of the shot he saw Wagner towering above him, microscope in hand. But the fatal blow never came.

At the police station David learned what had happened. A lady had seen light coming from the back of the building and alerted the caretaker who in turn called the police. David's story was met with much scepticism, as he had obviously shot the other man. Wagner was unconscious, and David doubted that he would live. David produced the letter with the sketch map. Emmy was summoned. Eventually she arrived, in floods of tears. But she was able to respond to most of the questions. David realised that he had won when a policeman offered him a cup of coffee.

Then the maid was brought in. She said nothing. Out of fear, David suspected. Carstens and Heymann were powerful men, and she was nothing.

'Was it Carstens, the ship owner?' ventured David.

No reply.

'Or Senator Heymann?'

No reply. She looked very vulnerable, thought David, and devoid of all hope.

'We'll take care of her,' said the policeman who was handling the case. 'You may as well go home now.'

David put a hand on Emmy's shoulder, as they left the police station. She shook it off.

'Emmy,' he said.

She was furious. 'My God, David, be quiet! And leave me

alone, please. Your interference has caused so much misery, so much distress, can't you see that?'

'I assure you, it was never my intention.' This was completely unjust.

'Leave me alone!'

David hesitated, trying to think of something he might say. But there was nothing. She was completely distraught. Understandably so, of course. Her fiancé fatally wounded and the maid she had trusted against all reason ruined all on the same day, all by him. Nothing he could do, then. He saw to it that she got a hansom cab back home, and then he began to walk back to his hotel.

It had started to drizzle again. His shoulder ached. Poor Emmy, he thought. Tomorrow she would feel sorry for having attacked him. Perhaps she would come to the boat to see him off. Or perhaps she would write him a letter and come to meet him in London. Or perhaps not.

A Right Royal Attempt

Ian Morson

London, 1900

Extract from Albert Potter's Diary

Thursday, 5 April 1900

I had such a strange experience today in the environs of the British Museum, that I feel moved to record it immediately. The day had been grey and dull, and the dirty, black stones of the institution's portals loomed ominously over me like some depressing northern cathedral – Joe Chamberlain's Birmingham, I would hazard at a guess. I was almost put off from my task of researching the Chartist movement in the Library's Reading Room, and, at the bottom of the flight of steps, hesitated between pursuing my work and lightening my gloom with a judicious malt in the Barley Mow Tavern just round the corner. Thoughts of what my dear Rosalind might say if she discovered I had shirked my duty impelled my feet forward, however.

As I reluctantly breasted the flight of steps, a shadowy figure detached itself from one of the Ionic pillars that adorn the Museum's frontage, and paralleled my course step for step. I deliberately ignored the person, as I assumed it to be some beggar who sought to prevail on my good nature to gain the wherewithal to indulge his own propensity for the demon drink. If my thirst was not to be quenched, then his most certainly was not. But, before I could reach the sanctuary of the Museum's lofty doors, he stepped into my path.

The shadowy figure turned out to be very substantial as I could now plainly see by the lantern over both our heads, which illuminated our confrontation. He was a large individual with broad shoulders that stretched the heavy overcoat he wore to its limit. The skirt of the coat fell almost to his feet, which were clad in shiny brown brogues. A luxuriant walrus moustache split his apparently cheery face in two, and from under it protruded large, square teeth. His unruly hair was cropped close around his ears and the whole ensemble was topped with a battered bowler hat which matched the colour of his shoes. He was clearly no beggar, though his ruddy visage suggested a propensity for drinking heavily.

'O'Nions.' The voice was gravelly, and betrayed a country upbringing, though not in Ireland, where a man of such a nomenclature should have his origins. To complete the introduction, he thrust a beefy fist towards me. 'Pleased to meet you, Mr Potter.'

'You have me at a disadvantage,' I retorted. 'You seem to know me, but I haven't the faintest idea who you are.'

His face fell. 'My apologies. I'm James O'Nions – Inspector O'Nions of the Special Branch.'

Special Branch! This was getting more and more interesting by the minute. The Special Branch had remade itself from the Special Irish Branch with the demise of the Fenian threat a few years ago. It now sought out political extremists of a variety of hues, and had made its name exposing the activities of the Birmingham anarchists' bomb factory in 1892. Did yours truly merit the attentions of the Special Branch now? A frisson of excitement ran down my spine at the thought of arrest and interrogation by this shadowy band of policemen. I had after all attended the Labour Representation conference in February as a leading figure in the Fabian Society, and was contributing to GBS's tract on imperialism, which would blast asunder the establishment's attitude to the Boer War. Surely a dashing and dangerous figure.

I was almost holding out my wrists for the manacles to be put on them, when O'Nions shattered my illusions. 'I need your help, Mr Potter.'

Letter from Rosalind Potter to Mr Richter, dated 5 April 1900

Dear Mr Richter

I am once again contacting you through the usual channels in order to ask for your assistance. You may not feel inclined to give it when I tell you with whom it is in connection, but be assured that it will be of help to the cause you espouse in the long run. Besides, I know from our earlier acquaintance how much you like a good puzzle. The Zermatt murder riddle was one we all took great pleasure in deciphering. But to the meat of my enquiry.

You will no doubt be aware of yesterday's attempt on the life of the Prince of Wales and his long-suffering wife in Belgium. That it should happen in Brussels of all places came as a great surprise to those charged with his protection, and at the Gare du Nord itself! The youth they arrested at the scene – Sipido by name – is being treated more courteously than our government would like. It appears he has said he did it to protest about the events in South Africa, and the British prosecution of the Boer War is somewhat disliked in Continental quarters! But to the point.

The establishment (through the agency of someone of unusual nomenclature belonging to that arm of the police with which we have had dealings before – I am sure you know what I mean) wants us to find out who is hiding behind the slim figure of Sipido. They do not think at fifteen years of age he was capable of organising such a feat as an assassination attempt. But with his incarceration in Belgium putting him beyond the grasp of the British political police, they are not able to interrogate him themselves. So enter the great detective triumvirate of Potter, Potter and ... well, I know how you value your anonymity. But do say you will help.

I understand that you are somewhere on the Continent at present, having recently returned from exile in the coldest part of your country. I said to Albert you should try living in Twickenham – nowhere could be as frosty, or as far from the seat of governmental power!

Yours in mutual 'brotherhood'
Rosalind Potter

Extract from Albert Potter's diary

Monday, 9 April 1900

We have had a letter back from U—ff at last, though I suppose I must remember to call him Mr Richter! I recall the last time I saw him five years ago in Paris. Someone said he was born old and bald, and if by old they meant serious-minded and wise, then I would tend to agree with whoever it was. I had then left him eating at a run-down café in the poorer part of the French capital, his cloth cap screwed up in his lap, and his shiny dome of a head glinting in the watery sunlight. He was brushing crumbs from his burgeoning goatee beard, and laying down the law to his attentive 'comrades'. How they would have been surprised to know the man and his whimsical sense of humour as I did!

His letter, written in poor English and read out loud to me by Rosalind, was not optimistic. He doubted he could find out anything about Sipido, but at least he promised to try.

Thursday, 12 April 1900

Another letter, postmarked Vienna, arrived today from Mr Richter, though signed 'Ritmeyer'. I attach it to this diary entry. He writes (in a German more comfortable than his stilted English, thank goodness) he can as yet find no more than a tenuous connection between Sipido and any socialist organisations in Belgium. This is beginning to be puzzling. Was Sipido really acting on his own as the Belgian police say he insists? Or is O'Nions's suspicion that he is merely the catspaw of some anarchistic organisation going to be more difficult to uncover than I or Rosalind assumed?

She meanwhile is meeting with Joe C. She does not know I know this, and her infatuation blinds her to his manipulation of the war for his own ends. But I must not play the jealous husband or she will be gone. And that I could not bear.

Letter to Mrs Potter from Mr Ritmeyer, dated Monday, 9 April 1900 (translated from the German by Albert)

My dear Rosalind

You know who this is from, even if the name at the bottom of the letter is unfamiliar. Twickenham sounds twice as frightening as S—a. At least in the latter place one can fish and hunt ducks. Twickenham sounds positively sterile! I have been thinking for some time of transferring my enterprise to London – you must advise me of the best place to find lodgings for myself and my new wife. Yes! I am now a married man, and so must cut my cloth more assiduously than I did in the past.

I passed a lot of the time in exile translating your and Albert's work, 'A Short History of Trade Unionism'. It was most enlightening.

As concerns Sipido, something odd is afoot. My first impressions of his origins are that he hasn't the bona fides of the true anarchist. He was briefly a member of the League for the Amelioration of the Working Classes, but this was a short-lived and rather bourgeois organisation in Brussels. He was over-eager, and soon inveigled his way into the hierarchy as a messenger-boy to the organisers. Where he remained for some months, during which time the League suffered several setbacks. On one occasion, the clandestine press used to print leaflets was raided, and all the machinery impounded. On another, a visiting revolutionary was arrested by the police, and summarily deported from Belgium before even getting to the assembly he was due to address. The League was desperate – assuming there was an informer in their midst, but unable to verify who it was. No one suspected the eager, fresh-faced child, who carried all their messages (and was therefore privy to all their machinations), as someone who, wittingly or unwittingly, revealed their secrets. Some revolutionaries!

When their third disaster occurred, they were all accusing each other of being the informer in their midst. Inevitably, the whole organisation collapsed, and Sipido disappeared. I will let you know if I can trace him crawling out of the woodwork anywhere else.

Yours

V. Ritmeyer

Extract from the private diary of Rosalind Potter

Friday, 13 April 1900

Met Joseph earlier in the week. His bearing is so unlike Albert's – so straight and yet so languorous – that I find him irresistible. Can't tell Albert that – he would be so jealous – but J's attentions are so flattering, I almost forgot the true purpose of our meeting. Though his Ministry is the Colonial, J is still at the centre of power, and knows what is going on. Even so, I don't believe he knows that Special Branch, in the form of the persistent O'Nions, is investigating the Sipido affair. He laughed off any implications of the assassination attempt. The 'crime of a young man with a disordered brain' he called it, attempted by a crazy juvenile Spaniard. I said I thought Sipido was Belgian, to which he replied, 'So might he well be, for all I know.' And attempted to drop the whole matter. When I persisted he became quite agitated – so unlike dear Joe!

When I told Albert of my rendezvous with Joseph, he became very excited, and suggested that JC's agitation contained evidence of the government's involvement in the assassination attempt. I'm afraid he has a lurid imagination. I would prefer to have some facts before entertaining such a preposterous idea. All it proved to me was that the incident was minor, and that Joseph was annoyed about my clouding our 'assignation' with such trivial matters. But I couldn't tell Albert that.

Extract from Albert Potter's diary

Saturday, 14 April 1900

I can't get Pushful Joe's reaction to Rosalind's enquiry about Sipido out of my head. Not only was he 'agitated' (Rosalind's own word) over her interest in the whole affair, he seemed to indicate that Sipido was of Spanish extraction. This comes as news to me, and the press, who have always called him Belgian. Does Joe know more about this child than he is letting on? I would not be surprised.

433

Later

Mr Ritmeyer's latest letter, dated 11 April, was delivered just now, along with a cutting from the *Journal de Bruxelles*. We both read the article, Rosalind peering over my shoulder, and she paled a little at the reference to Jean Baptiste Sipido as a 'youth with a disordered brain', but refused to elaborate. We moved on to the letter, and as usual I translated from the German for Rosalind. Thank goodness my one fashionable indulgence – German lessons – has stood me in practical, good stead. What he writes in the letter confirms in my mind that Sipido is no revolutionary working on his own as he is depicted in the papers. It is said he purchased a Lefaucheux revolver on the Sunday before, to carry out the deed. The problem is, how did a fifteen-year-old Belgian youth know on Sunday that the Prince of Wales would be in Brussels the following Wednesday? It appears Richter has bribed the clerk to the Procureur du Roi who interrogated Sipido for four hours, and he admitted to being put up to it by a shadowy 'person unknown'! I now recall this being briefly mentioned in *The Times* soon after the assassination attempt, and scuttle off to find the copy, but it has fed the living room fire. Nothing more was made of this connection though, and we now eagerly await more information from Richter/Ritmeyer. But I am already seeing a conspiratorial thread running from Sipido to the heart of the British government!

Monday, 16 April 1900

I met with Inspector O'Nions this morning – one of our prearranged meetings on the steps of the British Museum. The day was bright and sunny, unlike our first encounter, and yet the old dinosaur of a building still seemed grey and depressing. I have begun to wonder if that is what made Marx so lugubrious. Spending endless days in the bowels of such a gloomy monster cannot be conducive to a state of well-being or optimism. As usual, O'Nions appeared from behind the right-hand pillar at the top of the steps. I am beginning to wonder if he does not live there – I would not be surprised to find a secret door in the fluting of the pillar.

Despite the clement weather, O'Nions was still wrapped in his heavy, dark overcoat that hung down to his well-polished shoes. They were black on this occasion, but his bowler was still the trusty brown item he always wore. Pity the Special Branch don't tutor their officers in aspects of sartorial elegance. He cast a cautious glance over my shoulder, no doubt to ensure I had not been followed – though by whom I might have been was unknown to me – and offered me his beefy fist to shake. I will attempt to reproduce the gist of our conversation, as it was a source of some puzzlement.

'Any news from our mutual friend?' asks the doughty inspector.

'Some,' responds yours truly, not wishing to reveal all I know at one sitting. 'It seems our unsuccessful assassin's bona fides are in question.'

'You mean Sipido's membership of the ill-fated League for the Amelioration of the Working Classes, and the Socialist Advance Guard of St Gilles?' opines O'Nions, much to my chagrin. Neither Mr Richter nor I had uncovered the second organisation. How much more does he know, I wonder? I am soon to find out that it's very little.

'Does Mr . . . Richter know where he pops up after that?'

So his knowledge is limited after all. I do not wish him to know that I know no more than he does, and I play my trump card. 'He might, but you must tell me what your suspicions are about the little Spaniard.'

Surely this little piece of inside knowledge will startle him, I think. But O'Nions merely shows his tombstone-like teeth, and chortles with delight.

'I see Mrs Potter has been talking with the Colonial Secretary.'

I blush, and O'Nions continues by way of explanation.

'The Colonial Office have found a Spanish connection, but the boy is Belgian, I assure you. What I need to know is what his connections are in his home country.'

Angrily, I blurt out my suspicions of the 'person unknown' whose existence has been suppressed by someone. Could this person be linked back to England, I wonder? O'Nions's face darkens, and his lips compress into a tight line, banishing his normally cheerful expression.

'Don't worry yourself about connecting him to anyone in England. Just stick to the anarchist links.'

With this he abruptly concludes the interview, and returns to lurking behind his pillar. It is only as I transcribe this meeting that I am all the more convinced that we are being used, and there is some meddling hand in England that O'Nions wants us to ignore, merely providing him with a socialist smokescreen. I fear I am not prepared to be so blinkered. I will draft a letter to Mr Richter as soon as I put pen down on this entry.

Wednesday, 18 April 1900

Our letters have crossed! The Continental mail does not have the reliability of the Royal Mail, and Mr Richter's letter, dated the same day as my last, abortive interview with Inspector O'Nions, has just arrived. I will summarise its findings here, and speculate on the possible conclusions that can be drawn from it, which are remarkable!

Richter elaborates on his last letter, and his research into the putative assassin. Apparently, though Sipido is of the working classes, his father being a clerk for Belgian Railways (hence no doubt the son's predilection for the Gare du Nord as his chosen assassination locale), his mother comes of a respectable family in reduced circumstances. The boy indeed has uncles and cousins who work for the Belgian Civil Service, and it is reported he used to spend more time with his better-off relatives than in the bosom of his own family. An uncertain background for a budding revolutionary! In fact, Richter managed to trace a certain Uncle Alphon to the offices of the Belgian equivalent of our Foreign and Colonial Office – only a minor official of course, but nevertheless . . .

Richter draws no conclusions from his findings, but there is a definite trail, to my mind, from Sipido, attempted assassin of the Prince of Wales, through the Belgian Foreign Office, and thence to all the governments in Europe – including our own. I have begun to form a theory that the boy was not acting for the putative overthrowers of government, but unwittingly for one of those governments itself. Maybe even our own! He has been used by some government agent, playing on his youthful extremism. When I eagerly shared my theory with Rosalind, she pooh-poohed the idea. She taxed me with expounding the reason for Lord Salisbury's, or anyone in his government's, wanting to murder the heir to the throne. When I hesitated momentarily, she suggested that George Keppel might have reason – or any one of the husbands of the prince's favourite women – but not the government. I did not see that her tongue was firmly in her cheek, and eagerly began to draw up a list of possible aggrieved husbands, before she broke into unaccustomed laughter. I have to admit I threw my pen down at that point, and stormed out of the room. I will have to apologise for my behaviour later. But first I must hurry to be in time for my regular encounter with Inspector O'Nions. Perhaps he will not laugh so readily at my theories.

Extract from Rosalind Potter's private diary

Wednesday, 18 April 1900
After poor Albert had gone off in a temper to confer with

the ever cheerful O'Nions, and no doubt make a fool of himself again over government conspiracies, there was a knock at the door of our rooms. It was a telegram from JC, asking me to see him urgently. With little preparation other than changing my dress, adding some perfume, and piling my hair into a 'Gibson Girl' look, I rushed to the proposed location of the rendezvous – a quiet hotel in Bayswater. If I had entertained any subconscious thought that this was going to be a romantic assignation, I was soon disabused of my misapprehension. Joseph was preoccupied, and even his normal fastidious neatness was absent. The orchid in his lapel drooped in harmony with the moroseness of his expression.

'Rosalind, I will come straight to the point,' he said, his hands stuffed deep into the pockets of his formal pin-striped trousers. 'Inspector O'Nions should not have contacted you or Albert concerning the Belgian business – he was acting entirely on his own initiative. Why, I would not be surprised to learn that it was all a juvenile joke gone wrong, and that Sipido regrets everything. So I would be grateful if you could drop the whole affair. A matter of minor importance, it could only strain relations on the Continent even further, if it were pursued. I'm sure you understand.'

Much to his surprise, I think, I said I did. Not because I believed him, but because I suddenly wondered if Albert had been right all along. My agreement seemed to mollify him, and as abruptly as the meeting had begun, so it was terminated. Joseph turned his swallowtail-coated back on me and I was ushered out of the room and on to the street. I crossed the Bayswater Road, and, not knowing for sure why I did it, hid in the doorway of a gentlemen's outfitters opposite. I stayed there for almost an hour, but was disappointed – JC did not emerge. No doubt there was a convenient back exit to the hotel, which explained why it had been chosen, and if I checked the hotel register, I was sure it would reveal that no one had rented the room at all on that day. I hurried back to our rooms, and eagerly awaited Albert's return from his meeting with O'Nions. I will put my pen down, because I think I hear him now.

Extract from Albert Potter's diary

Thursday, 19 April 1900

I have left this for a full day before recording my impressions, as I needed to be clear on the implications of what happened yesterday. I think I am now certain in my own mind, and leave it to posterity to decide if I am right.

For the first time since we have been meeting regularly, O'Nions failed to put in an appearance from behind the British Museum pillar yesterday. I dallied on the steps for more than an hour, being taken at one point for a beggar. Rosalind is always chastising me for the cut of my coat, and forever telling me to brush the dust and fluff from it. It seems she has a point, if I appear so dishevelled as to merit charity. Still, the couple of pennies thrust into my hand by some passing scholar on his way to the Reading Room paid for a malt at the Barley Mow Tavern. But I shall have to avoid that selfsame scholar while conducting my own researches at the BM, or he may try to have me ejected as a vagabond.

I admit that I was so perturbed that one malt was followed by another, and that by a few more, as I tried to puzzle out what was going on concerning the Sipido affair. I then spotted a brief article in *The Times*, being read by my neighbour at the bar. It was headed 'The attempt on the Prince of Wales', and I include the cutting in my diary.

(Brussels, 17 April) It has now emerged that Sipido, one of nine children, spent Monday evening at the Maison du

439

Peuple, the haunt of extreme anarchists, in the company of five other young men, one named Meer. The said Meer, aged twenty-two, wagered five francs that Sipido would not carry out his threat to shoot the Prince of Wales in the head, if he ever came to Brussels. The others involved, who will not be arrested, assured the Procureur du Roi that they deemed it merely a joke, and it had resulted in a tragic act of bravado. The prisoner is now said to have expressed sorrow for his crime.

As it appeared O'Nions had now been warned off the matter, and a convenient story lined up, my whisky-fed imagination was filled with images of governmental conspiracies to get rid of the jovial prince. None of it made sense. Finally, I decided I had better go home and face the music, but walked rather than took a cab to allow the fine London air to cleanse my breath of the odour of Scotch.

Entering the hallway where Rosalind and I have our rooms, I collected a solitary letter that rested in our pigeon-hole, and trudged upstairs, resignation to my fate in every step. Much to my relief, I found a wife who had apparently forgotten my moody exit, engrossed as she had been in her own ratiocination. In fact, she was now inclined to believe me!

Note inserted in margin later

It was unfortunate (as we both later realised) that I put the letter down and forgot about it. It left us floundering in unnecessary speculation.

Extract from Rosalind Potter's private diary

Thursday a.m., 19 April 1900

I think I have it! The more I spoke to Albert about JC's

involvement in the attempt on the prince's life, and the more he speculated on the reasons for the government to do such a fantastic deed, the more I was convinced there was another answer. Then it came to me.

The government weren't covering up their own deeds, but those of another person who, if the truth came out, would cause an unbelievable scandal. One that would rock the monarchy.

Albert didn't see it at first. 'Do you mean it was the husband of one of Prinny's floozies? Keppel? The Duke of . . . ? No, I don't see it – that wouldn't surprise anyone.' Then he paled. 'You don't mean . . .' Even Albert found it difficult to say the name. He took a great gulp of air, screwed up his courage and spoke the unthinkable. 'You don't really think . . . Alexandra arranged it? His own wife? I know she is supposed to get angry at his dalliances, but do you really imagine she could be capable of arranging his murder?'

As a woman, my eyes sparkled at the thought of a wronged wife hitting back at her philandering husband. And such a prominent husband at that. I was only worried about one thing. Alexandra had been in the same railway carriage as the prince when the shots were sprayed in through the window. But surely I am right – it is the only logical explanation for JC's nervous suppression of our investigation on behalf of Special Branch, and O'Nions's removal from the case. I must take the startling news to the next Fabian Society meeting – GBS could make a wonderful play out of these bare bones!

Extract from Albert Potter's diary

Thursday, 19 April 1900
I have it! Princess Alexandra plotted the demise of her own husband. Rosalind took some convincing, but I am sure I am

right. The wronged wife (Alexandra, not Rosalind!), through the agency of her own family in Denmark, has been put in touch with royalists in Belgium, who have proposed a young man with impeccable family connections, and a false history of revolutionary activity. All she had to ensure was that she sat on the opposite side of the carriage to the prince. Case closed.

Extract from Rosalind Potter's private diary

Early morning, Friday 20 April 1900

I knew I was wrong about Alexandra. It just took a troubled night's sleep to work it out. Of course, my tossing and turning did nothing to disturb Albert, who snored the night away contentedly. I lay awake, the facts churning around in my head to my husband's trumpet accompaniment. Alexandra would never have found such a crude and dangerous way to rid herself of a philandering husband – the bullets, even if aimed accurately, might have ricocheted from some sturdy fitting in the carriage and endangered her own life. Besides, she evidently loves the fat beast, as much as I love the vainglorious, overly intelligent and . . . un-Chamberlain-like lump who snores gently at my side each night. Anyway, I have now read Mr Richter's last letter, which dear Albert forgot all about yesterday, and I have only just discovered lying like an anarchist time-bomb on the lounge carpet. It consists of some dates, and a very persuasive argument.

Letter from Mr Richter to Mr and Mrs Potter, undated

Dear Albert and Rosalind

I have been pondering your little mystery, and offer some further thoughts. One: Sipido is not a revolutionary – indeed the very opposite. Two: I have yet to come across a government that sought to assassinate its own head of state, much as it might wish to. Three: consider the following events –

1870 – attempt on the life of Chancellor Bismarck at Bad Kissingen

1878 – anarchist attempt on the life of King Alfonso XII in Madrid

1879 – attempt on the life of Tsar Alexander II in the streets of St Petersburg

1881 – successful attempt on the life of Alexander II

1882 – Roderick Maclean, a lunatic, fires a pistol at Queen Victoria at Windsor Station

1898 – Empress of Austria killed by an Italian on the quay at Geneva.

To me, it would seem no self-respecting ruler, or budding ruler, would consider themselves taken seriously unless they have been subject to an assassination attempt these days. Four: your Prince of Wales would die for (pardon my little pun) the same popular veneration as his mother receives.

Yours fraternally

Richter

PS Thank you for your information about suitable lodgings in London – the Grays Inn Road sounds most acceptable.

Extract from Rosalind Potter's private diary

Later, Friday 20 April 1900

The minute I read Vladimir's letter, I knew. Poor Albert, whom I took great delight in wakening before seven a.m., took a little longer to reach the same conclusion, no doubt befuddled by his imbibing of too much whisky again the night before, the evidence for which still hung on his breath.

'I don't understand – surely he can't mean that Sipido was responsible for all these attempted killings? The boy is only fifteen,' he groaned.

'No, don't you see? He was put up to it by—' Albert would not let me finish. It is a trait of his which annoys me greatly, and I will curb it.

'Our government? I thought we had discarded that theory. I cannot see why they should do such an outrageous thing. Certainly Salisbury is mad, and we should have a Liberal government. But to kill the next monarch? I think not.'

I let him rave a little longer about George Keppel and Princess Alexandra, then I put him out of his misery.

'Don't you see? What embarrassing truth would drive the government into hushing up the affair, when they discovered it? Why would they play an assassination attempt down so much that they will probably end up agreeing to the boy's being declared harmlessly mad, or something?'

'You don't mean . . . ?'

'Yes. In order to boost his popularity, and put him on a par with his old mama, Bertie arranged his own assassination attempt!'

The Playwrights

Michael Hemmingson

New York, 1909

T he first time I went to the bi-weekly evening gatherings of New York's most prominent playwrights, I was twenty-two, frightened, and intimidated. It was the spring of 1909, and I remember the weather being unusually warm; or perhaps all the sweating I was doing under my old wool suit was due to nervousness. My first play had opened at a small theatre to much critical (and little financial) success, thus I was invited to join the round-table of the city's renowned masters of stagecraft. There was a little over a dozen of them at the mid-city townhouse where the gathering took place, all sitting around on deep sofas and plush chairs and drinking various liquids, ranging from wine to Scotch and bourbon to tea. All but one were men; most in their late thirties to early forties, and the one woman among us was in her fifties. It caused me little comfort to know they all had been my age, or younger, when their first plays were mounted. However, to this day, most of them have faded into obscurity; for all their pomposity, they were doomed to a future of being neither in print nor on stage. There was one man there whose name you might recognise, though: Eugene O'Neill. I never got to know Mr O'Neill well, much to my later disappointment and regret.

My story here is about Willard Reed, and *his* story he told that first time I went to the gathering. Did I mention they called themselves the Playwrights' Chamber? That's who they were.

447

I wasn't sure what these people talked about. The art of writing theatre, yes, that was expected; or maybe they would complain about certain producers, directors, and actors; or maybe the talk would not be of art, but of political ideals such as socialism and communism, heavy aspects in those mutable days in American history.

After I was introduced to everyone, someone said, 'Last time, Willard promised to tell us his yarn of being a detective and how he solved a murder.'

'Well,' Willard Reed said, sipping at his bourbon, 'it is a story of how I played an *amateur* detective. Unfortunately, I didn't solve the murder.'

'Still,' someone else from the group said, 'it sounds like a fascinating tale.'

Willard Reed smiled. He was a tall man, thick in the middle, wearing a black suit and tie. He held a cane in his hand. He was in his late forties, maybe early fifties, hard to tell. I'd seen several of his plays over the years. I found them to be rather lengthy and opprobrious, but he always had sad, tragic endings that touched me in the darkest spot of my heart. He cleared his throat. 'This happened three months ago. You're all familiar with the Fritz Shakespeare Ensemble, I'm sure.' Nods and mumbled yeses came from most of the people. I nodded; I'd heard of them, had even seen one of their productions of *The Tempest*. 'A young and dynamic troupe that takes certain risks with the sacred William's words. I was most impressed with what they did with *Hamlet*. Three months ago, however, I was at the opening night soirée of their run of *Twelfth Night*. It was the usual afterglow gathering of a troupe having just completed hard work on a long and challenging project, and they were letting loose, with much booze, as is expected wherever actors – or even playwrights – are found,' a few low chuckles, 'and a bottle of absinthe and even a small tray with snuff. I was keeping a low profile. Only a few people there knew who I was, and I didn't feel like making advertisements as to my status in the theatre community.'

'How unusual!' someone commented.

Others laughed in afterthought.

Reed seemed to find this amusing. He grinned, and reached to the table in front of him, where the bottle of bourbon was placed. He poured himself two fingers of the fine, light brown liquid. Myself, I was drinking white wine. I can't stomach hard alcohol, although I like the taste of good bourbon with bitters. I was licking my lips in anticipation, on two different levels.

The man crossed his legs and went on. 'Being an astute observer, I noticed a minor drama taking place between three of the members of the company. A woman and two men, as such dramas are bound by cliché. One of the men I knew – he is the artistic director of the group; he was, in fact, the person who had invited me to this after-show gathering. He was also an actor, but wasn't in the present production, the duties of running the company, as he had told me in a previous conversation, taking up more and more of his time, so that he found himself on stage less and less. His name was, is, Daniel Davis. He was having what appeared to be an emotional conversation with the young woman who had directed *Twelfth Night*. She was no more than thirty, with a round pretty face and large eyes, dark hair, thin build. Her name was Carla Black. I must put emphasis on the past tense 'was', as she would, the next morning, be found murdered in an alley.'

There were some gasps from the group, but I felt they were feigning this shock to add tension to the suspense Willard Reed was building. I, for one, may have been uninterested at first, but he now had my rapt attention, because I recalled hearing about the murder of one of the members of the Fritz Shakespeare Ensemble – Carla Black, a young and promising director.

449

'But back to the party,' Reed said, sipping his bourbon with relish. 'At first glance, while I could not hear what they were saying, huddled in a corner of the room, I might believe they were having a heated conversation about the opening night performance; about art, about ticket sales, anything quite innocent. But I knew innocence was not a factor as I took note of another man also watching them. This man had a part in the present show, and he was good, a somewhat overweight but passionate actor I had seen in other productions from this troupe, and at other theatres as well. His name was, and is, Bertrand Barkley.

'You know how you can feel hate from someone if they are looking at you and directing that hate towards you? You can feel the same when witnessing a person directing hate at another. And Mr Barkley was commanding his hate towards Mr Davis and Miss Black. He had a mug of beer in hand, and he was watching them, albeit from afar, quite closely. Miss Black glanced away from Davis, and she saw Barkley looking at her. Then Miss Black started to go, to move away from Mr Davis. Davis grabbed her arm, and she shrugged him away. I overheard her say: "No, Daniel, no, it's over and it's never going to happen again."

'There was another person who was also watching this incident – a young blonde girl of twenty, an actress who had a bit part in the show. I wasn't aware she was part of this, but I'm getting ahead of myself.

'Anyway,' Reed continued, uncrossing his legs, 'Miss Black started to make her way to the middle of the room, perhaps to refresh her drink, when Mr Barkley made his move to intercept her. He took her by the arm, and she didn't appear to be pleased by this. I was close enough to catch some of their conversation. Basically, Mr Barkley wanted to know what she was talking to Mr Davis about. She told him that it was none of his business but he insisted it was. I heard Mr Barkley say:

"You told me that it was over between you and him."

' "It is," Miss Black said, "*it is*."

' "Well, it doesn't seem like it is to me," Barkley said.

'I noticed that, across the room, Mr Davis was now watching these two conversing, and he had hate in his eyes as well.

' "It doesn't even matter," Miss Black said to Barkley.

'Mr Barkley's reply was: "Well, it matters a hell of a lot to me!"

'With this, Miss Black stormed away, to another room, or perhaps outside. Mr Barkley remained where he was, and he looked at Mr Davis. Needless to say, the air between them, and the looks they gave one another, were far from friendly – for two men who worked in the same company.

'At this point, the young blonde actress appeared at my side, with a curious expression on her face. She was a small, bird-like creature, beautiful like an angelic child, I'd say. She was drinking Pernod, I could smell it from the glass in her hand. "Quite a show, wouldn't you say?" she asked. She had a British accent.'

'A British accent!' the only woman in the group said, with a thick British accent.

'Indeed,' Willard Reed replied. 'I asked about this. She said she was born in Hertfordshire, studied acting in London, and came to America. Her name was, and is, Cassandra Payne. This information was revealed a bit later in our conversation. The meat, we will say, of our rendezvous was what both she and I had been watching. I had seen her observing the little drama just as she had taken note of my own observation. She knew who I was, much to my surprise. She even said she had auditioned for one of my plays. "You were sitting there when I auditioned," she told me.

' "I'm sorry I don't remember you," I said, "but when I go to auditions for my work, I see many—"

451

'And she cut me off, gently, touching my hand, saying, "It's all right, I understand. You see many faces."

' "I'm sure you gave a great audition," I said. I felt foolish saying such. I wasn't at all sincere.

'Young Cassandra Payne didn't seem to register what I stated. She was preoccupied with the recent conflict we were both witness to. This is when I learned that Miss Black was formally Mrs Barkley. In fact, the divorce was still clogging through the court system and not finalised, and Miss Black had never officially taken Barkley's last name, being the liberated sort of woman we meet more and more these days. Or so I was to understand by hearsay information.

'Miss Payne gave me a quick synopsis of the history behind what had just transpired. Mr Barkley was far from the man of fidelity, having been married to Carla Black for three years. He was known to have had a number of liaisons with actresses who came and went from the troupe. At first, he was able to keep his extramarital trysts secret, but soon Miss Black found out, as such things always become apparent, and she wanted a divorce. Mr Barkley agreed, and confessed he didn't love her anyway. But when Barkley learned that Miss Black was having relations with Mr Davis, he became infuriated. One would wonder why, but apparently there was artistic and aesthetic rivalry between Barkley and Davis to begin with. Also, Barkley had won the favour of some young women that Davis had set his eyes on, so they were on a high competitive level.'

'Two cocks in a henhouse,' Eugene O'Neill said.

'Two bulls in a field of cows,' added someone else.

'Indeed,' Reed said. 'Miss Payne told me that the troupe was on the verge of falling apart because of this terrible threesome – the artistic director, the main stage director, and the main actor. Not to mention they were also the founders of the company! A bad stew brewing!

'Miss Payne shook her head as she relayed this information.

She looked very sad. I wanted to hug her, really I did. There was genuine pain in her eyes. I understood how such conflicts could destroy a theatre group. "I understand how they both love her," she told me. "She's beautiful, she has charisma, she is a great director. She draws people to her, and they fall in love with her. But I'm afraid Daniel and Bertrand may kill each other over her."

' "These things have a way of always working out," I said, and again I felt foolish, for being a playwright, a scribe of human drama, these intricacies of human love – well, I must admit to a certain amount of innocence and ignorance.'

'What about her murder?' someone next to me asked, a man close to my age who seemed quite enthralled by the story, and drinking Scotch.

'That is next,' Willard Reed replied. He poured himself more bourbon. I looked at my wine glass: half full. 'The next day, when I read in the papers that Carla Black, theatre director, was found with her stomach ripped open by a knife in an alley not ten blocks from where the after-show party had taken place, my blood went cold. The paper said there were no suspects. Naturally, as I'm sure this is going through the rest of your minds, I deduced otherwise.

'I bathed and dressed and immediately went to the local police station, and enquired about the detective handling the murder case of Carla Black. I was introduced to Nick Henderson, a well-dressed, well-groomed man in his thirties, who was assigned the case. I told him who I was, and my interest in the murder. He assured me that there were no suspects yet, that it could very well have been a random slaying. She was walking home, she was accosted, she may have been raped, they hadn't checked the body yet. "This is no Jack the Ripper case," I told him, "because I have two solid suspects for you."

'He told me that he had talked to everyone in the Fritz

Shakespeare Ensemble, but no one had seen her leave the party, alone or otherwise. I told him what I had seen, the arguments, and what I knew about the romantic love triangle. "This could very well be a case of crime of passion!" I said.

'Henderson considered this, nodding his head, and agreed. However, he had already talked to both Davis and Barkley.

' "How did they take the news?" I asked.

' "They were both in shock," he said.

' "They are both actors," I informed him, "and very *good* actors."

' "Perhaps," he said, "I should talk to them again."

' "But they're waiting for that," I said, "whichever one is the killer. The guilty party has prepared a story. But I have an idea." This is where I fancied myself the detective. Of course, I have been reading, for years, the mysteries composed by Sir Arthur Conan Doyle, concerning the adventures of Sherlock Holmes and Dr Watson. I don't know who I was seeing myself as, Mr Holmes or Dr Watson, but they were both my inspiration. So this is what I proposed to Detective Henderson:

' "Sir," I said, "whichever is the guilty party, they are presently waiting for you to confront them. We need to catch the culprit by surprise." I outlined to the detective my idea, and he agreed to it.

'I sent by bicycle messenger, early the next day, separate messages to both Mr Davis and Mr Barkley. I professed my deep regret for their loss of a company member, and my hope that the criminal responsible would be caught, charged, and convicted; then I offered an ideal situation: that I knew a man of wealth who was interested in underwriting a full season of their projects. Naturally, both men messengered me back, that afternoon, that they were interested in meeting with this possible arts philanthropist. Because of the animosity between the two, I assumed, correctly, there was a power struggle, and that garnering a rich benefactor would give either of them power over the other. Thus, I knew they would not tell one another of my correspondence.

'I had enough time to send a late messenger to both to come to my residence in the morning to meet the man with money – I told Barkley to arrive at ten, and Davis to arrive at ten thirty.

'Detective Henderson was at my residence at nine o'clock. We went over and over my plan. I assured him this would work. Of course, I was feeling quite proud of myself, like a Sherlock Holmes, trapping the killer in an intellectual web.

'Barkley was at my door at nine forty-five. I had a feeling he would be early, because he was my main suspect. He had a stronger motive – to kill, after all, his ex-wife, who was sleeping with a man who was his rival.

'I had tea and croissants to offer. I told him that the possible benefactor had not yet arrived. Detective Henderson, however, was situated in the closet, listening and waiting. At ten sharp, my bell rang. I answered the door, and let Mr Daniel Davis in, and took him to the room where Mr Barkley waited in a chair, and the police officer waited in a closet.

'Needless to say—'

'Needless to say,' someone interrupted, 'neither man was prepared for such a deception!'

'A deception, indeed,' Reed said. 'The ploy of the master detective! Or so I was fooling myself. Both men faced each other like two lions in a cage.'

'*Cocks*,' the British woman said.

'Cocks then. I knew I had to intervene quickly. I told them I had brought them both here because I knew that one of them was the murderer of Carla Black. I told them I had witnessed the scene at the party, and I knew, somewhat, the history between the three. At this point, much to my disappointment, Detective Henderson made his way out of the closet, and he was holding a Remington revolver in his hand. "I too know the history between the three of you," he said, "and it is my belief that one of you killed her with a knife."

'Both men broke down, simultaneously. They said Carla Black's death was the most devastating thing either had ever experienced, and they both stated they were not the culprit of her demise. And to my own shock, neither blamed the other.

'Together, they illustrated the history of this love triangle: how Barkley had, in fact, gone to the beds of young actresses who joined the company, and Davis had done the same, and a rivalry of female conquests began between the two. Thus, when Barkley learned that his ex-wife, or soon-to-be-ex-wife, was sleeping with Davis, he became extremely jealous, and quite insecure.

'We were told that the affair between Davis and Miss Black was brief; they had, in fact, only had two amorous encounters, and Miss Black felt this was a bad idea, for the sake of the troupe, and that she really had no feelings for Davis. The sexual entanglings were, as she had told both men, "a mistake in judgement".

'Despite this, in my mind, as well as the detective's, they were still likely suspects. However, both men had alibis for the night. They had both left the party in the company of actresses. In fact, Mr Barkley took Cassandra Payne to his home, the very girl who had led me on this path. "I drank a lot that night, I was very drunk," Barkley said, "but when I woke up, Cassy Payne was in my bed. This was no surprise, because she had been in my bed before."

' "Well," Henderson said of all this, "I will have to check out your alibis."

'I don't have to tell you the embarrassment I was facing. In my preconceived scenarios, one of them would have seen that there was no way out, and broken down and confessed to the murder, and I would be hailed as having solved a heinous crime, much like Mr Holmes. But I was placed in a precarious and inauspicious situation here.'

'So it seems,' said someone.

Yes, I thought. Then I spoke. I said, 'So neither Mr Davis nor Mr Barkley was the felon?'

Willard Reed glared at me for a moment, and said, 'No, boy. Both their alibis were solid, concerning the night in question. And this was the cause of my great embarrassment. Two days later, Detective Henderson called on me. He told me that, yes, neither Davis nor Barkley was questionable in the murder. He had talked to the young ladies whom the men had spent the night with. Both women attested that they had left the party with the men, and had been with them in their rooms all night.

'Thus, my attempt at brilliant amateur detective work went down the drain. Profusely, and sincerely, I apologised to Henderson for my apparent error. And do you know what he said to me? He said, "Don't worry." He said, "In my line of work, I make these kinds of mistakes all the time." Oh, yes, he said, "It's part of the job," but I didn't believe him. I was chagrined. I still am. And thus I give you my contrite story at being a sleuth. I failed miserably. I am no Sherlock Holmes.'

'And so the murder of Carla Black goes unsolved,' someone in the group said.

Willard Reed replied, 'Yes.'

It would be a month later that I, too, became somewhat of an amateur detective, or at least involved in Willard Reed's murder mystery. Perhaps 'informant' is the correct word.

There was this actress friend of mine, Lisa Jolen. I wished that we could have been more than friends, and I certainly had made my intentions clear to her more than once, until she told me that while she found men to be a distraction at times, she was more interested in women.

I was walking home one early evening and passed the building where Lisa had an apartment. I thought I'd drop in on her. My impromptu visit was inopportune, however, as she was entertaining a female guest. I caught just a glimpse of this guest, who gave me a stern look from within the apartment. The woman was small and blonde and intense-looking. 'Let's have lunch tomorrow,' Lisa whispered.

I met Lisa for an early lunch the next day. She confessed that she was uncertain about this new love affair. 'I keep telling myself that I'll stop getting involved with theatre artists,' Lisa Jolen said, 'but who else am I going to meet? This particular new amorous interest, she's an actress, of course. It began so suddenly. It was great. But she smothers me. She wants me all to herself, and it's not love. It's obsession, I think. I don't want to be obsessed over. Sometimes, the girl scares me.'

'Maybe you should call it off,' I suggested.

'Maybe. But Cassandra has quite a temper.'

'That's her name?'

'Yes. Cassandra Payne.' She must have seen it on my face. Lisa said, 'What is it?'

'Hmm? Oh. I forgot about an errand I have to run.'

'Right now?'

'No, no,' I said, 'something I can take care of later.'

I tried to get in contact with Willard Reed, but was unable to. I was afraid he wouldn't be at the next meeting of the Playwrights' Chamber, but – much to my relief – he was. I waited until the evening was coming to a close, and approached him, asking for a few private words. I quickly told him about my friend and her new lover, and who this lover was.

'So the girl gets around,' Reed said. 'I don't understand what you're getting at.'

'I was thinking of the story you told last month,' I said

excitedly. 'How Miss Payne was paying close attention to the arguments, and what she said about Carla Black.'

Reed raised a brow. ' "She's beautiful, she has charisma, she is a great director. She draws people to her, and they fall in love with her." '

'Yes.'

'Good Lord,' he said. He was thinking what I was thinking.

Two days later, Willard Reed invited me to dinner as his guest. He said he had great information for me. I met him at a fine uptown restaurant. I didn't think my suit was good enough to be in such a refined place, but the maître d' showed me to Reed's table none the less.

The man had a bourbon and bitters before him, and was smoking a cigar. He had a pleased expression, like a man just returned from a good safari in the African jungle.

He didn't waste time. 'Cassandra Payne murdered Carla Black.'

'You know this for sure?'

'She confessed. Right now, she is in the hands of the law.'

'I hope you'll tell me everything,' I said.

'I plan to. First, a drink?'

'Maybe a little wine.'

He waved for a waiter. 'You must try the duck here.'

'I'm a vegetarian.'

'Very good.'

After ordering dinner, Mr Reed went into his narrative. 'I went to where the Fritz Shakespeare Ensemble was rehearsing, looking for Miss Payne. She was there – she wasn't in the next show, but she was prompting for the actors. I asked if I could speak to her alone. I got right to the point. "You were in love with Carla Black," I said, "and you were extremely jealous of her entanglements with Davis and Barkley. I'll venture that you even had a liaison with Miss Black, and she no longer

459

wanted the affair, just as she was pushing the two men away. You were furious because of this rejection. I saw it on your face when we talked before, but it simply didn't register until now."

'As I spoke, she was quivering; and when I was done, she burst into tears. She grabbed on to me. I thought she was going to attack me. Instead, she was looking for comfort. She admitted that she did kill Carla Black. It *was* a crime of passion.'

'What I don't understand,' I said, 'is that she was with Bertrand Barkley the night of the murder. She was his alibi, for God's sake!'

'Ah, yes. That thought occurred to me as well, but I had a certain suspicion, which she attested to. Carla Black had left the party early after her confrontations with the men in her life. Miss Payne followed her, not long after she had spoken to me. She had a knife with her – it was a costume prop from the show, placed on the belt and never used in any dangerous way, possessing a working, sharp blade nevertheless. Miss Payne said she had convinced herself she was carrying the knife as protection – it was late, this is New York. But in the back of her mind, she knew she would use it to threaten as an act of love against Carla Black.

' "I really don't know what I was thinking," she told me in a thicker accent than I remember her having. "I was seeing red. I was quite inebriated from the Pernod. I was so in love with her. I wanted her to be in my arms for ever. She kept telling me what happened between us was a mistake, and that it would never happen again. The same damned thing she told Daniel Davis! We were walking down the street, and she was acting so coldly, as if she didn't want me near her, as if I was worthless! I pushed her in an alley, yelling at her. 'You're nothing but a tramp!' I cried, and that's when I took out the knife. I just wanted to scare her, and the next thing I knew, I had the knife in her belly."

'Looking down at the body of Miss Black, and realising what she had done, Miss Payne ran back to the party. She cleaned the prop knife and put it away. Mr Barkley was getting quite drunk and making passes at various women. When he came to her, she decided he would suffice as an alibi. She would go home with him. The irony of it! She was believing, by going to Barkley's bed, it would relieve her as a suspect, when—'

'When *she* was relieving *him* as a suspect,' I said.

'Indeed.'

'So did she think she committed the perfect murder? That she would get off scot-free?'

'She confessed that the guilt was overwhelming and she couldn't live with it any more. She said she was happy I had figured her out. She even said she'd been contemplating going to the police and turning herself in. "Now would be a good time to do it," I informed her. "I will go with you, if you'd like."

'She nodded. She got her coat, and I escorted her to the station. To be honest, I just wanted to see the look on Detective Henderson's face. I may have made a fool out of myself before in my novice notions of being a sleuth, but I was now delivering the murderess straight into his hands. And now here we are.'

'You solved the murder of Carla Black,' I said. 'You should feel proud.'

'Pah!' He laughed. 'I did nothing. Without your tip, I would've still been the bumbling fool. Needless to say, I was foolish to confront Miss Payne the way I did. Despite circumstantial suspicion, what if she was not the culprit? Or what if she felt no remorse and denied the crime? She could have simply laughed in my face and called me insane. She could have tarnished my image in the theatre community, claiming I was going around accusing everybody of murder!'

'But that wasn't the case.'

'No. Blind, dumb luck was on my side.'

A waiter arrived with our food.

'Time for dinner,' Reed said. He raised his glass of bourbon. 'Here's to two playwright/detectives.'

I raised my wine glass. 'Playwrights.'

The Problem of Stateroom 10

Peter Lovesey

North Atlantic Ocean, 1912

The conversation in the first class smoking room had taken a sinister turn.

'I once met a man who knew of a way to commit the perfect murder,' said Jacques Futrelle, the American author. 'He was offering to sell it to me – as a writer of detective stories – for the sum of fifty pounds. I declined. I explained that we story writers deal exclusively in murders that are imperfect. Our readers expect the killer to be caught.'

'Now that you point it out, a perfect murder story would be unsatisfactory,' said one of his drinking companions, W. T. Stead, the campaigning journalist and former editor of the *Pall Mall Gazette*, now white-bearded and past sixty, but still deeply interested in the power of the written word. 'Good copy in a newspaper, however. In the press, you see, we need never come to a conclusion. Our readers cheerfully pay to be held in suspense. They enjoy uncertainty. They may look forward to a solution at some time in the future, but there's no obligation on me to provide one. If it turns up, I'll report it. But I'm perfectly content if a mystery is prolonged indefinitely and they keep buying the paper.'

'The classic example of that would be the Whitechapel murders,' said the third member of the party, a younger man called Finch who had first raised this gruesome subject. His striped blazer and ducks were a little loud for good taste, even at sea.

'Dear old Jack the Ripper?' said Stead. 'I wouldn't want him unmasked. He's sold more papers than the king's funeral and the coronation combined.'

'Hardly the perfect murderer, however,' commented Futrelle. 'He left clues all over the place. Pieces of flesh, writing on walls, letters to the press. He only escaped through the incompetence of the police. My perfect murderer would be of a different order entirely.'

'Ha! Now we come to it,' said Stead, winking at Finch. 'Professor S. F. X. Van Dusen. The Thinking Machine.'

'Van Dusen isn't a murderer,' Futrelle protested. 'He solves murders.'

'You know who we're talking about?' Stead said for the benefit of the young man. 'Our friend Futrelle has a character in his stories who solves the most intractable mysteries. Perhaps you've read *The Problem of Cell 13*? No? Then you have a treat in store. It's the finest locked room puzzle ever devised. When was it published, Jacques?'

'Seven years ago – 1905 – in one of the Boston papers.'

'And reprinted many times,' added Stead.

'But the Thinking Machine would never commit a murder,' Futrelle insisted. 'He's on the side of law and order. I was on the point of saying just now that if I wanted to devise a perfect murder – in fiction, of course – I would have to invent a new character, a fiendishly clever killer who would leave no clues to his identity.'

'Why don't you? It's a stunning idea.'

'I doubt if the public are ready for it.'

'Nonsense. Where's your sense of adventure? We have *Raffles, the Amateur Cracksman*, a burglar as hero. Why not a murderer who gets away with it?'

Futrelle sipped his wine in thoughtful silence.

466

Then young Finch put in his twopennyworth. 'I think you should do it. I'd want to read the story, and I'm sure thousands of others would.'

'I can make sure it gets reviewed,' offered Stead.

'You don't seem to understand the difficulty,' said Futrelle. 'I can't pluck a perfect murder story out of thin air.'

'If we all put our minds to it,' said Stead, 'we could think up a plot before we dock at New York. There's a challenge! Are you on, gentlemen?'

Finch agreed at once.

Futrelle was less enthusiastic. 'It's uncommonly generous of you both, but—'

'Something to while away the time, old sport. Let's all meet here before dinner on the last night at sea and compare notes.'

'All right,' said Futrelle, a little fired up at last. 'It's better than staring at seagulls, I suppose. And now I'd better see what my wife is up to.'

Stead confided to Finch as they watched the writer leave, 'This will be good for him. He needs to get back to crime stories. He's only thirty-seven, you know, and toils away, but his writing has gone downhill since that first success. He's churning out light romances, horribly sweet and frothy. Marshmallows, I call them. The latest has the title *My Lady's Garter*, for God's sake. This is the man who wrote so brilliantly about the power of a logical brain.'

'Is he too much under the influence of that wife?'

'The lovely May? I don't think so. She's a writer herself. There are far too many of us about. You're not another author, I hope?'

'No,' said Finch. 'I deal in *objets d'art*. I do a lot of business in New York.'

'Plenty of travelling, then?'

'More than I care for. I would rather be at home, but my

467

customers are in America, so I cross the ocean several times a year.'

'Is that such a hardship?'

'I get bored.'

'Can't you employ someone to make the trips?'

'My wife – my former business partner – used to make some of the crossings instead of me, but no longer. We parted.'

'I see. An international art-dealer. How wrong I was! With your fascination for the subject of murder, I had you down for a writer of shilling shockers.'

'Sorry. I'm guilty of many things, but nothing in print.'

'Guilty of many things? Now you sound like the perfect murderer we were discussing a moment ago.'

Secretly amused, Finch frowned and said, 'That's a big assumption, sir.'

'Not really. The topic obviously interests you. You raised it first.'

'Did I?'

'I'm certain you did. Do you have a victim in mind?' Stead enquired, elaborating on his wit.

'Don't we all?'

'Then you also have a motive. All you require now are the means and the opportunity. Has it occurred to you – perhaps it has – that an ocean voyage offers exceptional conditions for the perfect murder?'

'Man overboard, you mean? An easy way to dispose of the body, which is always the biggest problem. The thought had not escaped me. But it needs more than that. There's one other element.'

'What's that?'

'The ability to tell lies.'

'How true.' Stead's faint grin betrayed some unease.

'You can't simply push someone overboard and hope for the best.'

'Good. You're rising to the challenge,' said Stead, more to reassure himself than the young man. 'If you can think of something special, dear boy, I'm sure Jacques Futrelle will be more than willing to turn your ideas into fiction. Wouldn't that be a fine reward?'

'A kind of immortality,' said Finch.

'Well, yes. I often ask myself how a man would feel if he committed a murder and got away with it and was unable to tell anyone how clever he'd been. We all want recognition for our achievements. This is the answer. Get a well-known author to translate it into fiction.'

'I'd better make a start, then.'

The young man got up to leave, and Stead gazed after him, intrigued.

Jeremy Finch was confident he'd not given too much away. Stead had been right about all of us wanting recognition. That was why certain murderers repeated their crimes. They felt impelled to go on until they were caught and the world learned what they had done. Finch had no intention of being caught. But he still had that vain streak that wanted the world to know how brilliant he was. The idea of having his crime immortalised through the medium of a short story by a famous author was entirely his own, not Stead's. He'd deliberately approached the two eminent men of letters in the smoking room and steered the conversation around to the topic of murder.

He wanted his murder to be quoted as one of the great pieces of deception. In Futrelle's fine prose it would surely rank with Chesterton's *The Invisible Man* and Doyle's *The Speckled Band* as a masterpiece of ingenuity. Except that in his case, the crime would really have happened.

It was already several weeks in the planning. He had needed to make sure of his victim's movements. This crossing was a godsend, the ideal chance to do the deed. As Stead had pointed out, an ocean voyage affords unequalled opportunities for murder.

He had made a point of studying the routine on C Deck, where the first class staterooms were. His previous transatlantic voyages had been second class, luxurious enough for most tastes on the great liners. His wife Geraldine always travelled first class, arguing that an unaccompanied lady could only travel with total confidence in the best accommodation, her virtue safeguarded. This theory had proved to be totally misfounded. Another dealer, a rival, had taken cruel pleasure in informing Finch after Geraldine's latest trip to New York that he had seen her in another man's arms. The news had devastated him. When faced with it, she admitted everything. Finch shrank from the public humiliation of a divorce, preferring to deal with the infidelity in his own way.

So for the first days of the voyage he observed his prey with all the vigilance of Futrelle's creation, the Thinking Machine, getting to know his movements, which were necessarily circumscribed by the regularity of life aboard ship. He thought of himself as a lion watching the wretched wildebeest he had singled out, infinitely patient, always hidden, biding his time. The man who was picked to die had not the faintest notion that Finch was a husband he had wronged. It wouldn't have crossed his lascivious mind. At the time of the seduction, six months before, he'd thought lightly of his conquest of Geraldine. He had since moved on to other lovers, just as young, pretty, impressionable and easily bedded.

He was due to die by strangulation on the fourth evening at sea.

The place picked for the crime, first class stateroom 10 on C Deck, was occupied by Colonel Mortimer Hatch, travelling alone. By a curious irony it was just across the corridor from the stateroom where Jacques Futrelle was pacing the floor for much of each day trying to devise a perfect murder story.

Mortimer Hatch was forty-one, twice divorced and slightly past his prime, with flecks of silver in his moustache and sideburns. His shipboard routine, meticulously noted by Finch, was well established by the second day. He would rise about eight and swim in the first class pool before taking breakfast in his room. During the morning, he played squash or promenaded and took a Turkish bath before lunch. Then a short siesta. From about three to six, he played cards with a party of Americans. In the evening, after dinner, he took to the dance floor, and there was no shortage of winsome partners. He was a smooth dancer, light on his feet, dapper in his white tie and tails. Afterwards, he repaired to the bar, usually with a lady for company.

It was in the same first class bar, on the third evening out from Southampton, that Jeremy Finch had a second meeting with Stead and Futrelle. They were sharing a bottle of fine French wine, and Stead invited the young man to join them. 'That is, if you're not too occupied planning your perfect crime.'

'I'm past the planning stage,' Finch informed them.

'I wish I was,' said Futrelle. 'I'm stumped for inspiration. It's not for want of trying. My wife is losing patience with me.'

'*Nil desperandum*, old friend,' said Stead. 'We agreed to pool our ideas and give you a first class plot to work on. I have a strong intimation that young Jeremy here is well advanced in his thinking.'

'I'm practically ready,' Finch confirmed.

'Tell us more,' Futrelle said eagerly.

Stead put up a restraining hand. 'Better not. We agreed to save the denouement for the night before we dock at New York. Let's keep to our arrangement, gentlemen.'

'I'll say this much, and it won't offend the contract,' said

Finch. 'Do you see the fellow on the far side of the bar, moustache, dark hair, in earnest conversation with the pretty young woman with Titian-red hair and the ostrich feather topknot?'

'Saw him dancing earlier,' said Stead. 'Fancies his chances with the ladies.'

'That's Colonel Hatch.'

'I know him,' Futrelle said. 'He's in the stateroom just across from mine. We share the same steward. And, yes, you could be right about the ladies. There was a certain amount of giggling when I passed the door of number 10 last evening.'

'All I will say,' said Finch, 'is that I am keeping Colonel Hatch under observation. When he leaves the bar, I shall note the time.'

'Being a military man, he probably keeps to set times in most things he does,' said Stead.

'Even when working his charms on the fair sex?' said Futrelle.

'That's the pattern so far,' said Finch, without smiling. 'I predict that he'll move from here about half past eleven.'

'With the lady on his arm?'

'Assuredly.'

The conversation moved on to other matters. 'Are you married?' Futrelle asked Finch.

'Separated, more's the pity.'

'Not all marriages work out. Neither of you may be at fault.'

'Unhappily, in this case one of us was, and it wasn't me,' said Finch.

After an awkward pause, Stead said, 'Another drink, anyone?'

At eleven twenty-eight, almost precisely as Finch had predicted, Colonel Hatch and his companion rose from their table and left the bar.

'I'm glad we didn't take a bet on it,' said Stead.

'I think I'll turn in,' said Futrelle. 'My wife will be wondering where I am.'

'Good idea,' said Finch. 'I'll do the same. I need to be sharp as a razor tomorrow.'

Stead gave him a long look.

The next day, the fourth at sea, Colonel Hatch rose as usual at eight, blissfully unaware that it was to be his last day alive. He went for his swim, and the morning followed its invariable routine. Perkins, the steward for staterooms 10 to 14, brought him breakfast.

'Comfortable night, sir?'

'More than comfortable,' said the colonel, who had spent much of it in the arms of the redheaded heiress in stateroom 27. 'I almost overslept.'

'Easy to do, sir,' Perkins agreed, for he, too, had enjoyed an amorous night in one of the cabins on D deck. At the end of an evening of fine wine and fine food there are sometimes ladies ready for an adventure with a good-looking steward. 'Shall you be attending the service this morning, or will you promenade?'

'The service? By jove, is it Sunday already?'

'Yes, sir.'

'I've done more than my share of church parades. I shall promenade.'

'Very good, sir.'

The colonel felt better after his Turkish bath. For luncheon, he had the fillets of brill, followed by the grilled mutton chops and the apple meringue. He then retired for an hour. Perkins had thoughtfully folded back the counterpane.

The latter part of the afternoon was devoted to cards, afternoon tea and conversation. He returned to his stateroom at six to dress for dinner. His starched white shirt was arranged ready on the bed.

At ten to seven, the colonel went to dinner. The seven-course meal was the social highlight of the day. The first class dining room seated five hundred and fifty, and there were numerous young women travelling alone, or with their parents. He was confident of another conquest.

Meanwhile, Jeremy Finch did not appear at dinner. His murder plan had reached a critical point. He was lurking behind a bulkhead in the area of the first class staterooms, aware that whilst the passengers were at dinner, the doors had to be unlocked for the stewards to tidy up and make everything ready for the night.

Finch waited for Perkins to open Colonel Hatch's stateroom. Methodical in everything, he knew what to expect. As each room was attended to, the steward left the door ajar, propped open with the bin used to collect all the rubbish.

Finch entered the cabin and stepped into the bathroom whilst Perkins was tidying the bed.

On Sunday evenings, there was no dancing after dinner. Colonel Hatch didn't let this cramp his style. He was as smooth at conversation as he was on the dance floor. He sparkled. But for once he experienced difficulty in persuading a lady to adjourn with him to the bar for champagne. The little blonde he'd targeted said the stuff gave her terrible headaches, and anyway Papa insisted she retired to her cabin by ten o'clock, and personally made sure she was there. The colonel offered to knock on her door at half past and share a bottle of claret with her, but the offer was turned down. At half past, she told him, she would be saying her prayers, and she always said extra on Sundays.

Hatch decided this was not to be his night. He returned to his own stateroom.

* * *

At eleven forty that Sunday evening, Able Seaman Frederick Fleet, the lookout on the crow's nest, sounded three strokes on the bell, the signal that an object was dead ahead of the ship. It was too late. Nothing could prevent the *Titanic* from striking the iceberg in its path and having its underbelly torn open.

On C deck, high above the point of impact, there was a slight jarring sensation. Below, in steerage, it was obvious something dreadful had happened. At some time after midnight, the first lifeboats were uncovered and lowered. The confusion of the next two hours, the heart-rending scenes at the lifeboats, are well documented elsewhere. The women and children were given priority. It is on record that May Futrelle, the wife of the writer, had to be forced into one of the boats after refusing to be parted from her husband. Futrelle was heard to tell her, 'It's your last chance: go!' It was then one twenty in the morning.

Futrelle would go down with the ship, one of about fifteen hundred victims of the sinking. The precise figure was never known. W. T. Stead also perished.

Between one and two in the morning there were pockets of calm. Many expected to be rescued by other vessels that must have picked up the distress signals. In the first class lounge, the eight musicians played ragtime numbers to keep up the spirits. Some passengers got up a game of cards. Well-bred Englishmen don't panic.

Stead, Futrelle and Finch sat together with a bottle of wine.

'Whether we get out of this, or not,' said Stead, 'I fear it's our last evening together. If you remember, we had an agreement.'

'Did we?' said Futrelle, still distracted.

'The murder plot.'

'That?'

'It would do no harm to put our minds to it, as we promised we would.'

'I thought of nothing worth putting on paper,' said Futrelle, as if that was the end of it.

'Yes,' said Stead. 'It defeated me, too. My brain can't cope with the intricacies of a fictional crime. But I fancy Mr Finch may have interesting news for us.'

'What makes you think so?' Finch asked without giving away a thing.

'I believe you had a plan in mind before you ever joined the ship,' said Stead, 'and I think you were tickled pink at the prospect of disclosing it to us and thus providing Mr Jacques Futrelle with a perfect plot. Is that correct?'

'In broad terms,' Finch conceded.

'Capital. And tonight you put it to the test.'

'You mean he actually killed someone?' said Futrelle in horror.

'That is my strong belief,' said Stead. 'Am I right, Mr Finch? Come on, the ship is sinking. We may all perish. We deserve to be told.'

Finch sat back in his chair, vibrating his lips, deciding. Finally he said, 'If you're so well informed, why don't you tell it?'

'As you wish. On the evening we met, you were a shade too eager to raise the topic of murder. You must have known of Futrelle's ingenious books – the stories of the Thinking Machine. You wanted your perfect murder enshrined in fine prose by a great writer.'

'The theory, you mean?'

'No, sir. More than a theory. I first had my suspicions when you spoke to me of the great shock you suffered at the news of your wife's infidelity on some transatlantic crossing. A real motive for murder.'

Finch shrugged.

476

Stead went on, 'Yesterday evening in this very bar you drew our attention to Colonel Hatch in intimate conversation with a young lady. You told us precisely when they would leave together, and you were right. It was obvious you had made a study of his movements.'

'True. I didn't hide it.'

'His routine was central to your plan.'

'Indeed.'

'Tonight you didn't appear for dinner.'

'How do you know? I may have come late.'

Futrelle spoke. 'Actually, I saw you. I was late going to dinner. I spotted you hiding in the corridor near my stateroom. It was clear you weren't bothered about missing the meal. You had something else on your mind.'

'And that,' added Stead, 'was the murder of Mortimer Hatch, your wife's seducer. Cunningly you waited for an opportunity to gain admittance to his stateroom. The steward went in to tidy up and prepare the bed, put out the pyjamas, and so forth. You crept through the open door and hid in one of the rooms, probably the bathroom, which happens to be closest to the door. How am I doing?'

'Tolerably well.'

'You waited for the colonel to return, and as it happened, it wasn't such a long wait. He came back early, having failed to sweet-talk tonight's young lady into the bar, let alone into bed. You killed him cleanly in his own stateroom, either with a blow to the head with some heavy object, or strangulation. Opened the porthole and pushed the body through. By then it was dark, and nobody saw. You left, unseen. I raise my glass to you. Perfect revenge. A near perfect murder.'

'Why do you say "near perfect"?'

'Because we rumbled you, old man. A perfect murder goes undetected. And isn't it ironical that you chose tonight of all nights?'

'You mean it may not have been necessary?'

'We shall see.'

'Is this true?' Futrelle demanded of Finch. 'Did you really murder the colonel?'

Finch smiled and spread his hands like a conjurer. 'Judge for yourselves. Look who's just got up to dance.'

They stared across the room. In the open space in front of the band, a couple were doing a cakewalk: Colonel Mortimer Hatch, reunited with his flame-haired partner of the previous night. Some of the women had refused to leave the ship, preferring to take their chances with the men.

Stead, piqued, gave a sharp tug at his beard and said, 'I'll be jiggered!'

'Caught us, well and truly,' said Futrelle.

Finch chuckled and poured himself more wine.

'What an anticlimax,' said Stead.

'On the contrary,' said Finch. 'Do you want to hear my version? I might as well tell it now, and if either of you survives you must put it into writing because it *was* an undetected murder. I killed a man tonight in the colonel's stateroom, just as you said. Strangled him and pushed his body out of the porthole. Nobody found out. Nobody would have found out.'

'Who the devil was he?'

'The degenerate who seduced my wife. They're notorious, these stewards.'

'A steward?'

'Perkins?' said Futrelle.

'They're in a position of trust, and they abuse it. Well, Perkins did, at any rate, aboard the *Mauretania*, and I suffered the humiliation of being told about it by an acquaintance. So I took it as a point of honour to take my revenge. I made it my business to learn where he'd signed on. Discovered he'd been hired as a first class steward for the maiden voyage of the *Titanic*.'

The two older men were stunned into silence.

Eventually, Stead said, 'You've certainly surprised me. But was it perfect, this murder? Would you have got away with it? Surely, his absence would have been noted, not least by the passengers he attended.'

'The method was foolproof. Of course there would be concern. The chief steward would be informed he was missing. It might even reach the captain's ears. But the possibility of murder wouldn't cross their minds. Even if it did, can you imagine White Star conducting a murder inquiry in the first class accommodation on the maiden voyage of the *Titanic*? Never. They would cover it up. The passengers Perkins attended would be told he was unwell. And after we docked at New York it would be too late to investigate.'

'He's right,' said Futrelle. 'He was always going to get away with it.'

'What do you think?' asked Finch, leaning forward in anticipation. 'Worthy of the Thinking Machine?'

'More a matter of low cunning than the power of logic, in my opinion,' said Stead, 'but it might make an interesting story. What say you, Jacques?'

But Futrelle was listening to something else. 'What are they playing? Isn't that "Nearer, My God, to Thee"?'

'If it is,' said Stead, 'I doubt if your story will ever be told, Mr Finch.'

At two eighteen, the lights dimmed and went out. In two minutes the ship was gone.

479

Dark Mirror

Lauren Henderson

North America, 1941

(for my sister Lisa)

L ast night I couldn't sleep. I thought once Terry was gone, sent away, I would sleep again. That was what he said, and he's a doctor, a psychiatrist, so he should know. But he was wrong. I lie awake next to him, listening to his steady breathing, and he never seems to be aware that I am wide awake, staring at the ceiling. Nor does he ask me about it next morning, though he must surely notice the dark shadows under my eyes. Or perhaps he doesn't see them either.

There was a time I thought that he knew everything. He behaved as if he did. That was why I married him.

Last night, lying awake, I didn't toss or turn. I never have. I get out of bed every morning and see that the sheets on my side of the bed are hardly rumpled. I was always the quiet one. One of you two has to be, our mother said: how else am I to tell the pair of you apart?

I didn't move at all. I lay still on the bed, remembering, for some reason, that terrible evening when they came to take Terry to the asylum. I should have felt relieved when it happened, but I didn't; I was just very tired, nearly tired to death. That was the most terrible time of all, that evening. Even worse than when they found that doctor stabbed to death and we were identified as having been in his apartment around the time that it happened. (When I say 'we', I don't mean both of us, of course. That's the shorthand twins use. I mean one of us.)

And of course people knew who we were. We ran the little kiosk down in the foyer of the building. Everyone knew us. And I don't mean both of us, either; I mean one of us. No one knew we were identical twins. They thought we were one girl, a girl called Terry. It was a little game we played, a silly harmless game. And we had been dating him, too, that doctor who was killed. Both of us.

That was another game. It didn't mean anything; neither of us cared for him, not in that way, not seriously. But he was clever. Most men didn't guess that there were two of us, the lively one and the quiet one. But he did. And he preferred one of us. He said some hateful things about the other, the one he didn't like. That was a hard thing to do, an unnecessary, cruel thing. It was why he was killed. And there are many worse reasons for killing people.

That evening when I came out of our bedroom, for some reason the first thing I saw was the mirror. It hung on the opposite wall and it reflected the sofa back at me. Terry was sitting there, still talking; she hadn't yet seen me, and her eyes were bright, her expression taut with that intensity I always envied. I never felt things the way Terry did. I wasn't passionate like her.

She was leaning forward as if she were talking to someone sitting next to her, but there was no one there. On the back of her head was the smart, fashionable little black hat with the sparkles that I loved, but whenever I tried it on it didn't look right somehow. I had never worn it out. Whenever I saw it on Terry I would think: you see, it looks fine! And I would see people turn in the street to look at her admiringly. But I knew that it didn't suit me. I couldn't carry it off.

Terry was wearing her favourite black dress; she had many, but this was the one she chose for important occasions when she wanted to give herself confidence. I thought she looked very beautiful. It was unusual for me to feel detached enough

484

from her to be able to comment on how she looked, because it felt as if I were passing a judgement on my own appearance. But that night, for some reason, I could.

I saw myself in the mirror too, above Terry's head. Only the top part of my body, to just below my breasts, then the angle of the mirror cut me off; I was floating on the wall like a picture, in my white dressing gown, my hair pulled back because it needed to be washed. It makes me nostalgic for her just to remember the characteristic way her head moved, its quick nods as she talked, agreeing with what she was saying, confirming it with every little assent of her head. But her words were mad, crazy words. He was right, she was crazy. I saw it clearly then for the first time.

She was saying that she was me, Ruth; she wasn't Terry. That no one had ever wanted Terry, it was always Ruth who the men had wanted. That there was something wrong with Terry, something bad, and everyone knew it. I stood watching her and it was as if my heart were being torn out of my body to hear her say those things about herself.

I knew she didn't have to be that way, you see. I had memories of her from when we were younger, or even just a short time ago, before things went so wrong, before that man, that doctor, was so cruel to her. All the times we'd laugh and joke together, over milkshakes when we were small, in the local drugstore, then cocktails, later, both of us sipping drinks through straws, perfectly happy, telling stupid jokes we'd heard a thousand times and laughing at them afresh, because we were so happy like that, just telling each other stupid, silly, girls' jokes. Oh, she could be different. It was as if no one wanted to see it.

Why had she got this way? That was something he could never tell me. He just said that she was bad and I was good. And he made it sound necessary, fixed in stone, almost as if she had to be bad so that I could be the good one. Yet he couldn't explain why. I didn't question him at the time. I had to have something to believe in with Terry gone. But that's not much of an excuse.

Still, looking at her then, I could see that he was right about one thing. She was crazy. Up till that moment I had denied it. I had tried to protect her. I told the police that we had spent the night together, the night that doctor was killed, that neither one of us had left our apartment. And as long as I stuck to my story, though one of us had been identified as being over at that doctor's place, we were both safe.

What could they do? she said. They couldn't arrest both of us. And she was right. They couldn't. But they were sure it was me or her. Terry said it must have been someone else who killed the doctor and of course I believed her. The police didn't. They made us go to him to let him look at what was going on inside our heads. To shrink them, Terry said. I was cross with her when she put him down, because I was in love with him then and I loved all his tests too, the psychiatric tests to see if you were crazy or not. The ink blots were such fun. It was like being a kid again, playing silly games. And it was wonderful just to sit and talk to him. He was pretty young, but in his white coat and his office with all the scientific charts, it was as if he knew everything that had ever happened, everything you felt. It was a release to me. I trusted him.

Terry was in love with him too, of course. We always fell for the same men. Or was it that she always fell for the ones I liked? I'll never be able to ask her now.

There were all these men in the room, too. I hadn't noticed them at first, I hadn't taken my eyes off Terry. But then they moved – not much, but enough for me to become aware of their presence. They all turned to look at me. All but one. I was standing just inside the room, almost in the doorway. She saw them turn, too, and she followed the line of their glances, her head darting in a jerky movement that was very like the convulsive little nods she had been making. She stopped talking in mid-sentence, and our eyes met in the mirror. I can't describe what I saw in hers. Desperation, maybe. A terrible sadness. Because of course my presence there contradicted everything that she had just been saying, the comforting story she had been telling herself. Looking at me, she knew that I was Ruth and she was Terry. There was the evidence, in black and white. Like the clothes we were wearing.

All I could say was: 'I'm sorry, Terry.' And my voice sounded so helpless I hated myself for it.

I never was sure why she called herself Terry. I preferred Teresa, her given name. In fact, I would have liked to have been called that myself. It was such a pretty name, much prettier than Ruth. But it used to amuse me, telling people that I shared a flat with Terry, because some of them would think I meant a man, Terence, and they could see I wasn't married. I had no ring. They would look so shocked for a moment. Then they would look at me, and realise I wasn't that kind of girl, and summon up the nerve to ask who I meant.

Terry still didn't say anything. Suddenly I hated the quiet, hated it. But I couldn't think of anything to say. I should have gone to her, then, sat down next to her, put my arms around her; told her I was here and everything was all right. But I couldn't. Maybe I was still scared of her.

He said later that she had been trying to drive me mad, to make me think that I was the one who had killed that doctor. And yes, it had been terrible those last two weeks. I couldn't sleep; I cried all the time, holding my head, trying to remember doing something that I simply hadn't done. But she didn't mean to drive me mad. She was just crazy, and she was trying to pretend to herself that she hadn't done it. I know that. Terry is part of me. I know how her mind works. People think I don't notice things because I'm quiet and sweet and she's the clever, talkative one, but they're wrong. I do see things; I can see what people are like. And no matter what he said, I know that Terry would never, never have hurt me.

It's not fair to expect him to have realised that, though. How could he? He looked in from the outside and thought my life was in danger, and he loved me, so he wanted to protect me. I do understand. But he says now that all his concern, his worry, was on my behalf, and that, I think, is hypocritical. After all, Terry had already killed one man for preferring me to her, and telling her that she was crazy. And here he was, telling her the same thing, a doctor too, just like the other one. No one's going to persuade me that he wasn't a little scared for himself as well.

Although the men around us were silent, I could hear their breathing. It was uneven, nervous. Their presence filled the room, not just their physical bodies but the intensity with which they were watching us. It felt somehow as if they had always been there, but only now had decided to reveal themselves. He was one of them, and he fitted in perfectly. All of them were wearing dark suits, except for the one sitting by the table who never took his eyes off Terry; I don't know how I'm so sure about that, for I never took my eyes off her either, but I am. He had very short hair and was all in white, like me. White tunic, white trousers. A hospital uniform. For a moment, aware as I was of Terry's beauty, her likeness to me but also her detachment, he seemed to be another reflection of myself, as still and white as I was, concentrating on her as much as I did. For from the moment I came through the door I never moved, and nor did he, sitting there like a statue.

Then, all of a sudden, Terry's face began to work, distorting itself into something that I recognised. She jumped up and picked up an ashtray off the table, throwing it directly into the mirror. And what she could see in the mirror, apart from herself of course, was me, in my white dressing gown. It was as if she were aiming at me, at my reflection, at us together. But not at me, not at the real Ruth. That's very important to realise. It was that picture of us together she couldn't bear. Even he didn't notice the meaning of that – the significance, as he would put it. But I saw it, and I understood. It wasn't me, Ruth, she hated. It was the way people saw the two of us together.

Of course she hit the mirror bang in the middle with that ashtray; she was always the one who could throw straight. It shattered into pieces. And she did too, from that moment. There was a rush of people, of bodies, motion released. I had to turn my head away from where the mirror had been, now just an empty frame, to see her in the flesh, and when I did she was in the arms of the man in white, sobbing, crumpled, the black hat slipping from her head, no longer beautiful or anything I could put a name to.

He came to me and put his arm around me. I clung to him, my arms clumsily round the dark material of his suit, as Terry was clinging to her warder in his white coat, and we stood there, frozen, dark and light, light and dark, the two pairs of us. But I wasn't crying.

When I woke up I was in my nightdress. He must have taken my dressing gown off and put me to bed with a tranquilliser. And he was sitting on the bed, smiling at me. It was all right now, that's what his smile said. He went to get a breakfast tray, and brought it straight back; he had had it all ready and waiting. I sipped my coffee, smiling into his face, and he said, 'Tell me something, Miss Collins?' and I said, 'What?' and he said, 'How do you come to be so much more beautiful than your sister?' and I smiled at him again, my best smile.

All that smiling . . . That's where it stops. That's where it should have stopped.

I miss her so much. I can't tell him; he would think I was crazy. I don't mean that literally, of course. I'm the sane one. But he wouldn't understand it, and that would worry him. After all, he would say, she tried to drive you insane, to make you think you killed that doctor; she fed you sleeping pills, told you that you had nightmares until you believed her and started dreaming them for yourself; she told me all those lies about you and in the end, already over the edge, she pretended that she was you, and that you were her, the one who should be committed.

And what would I say? Yes, I know, but . . . but . . .

It's how I feel, I can't express it properly. I was never good with words. Terry was the articulate one. When we were out with boys she would dazzle me and them with her wit, her sense of humour, and I would sit there, silent and jealous but proud of her at the same time. Everything she said seemed to sparkle, while in my mouth it would have been banal. But it was me they walked home, me they lingered with outside the front door, me they rang up and, halting, shy, asked out. Gradually, I learned that this would be the pattern, and so when we went out together I would be able to sit there, quiet, waiting for my turn later on. But now I wish I had tried to express myself, practised on them as she did, because I can't manage to explain to him how I still feel about her. I can only think about it like this, rambling away. I'm sure I'm not making much sense.

No, that's not right. I am making sense. I don't know why I just thought that. It's something I say quite often, after I've talked for longer than usual, because it makes their expressions

490

change, the men who are listening. Their faces soften, they smile at me in that kind reassuring way I'm used to, and I feel again in the right place to be.

But I am making sense. I wish I had a friend to talk to about this. Terry was the only friend I ever wanted; my twin, my sister, she was all I had and all I needed. I always imagined us married, living next door to each other, as close as we could be, popping in and out of each other's houses all the time, swopping recipes we'd cut out from magazines, our children playing together in the backyard.

When I was going to see him – for 'consultations', as he called them – he was so calm and professional I felt that I could tell him anything. I expect it's only natural that now we're married, that's all changed. But in a strange way I miss the tests, those ink blots, the machine that he connected up to me that would tell if I were lying or not, the graphs it made with its pen. It was all so scientific. And then there was the reassurance that although he was a mind doctor, he was a proper one as well. (He explained that to me when I asked, so nicely, not as if I were ignorant because I didn't know you could be both.) It was as if he had all the bases covered, just in case.

That building, where we had our kiosk in the entrance hall, was full of doctors. They all had offices there, consulting rooms. We called practically every man who passed 'doctor', automatically: it was quicker, and it helped if you forgot one of their names. And it's strange, rather ironic, to think about it now, but at the time there was something very comforting about working in that particular building, with all of those doctors; it made me feel very safe, knowing that if you hurt yourself, you couldn't be in a better place for it to happen.

I don't think he realised how much it would hurt me for Terry to be committed. I don't think he had the least idea. He saw it as a rescue, with himself as my knight in shining armour.

And he was, that's true. I mustn't forget that. She was pulling me down with her into her craziness. But he thought that he could just split us apart cleanly, and keep me separate from what was going on in her head.

Sometimes I wish I'd never seen Terry like that. He says it was necessary for my sake, to prove to me once and for all that she was the mad one of the two of us. It's not that I forget what it was like, those last days when she really was crazy. In fact, I remember it all very sharply, more and more every day. My terrible doubts of her, and of myself, the times when I held my head and cried with fear of my own nightmares, that moment when she asked me if I would ever betray her, and said that if I did she didn't know what she would do. I turned and saw her standing in the shadows under the window in her black dress, her face hidden and her voice metallic, mono-tonous, and she frightened me. But I would never have betrayed her, never, no matter what. She didn't need to scare me to make sure.

She couldn't understand that. Maybe she thought I had already betrayed her, with those boys, and then the men – him – because I was the one they liked; but that wasn't my fault! I couldn't help it. When we were first double-dating, I was sure it was her they would want, she was so bright and funny and quick. It was as much of a surprise to me as to her that it was Ruth, not Terry, who got the phone calls and the proposals. And if I came to learn that this was the way it was, I still didn't change, I just went on behaving in the same way. You can't blame me for that, Terry, can you? Just for going on the same?

Looking back on that morning – the day after they had taken her away, when he brought me in the breakfast tray and asked me why I was so much more beautiful than my sister – I feel sick for smiling. It seems so false, to do that at Terry's expense, as if I were laughing at her. It was a betrayal. And it wasn't even true that I was the more beautiful one. We were so alike, physically at least. We could fool anyone at first. Later, as people got to know us, we found it more difficult to act each other. Sometimes they would look puzzled, or ask us if we were in a bad mood, or feeling well.

That was the moment when something split, or at least when we realised something had split; not being able to slip so easily into being each other. It seemed too important to be ourselves. If I'm honest, I'll admit that I didn't want to act like Terry. I preferred being me, what it brought me. I was frightened that if I could be like her on occasion, witty, funny, I would always have to be that way. Oh, I enjoyed how it felt, making people laugh; in fact it wasn't that difficult. But I could see the change in their attitudes as well. They thought I was hard, tough. That I could take care of myself. And they hardened too, they weren't so kind, so gentle, so reassuring. It made me feel lonely and I wanted to be Ruth again, sweet Ruth whom men automatically wanted to look after.

I feel lonely now all the time. Even with him. The behaviour that seemed so natural to me before, when I had Terry to compare myself with, now seems – I don't know, not false, exactly, but somehow unreal. As if now I'm acting a part. Of course, I don't work at the booth any longer, so I'm alone during the day. I miss it sometimes, which is silly of me; think how serious his work is, and here I am complaining I don't still sell cigarettes and magazines, instead of look after his house and make it nice for him! We go out a lot in the evenings, to dinner, to a show, or dancing . . .

I miss her like a part of my body that's been amputated. As if he had cut her away with his scalpel. He had to do it, I know he did. He was saving me.

I went to see her yesterday. I didn't tell him, because I

493

knew that he would have argued me out of it. I was expecting to feel detached, as I had the last time I saw her. In fact I hoped I would feel that way. I wanted to be able to say goodbye to her, my mad sister, to put her memory to rest.

But instead, when I saw her I felt as if I were whole again for the first time since they took her away. She wasn't mad at all, she was Terry, Terry when we were small and she was still shy like me. Her face was scrubbed, and she wore one of those coarse white gowns tied at the back with strips of cloth; she looked very pure and beautiful, like an angel, apart from her eyes, which darted around the room the whole time. They weren't mad, though, just frightened. My darling sister Terry, frightened of me. I wanted to bawl like a baby. But I knew it wasn't really me she was scared of, it was this place, and what was in her head. She still loved me, Ruth. I know she did.

Gradually she was able to look at me for longer and longer periods, like a bird learning to trust a human. I cried. She stroked my hair as if she were comforting a child. She knew who I was, she called me Ruthie as she did when we were children, and I called her Tessie. She didn't know who Terry was; she'd changed her name when we were sixteen, declaring Tessie was too girlish, too silly. But now Terry was a stranger to her.

We talked about our childhood, and how happy we were. It's true, we were very happy. We hugged each other as tightly as always, talking about our time at school, children we had known there. But when we reached our memories of the time that we were fifteen, sixteen, her face started to crumple up as if I'd hit her. She just kept saying, 'I love you, Ruthie,' over and over again, as if it were the most important thing in the world to her, holding my hand all the time.

My clothes were a source of wonderment to her. They are to me, too. People who knew me before would hardly recognise me. I'm very smart now; we are very social. His work with the police has brought him fame – he says, modestly, that it's only notoriety – and we are invited to plenty of parties. People are fascinated by me, since they all know the story – our story, Terry's and mine. They are rarely bold enough to ask me questions, but they stare at me in a way I don't like, as if, on his arm, smiling – that smile again – I am living proof of his success, his professional skill. I suppose that I am.

After a while I found that the smarter I dressed, the more unapproachable I looked. It was a form of self-protection, and he encourages me to spend money on clothes. He likes to see me smart, which is strange, because when he fell in love with me I was dowdier than she was. Even when Terry and I wore matching outfits, which we often did, she was always the chic one. Now, however, I am learning to dress well, because it pleases him. I wear what she would have worn, I carry myself like her.

Terry touched my hat, my hair, delicately, as if I would crumble if she didn't use the lightest movements. I had meant to dress in something bright to visit her but I didn't have the heart for it, and I was wearing a black crepe dress, very simple, with a belted waist and exaggeratedly padded shoulders. Terry ran her fingers shyly along my sleeve. She whispered something. 'What, darling?' I said. She put her head up a little and murmured, 'Dark, dark . . .'

After an hour they said I had to go. I had thought before that I couldn't cry any more, but I was wrong, and they almost had to pull us apart. Terry was crying too, 'Don't go, Ruthie, don't go,' she kept saying. They led me out of the room with two men holding her back, not forcefully, but so she couldn't move. It took me another hour to collect myself enough for the journey back.

Since then I haven't been able to get the image of her out of my head. I always thought that the most important person in the world to me would be my husband, and then my children. That's how it's supposed to be. But there must be something wrong with me, because the most important person in the world for me will always be Terry, no matter what she has done or tried to do. She's my twin, my other half. Why did it take me so long to understand that? And how does he possibly think that I can just split myself off from her and pretend that she never even existed? How does he dare?

In that bedroom she and I shared, I was happier than I have ever been with him. I was myself. With him I don't know who I am. But I know who he thinks I am: the good one, the good sister. He thinks I am better than any woman in the world because he has cut the bad part of me away with his scalpel. Well, he's wrong.

Our beds were next to each other, with a rug between them, just like his and mine are now. Sometimes at night Terry and I would reach out and hold hands till we fell asleep. Or we would talk for hours, rambling away, talking about nothing at all, just to hear the sound of our own voices. We invented codes for grunting to each other when we were small and too tired or lazy to talk: one grunt for 'yes', two for 'no', three for 'I don't know', four and five I don't remember, but six was 'I love you'. Why, we used them the night before it happened. I will never be that happy again.

I can't undo what's happened, what I've done. I took something from Terry without really knowing what I was doing, but that doesn't excuse me. I took it all and there was nothing left for her.

We were at dinner, just the two of us, the night I had come back from seeing her in that awful place, and my head was still spinning. Suddenly I found myself picturing Terry with that doctor. I wondered how many times she stabbed him. Isn't that ridiculous? It was a pair of scissors she used. No one heard it happen, so there can't have been that much noise. I know I shouldn't think about it, that it's morbid; that's what he says when I mention her name, that it's not good for me to remember, because it's morbid. But sometimes I can't help it.

What did she feel when she was doing it? And was it easy? Because somehow I picture it as having been very easy, the scissors sliding into him like a knife into butter. Because he would have been taken by surprise, unsuspecting. Thinking, you see, that she was me . . .

I look more like Terry now. More and more, at smart dinner parties, the words that come out of my mouth, the jokes, the questions, are hers. He doesn't seem to notice. Maybe he thinks that because I'm the good sister, anything I do must be right. How amusing it would be if that were true.

At dinner I had the strangest thought. It would have made her laugh; she loved odd things. I thought: wouldn't it be a neat pattern if Terry killed someone because he loved me and not her, and then if I killed someone too for exactly the same reason? Because he loved me and not her? It's more interesting that way, don't you think, more interesting than if I killed someone for preferring her to me. That's just complete symmetry, which is too perfect to be real. After all, even Terry and I aren't perfectly identical. If you know us well you can see that her eyebrows are slightly lighter than mine, slightly more arched, for instance. Or that my nose has a little kink in it where I broke it when I was four, falling over on the school playground, running to get to her.

But no one has ever known us that well. Except each other, of course.

It was just a stupid thought. But I wished Terry had been there to laugh at it with me. Or that I was back in that place with her.

You know, I wouldn't care what the place was like if we could be together. No matter how badly they treated us, how uncomfortable and scratchy those white gowns might be. I wouldn't care about anything else but being with her. Nothing at all. Not even what I would have to do to get there.

(*This story is based on the film* Dark Mirror *by Robert Siodmak, with Olivia de Havilland as both Ruth and Terry. The story begins at the end of the film.*)

498

𝕬 𝕽𝖆𝖗𝖊 𝕭𝖊𝖓𝖊𝖉𝖎𝖈𝖙𝖎𝖓𝖊

The Advent of Brother Cadfael

Ellis Peters

'Brother Cadfael sprang to life suddenly and unexpectedly when he was already approaching sixty, mature, experienced, fully armed and seventeen years tonsured.' So writes Ellis Peters in her introduction to *A Rare Benedictine* – three vintage tales of intrigue and treachery, featuring the monastic sleuth who has become such a cult figure of crime fiction. The story of Cadfael's entry into the monastery at Shrewsbury has been known hitherto only to a few readers; now his myriad fans can discover the chain of events that led him into the Benedictine Order.

Lavishly adorned with Clifford Harper's beautiful illustrations, these three tales show Cadfael at the height of his sleuthing form, with all the complexities of plot, vividly evoked Shropshire backgrounds and warm understanding of the frailties of human nature that have made Ellis Peters an international bestseller.

'A must for Cadfael enthusiasts – quite magical' *Best*
'A beautifully illustrated gift book' *Daily Express*
'A book for all Cadfael fans to treasure' *Good Book Guide*
'Brother Cadfael has made Ellis Peters' historical whodunnits a cult series' *Daily Mail*

HISTORICAL FICTION / CRIME 0 7472 3420 5